SCOTCH ON THE ROCKS

Romance writer Elliot Fletcher resides in her too-small flat in Edinburgh, Scotland, with her husband, cat and dog. When she isn't writing about swoon-worthy, lovable men and the captivating heroines they fall for, you can find her browsing second-hand bookshops, collecting pebbles on the beach, or re-watching the 2005 *Pride & Prejudice*.

You can find her on Instagram @elliotfletcherwrites.

Scotch on the Rocks is the second book in the Macabe Brothers trilogy.

T0372171

Also by Elliot Fletcher

Whisky Business

SCOTCH ON THE ROCKS

ELLIOT FLETCHER

HarperCollins*Publishers*

HarperCollins*Publishers* Ltd
1 London Bridge Street,
London SE1 9GF
www.harpercollins.co.uk

HarperCollins*Publishers*
Macken House, 39/40 Mayor Street Upper
Dublin 1, D01 C9W8, Ireland

Published by HarperCollins*Publishers* 2025

1

A catalogue record for this book is available from the British Library

ISBN: 978-0-00-867997-2

This novel is entirely a work of fiction.
The names, characters and incidents portrayed in it are
the work of the author's imagination. Any resemblance to
actual persons, living or dead, events or localities is
entirely coincidental.

Set in Sabon LT Std by HarperCollins*Publishers* India

Printed and bound in the UK using 100% Renewable
Electricity at CPI Group (UK) Ltd

This book contains FSC™ certified paper and other controlled
sources to ensure responsible forest management.

For more information visit: www.harpercollins.co.uk/green

For my grandmother, who didn't get to read this,
you taught me the art of being your authentic self.

And for the ice queens,
the grudge keepers,
Every girl who's ever been labelled a bitch before she
opened her mouth.

Juniper & Callum's Playlist

Black Magic Woman – Fleetwood Mac
the grudge – Olivia Rodrigo
I Could Be a Florist – Olivia Dean
Mirrorball – Taylor Swift
Chew On My Heart – James Bay
High – Stephen Sanchez
Would That I – Hozier
Ok Love You Bye – Olivia Dean
Hits Different – Taylor Swift
Jaded – Miley Cyrus
Move Together – James Bay
Mad Woman – Taylor Swift
Nobody Gets Me – SZA
Weathered – Jack Garratt
i am not who i was – Chance Peña
Everywhere, Everything – Noah Kahan, Gracie Abrams
July – Hozier
Mess Is Mine – Vance Joy
Us – Miller Blue
Silver Springs – Fleetwood Mac
Don't Blame Me – Taylor Swift

Scan this QR code to listen along!

AUTHOR'S NOTE

While *Scotch on the Rocks* is primarily a lighthearted read, it features content that might be triggering for some. These include: mentions of child abandonment and adoption; the death of a parent (off-page); caring for a relative with Alzheimer's; an instance of on-page physical violence. This novel is an open-door romance with multiple on-page sexual encounters.

THEN

Callum

Falling in love with Juniper Ross felt like stepping into oncoming traffic.

Late July, running down the blistering platform of Edinburgh's Waverley train station. The air held the scent of smoke and boiling sewage that only came from dirty city streets. Heat rippled off the tarmac in hellish waves – and there she'd been. Through the train carriage window, she appeared like a mirage in the desert.

Warning bells should have sounded the moment I discarded the first-class ticket disintegrating in my sweat-slicked hand and threw myself through the sliding carriage doors just in time to retain all my limbs. Her carriage. *Who needs extra leg room anyway? Not me.*

Red flags should have waved when I got my first look at her up close and thought – *Too young* – then took the seat opposite her anyway. Sweat dripped from me, like the condensation on her iced latte, and she glanced up from her paperback just long enough to watch a bead trail the length of my neck.

1

Blistering. That's the word that would forever come to mind when I thought of her.

She reminded me of Snow White's sarcastic twin. Pale skin and a permanent blush to her cheeks. Black clothes, black boots and a delicate little septum piercing. Her hair had been long back then, midnight black and curling at the base of her spine. A wicked smile on her lips like she knew the punchline to a joke I hadn't even heard yet.

Or maybe I had.

Warning bells were ringing after all, and I ignored every one of them, throwing myself into the seat opposite hers. Not a guy who played his hand too soon, I granted her a full five minutes to feign interest in the paperback in her hands, then asked, "Do you live in Glasgow or Edinburgh?"

She barely glanced up from the page. "As if I'd hand over that information to some creep on a train."

Her voice was low, her accent smooth and melodic in a way that scratched a part of my brain perfectly. Even if she lived here, she wasn't a Lowlander.

"Usually, I would advise a woman against it, but this situation is entirely different."

She flipped a page. "And why's that?"

I bent closer, getting high on her perfume, and whispered, "Because I'm trustworthy."

She laughed and I felt like I'd won a medal. "A trustworthy creep? You're the fourth I've met this morning."

I'd never been so fucking thoroughly charmed by a person. I was only headed to Glasgow because my wee brother, Alistair, wanted me to meet his new girlfriend. It made me the worst sibling in the world, yet I was ready to drop all my plans for the next three days and beg her to fill every second of my time. Then, the train had pulled into Glasgow and she landed the first gut punch.

She had a boyfriend. *Of course she had a boyfriend.*

Shit, but it didn't seem fair for a girl like that to be in a serious relationship.

Hours later, standing in my little brother's too clean kitchen, the second punch landed.

My stomach was in my arse as I stared down at this weirdly wonderful woman for the second time that day. Her slim hand in mine as we shook in greeting.

Wee Juniper Ross.

I couldn't believe the cruel odds of meeting her there. Two escapees from our tiny Isle of Skye village. My baby sister's best friend. I hadn't made the connection on the train, too caught up in the vision of those mile-long legs wrapped around my waist. Alistair's new girlfriend. And I'd encountered her for the first time on the eight-forty-five train from Edinburgh to Glasgow. Seven months and twelve days too late to make her mine.

Falling in love with Juniper Ross felt like stepping into oncoming traffic.

I sensed my feet leave the kerb. Saw the flash of headlights. Heard the screech of tyres. Sensed that split second when I could have pulled back and saved myself. But then she laughed. Laughed like her entire body was set to take flight and it set fire to a place inside me that had frozen over the day my bullish father shipped his sixteen-year-old kid off to the army.

Juniper laughed and I opened my arms, welcoming the collision.

From that moment on, I locked my feelings deep inside my chest. I flirted and taunted and threatened to steal her away from my brother in the night. I ruffled her hair and flicked her nose like a big brother would.

But mostly . . . I avoided her, because every time I saw Juniper Ross, she owned me a little bit more.

3

Three Years Later, Glasgow

Juniper

"Are you looking at the documents I emailed over from the Boutique Hotel conference? I've highlighted a few paragraphs under the sustainable business model section—"

"This all looks very modern. You know your dad preferred to keep the inn traditional."

Yeah? Well, Dad isn't here anymore. Clutching my phone tighter, I swallowed the cruel retort, eyeing the door of my Glasgow city centre hotel. "I get that, but we need to make changes now if we want to compete with the influx of private holiday rentals on the island."

"I love your enthusiam, Juney, Dad would be so proud." But no – she didn't need to say it.

This was pointless. I knew before I'd got on the damn ferry from Skye that the conference was useless and, like a fool, I'd come anyway. I scrubbed a tired hand over my face. "Maybe we should talk about this when I get home."

"If that's what you want, love." It wasn't. But I acquiesced. As I always did. "Do you have any big plans tonight? You haven't visited Glasgow in so long."

"A mountain of room service and that lame wedding movie, you know the one where the guy falls in his in-laws' pool," I lied, already headed for the door.

"*Father of the Bride*? A classic. They don't make love stories like that anymore."

"If you say so." My adoptive mother had always been overly romantic.

"You're not meeting up with Alistair?"

"No, why would I?"

"I'm just saying, after so many years together it's a shame to let things—"

"Fiona." I issued her name like a warning.

"—it would be nice if you could be friends at the very least. He *was* your fiancé."

"Call me crazy, but I wouldn't put a fiancé who abandons you the second your father gets sick in the *great future friend* category," I snapped.

Silence. *Shit.* "Fiona, I'm sorry—"

"I know." Her voice wobbled. "It's just hard to remember him sometimes." I started to apologise again but she cut me off, sniffling in that way she always did while composing herself.

"It's hard for me too." My voice was quiet. Homesick not for a place, but a person. "Look . . . I'll see you tomorrow. My bus is early so I should get to bed."

"Tomorrow." Did I imagine the disappointment in her tone? "Love you, Juney."

My chest ached when I couldn't offer it back.

Out on the street, the familiarity of Glasgow's Victorian architecture moulded around me and I fuelled my frustration into each beat of my heels on stone that screamed *Home, home, home*. Instead of taking a left that would carry me toward the River Clyde and the gleaming tower of city apartments, I turned right, circumventing arm-in-arm couples to the string of upscale restaurants lining Hope Street.

That neighborhood belonged to a younger Juniper. A little more wild, monumentally less jaded and owner of one too many band t-shirts. By some miracle I'd put my journalism degree to good use and wrangled an entry level position at the Glasgow Herald only a year out of Uni. I always left out the part where I worked for the Gossip column, the ancient editor had taken one look at my septum piercing and declared, "*You'll bring a little edge*" whatever that meant. I hadn't cared that the stories were trashy. I'd loved the endless bustle of the Cube Farm office and the smell of shit coffee from my *World's Sexiest Journalist* mug (a gift from my best friend Heather). I'd loved that when I got really into a story, my fingers refused to type as quickly as the words flowed through my brain because it felt like I had my finger right on the pulse of something great. I'd loved that every Friday, Alistair took the subway from Hillend to Buchanan Street to take me out for lunch.

Almost a year since I'd set foot in the city.

Almost a year since my engagement party that changed everything.

The memory of my father, Alexander, collapsed on the dance floor clutching his chest, left me cold. A heart attack. Overnight, the strongest man I'd ever known became so frail he'd almost appeared childlike as he recuperated in a hospital bed. I'd dropped everything. Rushed home to help take care of him. Put my life and my relationship on hold. And then he'd died not even four months later. And every dream I'd had for myself died with him.

You're better off alone anyway, wean. Who'd want to stay with you anyway? The phantom voice slid through me like a white-hot poker. The voice of a nameless, faceless woman who'd abandoned her one-year-old daughter in a hospital toilet.

Brushing off the urge to glance down at my empty ring finger, I careened into the first bar I came across. Thirteen months – I'd been without it longer than I'd worn it – and yet I still felt the weight of it like a missing limb.

A young man greeted me at the door, head tilted back to meet my eyes. His widened ever so slightly and my lips tipped with wicked delight. *Oh, I really enjoyed that.* Shame he was a little short for my taste. Call me old-fashioned, but when a man fucked me against a wall, I preferred when my toes didn't drag on the floor.

Height was the very least I required when searching for a companion for the night. Not that I *was* looking, exactly. All I wanted was to drink and eat my own weight until I forgot the little fact I was back in Glasgow, the ghost of my old life haunting my every step.

Taking a seat in a small booth in the back, I paused the waiter before he could leave, ordering two martinis and a small feast of carbs from the bar menu. The food was with me in minutes: two bowls of skinny fries, whisky-battered onion rings, those little balls with veggie haggis in the middle, and a bowl of olives. I popped one into my mouth, savouring the salty flavour as a shadow fell over me. A hand gripped the back of the booth. I tracked it up to its owner.

A man around my age. Handsome in a generic kind of way. He was the kind of man you'd find modelling in an office supply catalogue, attractive, but not attractive enough to distract you from the swivel chair with adjustable lumbar support.

"Having a party?" He grinned across the circular table showing a dimpled cheek he probably thought was adorable. I wondered if he practised the move in the bath-room mirror.

"A wake if you don't remove your hand from my booth."

He jerked, eyes flicking between mine incredulously. "A shut-down, just like that?"

I dragged the second olive from the stick with my teeth. "*Just like that*." A man behind him – his friend, I assumed – snorted into his drink.

"Bitch!" he hissed, flipping me off and stalking away.

"Rude!" I called to his retreating back. "I thought you wanted to be friends?"

I'd barely dug back into my food when a second figure shadowed my table. One of his friends here to shoot their shot with the bitch in the back, no doubt. Perhaps I'd gotten extra lucky and they'd wagered money on it.

Not in the mood, I didn't even glance up. "Come any closer and I'll plant this cocktail stick in your eyeball." I held the miniature weapon up for his viewing pleasure.

"Unnecessarily vicious and yet I admire the creativity, harpy."

I froze. Every hair on my body rising at the deep brogue. The nickname. The lilt of humour that exposed a man who took very little seriously.

A different kind of ghost entirely.

Sitting back slowly, I had to fight to keep my voice even. "Callum Macabe."

He nodded to my new friend at the bar. "That looked brutal." His smile revealed pointed incisors I'd always envied.

He wore a charcoal suit, dark but not quite black. No tie. His light brown hair, the exact same shade as Alistair's, was a little longer than when I'd last seen him, curling at the edges of his open shirt collar.

I folded one leg over the other in a move more confident than I felt. "For him or me?"

"The lad looked heartbroken."

"I'm sure he'll find another *bitch* to keep him entertained for the evening."

Callum's grin vanished, shoulders pulling taut beneath the fitted jacket. "He called you that?"

He looked almost . . . angry – an emotion I didn't know Callum Macabe was capable of. It delighted me enough that I crooned, "Why Callum . . . you making plans to defend my honour?"

"If you ask nicely." The words were casual. The glare he tossed at my new friends was *not*. I could have sworn they all slouched in their seats.

We lapsed into silence, and I twizzled the now empty cocktail stick between my red-painted lips. Callum watched it with an intensity I wasn't accustomed to, the blue eyes he shared with Alistair flashing a sharp cobalt.

In an instant I was dragged back to that day on the train. The unconcealed heat in his eyes when he saw me again at Alistair's place. There, and gone so suddenly, I'd seen the regret settle like a mask over his features. Polite. Distant. A little cold.

Perhaps that's how everyone looked at their brother's girlfriend.

He wasn't looking at me like that now.

Tugging off his jacket, he slung it over the back of the booth and sat.

"What are you doing?" I demanded, steadying the table when he knocked it with his knee.

"Having dinner." His shirt cuffs came next, as he unbuttoned and then rolled the white cotton over toned forearms dusted with light hair. He kept a polite distance between our thighs, however his eyes lingered on the lacy bralette just visible beneath my shirt. A muscle in his jaw pulsed.

I crossed my arms over my chest. "Ordered your own, have you?"

Laughter lines at the corners of his eyes crinkled. "You're seriously going to eat all of that?"

"*Yes.*"

Clearly, he thought I was talking shit, yet when the waiter approached, he put in the exact same order – minus the olives – then sipped his drink with rapt attention while I pretended he didn't exist and sampled one of everything on the table.

I didn't ask him to leave. I should have. Because in the short time it took for the waiter to return with his food, an invisible third body had squeezed into the seat between us. Alistair, who at that very moment was probably a ten-minute walk away in his fancy high-rise apartment.

"What are you doing here?"

He seemed relieved by the question, or perhaps relieved by what I *didn't* ask.

"Met up with some old army pals. And you?"

"A small business conference in the city."

He nodded, thick fingers tracing the rim of his glass. "You're running Ivy House now, how's that going?"

Awful, I wanted to shout. *Fiona has turned into a control freak ever since Alexander died and refuses to let me change a thing. Heather and I barely talk, and I've got no fucking idea what I'm doing.* All I said was, "It's going."

His brow furrowed, clearly reading between the lines. "*Ah*, family fun . . . I'm really sorry about your dad, I wanted to talk to you at the funeral—"

I snorted into my martini. "Absolutely not. If you start with that you can take your food to go."

"What?"

"Pity." My nose wrinkled.

"It's not pity, it's sympathy."

"They are the exact same thing and I don't want it."

"Okay." He slung an arm over the booth's curved back, fingers a hair's breadth from the sharp ends of my bob. The last time he'd seen me it had fallen down my back in long waves. "What *do* you want, Juniper?"

Fuck, it was suddenly stifling in here. I couldn't remove my jacket without him thinking it was some sort of come-on.

Maybe I should remove it.

"I want to drink my two martinis in peace."

"You only have one."

"I have another on a tab." I pointed to the waiter who flushed adorably and raised his hand in a half wave.

"Hmm." Callum's eyes slid to the waiter and back to me. Then he shifted closer, the leather of the seat creaking under the weight. "I don't think that's what you want. I think you love that I came over here and ruined your lonely little evening. And when those two martinis hit, you're going to thank me for interrupting an evening of disappointing sex with some two-pump twenty-something."

I rolled my eyes. Hard. "*Christ,* I'd forgotten you were like this."

"Honest?"

"No, arrogant."

"Harpy, I've had sneezes last longer than that boy will between your legs." His eyes swept over my every feature, ending at the line of my jaw where my shorter hair now brushed. I did the same. He'd grown more handsome in the year since I'd seen him, features a little more chiselled with age, the scruff of facial hair a little longer. I used to find him too rugged, favouring Alistair's more *refined* features.

11

He looked different now.

Or maybe he looked exactly the same and something else had changed.

His throat bobbed.

"I like your hair this way," he said. Rough and low, as though he meant something else entirely. It was like he'd licked the words into my skin for all that my body reacted. Still holding his gaze, I lifted a hand to signal the waiter.

"What are you doing?"

"Ordering those drinks." I was going to need them.

"Did you bring a coat?" Callum cleared his throat, following me to the bar's exit. I shook my head.

We'd talked for hours, Callum eventually stepping in to finish my fries without comment when I pushed the bowl away. The conversation never once straying to Alistair, and when we eventually slid from the table, I no longer felt the weight of his presence between us.

Probably the effect of two martinis. The last had tasted extra strong and was subsequently the exact same moment kissing my ex's brother stopped feeling like a monumental mistake.

He still wore only his white shirt, his suit jacket now gallantly hanging over my shoulders after the bar's aircon became too much to stand. "Where are you staying?" We paused in the small entry.

"The Grosvenor."

He stared at me for the longest time, then scrubbed a hand over his jaw and shook his head. "Me too."

I sensed his lie, too distracted by the heat pulsating through every limb to mind as I replied, "What a coincidence."

His head whipped to look at me. "I could . . . drive you. I only had one drink." We'd retreated to opposite corners of the small space, like opponents in a ring, waiting for the other to tap out first. His jaw ticked as he tracked lower, down the line of my neck and pausing at the V of my shirt, half hidden beneath both of our jackets.

When the tension became too much, I broke our stare, dropping my gaze to my feet in time to see him step closer. Not stopping until his dress shoes whispered against my open-toed heels and my back pressed against the exterior door. The long silence pulsed. "Turn me down, Juniper."

I couldn't think. Couldn't speak around my racing heart.

This was so wrong. *God*, I knew it was half the reason I was getting off on it.

His finger swept down my throat. "We both know where this is going. Tell me . . . *fuck*, tell me to step away. Tell me to act like a half-decent brother . . . tell me to put you in a taxi and not look back." He was trembling, the words so raw they sounded dragged from his chest. "Juniper. Tell me this is a bad idea. Tell me . . . tell me I'm not for you." When I remained silent, he thumbed my chin up until our eyes locked. His expression was caught somewhere between fierce arousal and panic. "You need to be the one to say it. I can't walk away from you on my own."

Silence echoed for two thunderous heartbeats, Alistair's handsome face rising behind my eyelids. His smile the cruellest taunt.

And that voice slipped into my mind like an eel, reminding me that I deserved nothing. Deserved to be lonely.

"Bring the car around."

Callum

Alistair: Breakfast while you're in town?
Callum: Raincheck?
Alistair: Understood, brother . . . have a good night ;)

She's changed her mind, a vicious voice whispered. I snarled back at it like a challenged wolf, turning onto the busy through road and idling in the loading bay before the bar. If she'd changed her mind that was . . . fine. *For the best*.

I'd find a way to get over it. Eventually.

The clock ticked.

Thirty seconds passed.

A minute.

My hands tightened around the wheel. Guilt and hope battling in my chest. I needed to leave. Turn on the ignition and drive and drive until I was no longer swallowing down lungfuls of Juniper's perfume like I needed to commit it to memory. Imagining kissing those red fucking lips I was obsessed with.

Or . . . I could accept the fact she'd never truly be mine and grasp onto this one night – this one taste – like a gift and spend the rest of my life picking up the pieces.

The bar's door opened. My breath caught. Juniper's lean frame came into view, even taller in those fucking shoes that were hot enough to feed every single fantasy I played out for the next twenty years. Suddenly I was so bloody tired of fighting my feelings. Ever since that day on the train she'd only ever been a single thought away.

When I was with her, I only thought of how I could put distance between us. Hang onto that last remaining scrap of sanity. During the long stretches of time I didn't see her, I obsessed over all the ways I could force a meeting: a day trip to Skye, a quick text just to check in. Anything that put me on her radar for even a second.

Her head pivoted on the step, searching for *me*. My body acted independently, I flashed the headlights once. *Decision fucking made*. She veered in my direction, her measured steps brimming with expectation. *Alistair had his chance.* The sentiment beat like a drum as I bent across the console and opened the door, about to warn her of the steep step when her pale thigh flashed through the slit of her silk skirt and those endless legs ate up the distance with ease.

The door closed behind her and the car fell into darkness. Against the inky backdrop she reminded me of a heroine in a noir movie, too unobtainable to exist anywhere but a film reel. Her tongue licked over her lower lip and she glanced everywhere but me. "I've never been in your car."

She was nervous, I realised with a jolt. My harpy was never nervous. It made me falter too, hand trembling as I reached to cup her cheek and turned her to face me.

"Callum?" Her brows pulled together, and I wondered what my expression must look like. Desperate. Reverential most likely. I didn't care, my name on her lips the only thing that mattered.

My fingers curled, grasping her nape.

Hearts shouldn't beat this fast, I thought, feeling light-headed. This was the closest I'd ever been to her . . . the longest I'd ever touched her.

Tomorrow, I wouldn't remember who moved first. Only the crash of lips. The slide of tongue and reaching hands. I clasped her face between my palms, fingers sinking into the silken strands at her temples at the same time she grabbed my shirt, wrenching the material in fists and tugging as we scrambled to get closer, lips pressing to a punishing degree. I moaned her name between kisses, harsh grunts that made the soft curves of her name sharp as I opened my mouth, tongue flicking along the seam, searching for hers. Every time I got close she withdrew, keeping it from me.

"*Fuck*," I gasped. "You taste . . . you taste . . ." Exactly how I dreamed. *Better.*

She pushed to her knees, nails scraping my scalp almost painfully, tilting my head back until she towered over me on the narrow seat. My hands curled around her hips, beginning to tug her over my lap, exactly where I needed her, when a laugh filtered through the frenzy.

A young group of lads circled the window. One had the gall to give me a thumbs up. *Jesus*, Juniper had kissed me fucking blind, and I hadn't even tasted her tongue yet.

"*Fuck* – not here." I didn't grace them with a response, easing Juniper into her seat and strapping her in. It took three attempts to find the buckle. Other than her smudged lipstick and finger-tangled hair, she looked completely unruffled. That'd be the first thing I'd change once I got her beneath me.

"Take off the jackets," I ordered, voice the steely command of an army sergeant. She cocked a brow – the smooth movement never failing to make me hard – but complied. Swinging the car in an arc and looping onto Argyle Street, I had to remind myself to keep the speed down on the narrow lanes. "Underwear too."

I didn't look at her – *couldn't* – or I'd be done for.

"You seem to be mistaken, Macabe, thinking you're the one in charge here."

She was in charge, all right. Always had been. Still, I smirked. "You see, I'm all about give and take, harpy. And once I have you in a bed, I plan to do a whole lot of giving."

She paused, just long enough I thought she might not comply. And then her legs unfolded. Hands disappearing beneath her skirt. I tracked their trajectory up her thighs, heart thundering as I waited for them to reappear. She unhooked the article from her ankle. A lacy scrap so thin I could have torn through it with my teeth.

"*Fuck* – it's white." I couldn't say why that mattered. But it did.

Her lips twisted into a devious smile as she balled them, shoving the lace into my cup holder. "I like to keep men on their toes."

I snatched up the material the second she relinquished it. Brought it to my face, inhaled, then spread it out across my thigh. My eye-rolling groan had her laughing as we stopped at a traffic light. The red gleam made her skin glow like a flame behind glass. Her entire face lit, excitement burning in her brown eyes.

Too perfect to be real.

How many times had I imagined her like this? A thousand? More?

Holding my gaze, her square little teeth bit into her lower

lip. Her fingers curled around the hem of her skirt, dragging it higher. Inch by torturous inch. "*Fuck*."

"You said that already."

"Are you going to be trouble, Juniper? Please say yes."

"Undoubtedly." Her head sank against the headrest, dark eyes flashing, breasts rising and falling as her fingers dipped between her thighs. Not high enough to touch herself but high enough to drive me out of my mind.

I groaned again, zero control over the sounds coming out my mouth. If I wasn't so turned on, I might have been embarrassed.

"Macabe?"

"Yes?"

"The light's green."

"*Shit*." The car jolted, almost stalling as I fumbled into the correct gear. "Don't you touch yourself, harpy! Do you hear me? Do not touch yourself."

She hummed in pleasure. I risked a glance and swore as her back arched. "I'm in charge, remember?" Her moan cut straight out my fantasies.

"You're in charge. But unless you want a head-on collision in your near future, you'll grant me this small mercy." My hands white-knuckled around the wheel, fighting the need to glance again. To find the nearest side street and watch her stroke herself into oblivion. "I'll gladly watch you pet that pussy all night if that's what you want. Once I get you there safely."

At the next junction, the hotel came into view. Tyres spat gravel as I careened into the car park.

"Around the back," Juniper panted.

I parked haphazardly beneath a streetlight. Throwing myself from the car and around the bonnet with singular intent. Juniper already had the door open. I caught it, swinging it the rest of the way. Grasping her thigh and spreading it further until I could see all of her. Endless legs, drenched thighs and the prettiest pussy I'd ever bloody seen. I needed to taste her, right there on the cracked leather.

"Now, Macabe." Eyes fluttering closed, she fell back on her elbows. "Are you going to fuck me better than he ever did?"

More turned on than I'd ever been, it took a moment for her words to register. When they did, my body responded as if to an ice plunge. Pure dread followed by a cold so bitter, it hollowed out my insides.

My lips were a fraction from her clit. Close enough to scent her. *Taste* her if I dipped my tongue out.

"Fuck you better than *who*, Juniper?" Clearly I was a fucking masochist because I knew who.

"Forget it . . ." Her thighs tightened around my shoulders. "Just . . . just fuck me already."

Don't stop, my mind screamed at me. *You both want it. You're never going to get this chance again.*

It was the tight squeeze of her eyes that had me stumbling back. *If I continued, would it even be me fucking her? Or the memory of him?*

Heart wrenching, my hands shook as I tugged her skirt down. "I'm sorry."

A single beat of silence and she pushed to sit. "You're not serious?"

I shook my head, trying to block out the burn of rejection in hers. "I can't . . . we shouldn't—"

She barked a cruel laugh. "You couldn't even get me off before deciding to grow a conscience?"

"Fuck, harpy, I'm—"

"Don't you dare apologise again." She half fell from the

19

car, snatching up her jacket and purse. The lights in the car park just bright enough to reveal the deep red of her cheeks.

"I didn't mean – I shouldn't have – you don't really want this."

She halted but didn't turn. "You're suddenly an expert on what I want?"

"No. But I know it's not this." *Not me.* "And I refuse to do something I'll regret in the morning." The words were all wrong. I knew it the second they left my lips.

The world seemed to stop, the sound of the traffic disappeared as the moment stretched between us. Suddenly I was back on a Glasgow train platform, watching the only woman to spike my interest in years walk away from me.

Only this time she didn't speak. There was no smirk. No witty retort. Just climbed the steps to her hotel. And then she was gone.

NOW

Five Years Later, Kinleith

1

Callum

Mal: Where the hell are you?
Mal: Heather is going to dump my mutilated corpse into the sea if she has to wait for the food any longer!
Callum: Sorry! Give me ten minutes.
Callum: Make that twenty!

"Did you really wear those shoes to a beach party, harpy?" Every muscle in Juniper Ross's perfect body tensed at the sound of my voice.

Then in true Juniper fashion, she didn't whirl, but spun with slow calculation – no doubt getting sand in those chunky black loafers – to glare at me, eyeing the six-pack tucked under my arm with an eye roll. "A few grilled sausages and a crate of beer hardly constitutes a party."

"Sure is fun though." I winked. Another move guaranteed to get her icy blood pumping. As was the way my eyes dragged down her body, over the short little skirt, made even shorter by her mile-long legs. "Shit, you're even wearing tights."

"My tights are better than . . ." she trailed off, nose

22

wrinkling at the swim shorts covered in tiny half-peeled bananas I'd slung on after racing over from my parents' place. "What even are those?"

Adjusting the six-pack, I spun in place, giving her a full view of the goods. "Swimming shorts, harpy. Don't let the size of the bananas fool you."

She grimaced like they were the most offensive things she'd seen in her life. "I suppose I should be thankful you didn't wear the Speedo I know you have tucked away somewhere."

"Imagine it often, do you?"

Instead of answering, she snapped her sunglasses down over her eyes. The frames slightly tilted like cat eyes. *Fucking classy is what they are.* "As always, lovely chatting to you, Macabe."

I won't lie, I watched her walk away. Her slight hips swaying all the way to the shoreline where she accepted a canned drink from April, my brother Mal's girlfriend.

"Callum!"

"Callum!"

It took a third shout to drag my attention away. *Bloody infuriating woman.*

Cutting through the small group, I crossed to where Mal was manning a grill. The smell of charcoal-burned meat enough to make me wince.

"It's about time," he grumbled as soon as I was in earshot. Hair stuck to his forehead. Sweat pouring down his flushed, stubbled cheeks.

I'd promised last week to help carry the grill down the steep bank from his cottage to the small, private beach that bordered Kinleith Whisky Distillery.

I'd also promised to do the cooking.

And pick up the cake. *Shit, I forgot the cake.*

"Sorry, sorry!" Setting the crate down by the ice boxes, I

yanked the spatula from his hand, manoeuvred him away from the waist-high flames and lowered the gas before we became responsible for a wildfire.

Today was April's birthday and my sweetheart of a baby brother had wracked his brains for an entire month, trying to plan something special. The low-key beach party had been my suggestion. Which he'd agreed to so long as I was around to help with the cooking.

"I got caught up at Mum and Dad's."

He paused, holding a bag of half-opened hot dog buns. "Everything all right?"

We all had a . . . *complicated* relationship with our father, Mal more than any of us.

Jim Macabe was an arsehole, to put it bluntly. An arsehole obsessed with the idea of moulding his sons into *successful men*. As the oldest boy, I'd been placed into boxing lessons from the time I could walk. And when I came of age, the British army. Just like dear old Dad. Alistair had replicated our father's later-in-life vocation as a general practitioner. Malcolm, being the only son who dared to live the life he wanted, had paid the price in the form of years of verbal put downs. Dad never missed an opportunity to let Mal know how disappointed he was with him.

Now Jim Macabe was an arsehole with Alzheimer's. And it had all become a lot more . . . *complicated*.

That fucking word seemed to haunt me these days.

"Everything's fine, just helping Mum throw out some old clothes," I lied. If I told him Dad had developed a habit of wandering from the house over the last few weeks he'd only offer to help. The last thing I wanted was Mal feeling obligated to get involved.

He nodded, silently adding a couple of burgers to the grill while I flipped. "That bean burger is June's. Don't get it muddled with the meat or she'll have my balls." He shuddered and I laughed at the genuine fear in his tone.

"Wouldn't it be a shame if I ate it?" I joked. As if there were any way I would actually follow through.

"If you piss off my best friend at my birthday party, I'll have *your* balls." April appeared out of nowhere, ducking under Mal's arm to wrap hers around his waist. She looked pretty as a picture, her red hair seeming to burn against the light blue summer dress.

"Please don't talk about my brother's balls."

I laughed, cracking open a much-needed beer. "Still salty, I see." While April and Mal were getting together, I *might* have flirted with April in a bid to get his arse into gear. April was a beautiful, world-famous actress, it was barely a hardship. Not that I would have ever *actually* gone there. One brother's girl was all my conscience could take. "And Juniper's always pissed off." Selecting a clean turner, I flipped the bean burger.

"She doesn't look pissed off right now," April said. Like a magnet, my eyes sought Juniper, easily finding where she reclined on a beach towel.

No, she did not.

In fact, she looked far *too* happy. Laughing at whatever crap Jamie Stewart was pouring into her ear. He was a good lad. A great shinty player. But he didn't stand a chance with Juniper. She'd eat him alive.

Then why does it bother you so much?

Rather than untangle that mess, I brought my beer to my lips. Before I could take a single sip, "Uncle Cal!" split the air. My nieces Ava and Emily, giggling with childish excitement as they wobbled over the soft sand, Boy and Dudley – Mal and April's little and large dogs – hot on their heels.

"Uncle Cal, Uncle Cal!" Ava's hands waved like excited pinwheels. Boy barked, his giant Golden Retriever paws leaving wet prints on my white T-shirt.

"Oops." Emily giggled.

"Hi girls, causing mischief?" I bent down, ruffling Boy's cheeks.

"We found a dog!" Emily bounced on her toes. Soaked from the water guns clutched in their hands, beads of water clung to dark eyelashes.

"A dog?" Frowning, I glanced about. Only seeing Boy and Dudley. "Where?"

"In the grass." They both pointed up the sandbank. "It's hurt."

"Can you show me?" Expressions suddenly serious, they nodded, both of them reaching for my hands. I looked over my shoulder at Mal, letting them lead me away. "I'll be back."

"Shit," I huffed a minute later.

"That's a bad word. Mummy said we can't use bad words."

"She might let us say it if Uncle Cal uses it," Emily said to her twin. "Can we say it, Uncle Cal?"

"No."

"*What if I only whisper it?*" Emily whispered.

Trying not to startle the curled-up creature, I lowered to my haunches, putting my finger to my lips to hush their chatter. Ava and Emily immediately closed in on either side of me.

"Is the dog hurt bad, Uncle Cal?" Ava asked.

"It's not a dog." I tilted my head, eyes racing over the dark brown fur and whiskered face, looking for signs of injury. "It's an otter."

"*Shit.*"

"Emily!" Ava whisper-shouted in my ear, always the voice of authority. "Uncle Cal said no."

Emily argued back, something about an occasion last

month when Ava had spelled the word *idiot* with her fingers so she couldn't get in trouble.

"Girls," I interrupted. "Can you do me a favour? It's really important." Wide-eyed, they both nodded. "I need you to run back to beach and grab me a blanket so I can take this little guy to the Sea Life Sanctuary." I might have started my veterinarian studies at twenty-three – the very moment I was able to relinquish my role in the army – but I had very little knowledge of aquatic mammals.

"I'll get it!"

"No, I will. *Emily* . . . I'll get it. You take over everything!"

Listening to their retreating steps, I tried not to sigh. Assessing the trembling animal once again. It wasn't the little guy's fault I hadn't gotten enough sleep on Mum and Dad's squeaky camp bed. Or that I hadn't paused long enough to eat anything today. It needed help and it was my job to provide it.

The centre was only a twenty-minute drive away. If things went to plan, I could be back in an hour. I needed to grab April's cake from the bakery anyway.

Ten minutes later, with the sorrowful otter the twins had nicknamed Finneas tucked into a beach towel, I made my excuses to April and Mal.

"Just can't resist playing the hero." April laughed, leaning back against Mal's chest. "No wonder June calls you 'Community Ken'."

"She does?" Amused, confused and slightly aroused at the knowledge, I couldn't resist sneaking a glance her way. My teeth clicked. Still on that damn blanket with a man ten years my junior, Jamie's expression suggesting Christmas and his birthday had come at once as his eyes pinged between her legs and her face. I couldn't even fault the lad; both were irritatingly spectacular.

"Hey, girls." I waved to the twins, dripping water pistols still in hand. "Aunty Juniper's looking a little too dry for a beach party." They squealed, accepting their mission with a little too much enthusiasm.

"Shit," Mal said.

"Well . . . this has been fun." April turned in Mal's arms to watch the show. "Remember what I said about your balls." I blocked all images of Juniper and my balls before they could take form. This was a family affair.

"You've had a good time?" Mal asked into her hair.

She tipped her head back on his chest, her expression spilling over with adoration. "The perfect day. Thank you."

"Princess—"

A scream split the air. *And* . . . that was my cue.

Juniper was wringing out her short hair by the time I passed by, accepting the towel an equally soaked Jamie so gallantly offered. *We get it. You're a real fucking Prince Charming.*

"Captain," he said when he spotted me. "All ready for the game next week?"

"Yep." I wasn't. I hadn't even found time to book the pitch, which as captain of the Kinleith Shinty club was my responsibility.

I didn't spare the kid another glance, too busy soaking up the furious little snarl on Juniper's face as I clutched Finneas to my chest. *You're a sick, twisted man*, a voice whispered. Because if I couldn't have her affection, you'd be damn sure I'd take her fury. Anything that kept my name on those red lips.

"You're looking a little . . . wet, harpy."

"Screw you, Macabe."

I winked, already retreating. "Enjoy the party."

2

Juniper

The Macabe brother rule book (according to Juniper Ross):
1. **Don't look at a Macabe brother.**
2. **Don't talk to a Macabe brother.**
3. **Don't even think about a Macabe brother.**

"I swear, I've never gone through this many lint rollers in my entire life." I cast a look from my shirt, saturated with a coat of thankfully black hair, to Shakespeare. The deceivingly elegant black cat currently taking up the centre of my bed. She yawned and stretched onto her back, spreading more fur across the bedsheets. "Your grand plans for the day?"

Narrow eyes met mine. Tempted by her soft little cat belly, I extended a finger then immediately snapped it back when the action won me a fresh welt across my forearm.

"Remind me why I adopted you again?" Circling the island that separated the kitchen from the bedroom in my small, open-plan cottage, I ran the scratch under cold water and pulled my sleeve down to cover it. "You've been a pain in my arse from the moment I brought you home. I should have made you into a hat."

A pain in my arse was an understatement. While gorgeous to look at, the cat was a fucking menace who hated me.

With every passing day, it became more and more obvious that Kelly, Kinleith's sweet-as-pie veterinary nurse, had played me. She'd flat out *begged* me to take the '*misunderstood sweetheart*' home. A month and too many wounds to count, I'd come to realise Kelly simply wanted her to be someone else's problem.

Pouring kibble into the hellion's bowl for her to ignore, I called, "Don't wait up." And stepped out the door before the sun had even risen, not bothering to lock it behind me. One of the limited benefits of living a hundred metres from your place of work.

I'd moved into the small, stone-wall cottage six years ago, upon my return to Kinleith. Sitting on the very tip of the wildflower garden, it offered a little more privacy than the family apartments covering the top floor of Ivy House Inn.

Slipping through the back, I cringed at the creak in the old door, tracing my finger along the aged tartan wallpaper that decorated the walls of the old servants' entrance. Built in the late 1860s, the sprawling house, with its uneven floors, slate roof and ivy-coated walls, had once served as the "Old Manse", or vicarage, until the village church was decommissioned in the 1950s. Cue my grandfather, or *adoptive* grandfather, I should say, who bought the property and turned it into Kinleith's first guest house.

This was my favourite time of day at Ivy House, in the morning silence, the guests still sleeping. When the well-worn floorboards told the story of my home, rather than someone else's destination. In the quiet kitchen, the smell of garlic and rosemary hit me first. Ducking beneath hanging copper pans and dried herbs, I flicked on the oven and coffee machine in preparation for the breakfast service. All the while smirking at the thought of Hank, our curmudgeonly chef, grousing when he realised *I'd* gotten here first.

Brushing hands down my jeans, I left the way I came, refusing to so much as glance at the neighbouring property as I climbed into my car and drove the five minutes into Kinleith village.

That would be a direct violation of rule one of the Macabe brother rule book.

"Morning, Jess." I greeted Jessica Brown, the owner of Brown's Coffee & Cakes, with a bright smile I reserved only for her.

"Juniper, how are ye, lass?" Her pale skin practically shone beneath the fluorescent lights as she set both hands on the counter, taking the weight from her legs. After her double hip replacement last year, she'd remained obstinate in her refusal to follow doctor's orders and take it easy. So a plush stool now sat behind the ancient till – a compromise I'd yet to witness her make use of.

"Good. Not so busy at the inn now the tourist season is winding down. It's nice to have a little breather after the long summer." We'd been booked solid for the months of June, July and August, even with the perpetually leaking showers Fiona refused to replace. We'd been forced to cancel a few bookings in late July when a toilet backed up and put two rooms out of commission for a full week. And I now held the conviction I could strip and remake an entire bed with my eyes closed.

"How's that mother of yers? Still off on that trip?" Jess

gave a toss of her short, blue-rinsed hair with a derisive little snort. "In my day, we couldn't go gallivanting all over the world to meet men. We stayed here and made do wi' what we had."

"What a sad time. You'd have cleaned out in a big city, Jess."

She cackled, batting a hand my way. "Yer a daftie for encouraging her, she'll come home wi' one of those diseases they're always warning about."

I smothered my grin. "What kind of diseases are we talking about, exactly?"

"Did that fancy city education teach yer nothing, girl? Sex diseases!"

The door jingled then opened. Awareness prickled the back of my scalp.

Damn it. I knew I was cutting it close.

"What's this about sex diseases?" Callum Macabe stopped behind me, so close his chest grazed my back.

My nostrils flared.

Don't look at a Macabe brother.

Don't talk to a Macabe brother.

Don't even think about a Macabe brother.

I broke that last rule too frequently, but I let Callum take the blame. The results of *his* annoyance shouldn't lie at my door.

The rules didn't really apply to Mal, either. Especially since he'd started dating April over the summer. I hadn't seen Alistair in the six years since he'd stomped my heart into a thousand pieces, so it was truly the *Callum Macabe* rules. But even in the privacy of my own head it felt dangerous to single him out.

"Your favourite kind," I quipped. Breaking rule two almost immediately.

"Does a person have a favourite kind of disease? Though if I had to pick . . . it would be necrotising fasciitis, a rare and interesting flesh-eating disease."

What the hell is he talking about? Returning to pretending he didn't exist, I said to Jess, "It's about time she had a little fun, and it's not a sex trip. Though that does sound preferable to spending a month with my Aunt Sylvia. She's going on a singles' cruise to relax and if she happens to meet a man, then, good for her."

"Fun," Jess tutted again. I wondered if you reached a certain age where tutting just became second nature. "You youngins all want the fun, fun, fun, without the hard work."

"I don't know, Jess, sex should take a little hard work if you're doing it right."

I snorted. I couldn't help it. Callum's attention singed my skin like a branding iron. I hoped to hell my hair looked good from the back. "You consider sex, *work*? I pity the women unfortunate enough to wind up in your bed."

He stepped around me, his smile . . . luminous. Strike that. *Irritating.* The same smile he wore every time he managed to get a rise out of me. *Damn it.* What happened to "don't even look at a Macabe brother"?

"Have you imagined me in your bed, harpy? Does it warm those cold loins at night?"

Our attention met and I said with saccharine sweetness, "Only when I'm struggling to sleep, I picture you and—" I snapped my fingers. "I'm out like a light." He smirked again and I knew I'd lost this battle. "Speaking of work, I need to get going."

"Running late for a seance?"

"A cursing, actually. I'm short of a few ingredients."

"What might those be?"

"Five eyelashes and a pint of blood. Yours would probably suffice."

His lips twitched, revealing the lone dimple that lived between his scruff of facial hair and cheekbone. "I'm flattered, harpy. Truly. Unfortunately, I prefer to keep my blood where it belongs."

"A pity." I scratched my cheek with my middle finger, a total primary school move that made him snicker. *He won't be laughing in a moment.* "I'll take twelve oat and raisin cookies please, Jess."

Callum drew in a sharp breath and Jess's thin eyebrows rose. "All twelve?" she asked.

"You can't buy them all!"

I let one side of my mouth curl. "And why not? Is there a new cookie policy I'm not aware of?" Jess's gaze pinged between us. It had been a few months since we'd had a show-down in Brown's – or anywhere, I usually aborted before it got that far – but yesterday, he'd crossed a line with those water guns. My blood demanded retribution.

"Well . . . *no*," Jess said.

"Excellent. The same box is perfect, we have a guest who requested them."

Smelling the lie, Callum gritted his teeth, hands on his hips while he watched Jess pack away every one of the freshly baked biscuits. Jess kept the cookie selection on a daily rotation. Monday being oat and raisin day. And who just happened to *love* oat and raisin cookies, you ask?

"Oh, did you want one?" Box securely in hand, I turned to Callum, feigning a guileless smile as I flipped the lid. "I'm sure my guest won't mind sharing . . . if you ask me nicely, of course."

He eyed the still-warm treats and his lips parted. Tempted.

Yes! I mentally fist pumped. Bloody *willing* his begging into existence.

Then just as I thought he was about to break down and tear the box from my hands, he slumped back. "You take them. In fact." He pulled his wallet from the pocket of blue scrubs, and I refused to acknowledge how delightfully they stretched across his wide chest. "Allow me to pay and send your *guest* my best wishes."

Fuck. "Great." I flashed my teeth in a semblance of a grin.

"Just a coffee for ye, Callum?" Jess asked as I fell out of the line. "We have chocolate muffins too."

"No thanks, Jess, just the coffee is fine." He flipped his wallet open, and I aimed for the exit, waving my goodbye to Jess while she was distracted.

Flying through the door, I was met with a surprised *oof*. My elbow brushed flesh. "Oh, I'm sorry—"

"Watch where you're going—" Somewhat harried, Jill Mortimer blew a perfect blonde curl out of her eyes. "You almost knocked me over."

Bloody wonderful. The woman and her little posse of friends hated me. It was all very juvenile of course and it gave me one more reason to stay out of the village.

"I'm sorry," I said again, edging around her on the cobbled path. "I didn't see you." Her eyes ran over me, taking in my hair, my clothes and settled on my septum piercing. Her lips pulled down.

"You're a little old to still be playing the hapless high schooler, aren't you Juniper?"

The tinkling of Brown's bell saved me from answering. Callum came into view and Jill transformed from shrew to siren in a heartbeat.

"Callum Macabe." Her voice went all breathy. Not "just finished a 5k breathy" like mine would have surely sounded, but "mid-sex breathy". My teeth ground as his face lit up, offering her the "Community Ken" smile he never gave me. "Fancy running into you here."

With less than three hundred residents in Kinleith and one main shopping street, the odds of running into Callum three doors down from his veterinarian practice were pretty substantial.

Instead of pointing that out and incriminating myself with my own deductions, I used the moment to slip away unnoticed. I made it all the way to the car park before he caught up with me.

"Well played, harpy," he called with a wink. "I hope you know what you've started."

Parking outside Ivy House, I found my mum, Fiona locked in a battle with her overloaded suitcase. "Let me get that." Gravel crunched under my feet. Setting the box of cookies on a large planter, I hoisted the case into my arms.

"Careful now, June bug. Don't pull your back."

I rolled my eyes only once my back was turned. "I'm not going to hurt myself lifting a suitcase. Who would look after this place?"

"Better not to test the theory." Her attempt to wrestle the suitcase back fell flat when I set it down on the gravel. The wheels instantly sank deep into the little stones.

"What the hell did you pack?"

"Only a month's worth of clothes." Despite the cool September wind, she wore a large floppy sun hat.

"You know the ship has a laundry service, right?"

"What if I get bored with my clothing options?"

"Touché." I might have been adopted, but in *that* regard, I was truly my mother's daughter. Though different in style, we were just as finicky about our fashion choices.

Shivering, she pulled her cardigan more tightly over her floral sundress. She'd be half frozen long before arriving at Glasgow airport, but I didn't say a word as I watched her fight against the wind tearing the brim of her hat. Relieved she'd finally accepted my Aunt Sylvia's invitation at all. Fiona never took holidays. Days off were few and far between.

Shaking off the thought, I urged her toward the waiting car. Neil, the only taxi driver based out of Kinleith, idled between the few visitor vehicles in our compact car park, an open book in his hand.

"You won't be late for the breakfast service, will you?" Fiona asked me.

"I still have thirty minutes and Hank is already well prepared." Hank had been in charge of the breakfast service long before I arrived as a frightened, gangly seven-year-old. He was basically part of the furniture. If the furniture had mutton chops and swore like a sailor.

"What if someone has an allergy?"

"Then I'll give them the allergy menu." I set the case down beside the car, offering Neil a small wave and nodding to the boot. He beat me there, slipping easily from the seat, and with a cheerful "Good morning" he stored it away.

Fiona wrung her hands together. "Remember the leaky shower in room five, don't put a guest in there unless you absolutely have to."

"I remember." I squeezed her shoulder, understanding that this separation couldn't be easy for her. Ivy House had been her baby long before I came along, even more so after Alexander's death. "You deserve this break. Let me hold the reins for a little while, yeah? You can trust me."

Her hand went to my cheek, stroking lovingly as always.

And as always, I fought the urge to draw away. "Of course I can, my darling girl, you know how I worry about you."

I held in my millionth rendition of my "*I'm a grown woman . . .*" speech and instead nudged her toward the back seat.

"You'll phone me if anything goes wrong." It wasn't a question.

"Cross my heart."

"And you have all the emergency phone numbers?"

I almost deflated with my sigh. She claimed to trust me and yet it was becoming clearer by the second that she didn't. "*Yes*, they're laminated and taped to the front desk. Exactly where *I* put them two years ago."

"Of course." She gnawed at her lip and I felt like the worst daughter in the world.

"Go and have fun. Get drunk every night and sleep with a sexy, too young waiter." She laughed but pain, clear and acute, dulled her eyes. A pain so ingrained in her features I wasn't sure I'd recognise her without it. Years filled with heartache and Ivy House were all she had to show for it. And me.

Though I wasn't sure I counted.

I flicked the brim of her hat. "Hold onto this thing on the ferry."

"I love you."

I love you too. I didn't say it, pulling her into a quick hug I hoped sufficed. "Make sure someone helps her with her case at the other end, will you, Neil? It's too heavy for her to lift alone."

"You got it, June." He winked in the mirror. "How about a drink later?"

"In your dreams." He knew good and well I no longer dated men from Skye.

I gave Fiona a final wave goodbye, listening to the crunch of the tyres as the taxi manoeuvred down the narrow lane that would take her through Kinleith village to the ferry port in Armadale.

The second the car slipped out of sight, I raced back to the inn. Peeling off my jacket and tossing it along with the box of forgotten cookies onto the reception desk, I cut down the hallway, past the kitchen and guest dining room, to the back door.

Gordon Murray already waited on the porch, his two grandsons in tow. "You're on time." *A first time for everything*.

Old man Murray grunted his greeting and brushed past me. "I dinnae like being ushered through the back o' house. I feel like I'm daein' something wrong."

"It's a surprise for Mum, I mentioned that on the phone."

"I still dinnae like it."

"This way," was all I said. Hank glowered from the kitchen as we passed and I stuck my tongue out. He didn't need to utter a single word for me to know he *fucking strongly disapproved*. He'd said as much every day for the past two weeks.

I already regretted my decision to hire Gordon Murray – a well-known complainer. But he was one of only three plumbers on the island and the other two were booked right through to November. That regret was starting to hold a little more weight when he halted and cursed halfway up the staircase. "My knees won't thank me fae this."

I'd issued the plumbing work to begin on the second floor, room five, where the leak was the worst, having put away money for over a year without Fiona's knowledge.

She'd be pissed when she realized.

Yet, this was my only chance to truly make Ivy House special.

More than a relic of the life she was holding onto while the building crumbled around our ears. Fiona argued city life had made me too ambitious, that you didn't need fancy gadgets and sleek interiors to compete in the hotel market. And I agreed. But adequate plumbing was where I drew the line.

Slipping the heavy key in my pocket, I flicked on the bathroom light in room five. "A skip will arrive tomorrow to collect the old parts. And remember to be careful with the black and white tiles on the shower walls, I want to keep those." Alexander had fitted those himself. Another reason Fiona was so reluctant to update.

"Right you are, lass." Pushing his thick-framed glasses up his nose, Murray ushered me out the way. I retreated, worry churning in my gut as I watched them get to work.

It will be fine, I assured myself.

It took only three days to dissuade me of that notion.

3

Callum

Kelly: Think you can squeeze an extra appointment in this afternoon?
Callum: Who's the patient?
Kelly: A four-year-old cat. Possible UTI.
Callum: No problem. Just shorten my lunch hour.

"What do you mean you're not coming home?" Swinging my car onto Bridge Road, I cut past the harbour and the rolling waves lapping in great swathes of foam over the pebbled beach, dragging with them the heavy clouds from the mainland. My brother's voice pulled away from the phone, murmuring to someone. "Alistair?"

"Sorry – *shit* – I'm listening." Paper rustled. "My resident nurse is on the phone to the hospital regarding a patient and I can't find his bloody file."

"You promised you were coming home next week. You've been promising for *months*."

"I know and I'm sorry. Things are just crazy here right now. You know I hate letting my patients down."

But he'd let his family down?

Guilt rose, edging out the treacherous thought. My brother was a good man doing a noble job. And yet . . . I was undeniably pissed. I wanted to go at him like I would have as a teen, until we were both a little bruised.

"I get it," I finally said, tamping down the bitterness threatening to poison my tone. Manoeuvring my oversized four-by-four, which was perfectly made for traversing the sprawling country roads of the island but felt ridiculous on the picturesque rat runs of Kinleith village, around a particularly tight corner, I aimed for the small car park at the end of the pedestrianised high street. "But you need to visit at some point, Alistair. I don't want to tell Heather and Mal yet, but he's getting worse every month." *Every week.* Just saying the words aloud felt like a betrayal to my ever-hopeful mother.

"I can't just abandon my life."

"I'm not asking you to abandon your life but, *hell*, take a few weeks off. You haven't taken a holiday in years; they owe you that much." How could he not grasp how important this was? "If you don't come back soon, you'll regret it for the rest of your life."

"I know and I will. Maybe next month when things calm down a little, yeah?" Low murmurs followed and I fought an eye roll. "Look," he said to me, "I've got to go. I'll phone Mum later and explain."

"Don't worry." Sighing, I rubbed a hand across my brow to ease the growing tension, suddenly weary to my damn bones. "I'll tell her."

I'd served as a medic in the military. Seen combat in wars I never wanted to be a part of. Held friends and innocent civilians as they took their final breaths. I'd experienced loss and pain over and over and over. It felt ridiculous that this could be the thing to finally break me.

"Yeah?" He sighed in relief, "Thanks big bro." The line cut out before I could say another word.

Fucking great. I slammed a hand on the wheel.

The unlined patch of tarmac before the town hall was tight, room for twelve cars, max. And that didn't account for the large RV currently taking up three spaces. "Damn tourists." Didn't they know summer was over?

Aiming for a small spot at the very end by the rope fence, I slowed, shifting into reverse just as another car entered the lot. A black, electric go-kart that looked about as safe as a tin can. And behind the wheel – the source of my every fantasy.

Juniper Ross peeled through the opening like a bat out of hell. Tyres spinning, she aimed for the singular parking spot. *My* spot. Had I been feeling more charitable, I might have let her have it.

Bad luck for her.

Extending my middle finger in her direction, I slung my free arm over the passenger seat, turning the wheel with the heel of my hand, backing smoothly into the space seconds before Juniper screeched to a halt, her bumper kissing mine.

Our eyes locked like competitors on a starting block, then she threw up her hands, mouth slinging silent curses that stoked my first laugh of the day. What I wouldn't give to hear every insult flying from that vicious mouth.

I was still laughing when I shut off the engine and climbed out. Juniper rolled down her window and anticipation fizzed in my stomach.

"What the hell, Macabe?" *Macabe.* Why did it get me so hot when she said my name like that? *Because you're a sick, sick man.* Her tone was cutting but somehow still sweet. Her expression like a knife dipped in honey.

"Oh, hey, neighbour." I flashed a grin. The toothy one that always pissed her off. "I didn't see you there."

"*Right.* That was my spot and you know it."

Ignoring the accusation, I ran an assessing eye over her compact vehicle. "Does that thing have gears or did you Flintstone all the way here?"

"Move," she said. It wasn't a request.

"Nope." And just like that I felt better already. My conversation with Alistair, my worry over Dad, all fled to the furthest, dusty corner of my mind until it was only this. Only *her*.

"*Move.*"

I let my head tilt, giving myself a heartbeat to take her in beneath the low baseball cap she wore. *So damn delicate.* With her slim nose and big brown eyes, she looked like a water nymph, completely at odds with the fire and ice battling beneath her skin. "Ask me nicely. Say, 'Callum, will you pretty please put those superior driving skills to good use and move your car?'"

"*Superior driving skills?*"

"I know, I know. Witty, handsome and an excellent driver. The scales are unfairly tipped in my favour." She rolled her eyes. "Say it, harpy, and the space is yours."

When she remained stubbornly silent, I prodded, "Today is Thursday."

"So?"

"*So* . . . it's still another four days until oat and raisin cookie day. But you already knew that."

"You stole my spot over a damn cookie?" She gripped the steering wheel like she might run me over. Fool I was, I'd probably let her.

"One of *Jess's* cookies. Wars have been fought over less."

"You are completely unreasonable." No. Fucking petty was more accurate.

"Perhaps."

"Move."

I tapped my lips, pretended to think it over. "No. I don't think I will."

"I saw it first, it's driver's etiquette."

I rapped my knuckles on the hood of my car. "And yet I'm the one with the space."

"Have I told you that I hate you?"

Every damn day.

The words didn't sting like they used to. Rather, they set me ablaze, my blood rising to meet them like a challenge. She said she hated me – my only thought was *How much?* How far did I need to push until she unravelled? And what would that hate taste like on my tongue?

Like I said, a sick, sick man.

"No you don't. But feel free to lie if it makes you feel better." I glanced at my watch, knowing I had to wrap this up if I wanted to leave with any of my remaining defences against this woman intact. "While I love sparring with you, some of us have places to be, harpy."

"Screw you." Her tyres spun, the sentiment smoke in the air as she sped back the way she came.

One eye on her retreating car, I knew I was smiling like a sociopath as I retrieved a small hutch from the back seat, checking through the mesh cover that the white and black lop-eared bunny was sitting comfortably. "Good work this morning, Simon, the kids loved you." He didn't look up from the sliced apples I'd allowed the children to feed him before leaving Kinleith Primary School. He nibbed with ferocity, his pink little nose twitching.

Crate in hand, I barely made it across the car park before I pulled my phone from my pocket, hitting my mum's number.

"Hi, love," she answered after a few rings. My chest tightened at the tired edge to her voice.

"Bad night?"

"So-so. He woke up a few times and it was a struggle to get him back into bed. He kept putting his coat and shoes on. Said he wanted to go for a walk. I had to hide the front door keys in the bathroom cabinet."

Shit. "The meds for the leg pain didn't help?"

"The doctor said it might take a few days to fully settle him, we need to be patient and wait it out."

Halting at the foot of the high street, I dipped into a small alcove between the beauty salon and the pet store. The air tasted like damp autumn leaves, at odds with the cheerful bunting that still zigzagged above the brightly painted shopping street, better known by tourists as the rainbow walk. The wind-torn fabric fluttered beneath the melancholy cloud cover, as though not quite ready to relinquish its hold on summer.

In a few short months the Hogmanay celebrations would begin. Locals would line the narrow street to witness Kinleith revert to its pagan roots, performers swinging flaming fireballs about their heads while drummers and pipers led them in a dangerous dance.

My favourite time of year.

Out of sight, I slumped against the brick wall. "I can sleep there tonight, give you a wee break."

"No. You already slept here three nights this week, I'm not letting this consume your life."

Typical Mum, so stubborn about some things and lenient about others. "And *you* can't keep going on like this." I couldn't remember the last time either of us had gotten a full night's sleep. Dad had been diagnosed just under a year ago but the swift decline these past months was staggering.

This had already consumed my life. It made no difference if I slept on the damn pull-out.

"Mum, I know you didn't want to discuss assisted living—"

"And I don't now. I'm managing just fine." *Fuck*. This was why I needed Alistair home. He was the only person she'd listen to. "Did you call just to be a busybody, I thought you were working?"

"I'm on my way to the practice now. I had my weekly animal therapy session at the school with Simon."

"Of course, I've been getting my days mixed up lately. Did I tell you how proud I am of you? You were always my most sensitive wee soul, even as a boy."

The words were like a punch to the gut. My first instinct to shut her down, just as Dad would have. Jim Macabe, along with my mandatory six years in the army, had done all they could to grind the sensitivity out of me.

"Thanks Mum." The words were so low, they were almost swallowed by the breeze. "Look, I need to get to work, I was only calling to let you know Alistair can't make it next week."

"*Oh* . . . well, I know how busy he is." Her disappointment left a metallic taste in my mouth.

"Right . . ." I cleared my throat. "He's going to let us know when he reschedules."

"Okay, love. And I don't want you rushing around here after work, relax, take the evening to yourself."

The thought of catching up on my mounting paperwork was tempting, but— "I'll just sit at home. I may as well come and do that with you."

"You could actually go out."

"What's out?"

"Hilarious. When I was your age, Dad hired a babysitter every Friday without fail so we could go to the village disco."

"This isn't the 1920s." I deadpanned.

"If it was, you'd have your own family to worry about."

"Ouch, Mum." I rubbed the spot on my chest her barb had struck. "It's a little early for home truths, don't you think?"

"I see more grandchildren in my future and for that, I need my son to regain his social life. Go on a date, join a hiking group, do something."

"Mum—"

"Do something," she repeated firmly.

"You promise to call me if anything happens?"

"Promise," she echoed before the line went dead.

Dating? I snorted to myself. *As if I have the time.* Shoving that thought aside, I clutched Simon's carrier tighter and hurried back onto the street. If the army had taught me anything useful, it was the art of compartmentalising.

I was two doors from the practice when a familiar lean form snatched my attention. The silky black locks I'd dreamed about long before I knew what it was to run my hands through them. You could block my ears and blindfold me and I could still pick her out of a line-up from the gut tingles alone.

Fucking gut tingles. When had I become this pathetic? Didn't stop me from coming to a dead stop in the middle of the street.

Juniper.

Twice in one day.

The universe clearly wanted to punish me.

Her strides were short and jerky, head ducked low as she hurried along the path, no doubt from the overflow car park that charged a small fortune for a single hour. Yeah, a definite arsehole move on my part. The space was rightfully hers and had she been anyone else, I would have let them have it. The problem was, Juniper Ross had infected my brain. And five years ago she'd destroyed me so thoroughly in a hotel car park, I'd never quite pieced myself back together.

A little light hazing was a small price to pay. And I had a sneaking suspicion she got off on this little game as much as I did.

From a safe distance my eyes devoured her sleek lines, like it had been weeks not minutes since I'd seen her last. Despite the chill, she was dressed in only a strappy tank top, and it wasn't until I noticed how the fabric literally clung to her that it registered she was soaking wet. Damp footprints lay behind her like a treasure trail. Water dripped from her workout shorts, hair flicking from beneath the cap in damp curls as she ducked into the small hardware store.

Had it rained today? *No.*

How didn't I notice the state of her before?

Now I really felt like an arsehole. I changed direction without thinking, ducking through the door only seconds behind her. The bell sounded and the owner, Duncan, nodded over the top of his hardback. "Morning, Callum. All ready for the first match next week?"

"Aye." Distracted, my gaze scanned the three small aisles leading away from the counter. Uninspiring metal shelving stacked with tools, paint samples and rolls of wallpaper. Anything more required delivery from the mainland.

"Jamie had a few ideas about testing out a new team formation—"

"That's great, tell him to email me." A flash of black in the furthest corner and my feet closed the distance. *What are you doing here, sweetheart? You don't DIY.*

I found her in the sparse bathroom section, grabbing seemingly random items and shoving them into a large orange bucket with an unravelled urgency I'd never seen from her. Rolls of duct tape, quick repair putty, a wrench, several pairs of gloves, mop heads. Even a trowel made the cut.

"What are you doing?"

She leapt a damn foot in the air, hand flying to her chest. Then she turned the full force of those doe eyes on me. "Not now, Macabe."

The words might have been cutting had she not resembled an injured dog. Despite the few inches I had on her, she managed to look down her nose at me, standing as straight as an arrow, an artificial stillness bolting her limbs in place. Juniper always held herself with complete control, even when she thought no one was watching. Aloof. Cold. Unrelenting. As though she didn't trust a single other person to help her carry the load. Years ago, I'd seen her tough outer shell as a challenge, crack it just right and you'd be rewarded with her soft centre. Now I knew better. Because crack it *wrong*, and there'd be nothing left to hold the shattered pieces together.

"I think now is exactly the time, if anyone gets to bear witness to *this*—" I drew a circle around her with my index finger. "I'm so glad it's me."

Come on, sweetheart, play with me.

Instead, she gave me her back, continuing her rendition of *Supermarket Sweep*. "Can you stalk me another day?"

"Now, now, harpy, that almost sounded wishful."

"Can you just fuck off? Just for once . . . *please* fuck off. I can't do this with you today." She clutched a tube of bathroom sealant so tightly in her fist I thought the lid might pop. "Save up those witty little remarks and post them to me. But for now, just leave. *Please*."

I looked at her again, finally noting then the lines of tension in her shoulders and jaw. The fresh tears on her cheek. *Fuck, I couldn't handle her crying.* "You going to tell me what happened?"

"No." Her chin tipped proudly.

There was something uniquely satisfying about gaining

the full focus of Juniper's attention. It thrilled and it terrified. Her eyes pierced, like she could read my thoughts. Like
she could read every thought I'd ever had in my life.

"Why?"

"Because you'll find a way to turn it into a joke."

What the hell? Yes, I liked to piss her off, *loved* it in fact,
but could she truly think I wouldn't help her?

"Pinky swear I won't." I held up my hand, extending
the little finger I'd broken in high school that never fully
straightened.

"Fuck my life," she muttered, fingers digging through her
wet hair. "Fine. I hired Gordon Murray to update some of
the bathrooms while Fiona's away and he flooded half the
first floor."

I laughed. Shit, but I couldn't help it.

"*See?* I knew you'd be like this."

"I'm sorry." I clutched my stomach. "But seriously? Old
man Murray? The guy's on the waiting list for cataract surgery. Why do you think he takes his grandsons along?"

"How the hell was I supposed to know that?"

"*Everyone* knows that."

"Yeah, well I don't gossip like an old fishwife." She punctuated what was obviously meant as a dig with a cock of
one perfectly manicured eyebrow. *I wanted to lick that
fucking eyebrow*.

"Gossiping like an old fishwife might have helped on this
occasion."

I didn't think it possible, but her scowl deepened. "They
should put out a damn bulletin about this shit."

"Probably." I nodded to the contents of the bucket.
"What's the trowel for?"

"I grabbed everything I could think of to fix it."

"Need some help? I'm very handy with a wrench." I had

51

a full afternoon of appointments but for her, I'd shift stuff around.

"For you to sabotage the situation even more? Thanks, but no thanks." Shoes squelching, she circled me, gliding to the counter with all the grace of a queen.

Bloody stubborn woman.

Before I could do something ridiculous, like offer to pay for every useless item in that bucket, I strode out the door and across the road to the practice. Handing Simon's carrier over to my vet nurse, Kelly, who cooed over him like a returning war hero, I pulled out my phone to text Mal: If you have a spare hour. Drive out to Ivy House and find out how bad it is.

His reply came almost instantly. Before April, a weekly phone call from my baby brother was akin to winning the lottery.

Mal: A little more info might be helpful.

Callum: A leak of some kind.

Mal: Shit. I'll head over in an hour.

Callum: Take April.

Juniper was like a bloodhound. She'd eat Malcolm alive the moment she realised I'd sent him.

Knocking softly, Kelly popped her head through the door. "Jill Mortimer is here with Biscuit."

"Again? She was in last week." Pulling on my white jacket, I coiled the stethoscope around my neck. "Is her leg still bothering her?"

"Nope." Kelly shook her head, fighting a smirk. "Stomach issues, apparently." *Damn it*, I scrubbed a hand over my jaw, scratching at the too long bristles. Jill Mortimer couldn't take a hint. And she had more hands than a freaking octopus. "You look tired, I can try and rearrange—"

"I'm fine. Send her through."

4

Juniper

Fiona: We've docked in Lisbon for the day.
Fiona: Everything okay at home?
TWO MISSED CALLS FROM FIONA
Juniper: Why wouldn't it be okay?
Fiona: Hank sounded weird on the phone.
Juniper: He's always weird.
Juniper: And stop calling Hank. You're supposed to be having fun, remember? A conversation with Hank sits somewhere between anal waxing and hugging a rabid badger on the fun scale.
Fiona: Don't say *anal*, Juniper. It's uncouth.

"Shit." Mal kicked at the soaked area of rug with the toe of his boot while April scowled like an angry kitten from our spot in the hall. I couldn't be sure how they'd gotten wind of the situation, though I had a good idea from whom. I didn't have time to focus on that right now.

In the few hours since floodgate, I'd launched into full *fix-it* mode. Moving the few guests as far away from the damage as

53

possible, comping rooms where needed, all the while ignoring Hank's stream of lectures and threats to call my mother.

"Three days, Juniper Ross. Your mother has been gone for three bloody days and the place is falling down around our ears. Are you targeting my kitchen next?"

Yes, yes, I'd fucked up. I didn't need to be reminded in quite so explicit terms. And Fiona was the least of my worries right now.

"Shit is right," I agreed.

Straightening, Mal flushed as though he'd forgotten I was in the room. "I mean—"

I waved him off. "We managed to shut the water off before it caused too much damage, but this room and the one above are just about fucked."

Moving to my side, April curled her arm around my back in that comforting way that came so easily to her. "I'm so sorry. I know how much time you put into this." Luckily, I wasn't the wallowing type, or I might have barricaded myself inside my cottage.

April dared a step further inside. Mal held out a staying hand. "Wait until we know the ceiling is secure, princess."

"*You're* in there," she said.

Mal's eyes flicked to me and he swallowed twice. I smirked at this little show of his protective streak. Six months ago, I wouldn't have suspected he had it in him. Then again, six months ago I knew next to nothing about the shy whisky distiller who had almost been my brother-in-law. Then April had returned to Skye, full of love and life and in need of her own escape. Exactly what he needed. It was clear to anyone with eyes that he was head over heels for her. He would remain on my good list so long as that smile graced her lips.

I was actually starting to *like* the man. The notion didn't sit well.

"I have a harder head than you," he replied.

"Not true." She reclined against the door, folding her arms across her middle. "I read all of your creepy anatomy books, it's a scientific fact that women have thicker skulls than men."

Shock slackened his features. "When?"

"I read a chapter every time you're in the shower . . . What? I want to know what interests you so much."

I was thirty years old and could honestly say, despite the crap romance movies might spout, I'd never seen a man melt in real life . . . until now. Mal's entire body softened, eyes crinkling at the corners, lips pulling into a crooked smile that belonged solely to April.

I cleared my throat. "I don't know what sick kind of foreplay gets you two hot, but can we focus please?"

His cheeks reddened again. "Right, sorry." I had the sneaking suspicion the youngest Macabe male was a little afraid of me.

"Oh, come on." April nudged me with her elbow. "We're adorable."

They were adorable. So adorable being in the same room as them was enough to get a toothache. "You're definitely *something*." She stuck her tongue out and I smiled for the first time in hours.

"Do you have a ladder?" Mal asked.

I nodded and left to retrieve it from the cleaning supply cupboard. By the time I returned April had fully ignored Mal's warning, squelching through the light layer of water with a mop and bucket in hand. Mal watched her, a puckered little frown between his brows, but offered no further complaint.

Folding the A-style ladder out, I handed it over to him, observing as he climbed high enough to prod at the wet plaster around the gilded light fixture. "Do you know what you're looking for?"

"Not a clue."

I laughed dryly. "That makes two of us."

He paused, brows crinkling. "You turned the electricity off, right?"

"Yes. As soon as I shut off the water."

"And Murray didn't hang around to check any of this himself?"

Needing to be doing something, I snatched up the spare mop, soaking up as much water as I could and squeezing it out into the bucket. Trying not to dwell on the watermarks staining the original hardwood flooring. "He offered, but honestly I just wanted them gone."

"Understandable." Mal had a way of talking that was completely unlike his three siblings. Short pauses between statements that let you know he considered every word that came out of his mouth. *Careful*. That's how I'd describe him. Careful and dependable. My best friend's gentle heart deserved to be in careful and dependable hands.

"I can't believe that old goat thought he could get away with instructing his untrained grandsons on the job. He should lose his licence," April said.

"I'll settle for my money back."

"Want me to threaten him?" Mal delivered the words so earnestly, only the wry tilt to his lips revealed he was joking.

"No assistance necessary. If he's attached to his balls, he'll give me my money back."

"Gross." April shuddered. "Please can we not talk about his wrinkled old man ball sack. That image is now seared on the back of my eyelids."

Mal hopped down from the ladder, boots squelching so loudly, we all winced. "The plaster seems stable enough and

I wouldn't turn the electric back on any time soon, but . . . what the hell do I know?"

It felt cruel to point out I'd already figured that much out for myself. So I simply nodded.

"I could maybe help with the floor." He scratched the side of his jaw.

April was already shaking her head, red curls coiling loose from her braid. "Remember the last time you attempted woodwork?"

"I thought you loved the bench."

"*I do.* But June probably won't appreciate a health code violation at her inn."

"Right." He nodded. "We'll stick around and clean up."

"Have you found another plumber?" April asked, wringing water from her mop before repeating the motion.

"No. Everyone on the island is booked right through autumn. That's the only reason I hired Murray at all. I might be forced to call an emergency plumber from the mainland."

They both winced.

It would cost me a small fortune in travel expenses alone. But I didn't see what other option I had.

"I never should have started this." I said. Hating to admit what an absolute fuck I was, even to my friends, but today had sucked away all remaining pride.

"Of course you should," April shot back. "You've put everything into this place since your dad passed, you deserve to see it thrive."

I wasn't sure that was true. How on earth could I be capable when I hadn't even lasted a week without Fiona? The past six years I'd thought *she* needed me, but what if the opposite was true? And I was clinging on too tightly to people who would be better off without me? "There's no way I can get the repairs done before she gets home."

"So what if you can't? She's your mum. She'll be pissed off, but she won't stop loving you." I scrubbed at the floor, refusing to point out that April herself knew that statement wasn't always true. "We can help," she offered.

"And the rest?"

April quieted, biting her lip. It was Mal who surprised me by saying, "You could ask my brother."

He sensed my astonishment because his features slackened under the eerie silence before I stupidly blurted, "Which brother?"

Unless Alistair had taken on a new vocation since we'd last spoken – very unlikely – he didn't mean him. And the other? No way. Perhaps he had another brother I wasn't aware of.

"*Callum*—"

Even his name irritated me. "No."

At my brisk shut-down his eyes flicked to April who supplied, "That's in direct violation of Juniper's rules."

Rules I'd violated only this morning.

All attempts at silencing her with my death stare failed because she was already ticking off her fingers, "Don't think about the Macabe men. Don't talk to the Macabe men. Don't look at the Macabe men."

"You don't qualify," I cut in pointedly.

"I'm not sure if that's a compliment or not."

"Oh, it's definitely a compliment." April tucked herself into his side and his arms automatically curled around her. "A high one coming from Juney."

"Don't call me *Juney*."

"But it suits you perfectly. Like a fluffy little kitten."

Sweet hell. Refusing to dignify that statement with a response, I rounded on Mal. "He plumbs?" *Of course he does.* He saved furry little animals for a living and helped out around the village. Didn't anyone else see what a smug bastard he was? "Of course 'Community Ken' plumbs."

From the corner of my eye I caught Mal mouth to April, "*Community Ken?*"

"He reminds her of a Ken doll." I threw another glare that she ignored. "He fitted a new toilet and sink into the tasting room for us last month, he did a fantastic job."

How did I not know that about him?

I don't know why *that* was the detail my mind kept circling back to.

Callum was the epitome of every arsehole guy I'd gone to university with. Charming, athletic and all too capable on the surface. The kind of guy who wanted to bed the alt girl just to see what she was like in the sack and then brag about it to his friends.

I wasn't mad at him for the *incident* in Glasgow . . . okay, I was mad that he'd waited until he had me spread and desperate for him on his front seat, just to prove he *could*, before seemingly growing a conscience. *I refuse to do something I'll regret in the morning.* An absolute arsehole move I could have moved past.

But I was angry that he'd so easily brushed it aside when that night had wrecked me and left me questioning everything.

I was furious that the first time I bumped into him in Brown's after his move back to Kinleith, he'd dragged his eyes down the length of me, like he'd recently acquired X-ray vision, and said, "*Amazing* to see you again." Then whispered in my ear, "What colour today, harpy?"

He never let me forget.

Not once.

But I was more annoyed at myself for letting things go that far.

"Wonderful. Still not asking him." My mop worked more viciously. "I'd rather the roof cave in than ask Callum Macabe for help."

"You're in room three on the first floor." I slid the brass room key over the desk to our newest guest – Mr Damien Lewis, according to his booking information – thankful that his late check-in meant he'd missed the craziness of the day. One less guest to compensate. "Take the stairs and it's the second door on the right."

Grinning, he ran his thumb over the rounded bow. "I didn't know hotels still used real keys. It's all swipe cards and QR codes these days." His thick black hair and rich accent hinted at his Welsh heritage.

I gave him my friendliest smile. The one Fiona complained was too toothy, like an alligator. "We like to do things the old-fashioned way around here."

"Never said it was a bad thing." He crossed thick arms atop the front of the high desk, settling in.

This was the reason I usually let Fiona and our part-time receptionist, Ada, handle the check-ins. I *detested* chit-chat.

"Remember to mention that in your glowing review." I drummed my fingers against the wood for effect. He laughed as if I'd delighted him.

"You're funny."

Now I knew he was lying. I'd been called many things in my life, *funny* was rarely one of them.

This wasn't the first time a guest had attempted to flirt with me. Despite Fiona's encouragement, I would *never* go there. Even if he was handsome with a full head of black curls and a smile that suggested he knew exactly how long it'd been since I had a man in my bed. Mixing business with pleasure rarely ended well.

The door at his back opened and closed, probably another guest returning for the night. I jumped on the interruption and gestured to the stairs. "Breakfast starts at eight a.m., hang your menu card on your door and I'll put your order in with the chef." An obvious but polite dismissal. One I could have sworn he was about to ignore until a throat cleared.

Our heads swivelled in perfect synchronisation.

"Macabe."

Grin firmly in place. Tanned arms crossed over navy scrubs. Hair wind-ruffled or possibly finger-raked after a long day. Callum Macabe looked . . . he looked . . .

"I heard you needed me, neighbour."

Smug. He looked smug.

Ignoring him, I turned back to Mr Lewis. "Can I help you with anything else?"

"Any excursions you'd recommend? I plan to see as much of the island as possible."

"Oh," I floundered slightly. Again, this was why I preferred Fiona to handle this part. I wasn't exactly the outdoorsy type. Too aware of Callum's stare, I riffled through the nearest drawer, returning with the stack of leaflets Fiona and Ada handed out to guests. Unable to recall the personal recommendations they usually offered, I silently held the stack out. He leafed through them slowly, then tucked the wad of paper into a pocket.

"Have a pleasant evening, Mr Lewis. Reception closes at ten p.m., but there's an emergency contact in your room should you need it."

"And if I call it, will *you* pick up?"

I laughed in surprise. The man had some balls, I'd give him that. "Goodnight, Mr Lewis."

With a final crooked smile, he hefted his small luggage bag over his shoulder and took the stairs. Callum watched him leave, a small notch creasing the skin between his brows. When his attention returned to me, the room felt smaller, like his presence had somehow depleted the square footage by several feet.

"What are you doing here?" I asked after a long moment. "This morning wasn't enough, you needed to go for round two?"

That smirk I detested played on his lips again. The one he reserved solely for me. With everyone else, he was playful but endlessly polite. *Community Ken. Kind Ken. Can't do enough for you Ken.*

His blue eyes lit, as warm and untrustworthy as a Scottish summer day. "I don't think we'll ever have enough, harpy. But I heard on the grapevine you need my help."

"You heard wrong."

He tsked. "I don't think so. My source is very reliable."

Bloody Heather. She'd called around this afternoon and stated multiple times that she was firmly aboard the "ask Callum to fix it" train. "The only thing this village is missing is a bloody phone tree," I muttered.

"We already have one." He stalked closer, until his thighs were flush with the desk. "I wonder why no one invited you to join?"

I willed myself not to react to what was so obviously an attempt to get a rise from me, turning back to the computer and wiggling the mouse inanely. "Heather has it wrong. I've got it covered."

"Really? By whom?"

I clicked, opening a random file and pretending to read. I hated the way he towered over me in this position but there was no way I could stand without admitting that his proximity affected me. "It's not been decided, but I have some promising candidates."

"Not one that can get it done before your mum returns, I bet." He folded his arms, still sprinkled with summer freckles, across the desk. The same way Mr Lewis had. We were finally eye to eye, and it was somehow worse. Ignoring the jump of my pulse, I shoved his arms back over the other side. That smirk only grew.

"I'm not hiring some cowboy that renos as a hobby."

"Cowboy?" I swear I witnessed the joke take form in his eyes. "As I recall, you were the one ready to do the riding." Arsehole.

Too attractive, conceited *arsehole*.

I launched to my feet, hands slamming on the desk. "Get. Out."

Of course he didn't budge. "I'll even do it for free."

"Why would you do that?"

"Because I'm a nice guy." He said it like a fact. *Sky is blue, grass is green, oh, and didn't you hear? Callum Macabe is a swell guy.*

"Ah, the self-proclaimed *nice guy*."

His heavy brows drew in. "I don't know what that means."

"They never do." Anger leached into my tone, giving me away. I was seething, arms folded across my chest to stop me from wringing his neck. If it wasn't for the desk separating us, I'd already be on him.

He must not have sensed the danger because he bent closer, voice lowering to a conspiratorial whisper. "Full disclosure, it turns me on when we fight."

My stomach whooshed. "You're disgusting."

"*Yes*. Just like that." His eyes closed and he let out a low, ridiculously sensual moan. "Pretend I'm your husband and you're pissed because I didn't pick up my dirty socks. *No wait* – I didn't load the dishwasher correctly."

"You're a grown man, pick up your own damn socks!" Why was I feeding this ridiculous scenario? He was trying to throw me off kilter and I'd walked straight into the trap. "Is that your dream relationship, Macabe? No wonder you're single and nearly forty." Cruelty coated the words like syrup.

"It's a hypothetical, harpy. I can look after myself and the woman in my bed. I happen to *enjoy* caretaking." He let the image those words conjured marinade in my mind. "And I'm single because that's the way I like it." Oh, I bet he did. I bet the women he spoke of enjoyed it too.

"I think it's time to go."

He assessed me, but then nodded. "Think about my offer."

"Why? What do you get out of this?"

He shrugged. "I can't be neighbourly?"

"*I see*. It's leverage you can hold over my head."

"*Jesus*, you're cynical. Think of it as a family offer."

"We aren't family." We may have been close to that once, but those bonds had strained long ago. And torn completely when I almost let him inside me.

"My brother is practically married to your best friend."

"They've been dating for three months."

"And he already has a ring stashed in his sock drawer—" His lips curled around his teeth like he could suck the words back in. Then he held up a finger. "Keep that to yourself."

"Mal's going to propose? That's way too soon."

He glowered at my obvious disapproval. "They're happy and if they get engaged it's no one's business but theirs. Don't get involved."

Did he truly think I would? That because I'd given up on love, I would spread that onto my friend?

I believed in happy endings for people like April. As fresh

and lovely as a summer daisy, she was quick to laugh and even quicker to forgive. Easy to like and impossible not to love. Whereas I was . . . *wrong*. Like an ill-fitting pair of shoes that looked good in the store but pinched your toes and left behind blisters. An exciting diversion for a night, until they cut themselves on my sharp angles. The rough before the real thing. Too cold. Too closed off. Too much yet not enough in all the ways that mattered.

As a child, I'd wanted to gain the weight of unwavering love so badly; I'd felt as if I bore a mark of desperation like a tattoo on my forehead. Practising pleasing smiles in the mirror until my cheeks ached. For all the good it did. My unlovable nature felt like a poisoned apple in a fruit bowl, waiting to see who'd bite next.

Refusing to look at him, I nodded to the door. "I'll give your offer some thought."

"You'll think about it?" He hooted a laugh as though I were the most amusing person he'd ever met. *There was a lot of that going around tonight.* "Harpy, you aren't going to find a better offer than this. Call me when you come to your senses."

5

Juniper

Google search: Plumbing for dummies

"What a fucking mess," Hank grunted again, crumbs from his freshly baked oatcake clinging to his bushy mutton chops. "Fiona shouldn't have left you in charge."

"So you've said." Ignoring the burn of humiliation in my cheeks, I continued my fruitless Google search. Over the past twenty-four hours I'd contacted just about every plumber north of the English border. *False*. I'd made a very desperate call to a company in Newcastle. The man's chuckling, "The Isle of where? Ah don't think so, pet," had felt particularly brutal.

The skip hidden around the back was now filled with ruined bedding, rugs, a spoiled mattress as well as the bathroom suites I'd foolishly let Murray tear out. This morning I'd been in the middle of comping a night's stay and free breakfast for a disgruntled guest, as I could no longer offer the ocean-view room she'd initially booked, when Mal had appeared. Cheeks pink from the wind.

He'd only winced at my grizzly interaction and hefted

what looked like a dehumidifier over his head. When I finally located him in the first-floor suite, he was on his knees, unspooling the cord, explaining it would remove the moisture from the air. "You should also crank up the heating. It will reduce the risk of mould forming now the evenings are growing colder."

That had me thoroughly panicked. The old tartan wallpaper already resembled a Jackson Pollock painting. Not quite the vibe I'd been aiming for in a honeymoon suite. "How do you know all this?"

He'd hesitated, eyes flicking between me and the cord in his big hands. "Will you be mad if I say Callum?"

"No . . . Maybe. What's that guy's deal, anyway?"

"Callum's?" He'd pushed the plug in the socket and fiddled with the dials on the boxy machine until a low whir filled the room.

"Aye."

"He likes to help. And take it from someone who spent years trying to force him into doing the opposite, it's easier to just go with it."

I hadn't agreed or disagreed.

Shrugging off the memory, I spun to face Hank. "Why am I like this?"

If he was surprised by my question, he didn't show it. The grooves around his mouth cut into deep lines as he gave it real thought. "That's a question with many possible answers. That morbid music you kids like so much definitely dinnae brighten yer mood."

"I didn't mean that." I flicked a stray crumb his way. "My music taste is exquisite."

He said nothing. His usual signal for me to continue. He was like a priest in a confessional that way, though his advice was likely far more colourful.

"Callum Macabe offered to help."

"And you turned him down?"

I nodded.

"Good," he grunted, shoving the remainder of his food past his lips. "The lad's always grinning. Makes me antsy."

I laughed, happy to find another person on this island who didn't sip from the Community Ken cup. "You don't think I should say yes? Set aside my pride and accept help when it's offered?"

My words trailed off when Ada swept through the door, already talking as she slipped out of her damp coat. "Sorry I'm late, damn sheep in the road again. Then a motorhome full of tourists got out to take pictures." She shook her head, silver-streaked box braids slipping over her shoulder. "As though the folk that live here don't have places to be." Turning for the desk, she held Hank's stare a fraction longer than strictly polite. Born in London, she and her late husband relocated to Skye almost thirty years ago. She'd lost him seven years back and worked part time at Ivy House ever since.

The quickness with which Hank straightened was almost comical. As was the way he brushed crumbs from his chest. "You missed a bit," I whispered, pointing to one lone crumb on his lip while sliding from the seat to let Ada take over the evening shift.

"Hey Ada. Question: do you think I should hire Callum Macabe to help with the bathrooms?"

"Callum?" Like every female in this village, her face brightened at the mention of him. "He's such a lovely boy."

Looking back at Hank, I lifted my brows in the universal *see* gesture.

Grunting, he waved a hand, already retreating to the safety of his kitchen. To avoid me or the attractive widow? That was still up for debate. "Do what you want, lass, yer always do. Just leave me out of it . . . And be careful around that lad, I dinnae trust him." He offered the final comment as though it were an afterthought.

Using Ada's arrival to escape, I plugged in my head-phones and retreated to the quiet seclusion of the laundry room and the stack of clean bed linen waiting to be pressed and ironed. My mind wandered through the menial task, looping over Hank's words.

Just leave me out of it.

There lay the problem. I didn't *want* to leave him out of it. I wanted someone to take the decision out of my hands, so I didn't suffer any blowback.

I wanted all of the reward with none of the risk.

Later that evening, I curled into the sofa cushions in my cosy living room. Shakespeare perched on the arm of my velvet-lined wingback, watching as I balanced my phone atop a pile of books with one hand, careful not to spill the cereal in the other.

"Glare all you want, arsehole," I said, waiting for the camera to connect.

"Is this how we're greeting each other now?" Backlit by the glow of flames in the tiny cottage she occupied with Mal, April looked delighted at the prospect. Heather connected next, her face blurring as the camera drifted in and out of focus.

"Sorry." I flipped the screen so they could get a good look. "That was aimed at the demon cat."

"Still not going well?"

I held up my heavily decorated arm in explanation, welts curling around my wrist like a bracelet. "Why did this have to be the cat I agreed to adopt rather than foster?"

"Because you took one look at that beautiful face and couldn't say no?" Heather joked. I hummed noncommittally but Heather was right, I'd always had a weakness for pretty things.

"I know all about that." April reclined in her chair with a chuckle, a script balanced across her knees. In just a few short months she would leave to shoot her latest movie, and if I was honest, I dreaded her departure.

The magnitude of April's level of fame often crept up at the strangest times. Having my best friend back in Kinleith felt so normal, it wasn't until tourists pointed her out in shops or on the beach that I even remembered her fame. Heather and I had a lot of fun watching Mal attempt to fend off some of her more *dedicated* fans.

"How's things at Ivy House?" Heather was the first to broach the subject.

"Oh, you know, I've comped so many rooms I'm pretty much paying the guests to stay at this point and I had to bribe Hank with a raise to stop him calling Fiona."

"It's just a bump in the road."

"Especially if you agree to let Callum help," Heather urged, voice edging towards exasperated. "I know you two don't exactly see eye to eye, but for this, can't you try getting along?"

"I have some free time tomorrow if you need a hand? I'm very adept at customer service," April cut in, effortlessly changing the subject. Though she'd never said anything, I knew she had her suspicions about Callum and me.

"No need, Ada is happy to pick up extra hours."

"Has Old Murray returned your money yet?"

"Not likely," Heather replied before I could. "You could have a pitchfork to his throat and the tight bastard wouldn't budge."

I snorted so hard oat milk almost poured from my nose, then said, "Which is exactly what I intend to do . . . as soon as I can escape for more than five minutes." Heather winced, gathering her short strands into a stubby pony-tail. "You look tired," I noted. Her skin seeming even paler under her harsh kitchen lights.

"I'm fine." She yawned, her eyes meeting mine and bounc-ing away. I hated that bounce. The reminder that while we laughed and teased one another like friends who'd given each other Spice-Girls-inspired haircuts at seven years old, the severing of mine and Alistair's engagement had cost me far more just my romantic relationship. "Just a long day and the girls won't stop arguing. I'm considering giving them sepa-rate bedrooms so they have a bit of space from one another."

"Could be a phase," April said.

"Could be." She rubbed at her temples. "I know it's normal for kids to fight. I only wish I had someone to back me up, you know? When they're screaming at one another and I have to remind myself that I'm the adult here, when really, I just want to lock myself in the bathroom and cry. A one-hour phone call every other week from their dad doesn't quite cut it as joint parenting."

"Prick," I spat, hating that her ex-husband's departure had been the catalyst for our reconciliation. I'd never expected Heather to choose me over Alistair. But I'd hoped there would be a *choice*.

Life schooled you for romantic heartbreak. *Eat the choc-olate, watch* Legally Blonde, *cry in the shower to Taylor Swift*. Rinse and repeat. But no one ever warned you that heartbreak over friendship cut twice as deep.

"*Prick*," Heather and April agreed, and I forced a smile as the conversation drifted. I sank back into the mountain of throw cushions, trading out my empty cereal bowl for a glass of red wine, doing all I could not to fall asleep as my friends discussed Heather's new role as manager at the distillery, but my mind was like a sieve, unable to grasp onto a single thought as the long day caught up with me.

The conversation yanked me back when a door opened and closed on April's end. With a grin she angled her face up a split second before Mal's head descended into view. The image blurring out of focus as his lips caught hers, hands bracketing her cheeks to kiss her deeply. Passionately. As though a sea had separated them, not a handful of stone walls. And damn, I couldn't look away from the fierce longing they shared. Knowing she'd take a piece of his heart with her when she went away.

"Gross." Heather gagged. They snapped apart, Mal's cheeks turning a burned pink while April laughed.

"Sorry guys." His flush deepened when he registered the two of us. "I didn't notice the phone." Because he didn't notice much besides April these days.

"And I think that's my signal to go," Heather said.

"Not on my account." Mal dipped over April's shoulder to speak to his sister. "I'm about to shower anyway."

Heather shook her head, stifling another yawn in her palm. "I need to get to bed, the girls have gymnastics club before school tomorrow."

"Let me know if you need help with pick-up or drop-off," he replied before dipping out of view.

I waited in silence as Heather said her goodbyes. Returning her drooping smile with one I hoped was convincingly reassuring. Then her screen went black and I cried, "I almost slept with Callum." Like I'd just undergone hours in an interrogation chair. I don't know where the admission came from. Stress? *Yes, definitely stress.* And the fact he'd been getting in my face for days.

April blinked, lips moving, only her reply was drowned out by a distinctly male choke.

I froze, leaning closer to the screen as though I might peer into the room. "Is that Mal?"

Two seconds passed. Then the reply came from off-camera. "Yep."

"I thought you were going for a shower," I said. April's eyes darted between us.

"I forgot a towel?" It was more of a question than a statement, as though I were his teacher and he was explaining how his dog ate his homework.

Yeah, I couldn't do this. "Will you just come into the shot please?"

Another lengthy pause. "I don't want to."

"Well, pony up, because you're unfortunately a part of this shitshow now."

"I don't think—"

"*Mal!*"

He stumbled into view like I'd yanked on an invisible rope tied around his waist. Hastily drawing a dark T-shirt over his wide chest, he dropped onto the sofa beside April. Our gazes collided and slid away but I refused to be embarrassed. Even if my cheeks were burning.

"Can we return to the matter at hand please?" April tucked her legs beneath her, practically vibrating with excitement. "You almost slept with Callum today?"

"Absolutely not . . . this was years ago."

"I knew it! I *so* knew there was something between you. Did it happen while you were with Alistair?" April's tone held no judgement whereas Mal had the posture of an animal caught in a trap.

"Of course not! A year after it ended."

"*Fuck*." Mal swiped a hand over his jaw and stood. "I shouldn't be here for this."

"*Sit*," April and I said in unison. He complied instantly.

"It's just girl talk." April pressed a kiss to his shoulder then turned back to me. "So you were together?"

"The key word is *almost*."

She waved a hand like the difference was inconsequential. "How did it happen?"

"I was attending a conference in Glasgow, we bumped into each other at a bar."

"Was it good? The lead up, I mean." She rolled a finger and Mal wheezed, face dropping into his hands.

"What do you think?" I returned dryly, recalling the desperate tremble in Callum's hands as he tugged me into his lap. He'd fucking wanted me. Until he hadn't. "I might not like the man but even I can admit he has a body made to do bad things too."

"Better than Alistair?"

I pursed my lips, considering. "Different. It's hard to fully compare. Sex with Alistair was always incredible, but this was . . . I don't know, *charged*. In a way I've never experienced before."

"Kids, that's what we call a build-up of sexual tension." She spread her hands at her sides as though she were holding court.

"That's it—"

"No, stay," I begged before Mal could leave. "I need your opinion."

He grimaced, eyes squeezing. "Please don't."

"If it helps, I know all about your sex life."

His eyes shot open, pinning April where she sat.

"What?" Her tone was entirely unashamed. "I need someone to brag to and it can't be Heather. That leg thing you did against the wall last week—"

"So you and Callum?" he cut in evenly, though his face had taken on the sheen of a red balloon. I'd never seen a person so embarrassed.

Taking it easy on him, I rolled with the subject change. "Almost and only once."

"*Christ*." He scrubbed a hand across his jaw, in a way I was coming to learn was a nervous tic. "This is the most bizarre conversation of my life."

"You've never been tempted again?" April asked.

"No." *Every time I want to come.* "He's always an arse to me."

"That is classic teasing-the-girl-you-like-to-get-on-her-radar."

"Oh, really?" I shot a pointed look at Mal. "That's not what you said six months ago." Heather had said the exact same thing about Mal and April had shut it down. Hard.

"And then I learned that Mal was in fact pining away like a sad grizzly bear night after night—"

"I wouldn't say night after night, exactly. Just a little light pining . . . you know, a normal amount of masculine pining." Said the man currently taking part in this excruciating discussion for no other reason than the woman at his side. The pining levels weren't up for debate. "You never mentioned Callum was into June."

"I thought it was obvious. Besides, it goes against girl code."

"Enough. Callum isn't *into me*." I nearly gagged on the juvenile phrase. "I wouldn't care if he was. All I want to know is, Mal . . . knowing everything, do you think I can trust him to help me?"

His nod was immediate.

"*Shit*." I slumped back against the cushions.

"Not the answer you were hoping for?" He offered me the same grin he'd given Heather. It brightened his entire face.

"Nope. You've officially made my Macabe family shit list."

6

Callum

Callum: How'd it go?
Callum: ???
Callum: I know when you've read the text, Mal, a little tick appears at the bottom of the message.
Mal: How did what go?
Callum: The dehumidifier. Did she take it?
Mal: I didn't really give her much of a choice, just plugged it in and left.
Callum: Good.
Callum: Murray paid her back yet?
Mal: What do you think?

The rap of my knuckles was sharp. Hard to misconstrue. "Open up, Murray!" I yelled at the flaking paint, more than ready to bust the door down if he didn't show his face in the next thirty seconds. The handle twisted and his wife's friendly face appeared in the opening.

"Callum." She smiled, drying her hands on a tea towel. "Did Gordon arrange a house call?"

"Uhh . . . not exactly." I scratched the back of my neck, suddenly feeling bad about the hammering I'd given her front door. "It's more of a social visit." An issue irritating enough to play Russian roulette with my truck's suspension on Murray's shitty dirt track road. I still needed to squeeze in a visit to Dad before heading to work. "Is he about?"

"Just washing up for breakfast, I'll grab him."

"Much appreciated, Mrs Murray." I flashed my best grin. It wasn't her fault she'd married that rat.

She flicked the tea towel at my thigh. "Yer daftie, it's Vanessa to you." She ducked inside and reappeared only seconds later, a scowling Murray in tow. The collar of his shirt was damp from shaving, he ran a towel over his chin as he stepped onto the porch.

"Thanks, Vanessa, I only need to steal him for a minute. Remember to bring the cats in for their annual vax soon, I'll arrange a little discount."

I held her smile until the door closed and then bundled Murray back so quickly its hinges creaked.

"Hey, now! Are ye mad—"

"You don't need to talk, only listen. Understand?" My grip on his shoulder wasn't too bruising. I exerted just enough pressure to let him know he'd pissed me the hell off.

He nodded, his weather-worn cheeks reddening further.

"You owe Juniper Ross quite a bit of money."

"That's what this is? She cancelled the job, not me. I'll tell yer what I told the wee lassie, that pipe was faulty, it's nae my boy's fault."

I might call her *wee* all the time, but from Murray's lips it sounded condescending. As though she were a naive little girl, too simple-minded to understand the complexities of "important male business".

"Juniper is not a *lass*." My tone was sharp enough to

cut glass. "I have friends on the council board. Return her money today or I'll have no choice but to report your unsafe work practices. They'll probably take your licence away and then what will you do?"

"You'd ruin me fae a wee mistake the lads would have put right if she hadn't started screaming like a banshee? She threw a shoe at Brodie's head." What I would have paid to see that. "I could sue *her*."

Perhaps. He'd have to prove it and it would raise questions he wouldn't want to answer.

Inching back, the heel of my foot crunched over gravel as I straightened his collar. "Here's what you're going to do. You're going to start by paying Juniper every penny you owe." He began to protest, and I held up a hand. "You are going to pay her back. Today. That part is non-fucking-negotiable. Then you're going to get your grandsons properly trained. Brodie is off the team until you do."

He gaped. "Off the team? Yer mad, he's the fastest half forward on Skye."

I shrugged as though I wasn't handing this year's North Division league cup to Portree. "There are other players." *There weren't.* Pulling my car keys from my pocket, I rounded to the driver's side, calling over my shoulder, "Get it sorted and he's back on the team, he might still get a few games in this season."

I hadn't even opened the door before his reply washed over me, low and far too arrogant. "You know, being sweet on yer brother's lass might be frowned on by some folk in this village."

My answering laugh was so heated, the drizzle in my periphery turned to steam. He thought he had me by the balls. Little did he know Juniper had been carrying those around in her purse for the last eight years.

"Good job I don't care what folk think of me, Murray."
I held his gaze, daring him to say more. When only his jaw
ticked, I climbed into my truck. Dust kicked up beneath my
tyres as I peeled away, leaving his inane threats over Juniper
with him.

I couldn't care less who knew about my feelings, I'd had
a long time to make peace with them. Any guilt I'd once
harboured began to wane in the same moment my brother
made the biggest mistake of his life. The night I'd driven,
half blind with rage, from Edinburgh to Glasgow, hating
him for hurting her. Hating *myself* for feeling so bloody
relieved.

Then I'd seen the hollow look in his eyes. Beard grown
out; eyes bloodshot, wearing only one sock.

Instead of fighting, he invited me inside where we'd
gotten blind drunk on whisky that reminded us of home.
With every sip I'd held my breath for the light bulb moment,
the frantic search for car keys that would ensue when he
realised how badly he'd fucked it all.

Days turned into weeks. Every phone call I expected to
hear his voice on the line. "*Hey bro, funny story, June and I
are back together . . .*"

Every day it didn't come, my guilt lessened, until it was
nothing more than a twinge in my chest. Then Glasgow
happened. And I stopped seeing Juniper as his and she
became mine. Mine to provoke, love and protect, if only
from afar.

7

Callum

Dear Callum,
You know me, it's not in my nature to overstep, yet I couldn't help but notice you'd yet to book the pitch for the Portree game next week. Rest assured I have it all in hand, as well as the training pitch for Thursday evening. Portree plays a strong defence and we need to be prepared, especially without Brodie's speed on the ball.
You've been rather distracted of late. If the captaincy is proving too much, I'd be happy to take the lead in your stead.
For the good of the team, of course.
Duncan

Duncan,
Thanks for your concern but I have it all in hand.
Callum

A knock to the examination room door dragged me from my furious scrolling. Saving the assisted living home in

Kyle to my bookmark, I dropped my phone onto the desk. Today had been . . . not great. Though she tried to disguise it, I could tell from the weary set of her shoulders that Mum was exhausted. Permanent lines strained her features that hadn't existed a year ago. She'd lost weight—

Knock. Knock.

Fuck. "Come in." Even when I was here, I wasn't really *here.*

Kelly popped her head around the door, a bright smile on her face. "Jill Mortimer is here for her appointment."

"*Again?* It's barely been a week?"

Kelly shrugged, tight brown curls bouncing off the collar of her pink scrubs. "It's Coco this time."

Resisting the urge to curse, I drew up Jill's extensive file on my computer. "Send them through."

I was draping my stethoscope around my neck when the polished blonde I'd attended school with strolled in like she was walking a red carpet. A floaty, floral skirt, a touch too summery for the cold snap we were having, curled about her calves.

"Callum." She grinned from ear to ear, the lead to a beautiful King Charles Spaniel clasped loosely in one hand. "We need to stop meeting like this."

"Ms Mortimer." I offered the best smile I could muster and crouched to greet the dog I'd examined no less than ten times this year alone. "How are you doing, lovely?" The words were obviously aimed at Coco, yet Jill fanned her face with feigned delight.

"My, my, Callum, you were always a charmer. I think my girls are as fond of you as I am. *Almost.*" She added the last bit with a wink I pretended not to notice.

"I doubt that's true, Ms Mortimer." I stood just as her hand clasped my bare forearm, long red nails curling against the skin until the tips bit in. Something about those long red nails always made my stomach twist. Or perhaps it wasn't the nails, rather *the owner*. Because whenever I saw Juniper's neatly manicured nails – always tipped in black – I imagined them buried in my back. She could grow talons and I'd be into it. I had nicknamed her harpy, after all.

"Callum, how many times have I told you to call me Jill?" Her nails dug in a little more before releasing, dragging over my wrist in a move undoubtedly meant to be seductive. "We are old *friends*, after all." Never had my sixteen-year-old self expected a single drunken kiss at a high school beach party to come back and bite me in the arse quite as often as that one did.

Trying to get this over with, I nodded to Coco. "What seems to be the wee one's problem?"

"Oh . . . Coco, *of course*. Her back leg is bothering her."

She'd trotted in just fine, but dogs could be sneaky about hiding their pain. "Let's get her on the table and take a look." I scooped her up before Jill could. Starting at her back legs, I gently smoothed my hands over her fur, looking for any sign of discomfort. "Has she been eating as normal?"

"Yes. Just like her mum, she loves her food." Jill's laugh was just this side of self-deprecating as she traced her palms over her curved hips.

Bloody hell.

I cleared my throat. "Any pain during urination?"

"None."

"That's good." I reached the dog's front, checking inside her ears and eyes just for good measure. Coco licked my arm as I worked, completely at ease.

"I can't see any obvious problems," I said at last, drawing back to rinse my hands. "It could be a slight muscle strain but that's nothing to worry about unless it persists."

"Hmm." Jill worried her lower lip between her teeth.

"Do you think I should make a follow-up appointment for next week?"

"That won't be necessary, but you can always phone in if you're worried."

Her smile brightened and I inwardly winced at my fuck-up.

"What would I do without you, Callum? You have such a big heart." *Right.* Turning to the *computer*, I gave her my back and input a few details in Coco's file. "You should let me take you to dinner, to properly thank you." My fingers stalled on the keys. "Just as friends, *obviously*. I'm not ready for anything more after my divorce."

Jill and her ex had officially split six months back and she'd been a constant thorn in my side ever since. I felt like an arse to even think it, but I knew, despite her words, Jill would be in my bed in a heartbeat if I wanted it.

"I don't think that's a good idea. I have a lot going on right now." The reply felt shitty. I might as well have said, *It's not me it's you.* I should have shut her down harder the last time she asked, but I'd felt guilty. Too worried about hurting a lonely woman.

"Oh." She deflated like a day-old balloon. "Perhaps in a few weeks? Remember you offered to help clear out my gutters?"

With a start I realised I *had* offered that. Heat rose in my cheeks, the desire to please almost forcing a vague, *Yeah, maybe*, past my lips. I needed to be honest before I hurt her. Shut her down in a way she couldn't misconstrue. "Jill, I'm sorry—" *Fuck.* "But I'm not interested in you . . . *like that.* I can still help with the gutters but that's all it will be." Her entire face shuttered, lips pinching, and I knew I'd made a mess of it. *God, I was going to hell.* "Let me see you out."

* * *

My phone rang in my hand as I trudged the short slice of land between my place and Ivy House. Booted feet thudding on the sturdy, moss-covered planks that bridged the burn between the properties, the bank fringed by lush ferns and pine needles.

Mum. My stomach sank and, for a terrible, selfish second, I considered not answering.

"Hey," I pinched the bridge of my nose as I picked up. "Everything all right over there?" I hadn't even been home yet. It was after eight p.m. and I'd rolled out of bed at the arse crack of dawn to get to Murray's.

I needed to get out of these scrubs and shower off the clinging scent of wet dog. I needed to eat. Needed to sleep. I needed . . .

"Hi, love." Her voice wavered on the other end. "Everything's fine, just checking if you know where that Jimi Hendrix record your father loves has gotten to?"

"*The Last Experience*? Mum, all the records are in the hall cupboard. Do you need it now?" Alarm made the words tight, and I took a breath, willing the roiling in my chest to settle. This was becoming our new norm, Dad growing agitated, Mum coming up with fresh schemes to bring him back to himself.

"He's restless again tonight, the doctor said listening to his favourite music might soothe him."

"The box along with the record player are on the top shelf, don't get it alone, it's too heavy."

"I'll use the ladder."

"*Mum*—" My gaze drew longingly to the inn door, my entire being straining toward it. It was like it could sense Juniper through the walls. Anticipate whatever snarky barb she'd throw at me and turn this clusterfuck of a day around. "I'm about to go into a meeting, can you wait an hour?"

"At this time?"

"I'm helping a friend with something," I said too casually.

"All right, love."

"Try playing the song on your phone until I get there."

"He doesn't like it the same. We shouldn't have put the player away."

I swallowed my sigh. The man hadn't glanced at that record player in almost a decade. "I'll be as quick as I can."

Setting my phone to loud just in case she rang again, I attempted to squash my worry as I pushed through the small outcrop of trees and Ivy House appeared, velvet night contouring its crooked edges. I'd grown tired of waiting for Juniper to come to her senses, it was time for a different approach.

I was almost at the deep green door when my phone rang again. Expecting it to be Mum, I stalled on the first step, certain I was hallucinating when Juniper's name flashed across my phone screen. I squinted and – *holy shit*, still there. Juniper. *Calling me.*

I didn't think she'd *ever* called me.

I fumbled the phone, almost hanging up with my clumsy, too big fingers. "Juniper?" Silence. "Hello?" I glanced up at the inn, half expecting to see her at a window.

"How did you know it was me?"

I shivered, her voice like a warm exhale down the back of my neck. Deeper and far more intimate when it was right beside my ear. I had to clear my throat before I said, "There's this cool invention called caller ID. I can come over and explain it to you if you like?"

She must have been going for blood tonight, because instead of arguing, she completely cut me off at the knees. "I accept your offer."

Just like that, sweetheart? Something was off. "What offer might that be?"

"Do you get off on being a smug prick, Macabe? Or were you born this way?"

My first smile of the day broke across my face and I dropped back against the wall, a hand pressed to my racing heart. "You sound intrigued, harpy, are you certain you still hate me because this is starting to feel like a ruse to get my attention?"

"I don't know why I ever thought we could have a normal conversation."

"Don't lie, you love our banter as much as I do." I saw the fire in her eyes every time we bickered. She burned with it. A stark contrast to the ice queen her body played host to the other twenty-three hours of the day.

It had been five years of intense foreplay.

"Oh, it's banter? My mistake. All this time I thought I avoided you because whenever we speak, you act like an entitled arse."

I loved it when she gave me shit. "Is this why you disrupted my evening? To insult me?"

"No. You're sending me off track." She fell silent again and I could practically feel her reinforcing her walls for what came next. "If the offer of help still stands . . . then . . ."

"Tick tock, I don't have all night." *Come on, sweetheart, give me something.*

"*Fuck!* I accept. *I accept*, okay?"

Relief punched through me. I'd gotten exactly what I wanted . . . just like that. And yet the opportunity to mess with her just a little was always too good to pass up. "Say you need me, Juniper. Say you need me and I'll do it."

"Fuck yourself, Macabe—"

"Wait, wait, I'm joking. Don't hang up." I grinned in the

dark knowing she couldn't see me. But shit, the way she said my surname with that vicious little tongue made me hard as a rock. It always did. "You still there?"

"*Yes*." And that breathy tone laid claim to a completely different organ.

My next words were rough. "Yes. The offer still stands."

"What's the cost?"

"We'll discuss it face-to-face." Unfolding myself from the wall, I climbed the few steps to the front door, rapping my knuckles. "Open up."

"What?"

"I'm outside, harpy."

"Since when?"

Ignoring her, I kept knocking. "Open up, I don't have all night."

Then from behind me, "Hey! Want to quit acting like an oversized oaf? I have sleeping guests!"

8

Juniper

Fiona: Why aren't you returning my calls?
Juniper: Because I'm working.
Juniper: I thought the ship had an open bar. If you can dial you aren't drinking enough!

Callum whipped around so quickly, he almost lost his balance on the trio of steps. I might have enjoyed unsettling him a lot more had he not looked like . . . *that*. I glimpsed him in his work scrubs more than any other clothing. Usually from a distance in the village or climbing into his car when I let my eyes drift over the invisible "do not cross" line I'd erected when he'd moved in next door.

It wasn't a sight I'd ever grown accustomed to.

The lamp above the door backlit him from behind, glowing like a warm halo around his upper body. He gripped a bag in one hand, his phone still to his ear with the other, making his bicep bulge obscenely. Veterinarian Ken in the flesh. *He had to buy them a size too small, that's the only reason it would strain that way.*

I should have found it ridiculous.

I *did* find it ridiculous.

And yet there I was, drooling over him like every other foolish woman in Kinleith. His uninvited appearance was both an annoyance and thrill which just further pissed me off.

Lowering the phone, he took the image of me in my pajamas in. "Were you in bed?"

"Yes." I pulled at the thick cardigan I'd quickly thrown over the top.

"It's eight fifteen."

"There isn't exactly a buzzing nightlife scene around here."

His eyes were all over me. My face, my throat, lingering where my pyjama shorts moulded to my thighs in the brisk wind. My long legs shone like icicles in the moonlight. The shorts were . . . *short*. Then again, I'd been tucked away in my cottage for the night, I hadn't exactly planned on setting foot outside.

"Cute," he finally decided, as if I'd been waiting with bated breath for his opinion.

I rolled my eyes but continued as though we hadn't been interrupted by this little eye-fucking interlude, "I'll pay you."

"I don't want your money."

"That's not how this works." If I agreed to this, I needed clear boundaries. This was nothing more than a business exchange. The only option available to me.

"It is if you want my help." He came down a step, the wind ruffling the silver-streaked strands of his hair.

"Macabe—"

"I don't want it, spend it on other repairs."

I bristled. "I don't need charity."

"A favour isn't charity."

89

There it is. "You mean I'd owe you?" The prospect was grotesque.

"If you like." He shrugged too casually.

"I'm not having sex with you!"

He laughed, deep and throaty and, despite my words, I knew this was exactly the way he'd look in bed, head thrown back as pleasure tore through him. I tried to picture his own space, *his bed*, it would be all straight lines and masculine shades of grey and green, like the peaks and glens he loved.

"You think I'm doing this to have sex with you? Harpy, if sex was all I wanted, trust me, I could have it with a lot less effort."

My stomach whooshed. "You throw stories of your prowess around an awful lot, I'm starting to think it's all talk as I never actually see you with anyone."

"Someone's been paying attention." He winked and I wanted to jab his eye out.

This was never, ever going to work.

My hands curled into tight balls, ready to tell him just that but, in true Callum Macabe fashion, his stream of chatter didn't halt. The man could be six feet below water and still find a way to steal the conversation. One of the most obvious differences between him and Alistair, Callum didn't simply speak, he performed. A born storyteller. When passionate, his eyes dazzled and he embellished with his hands like a conductor leading a symphony, making it all the more impossible not to get drawn in.

"In fact, you'd be the one standing to gain from such an agreement. *I*—" Hands pressed to his chest. "Would be working for free, while you'd get the pleasure of using my body however you see fit." *Using my body* – it hardly took a genius to understand the innuendo. A traitorous lick of heat curled through my stomach at the memory of that night. Glasgow. My underwear spread over his thigh.

Just sex, I reminded myself. *What you're craving is good sex. Not him.*

"You really love to hear yourself talk," I finally said.

"Some consider conversation a forgotten art form."

I couldn't contain my snort, he just looked so . . . pleased with himself. "Yeah, but you're more like modern art, a placard is required to make sense of the point you're trying to make."

Another laugh, this one puffing a white cloud into the air between us. We were still standing in the carpark, I suddenly noted. It became all too easy to lose time when he was purposely irritating.

"All right, smart arse, are you going to show me the damage?"

"Now?"

He shifted his bag until the contents clinked. "No time like the present."

"Fine . . . but be quiet, I don't need any more complaints." Skirting around him, I held the door open while he followed me into the porch.

"You don't live here?" he asked, the tread of his boots skimming my heels.

"No. I stay in the cottage around the back." I pointed to the stone path I'd just traversed around the side of the inn. "I prefer my own space."

"Sounds like a good set-up."

I glanced back, feeling his gaze like warm sunshine on the back of my neck, a few degrees past comfortable. *Was this his attempt at chit-chat?* Our eyes locked, my mouth dried, I glanced away.

This is the worst idea I've ever had.

"Hey, Ada," I greeted. Her head popped up over the large monitor, square glasses slipping down her nose. "Can I have the key for room five? Mr Macabe is going to inspect the damage upstairs."

"*Mr Macabe.*" Callum snickered at a volume only I could hear.

"Thank god! Are you here to rescue us?" Ada's palms pressed in a prayer. Her smile, all teeth and dimples as though the King himself had dropped by for tea.

"Of course. Juney's placing you in capable hands." Callum's shoulder bumped mine, like we were a team.

"Can you fix the light above the desk too? It keeps blinking," She pointed to the spotlight in question. "It's giving Juniper a headache."

How the hell did she know that?

"It just started?" Callum frowned up at it, transforming effortlessly into *fix-it* mode.

"I can take care of that myself," I said, before Callum could do something very on-brand and whip off his scrub shirt to reveal the Superman suit hidden beneath.

He's just like you and I, folks. Only better in every way.

"Could still just be drying out, but I'll take a look." He continued like I hadn't spoken.

Ada looked ready to swoon. "You Macabes are saints." I put a finger in my mouth and made a gagging noise. Callum's sharp elbow met my ribs, but I didn't feel the pain because Ada suddenly asked, "How's your dad doing?" And all the warmth sucked right out of the room.

For one terrible heartbeat you could hear a pin drop. Then he said, "You know how it is." *I didn't actually.* "Good days and bad." He turned to me, face flatter than I'd ever seen it. "Shall we?" Utterly taken back by the change in him, I nodded like a scolded bobblehead and made for the stairs.

"Did Murray return your money?" he asked from the step below.

"This afternoon. I must be scarier than I thought." I'd opened my banking app and the money was just sitting there. "I didn't even need to pay him a visit."

"Truly terrifying." His tone was dry.

We rounded onto the first-floor hallway, my flip-flops slapping obnoxiously off the herringbone, and I decided, to hell with it. If he could be nosy, so could I. "You don't like talking about your dad?"

"Do you like talking about yours?"

Touché. "That depends which one you're talking about. I never met the first, but I think it's fair to assume he was an arsehole." I don't know what possessed me to offer up that little tidbit. Callum clearly didn't know how to respond, because I unlocked the door and flipped on the light in silence.

I gestured him in ahead of me and he passed a smidge closer than strictly polite. My cardigan snagged on his bag. His bicep grazed my shoulder. Electricity zapped. We both ignored it.

At least I did. His expression gave nothing away as it ran over the ruined wallpaper and stained panelling, pausing at the large bay window, as if he could see the tumbling green hills beyond, even in darkness. The dehumidifier still whirred in the corner, and I absently stripped off my cardigan in the muggy air, hanging it on the back of the door while directing him to the bathroom.

My mind had time travelled to the last time I'd been alone with him like this. It must have been the way his feet rooted in place while his eyes shadowed my every step, his pupils expanding until they all but swallowed the blue, because I *knew* he was recalling that night too. Knew he also felt the giant fucking question mark hanging over our heads.

He eventually followed and hissed through his teeth. Aesthetically, it resembled a crime scene. Nail-ridden floorboards stacked haphazardly in the corner. Missing pipes and cracked tiles. I wrung my fingers as he performed a quick inspection, counting his every curse and disgusted headshake. At nine, the *it looks worse than it is* hope I'd been clinging to withered and died.

"That bad?"

"Murray should have his licence revoked. The closet connection for the toilet is too small for code." He grunted, crouching to get a better look at the U-shaped pipe.

"I don't know what that means."

"It means he's a lazy shit. He's got the rough-in wrong too, you need twelve inches between the toilet flange and the back wall. He doesn't even have ten." *There was a dick joke in there somewhere.*

"Toilet flange? Now you're just making shit up."

"Harpy, if I was going to spout nonsense it would be a damn sight more interesting than closet connections and toilet flanges. Unless that's what works for you." He pushed up from his knees and turned to me, a taunting smile on his lips. "I could pop round later if you like, whisper naughty things in your ear, like . . . plumbing code." His voice dropped sensually. Sarcastically. A mockery of what it had been that night in his car. "Cold water supply line." He bit down on his lip. "Flush bushing."

I swallowed tightly. "Can you fix it or not?"

His chin dipped, following the action. "Aye, I can fix it." Thanks to the high heating, we were both beginning to sweat.

"How long will it take?"

My question went unanswered, his attention shifting to the open notebook on the windowsill. Instinct had me scrambling for it, but he was faster, the pages protesting in his grip as he held it above his head. "What are these?"

I bit my lip, realising it was too late for me to lie. "Nothing. Just a few sketches for the inn." He flipped a page, and I lunged again, unaccustomed to being at a height disadvantage. I pushed onto my tiptoes, my fingers scraped the ring binding, he lifted it higher, crushing our bodies together. I'm talking my chin to his collarbone, my breasts to his ribs. I could feel the scrape of his nipples through the thin material of our shirts, so he could definitely feel mine. I couldn't have given a shit. "Give it back."

"There's at least a dozen in here."

One for every room in Ivy House. That notebook contained more than sketches, it contained my entire business model, starting with ways to make the inn eco-friendlier with a smart water irrigation system and solar panel installation and ended with my dream to turn Ivy House into one of Skye's most sought-after wedding venues.

A pipe dream.

"Laugh at me all you want, just give it back." I grabbed the edge and tugged, almost tearing the thing as it wrenched free.

He steadied me, a hand curling around my waist. His face so close I could see flecks of silver in his eyes. He didn't look happy. "Why would I laugh?"

"Because . . ." *It's nothing.* I squeezed the book to my chest until I felt the pages crinkle. "There isn't a single achievable thing in this entire book." He didn't reply so I pushed us back on track. "Can you fix it or not?"

"Aye." He scratched at his thickly bristled cheek. "A week or two, maybe, to put right Murray's mess and get the new suite installed."

"A few weeks?" That didn't seem like long.

"How many rooms look like this?"

"Two. That's all I could afford right now." The words felt small. Ready for mockery.

His lips didn't so much as twitch. "Why not apply for a business loan and renovate all the rooms at once?"

"It isn't my business." Fiona made it perfectly clear she wanted everything to stay the same. I'd already fucked up by going *this* far.

He settled back against the wall, arms folding over his flat stomach. "And let me guess. You just work here?" I could have sworn a muscle jumped in his jaw.

"Exactly."

"*Right*, well . . . I'll help you."

I knew I should, but I couldn't quite bring myself to thank him, so I bobbed my chin in the semblance of a nod.

"Are we calling a truce?" he asked.

"Absolutely not."

His smile came automatically, as though it were a test I'd passed with flying colours. "Then I've thought of a way you can repay me."

"No."

That damn brow cocked, taking him from irritating to charmingly handsome. I wanted to smooth my finger over it and hold it in place.

"I haven't even told you yet."

"I already know I'm going to hate—"

"You—"

"Just let me pay you."

"—allow me to show you around Skye."

I blinked. Not sure I understood. "I live here."

"And you barely even venture into the village," he said, straightening and coming closer. "I heard the way you floundered with that guest the other night. Let me show you Skye, if you only *work here*, you should at least know what you're talking about."

"No—" *Wait.* "That's it?"

"That's it." He shrugged. "It seems like a harmless trade."

It was harmless. It made no sense. "Why?"

"*Christ*, Juniper." He dropped his face into his palm. "I'm not a storybook villain twirling my moustache and plotting ways to ruin you. I do actually have my own stuff going on. I've been busy over the summer and everything with my dad—" He broke off, running a hand down his face. "Mum has been nagging me about dating." He looked embarrassed yet I couldn't find it within myself to take it easy on him.

"That's the saddest thing I've ever heard, Macabe." His eyes narrowed and he flipped his middle finger. Feeling like I'd scored a point in this little game, I pretended to study him. "You're not hideous to look at, once you look past the tech-bro, skintight T-shirt thing you have going on. Have you considered actually dating?"

I expected him to laugh and flip me off again or mess up my hair. Instead, he glanced away, jaw pulsing. "I'll date when *I* want to. Not because my mother tells me to."

"So, you won't date but you'll do . . . whatever the hell you're proposing with me."

"I just need her to think I'm taking time for myself, so she has one less thing to worry about. And hell, maybe she's right. I love this island, somewhere over the past year . . . I've forgotten that. I could use the distraction, that's it. I'm not going to tie your laces together and push you in the harbour."

How quickly he humbled me. Perhaps being an only child who'd spent her formative years in and out of foster care was the root cause, because I'd never quite grown out of the habit of making every situation about myself.

97

"Fine. But we need to set a limit, I can't just disappear with you every weekend."

He snorted. "I'm bowled over by your enthusiasm. Six dates."

"*Two*. Don't push it. These will be excursions, not dates. You could go with anyone; it doesn't need to be me."

He crept close enough to smell him. Pine mixed with the kind of sweat that came from a day of hard work. "Perhaps it's because you're the only woman in Kinleith, other than my sister and April, that doesn't show a blind bit of interest in me."

"Do you hear yourself?"

"Being humble won't make it any less true. I can't even have a drink with a woman without tongues wagging. And we got on . . . once."

"Once being the operative word."

"Five dates."

"You're bloody relentless."

"Pretty much." His shrug was accompanied by a boyish smile.

"Three."

He scoffed. "Don't waste my time, harpy."

"*Fuck*. Four." For Fiona I would do this.

"Four it is," he said. "And I get to choose the activity."

"Fine." What the hell was I agreeing to? I wouldn't put it past him to enjoy cliff jumping.

"Perfect."

My chin rose, prepared to see this battle of wills through to the bitter end. "Great."

"*Sublime*." Before I could blink his fingers stole out and snatched the notebook. Tucking it away in his pocket. "I'll look over your sketches too."

I scrambled for a way to get it back when his phone rang.

I knew this because he had his phone on loud with an actual *ringtone*. The blaring alarm ringtone that should have been outlawed in the Stone Age.

His entire demeanour changed. Tensing, he fumbled in his pocket. "Mum, everything okay?" He spoke to her, but his eyes were on me. "I'm on my way."

9

Callum

"Dad!" I made it to my parents' house on the outskirts of
Kinleith in record time. Not even turning off the engine
before I threw myself from the vehicle, cutting off Dad's
escape down the uneven driveway. "What are you doing
outside?" He wore nothing but pyjamas, the cuffs of his
striped trousers shrunk – revealing bony ankles – after one
too many wash cycles.

"Dad?" Shivering, he stared straight through me, as
though I were an imaginary friend time had stolen from
him. Unseeing eyes gazing toward the open gate. *Mum
needs to get better at closing it. Or I could start swinging
by after work to ensure she has.*

Suddenly, like the cold had knocked him back into himself, his stare locked with mine, recognition seeping into his watery eyes. "Callum." His voice cracked. "Your mum won't let me go for a walk."

Relief hit me like a gut punch.

It was becoming increasingly difficult to predict which Jim Macabe you'd be faced with. What side I even *wanted*. Some days, I'd give just about anything for that spark of recognition, the hope the disease wasn't stealing him as quickly as the doctors feared. Other days . . . I hated myself for the flash of relief when he looked at me like a stranger.

My father. The man I'd looked up to my entire life. The man I knew loved me in the only way he knew how. Pushing for perfection. Pushing for just . . . *more*. Pushing, pushing, pushing, until it became normal to live your life by someone else's preconceived plans.

"Because she doesn't want you to get sick. It's freezing out," I said gently. *Christ*, he wasn't even wearing shoes. Thin blue veins pressed through skin as thin as wet paper.

"She's trying to lock me in. I'm going to phone the police!"

"How about we go inside and warm up. Then we'll talk about it." When I lightly clasped his elbow, he didn't fight me. "Mum wants to listen to records with you. You remember the old record player, right? Every Christmas you'd dig it out just to listen to Frank Sinatra." *The only way to appreciate his voice*, he used to say, blowing dust from the vinyl.

He didn't reply but allowed me to steer him to the open front door. Mum waited for us on the porch, looking harried as she tucked a thick dressing gown around her middle. "I tried going after him, but it made him worse. I was only in the bathroom for a minute, I don't know how he got the door unlocked."

"Don't worry about that now." Wrapping an arm behind his back, I ushered Dad into the living room, guiding him into his favourite armchair beside the lit fire. His entire body wracked with shivers. Mum already held a thick blanket. Draping it over his lap, she chafed her hands up his thin arms.

"There you are, love. Give it a minute and you'll be right as rain." She pressed a kiss to his head. "Do you want a coffee?" That offer she aimed at me. All a part of our new routine.

I wanted five, but caffeine on top of the buzz in my veins from spending time with Juniper would mean I'd never sleep tonight. I shook my head. "Tea please, I'll grab that record player."

Within minutes I had the heavy machine in one hand, the case of records in the other. Dust tickled my nose as I returned to the front room.

"Are you staying tonight?" Mum placed a mug at my elbow.

I nodded, plugging a wire into the back of the player and setting it on the side table. I always stayed on his restless nights. "You take the spare room, I'll drag the pull-out into your room and keep an eye on him."

Mum's face cut into a wan smile, making the shadows beneath her eyes more pronounced. "You don't have to do that," she offered, but the words held no real fight.

"Get some sleep, Mum." I pressed a kiss to her forehead and returned to the hall cupboard, piling up the spare blankets I knew I wouldn't use. The record player long forgotten.

10

Juniper

One-star review – Don't waste your time
My first visit to Scotland and to be frank, I don't understand the appeal. Such a long drive for atrocious weather, big hills and sheep. And don't get me started on the accent. The inn was nice, I suppose, and the bed was comfortable, but I couldn't eat the breakfast. Perhaps they should start serving pancakes instead of haggis.

I was in a staring contest with my cat. The third one this week.

Music hummed softly from my sound system and, in her spot across the room, Shakespeare's eyes drew into thin slits. Her tail whipping like a thresher shark's, right before it stunned its prey. Refusing to blink first, I widened my own eyes, leaning forward until my chair groaned.

"Flick that tail all you want." I had a fresh scratch across my chest, courtesy of the little monster who'd used me as a pin cushion in the middle of the night. "Today's victory is mine."

"So this is where the magic happens."

"Fuck—" My elbow slid out, sending the spoon from my empty bowl clattering across the counter. "You scared the shit out of me, Macabe."

Shakespeare hissed, leaping to her favourite hiding spot atop the fridge. The very same spot she'd taken refuge last week when I'd attempted to administer her flea ointment. The ordeal resulted in a shattered vase, a hole in my favourite blanket and a five-inch battle scar down the length of my forearm.

Reclining in my doorway, Macabe gave me an *oh so casual* two-fingered salute, eyes bouncing around my tiny home.

"I expected more, I'll be honest. Not a salt circle in sight."

"Don't you knock?"

He flashed his signature *just decapitated the neighbours' gnome collection* schoolboy grin. "I did. Three times."

"And when I didn't answer you decided to let yourself in?"

"Figured you could have been hurt."

"And if I'd been in the shower?" I shot back, my chair screeching as I stood to deposit my bowl in the sink, right beside yesterday's.

"Even better."

"Do you take anything seriously?"

He stared at me for a beat. "When the mood strikes."

I threw him a glare, opening my mouth to say . . . I don't know, something rude and witty hopefully. But I finally noted the thick coat and grey knitted hat he sported. He looked – *Macabe rules*, I reminded myself before I could travel any further down that road.

"Sorry." I shook my head. "You're going out of your way to help me, I'll try my best to curb the insults. It's second nature when it comes to you."

"No, please go on." He rolled his hand for me to continue. "I love hearing how much you hate me first thing in the morning. Really kicks my day into high gear."

"It's not as though you like me."

He only tilted his head, those depthless eyes tracking my features until I squirmed.

"Are you here for something?"

"Surely you haven't forgotten our first date?" he said, brows pulling in. I followed his stare to my bare feet. My black-painted toenails were a little chipped and I curled my toes in self-consciously.

"Already? But you haven't made a start on the bathroom yet." And I needed a chance to set some new rules if I was going to spend time with him. The Macabe brother rule book wouldn't see me through this, I'd violated every single one in the last thirty seconds.

Callum unsnapped the first button of his coat, working the zip down an inch. "Consider this a deposit. I've already checked in with Ada, you don't work until noon, and I'll be back tonight to get started on the suite. Unless you think your guests will enjoy waking up to the sound of hammering."

I crossed my arms. "You *might* make an excellent point."

He grinned that Ken doll smile, flashing his dimples. But beneath the charm, his beard looked a little too long and dark smudges bloomed beneath his eyes. "That's been known to happen a time or two." He clapped his hands. "Let's go. Dress warm."

I gave him my own brand of salute and strode past, noting the clothes horse beside the radiator, covered in every piece of underwear I owned, which he would have had to walk past to get to my kitchen. The books and game controllers spread out across the coffee table. I winced. I wasn't usually this untidy.

Heat rising in my cheeks, I scooped up the pile of washing from the end of the sofa and deposited it inside the walk-in closet, leaving Callum to amuse himself while I brushed my teeth.

"Hey, harpy . . ." he called a minute later.

"Yeah?"

"Not to alarm you, but there's a very angry cat sitting on top of your fridge."

I popped my head out. "Oh . . . yeah, that's Shakespeare. I wouldn't touch her if you want to keep all of your fingers . . . or y'know, do." I smiled around my toothbrush.

"What's wrong with her?"

"She's possessed by a demon, Father Robertson is performing an exorcism in the morning." I left to spit, returning to the main room in time to watch him draw closer to her.

"What scares me, harpy, is that I can't tell if you're joking."

"It's more fun that way, wouldn't you say?"

He snorted. "Does she need anything?"

I eyed her hunched form on top of the fridge and said, "A lobotomy perhaps."

"As warm and comforting as always," he muttered, holding out a hand to her. I bit my lip, stifling my warning as he paused a short distance away, offering up his scent without startling her. Shakespeare took the bait, or maybe *he* did, because she slunk forward a step, sniffing his hand then pressing her furry cheek into it. "Hey, beautiful." He stroked her softly. "There's a good girl." When she licked his finger, he threw me a triumphant grin over his shoulder. "See, she's a little prickly but all she needs is a tender – *ah, fuck!*"

Callum snapped his hand back, a single drop of blood beading on his index finger. Shakespeare hissed, showing all of her gleaming teeth. And I laughed, I couldn't help it. The stunned expression on his pretty face almost too pure for this world.

"She's a wicked little thing," he noted with dry amusement, running the cut under the tap.

"That's her MO, draw you in before she goes for the kill."

"Like someone else I know." He crossed to me, eyes roving over me again. I didn't understand what he was searching for until he hissed, "*Fuck*, Juniper." Spotting a particularly bad scratch on my inner arm, he extended a hand, as though to run a finger along the tender surface. Then dropped it limply to his side at the last moment. "Why would you bring home a vicious cat?"

"You can blame Kelly for that."

"Kelly? My nurse, Kelly?"

I nodded. "I occasionally foster cats from the shelter she volunteers at, just a night here or there, until she offered me a 'really sweet girl' struggling to find a permanent home. She played me."

He laughed with surprise. "Fuck, I didn't know Kelly had it in her. Wait . . . how did I not know about this?"

I froze, thinking through my options before admitting, "We use a . . . different vet."

His eyes flashed and he barked, "Who? Don't tell me it's Dennis Foster?" I curled my lips, saying nothing. "Please tell me you're joking. Foster's barely qualified, the kid got his degree from the University of Aberdeen for crying out loud."

"He handles Shakespeare well enough." Not exactly true. She'd made him cry the first time he checked her teeth.

"Bullshit. Next time bring her to me."

I rolled my eyes. "Are you done being high-handed? It's extremely boring."

"If you promise to let me examine her."

Jesus, I almost missed Community Ken. "I promise to think about it. Good enough?"

"Not even close."

Screw these Macabe men. Squaring my shoulders, I turned for the bathroom.

"Why did you keep her? If she's such a menace?"

I paused with my back to him. "Kelly blackmailed me, said no other family would take her."

"Careful, I might mistake you for a softie, harpy."

"That would be your mistake, *Macabe*."

"You're a real fucking snoop, you know that?" Fully dressed in a thick cardigan and jeans, I found Callum dragging a finger over my alphabetised game collection.

He paused, pulling the *Silent Hill* box from the shelf and eyeing it with interest. "Can you blame me? This feels like getting a peek behind the curtain."

My brows flew up, about to ask what the hell that meant, when Callum's attention slid from the game to the sideboard. The ring box I usually kept hidden in my junk drawer sat open, the diamond glinting in the fresh band of sunlight filtering through the window. Everything with Callum had left me feeling . . . muddled and I'd pulled it out last night to torture myself. I must have forgotten to put it away.

The floor tilted. My steps slow and choppy as I rushed to snap the lid shut. I knew it was too late. The pinch of his lips told me he'd already seen the contents.

Neither of us spoke for a long moment. The seconds passing almost audibly when I refused to look at him.

Then he was at my side, his large hand covering mine, skin surprisingly rough as he slipped the box from my fingers and brushed a thumb over the closed lid. "Why do you still have it?"

"To remember—" The words rose up my throat, tangling at the tip of my tongue. "Someone can swear you're the love of their life a thousand times, that doesn't make it true."

He set it back on the sideboard carefully. "Did he cheat on you?"

The question surprised me. Had he and Alistair never spoken about this? "Does it matter?"

"Of course it matters."

No, he hadn't cheated. Sometimes I wished he had so I could look back and pinpoint the moment it all went wrong. A reason to rage and scream. A reason to burn his pictures and cut up his clothes. When a person abandons you for the simple reason of not loving you enough, everything becomes very . . . quiet. A small wound that lingers, festering beneath the surface.

"Will it make you feel better for nearly fucking me?" I don't know why I said it. To make him feel as shitty as I felt, I supposed.

"*Fuck*, Juniper, that's not why I'm—"

But I was done. Done with his prying. Done with how pathetic these memories made me feel. "Can we go now? I want to get this over with." I fled for the door without waiting for an answer.

"Hold your hand out, let her come to you," Callum urged from beside me, one arm slung casually over the fence post as though we weren't staring down a two-thousand-pound monster.

"You can't expect me to touch that thing?"

Callum shifted the giant bag of barley at his feet, and I swear it licked its lips. *Oh, fuck no.*

I folded my arms, stepping away. After a lengthy and gruelling hike through a dense forest, my boots squelched so deeply into the mud on the steep hilltop, it soaked through to my socks. "You're insane for thinking I'd ever agree to this."

Early October cloaked the sky like a shroud in proud purples and blues, the icy wind tossing the strands of our hair poking from beneath woolly hats with rough fingers. Beads of moisture clung to Callum's eyelashes like tiny distracting pearls. I didn't want to know what I looked like. It had been a short tension-filled drive – for me, at least: Callum had steered his oversized truck with admirable ease. Thrumming his fingers on the wheel in time to an old rock song as he sped around sharp bends that usually left me wincing. I'd started to scramble from the car before he could do something ridiculous, like open my door for me, when he flipped open the centre compartment, slipped a black woollen beanie onto my head and said, "You need a hat." I'd been about to tear the thing straight off, drawing the line at wearing his sweaty old car beanie. Then I noticed the store tag he shoved into his pocket.

He'd bought me a hat. Ten minutes later I was still trying to figure out the punchline.

"Perhaps my nickname was misplaced, harpy. I thought you were made of sterner stuff."

"I'm a coward for not wanting to catch rabies? You can't bait me into agreeing."

He rolled his eyes. An entirely new gesture on the oldest Macabe. "You can't catch rabies from a cow."

I threw a hand to where it waited on the other side of the fence. "Look at the crazed glint in its eye. It's sizing me up." It had *horns*. I couldn't be the only person to notice that particular detail.

"Because she's hungry and you're taking too long."

"Then you do it." We could have done anything on this damn island. *Anything.* Shell picking on the beach, wild swimming, the options were numerous, and he'd chosen this?

"I have. Dozens of times." His bare hands came to rest atop his chest. "Why would we drive all the way out here so I, a vet, could feed a cow?"

"Why would we drive all the way out here so *anyone* could feed a cow?"

"Because you can't live on Skye and never hand-feed a cow, it's like a rite of passage." He tore the bag of grain open with his bear paw hands and kernels flew like tiny missiles. The beast crept closer.

I jerked, boots sinking further into the mud. "I've made it this far."

He sighed and for the first time he sounded a tiny bit exasperated. "If you really don't want to do it, we'll leave." I didn't think he was trying to make me feel guilty, but it slithered through me all the same.

I glanced at the cow again. Its russet hair ruffled in the wind, making it shine like burned gold. I could admit – from a distance – it held a certain . . . *charm.*

"Fucking fine." I rolled the sleeves of my coat up, goose-bumps pebbling as my entire forearm was exposed. "If this is your go-to move to impress a woman, try harder next time."

"Again, so curious about my dating life. If you want to know, all you need to do is ask."

I scoffed and held out my cupped hand. "Can we just get this over with? You promised I'd have fun; all I'm feeling right now is cold and dissatisfied."

"Is this the wrong time for a '*that's what she said*'?"

111

Was there a wrong time for a well-placed *that's what she said*? But I could never give him the satisfaction of confirming he was occasionally funny, so I schooled my features into boredom. "I'd forgotten I had the honour of spending time with Scotland's most promising comedian."

"That's your mistake, harpy." He echoed my earlier words, eyes dancing.

I stuck my tongue out. "Are we doing this?"

He answered with a wink and tipped a heap of grain into my palm. "We'll start small and see how you go." Despite the chill, my palm was clammy, the grain sticking to it. "Just hold your arm over the fence and she'll come to you."

"Are we allowed to be here?"

"I play shinty with the farmer." Of course he did. Social and sporty? Perhaps I should elevate him to Superstar Ken. "And I helped him deliver a calf last spring."

"I thought you only worked with domestic animals?"

"It was an emergency. I was the closest." He shrugged like it was nothing while I was still backtracking to the image of this man with a baby cow in his arms. Shirtless of course.

"Is there anyone you don't know?"

He thought about it, gracious enough not to point out that I was stalling. "Nope." He shrugged. "People like me." It wasn't a dig and yet something sharp scoured my throat. Unlike me, Callum had one of those personalities that people easily gravitated to. "Let's go."

Resigned to my fate, I swallowed and edged closer to the fence. "Okay, here I go. I'm doing it," I said more to myself than Callum. "I'm approaching the cow."

"Yes, you are." He sounded amused. "Don't forget to breathe."

"Easy for you to say, Mr Animal Whisperer." I hooked

my trembling arm over the beam and grain spilled into the wet grass. "Like this?"

"Harpy, it's a cow, not a grenade. Hold it steady . . . yep, like that." A finger pressed lightly beneath my elbow, nudging it higher. "Perfect. Flatten your palm a little, it will make it easier for her to take it."

I complied, looking the cow right in the eyes as she leant in to sniff the offered food . . . but came no closer. After a minute, I deflated. "Am I doing it wrong?"

"No. She's just sussing you out. Deciding if she likes you."

Remembering the fresh cut Shakespeare had left on my knuckles only this morning, the sharpness in my throat expanded. My hand trembled.

Take it.

Take it.

Please – I urged the stubborn animal – *don't embarrass me like this*. Still, she came no closer, and my hand fell completely, rejection and embarrassment scorching like fire down my chest. I'd failed. Even at *this* I'd failed.

What was it about me that made me so easy to dismiss?

Before I could crumble completely, heat enveloped me. Callum. His wide chest flush to my back. Steady breath at my ear. Salt and soap and Skye filling my nose. He smelled like the mountain thyme candles we burned at the inn. Earthy and a little wild.

"Don't give up." His hand cupped my wrist, rough fingers folding all the way around my bare arm as he lifted and held it steady. "Sometimes you need a little persistence to make something spectacular happen."

His other arm curled around me, fingers grasping the fence panel. My chest met the wood, his every breath pressing me deeper as we waited. I don't think I breathed at all.

"*Come on,*" I thought I heard him murmur. It could have

simply been a whisper on the wind because I was no longer paying attention. Not when the cow finally lumbered closer and seized the offering. Her hot nose brushed my wrist. Tongue, as rough as sandpaper, lapping up every single grain.

"I did it." The words punched out of me. Giddy. I was utterly giddy. "Did you see that?"

The cradle of his arms tightened. "Damn right, I did."

I shook out my hand, saliva dripping in globs. "That was disgusting."

"Want to do it again?"

I grinned despite myself. "Absolutely."

His laugh rumbled through me, and he stepped back to retrieve the sack. "Both hands this time."

I cupped them both eagerly, a childlike lightness I'd rarely felt as an *actual* child brightening my insides.

"Just as before?" I eagerly hooked my arms over the fence, and he followed. Both of his hands gripping the wood this time. His chest to my back. Hips cradling mine in a near perfect curve.

"Just as before," he said and I felt the words like a caress down the collar of my coat. There was no reason for him to be this close, and yet I couldn't summon a single word of complaint as the cow dove in again. "There . . . you got it." His tone filled with pride.

I was laughing. No, *giggling*. Unable to recall the last time that sound had passed my lips.

"Still hate me, sweetheart?" The words were a whisper on the shell of my ear.

Sweetheart. That was new.

I swallowed. "Undoubtedly."

"*Good.* Just making sure."

I didn't even have time to consider what that meant when

another russet head appeared. The second cow was bigger, easily brushing the first aside to get at my hands.

"Woah, not so fast," I chided, when another blustered its way through, mouth open so wide I could smell its breath. Count its teeth. Callum unfurled from me, reaching forward to stay the newcomers at the exact moment I recoiled. Too entrenched in the mud, my feet refused to follow, suctioning me to the wet earth. My arms flailed as the fence tipped. No, *I* was tipping, falling, hands searching for purchase. Callum shouted my name. His fingers grazed my sleeve. But not quick enough.

Cold. That was the first sensation to return.

Cold, wet mud. It seeped through my leggings. Coated my hands where I'd braced myself. And the—

"Fuck, Juniper. You okay?" Callum was bending over me, reaching to lift me to my feet. But halted, expression grim.

"Is that—"

"*No.*" I immediately cut him off. "No, no, no . . ."

His entire face changed. It was like witnessing a domino effect as his grin rippled into his eyes. "It *is*—"

I squeezed my eyes shut, blocking him out. "Don't say it. Don't you fucking dare."

"I have to. It's like pulling off a plaster . . . Ready?"

I shook my head. Frantic. If he didn't say it, it hadn't happened.

"Juniper . . . *sweetheart.*" I heard him take a breath, as though steeling the both of us. "You fell in shit."

His words were the breaking of a dam. The smell rushed in, so potent I gagged, bringing my hands up to cover my mouth.

"No." He caught my wrists. "Don't touch your face, just in case."

115

I gagged again at the thought, glad I'd had so little for breakfast, or I'd be wearing that too. I cracked my eyes, finally taking in the state of myself. Every inch was coated or splattered. My feet were still stuck in their little mud hole, my hands streaked with wet muck, crusting beneath my nails. It even dripped from my hair.

"I . . . I don't know what to do." I was about to bloody cry. I could feel the tears rising inside me like a tidal wave.

"Just . . . try and hold still for now." His full lips wobbled. "I've got a blanket in the bag."

He was back in a flash, the thick tartan tossed over his shoulder. His unchecked grin leading the way as he bounded back up the hill. Bracketing his feet on either side of mine, he reached underneath both of my arms. Our cheeks brushed and I felt the imprint of his smile, joining with the quiet rumble in his chest.

"Want to try and rein your enjoyment in just a little, Macabe? Keep grinning like that and you'll get wrinkles."

That seemed to push him over the edge and the laugh tore free, shaking his entire body. "I didn't say a word."

"You didn't have to. You practically floated back up the hill." He snickered again and I groaned. "Can we just pretend this never happened?"

"Oh, no. I'm going to be feeding on this memory for years, stinkerbell, might as well get used to it now." And then before I could even register the new nickname, I was lifted. Leaving nothing but a sickening squelch and my dignity behind.

As soon as I was steady, I pushed him away. Satisfied with the dirty handprint I left on his sweatshirt. "I hope you're happy with yourself?"

That grin of his refused to slip and he brushed away a single happy tear from the corner of his eye. "You think I lured you out here so you could trip over *your own* feet and land in cow shit? That's a little far-fetched, even for me."

"I wouldn't have been out here in the first place if it wasn't for you." I gestured down to myself. "Now look at me."

Unaffected by my goading, he looked me over, from the slightly askew beanie to the mud pies that had replaced my feet, and his nostrils flared. Probably from the smell. "You look fucking beautiful, Juniper, you always do."

"Am I supposed to believe that's a compliment?"

"Believe what you like." He chuckled ruefully, barely even wincing as he swaddled me in the plaid and hefted me into his arms. I shrieked; arms too tangled to cling on. "You never trust pretty words, especially if they come from me." I opened my mouth, but he cut me off. "Let's get you home and showered. You're looking a little *pooped*."

11

Callum

Isle of Skye Guidebook
  Kinloch Forest and Leitir Fura
  Distance: 6.5km.
  Time: Allow 2-3 hrs.
  Terrain: Be prepared for steep hills.
  This beautiful scenic trail through woodland offers ever-changing fauna, stunning views over the Sound of Sleat and the mountains of Knoydart.

I'd broken her.

Swaddled in my front seat like a newborn, Juniper hadn't uttered a single snarky comment the entire hike back to the car, her teeth chattering through every miserable step, though I'd carried her through most of it.

Peeling my eyes from the road, I slowed onto a cattle grate and snuck a glance at her. The set of her jaw was steely, but she stared through the flock of sheep grazing at the roadside like she didn't even see them.

"Are you cold?"

Her head shook while a shiver wracked her body. I cranked the heat higher. Eyes watering from the smell, I focused back on the road. I knew these winding roads like the back of my hand. Even then, it wasn't wise to rush. At any point the road could curve or dip unexpectedly, or the vehicle in front could slam its brakes, the driver too in awe of the wild landscape.

Juniper shifted, teeth chattering through the small hole I'd allowed for her dirt-streaked face, clothes heavy and wet from the waterlogged mud. I was tempted to press the pedal to the floor, safety be damned. Damn it, but she'd been having a good time . . . Until she wasn't. She'd deny it later, of course, but I'd heard her laugh, seen the gleam in her eyes and my heart had punched right through my rib cage in answer.

Then, I remembered the overwhelming horror on her face when the cows crowded in. How she'd screamed, "I'm a vegan!", right before she hit the floor, as though they should have sensed her allyship and taken it easy on her. And I wanted to laugh all over again.

I'd fully pulled into my driveway when Juniper finally spoke. "We're at your place."

I switched off the engine. "I figured you wouldn't want to risk any guests seeing you like that." And I selfishly wanted to take care of her.

"Right, of course." She nodded distractedly, like she was coming out of a dream, reaching for the door handle.

"Stay there. I'll help."

She must have been out of it because she did as I asked, staying put while I rounded the hood, eyes pinning her the entire time. I opened her door, and she turned to face me.

"Need a hand?"

Her head rustled in a listless nod.

Christ, even with a scent so potent it made my nose burn,

119

she was the most gorgeous woman on the fucking planet. Gripping her waist on either side of the blanket, I lifted and lowered, keeping her body a safe distance from mine, though instinct demanded I crush her to my chest, shit and mud be damned. We could shower it off together. Not exactly the way I'd dreamed of first showering with Juniper, but I'd take what I could fucking get.

With her feet safely on the ground, Juniper seemed to come back to herself, pulling the plaid from her shoulders and offering it out to me. I balled it, tossing it into a heap by the front door to deal with later.

Peeling her jacket away from her body, she frowned at the flakes of mud falling about her like confetti. She'd stomped most of the dirt from her boots before climbing into the truck, but they still clogged around her ankles, crusting the cuffs of her jeans.

"Do you have an outdoor hose, maybe?"

An outdoor hose? *You've got to be joking, sweetheart.* "You can use my shower."

"And trail shit all over your floors?"

"I could give a fuck about my floors, Juniper. I can hear your teeth chattering from here. It's not happening." Her quick nod of agreement was frightening.

Come on, harpy, snarl at me.

With stiff fingers she reached up for the zip. I flicked them away, undoing her jacket and tugging it over her shoulders. She kicked off her boots and I bent, snagging them along with the coat.

"I'll clean them while you shower," I said, leading her to the front door.

I toed off my own boots in the mud room and set hers beside them – trying not to get caught up on the domesticity of the action – before showing her down the hall to my bedroom. She halted on the threshold, curious eyes flicking to every corner. I ran my gaze over the neat space, trying to see it as she might. Juniper's cottage was a study in black. Deep and decadent, just like her. It reminded me of the fairy-tale cottage from Hansel and Gretel and the witch within waiting to eat unsuspecting children. I suspected Juniper's victims were far more willing.

Mine felt . . . *empty* in comparison.

"The only shower is in my ensuite." I cleared my throat, pointing to the door in the far corner. "There's a tub in the main bathroom if you'd prefer?"

She shook her head. "The shower's fine." Then tagged on, "Thank you."

I nodded. "Great. Thank you." *Why are you thanking her?* My voice was pathetically husky, and I cleared my throat again. "Clean towels are in the basket, leave . . . just leave your dirty clothes on the floor outside. I'll throw them in the wash and find you something to wear." She only stared at me. Unsure what to say, I stared right back. And then she pointed to the bathroom door at my back.

"*Shit*, sorry." Feeling my cheeks burn, I stepped out of her path. Having her so close, inches from my bed, was making my imagination run riot. "Have a nice shower."

And with that parting line, I fled.

Have a nice shower? Real fucking smooth. Tugging a hand through my hair, I put as much distance between us as possible, checking on Simon in his large enclosure just for something to do with my hands. Refusing to think of Juniper undressing two walls away. Stepping into my shower. Would she use my shampoo? My body wash? *Fuck*, did I even have any shampoo? I forgot to run to the store yesterday.

Turning to rifle through a basket of clean washing, I pulled out the first black T-shirt my hands found. Sniffing to make sure it smelled fresh, I carried it back to the bedroom and almost swallowed my tongue.

Door wide open, Juniper stood under the soft bathroom lighting, hair curling around her cheeks. *I fucking loved it when her hair curled*. She'd already turned on the shower and steam clouded, turning the air hazy as her stiff fingers fumbled over the buttons of her cardigan.

I might have been having a heart attack, I realised, heart threatening to crack my ribs. It would have to wait.

"Need a hand?" My mouth moved before my brain caught up, but there was no taking it back now because I was walking, closing the distance until the wet heat folded around me.

Her expression was unreadable. Dark eyes swallowing me whole as my trembling hands lowered ever so slowly to the top button, fully expecting her to shut me down. Slap my hands away. She did neither. Touching only the fabric, I slipped the first button through the loop. Then paused. Waiting. Barely breathing. *Be fucking cool.*

Her throat bobbed but didn't protest and so I moved on to the next, repeating the motion. The fabric gaped, revealing the silken skin of her collarbone and thin straps of her undershirt. My eyes flicked between hers and every fresh inch of skin as I unbuttoned the next and the next until the cardigan fell away completely, hitting the floor with the sensual hiss created only by discarded garments.

She could absolutely take it from here. I knew it. She definitely fucking knew it. But it felt like we were in our own little world, nothing else existed but the sound of water hitting tile, rising steam and Juniper. *Juniper.* She filled every corner of my vision, pale skin and the faintest brush of freckles beneath the dirt staining her cheeks and nose.

You get prettier every time I see you, I wanted to tell her, unaware of stepping closer, or my knuckle tracing down the line of her stomach pausing on the button of her jeans. "These next?" It was my voice, but it wasn't. Gruffer. Hungrier. Desperate. Juniper nodded, head bobbing almost frantically. That wouldn't do. "Answer me . . . please." I needed a yes. Needed to know she was right here with me.

"Yes." Her throat constricted. The word almost lost in the sound of my shaken exhale. But I'd heard it. It was enough. The button snapped, opening on only the smallest pressure. My hands trembled, head spinning as I tugged the zip, falling to my knees as the fabric gave way.

"*Fuck*." Her curse bordered on a groan. Her head fell back as I slipped off one sock, then the other.

"Eyes on me," I said. They opened into thin slits, reminding me of her hissing cat as they focused on me.

Pulling at her waistband, I peeled her stiff jeans down her thighs, kneeling far enough back to catch every bared scrap of skin. Holding my breath and only releasing it when the light pink lace came into view. "God, Juniper." The first time in my car wasn't an anomaly. Her little secret was out. Juniper Ross liked frilly, pretty, little underthings. I barely paused to glance at her gorgeous legs, because this would be over far too soon.

I stood, fingering the hem of her undershirt. "And this?"

"Please."

Please. That single word on her lips fucking did things to me. "Arms up." I helped push them above her head and tugged it off in a single sweep, groaning at the dizzying sight of her matching bra and the perfect breasts contained within. This was more than I'd ever seen of her and every inch was perfection. From the lines of ink to the raised scratches, some healing and some fresh. Gifts from the cat that reminded me of her.

"My favourite colour." My shaking finger grazed the

dainty strap of her bra without touching her skin. If I touched her, I'd be done for. "You're so gorgeous, Juniper, but of course you know that. How could you not?"

"You didn't say that last time."

Last time. The words emptied every thought from my head but that memory. The car park, Juniper's skin beneath my tongue, her back as she walked away. The open ring box on her sideboard, evidence of where her heart still lay. *Too soon. This was too soon.* I dropped my hands, but it didn't help, Juniper was panting, her peaked breasts grazing my chest through my T-shirt. *Fuck.* I squeezed my eyes shut, hands balling into fists at my sides.

"All right over there?" Her tone was sardonic, like she could read every humiliating thought in my head.

I managed a nod. Swallowed. "I should leave . . . I *am* leaving."

"You sure about that?"

"*Yes.*" It was a snarl.

"You look like you're about to kiss me, Macabe." My eyes snapped open, taking in the smug quirk of her lips. Like she'd fought a duel and came out victorious.

That wouldn't do.

I leant in a fraction, satisfaction roaring as she tensed. Chin tilting, lips parting.

"Do you want me to kiss you?" Eyes that had been on my lips found mine, flicking side to side as she tried to focus. Her tongue worked around a reply that never came. I could practically see the cogs in her brain turning. "Until that answer is a resounding yes, I'm not going to kiss you, harpy."

Something flashed through her expression, a vulnerability she masked far too quickly. "You'll be waiting a long time."

"I don't doubt it." And it would be worth it. For all my

talk, I was so pathetic for her, I'd be crawling to her on my hands and knees before the week was through.

Stepping back, I stared at her for the longest time. Her fingers clutched the sink, but she didn't move as I mapped every inch of her, mentally scrawling my name over every slight curve. Even as I shook my head and scrubbed a hand over my beard. *Your move*, her silence said.

It took more strength than I knew I possessed to collect her clothes and turn for the door.

Ten minutes later, I was tossing her clothes into the machine when, "I hope you aren't sniffing my underwear, Macabe," came from over my shoulder.

Macabe.

The message was clear. From the snark to the surname, she was putting us straight back onto familiar ground. I could work with that.

"I'm not sure what gets *you* hot under the collar, harpy, but for me it's definitely not your shit-soaked cardigan."

She shrugged, like my taunt was of little consequence. Her damp hair left wet patches on the borrowed shirt, jogging bottoms rolled over several times at the waist. Was she wearing the boxers I'd left, too? Curious minds demanded to know.

I crossed to the counter, only the hum of the washing machine cutting through the tension as I filled the kettle.

"Tea? Coffee?" I offered both, knowing she'd take the coffee with a splash of coconut milk, like she always did.

Her teeth scraped her lower lip. "I should get back."

I nodded, flicking the kettle to boil anyway. "I'll bring your clothes over once they're dry."

"And I'll wash these." She gestured down the length of her. A move I couldn't resist following. If I'd thought she

125

looked appealing cocooned in a blanket in my truck, the memory was nothing compared to now. There was something – *something* – about seeing your woman in *your* clothes. The way her bare toes curled into the area rug while she tugged the sleeves around her fingers. She looked so cosy I wanted to drag her into my bed and bury my face in her throat.

She wasn't even mine. But my heart roared otherwise. We were tiptoeing dangerously close to territorial caveman territory.

"Keep them as long as you want." Hell, *keep them forever.* I wanted to empty my wardrobe, ask her to wear every item of clothing I owned.

From the corner of my eye, I watched her swipe her boots from the mud room, balancing one arm on the back of my sofa while she laced them, right as I placed a mug on the end of the counter.

She eyed it like one would a viper. "I said I couldn't stay."

"I know. You can return the mug when you return the clothes." One more reason for her to come back.

She lifted it in a thanks gesture, taking a sip before she spun for the door. Then paused. "How'd you know how I take my coffee?"

"Because I know *you*, Juniper." Her eyes narrowed and her lips parted, ready to say – I could only guess what. Then she changed her mind at the last second, snapping her mouth shut. *Oh, no, sweetheart, not happening.* Compliment or insult, I wanted her words. "You look like you've got something to say."

"Okay, fine. You say a lot of cryptic shit about *knowing me* when in fact . . . it's the complete opposite." She spat the words with such personal malice, it sent a thrill through me. That tone belonged to *me* and me alone.

I sipped my drink. "Why do I feel like we're not talking about coffee anymore?"

"What else would I be talking about?"

That night in Glasgow. How our bodies felt so in tune – like we'd touched each other a thousand times before – it scared you.

But I couldn't say any of that without her scrambling for the nearest pointy thing to stab me with. So I simply said, "Okay, then let me get to know you. How about this . . . I'll trade you one secret for another."

She froze, surprise, alarm, panic, morphing in her face one after the other, like a fun house mirror. Her foot backed up, ready to run. "We've already agreed to four dates as payment. That's more than enough, don't you think?"

I shrugged, but it didn't feel as indifferent as I'd hoped. "Then don't consider it payment. Tell me just to tell me."

Just when I thought she'd leave without answering, her spine straightened. "I had fun today," she whispered it like a dirty secret.

I had fun today. Such an innocuous statement, so why did it make the back of my throat burn?

Because she'd spoken it with such insecurity, as though she expected me to laugh at her.

Her gaze searched the floor as she asked, "And yours?"

"I always have fun with you, harpy."

Her eyes flew to mine, the tops of her cheeks turning a pretty pink. "You mean that?"

Could she truly not see herself the way I did? The way Heather, April and Fiona did? *This woman would be the death of me.*

"*Aye*." I said the word slowly. Making certain she heard it. *Never fucking doubt it.*

12

Juniper

Three missed calls: Fiona

"Rule one, don't look at a Macabe brother," I muttered through gritted teeth, clinging tightly to the inn bannister. "Two, don't talk to a Macabe brother. Three, don't even think of a Macabe brother." *What part of that couldn't I understand?*

Every step down from the second floor was torturous thanks to our morning hike. My descent was slow, thighs burning and cramping. I could admit I'd let my physical activity go in the past couple of years. A busy work life coupled with my natural inclination to be indoors meant I'd relied on taking the inn stairs twenty times a day to keep me fit. It hadn't done a very good job, apparently. The burning was made only worse by the four-inch heels I'd squeezed my bruised feet into for my evening shift. Fiona always fussed over my choice of footwear – *a safety hazard*, she scoffed at least twice a day. But I could happily work an eight-hour shift in them without even wincing.

Usually.

"Are you all right, June?" Ada hovered behind the desk; a stack of papers pressed to her chest.

"Fine," I straightened. "Just . . . performing a safety check."

"On the bannisters?" Her brows flew up.

"*Yes*." My thoughts scrambled. "For . . . woodworm."

I regretted it the moment the words passed my lips. Ada shrieked and I sighed, watching papers scatter across the floor. "Do we have an infestation? I'm *deathly* afraid of insects."

"We don't have woodworm," I quickly assured her. "That I'm aware of." She screamed again, leaping from behind the desk like the unfortunate heroine in a B-grade horror movie. I swept down the final step, biting my lip as I knelt to gather the strewn documents.

"I told your mum when she hired me that I wouldn't work with animals, especially insects." She swatted at her arms. "I feel all itchy now."

Despite the headache forming, I said, "How about you take off for the night? I'll cover reception and get all the necessary checks in place before your shift on Wednesday?" It wasn't Ada's fault I was in a shit mood.

"Would you? Perhaps call an exterminator too, it's best for everyone to have a safe working environment." She was already collecting her coat and bag from beneath the desk. "Now I can get to my book club a little early." Hooking her jacket over her arm she squeezed my shoulder as she passed. "You're a good girl, June. Those invoices still need filing before tomorrow."

"*Great*." My fingers rolled over my temples. I still had three rooms to turn over before tomorrow after spending most of my afternoon stripping the waterlogged wallpaper out of room five.

Trying not to move my legs any more than necessary, I

shuffled the papers into a pile. One in my periphery lay just out of reach, I stretched a little further, a finger just grazing the corner. "Come on, you shit." I extended just a little more. "You fucking, *fuck*."

"Call me egotistical." A pair of unlaced boots stopped just shy of crushing the invoice. "But I have the strangest notion you're imagining that piece of paper has my face on it."

How did a man of his size move so silently? Help or not, I seriously regretted giving him free rein to come and go as he pleased.

"That would involve me thinking of you at all—" Shoving with my feet, I shuffled an inch closer and snatched the invoice from the toe of his boot. "Which I don't."

A bare-faced lie. The deep timber of his voice transported me back to his bathroom this morning, steam misting my eyes, turning my brain foggy as he'd undressed me with surprising gentleness. His hands had been warm and shaky as they slid around my waist, blazing through my shirt, making certain I was steady on my feet before dropping to his knees. He'd looked ready to eat me alive. And like an utter fool I would have let him.

Now the roles were flipped, and I knelt at *his* feet.

He took in my position with a keen stare. "You can't get up, can you?"

Oh, he thought he was so funny and charming with that dimple popping smile. "Perhaps I'm taking the opportunity to inspect the hardwood."

His boot scuffed against the floor, making a high-pitched squeak. "More of those renovations in mind, harpy? Feels like you're trying to keep me around."

When I only rolled my eyes, he held out a hand. Biting down on my wince, I bypassed the offer and pushed to my feet, my features set in a victorious little grin.

"Very smooth," he noted.

"I assume you're here to work?" I said over my shoulder, pushing an extra little sway into my hips as I rounded the desk. Suddenly very pleased I'd worn my favourite skirt that fit like a glove.

He followed, patting the bag on his shoulder. "Within a few hours you'll have yourself a fully fitted toilet."

"What every girl dreams of hearing." I sat, dropping the stack of invoices onto the desk. "Anything I can do to help?"

"Not unless you're handy with a wrench."

"My talents lie elsewhere." I hummed, leafing through the documents rather than looking at him. I couldn't pinpoint precisely when it happened, but the starling blue Macabe eyes had morphed into an affiliation with *him*, not a memory of Alistair.

He clicked his tongue, "Pity."

He hovered at the edge of my vision, and I pretended not to notice. We were always doing this . . . this charged back and forth. A conversation of concentric circles that achieved nothing but shifting my pulse into a higher gear.

"Well, you know where I'll be," I said, a dismissal he ignored by setting a bar of dark chocolate on the desk. The purple package rustled in his fingers.

"For you."

Seconds ticked by while I stared at it. "Why?"

"After today I figured you could use a pick-me-up." He gave me a small smile that made my chest ache. The same smile from this morning that accompanied, *Because I know you, Juniper*.

I cleared my throat. "Thank you."

"No problem. Is . . . is everything all right?"

I didn't reach for the chocolate, just returned to leafing through the stack of papers without reading. The words could have been written in hieroglyphics; I wouldn't have noticed. "Why wouldn't it be?"

"I don't know, you usually greet me with 'Fuck off, Macabe.'"

"You're doing me a favour so I'm being nice."

"This is *nice*?" He hooted. Would it kill him not to sound so surprised? He made me sound like a bridge troll.

"Yes." I exhaled the word through my teeth, no doubt aggravating my TMJ disorder. "I'm being downright pleasant."

"Lucky me." His knuckles rapped once on the wood, timing the action perfectly with his signature wink, then backed away. He clearly didn't expect me to watch his retreat because his demeanour shifted the instant he hit the stairs, shoulders drooping, head hanging like a puppet with its strings cut. I thought again of the dark circles beneath his eyes and wondered if I wasn't the only one who'd learned the art of pretending.

13

Callum

Heather: Free for dinner tonight? The girls miss you.
Callum: Can't. I'm helping at Ivy House.
Heather: I knew June would come around.
Heather: Be nice to her! She doesn't appreciate your brand of humour.
Callum: My brand of humour?
Mal: That's our baby sister's nice way of saying, "you aren't as funny as you think you are."
Heather: It's an acquired taste.
Mal: Like Irish whisky.
Callum: Remind me again why I begged Mum and Dad for more siblings?
Alistair: What happened at Ivy House?

An hour later and feeling every one of my thirty-nine years, I accepted I needed Juniper's help. Trudging to the stairs with all the energy of a North Pole elf come Christmas Eve.

The changes from my last visit told me Juniper had been putting in as many hours as me. All the furniture had been cleared and the old tartan wallpaper stripped. Between that and running the inn, when did she find time to sleep?

"Nothing you can do unless she asks for help," I reminded myself, checking my watch as I hit the small landing between floors. Seven thirty. More than enough time to finish here, check in with Mum and make it home for a quick dinner before bed. I might even get that elusive eight hours.

I found Juniper exactly where I left her. Phone pressed to her ear, bare toes just visible where she'd kicked her heels aside – *damn those elegant little toes*. Feet usually freaked me out, but Juniper's were just as perfect as the rest of her. Her tongue traced along her lower lip as she listened to the person on the line, a nervous gesture she made often but couldn't have been aware of because she'd have found a way to master it.

"*Yes*, I'm prepared for the food delivery – because it's the same day every week—"A muffle cut her off. "You're on holiday, why are you logging into the booking system at all?"

Her mum, I realised, pausing curiously on the bottom step.

"Well don't – everything is fine, go to the beach and have a cocktail or something. *Bye*, Fiona – *aye*, bye!"

The heels of her hands pressed into her eyelids, and I cleared my throat. "Who was that?"

"*Shit* . . . how the hell do you do that?"

"I snuck out a lot as a teenager. You become an expert after facing Jim Macabe's wrath a time or two." Her lips pinched like the thought didn't please her. "Very different from your dad, I bet?"

Her head tilted. She didn't smile but her features softened, eyes brightening like two pools of melted chocolate. Folk in

134

the village described Juniper as cold, it made me wonder if they ever paused long enough to look her in the eyes. They were the furthest thing from *cold* I'd ever encountered.

"You could say that. Alexander was more of a 'my kid is safer if I know where she is' kind of parent. Most likely why I couldn't stay away from trouble."

It was on the tip of my tongue to say something flirtatious, like, *What kind of trouble?*, but I'd heard all about the excessive partying of her younger years. I wouldn't judge her for it, I'd hardly been a saint.

"He sounds like a smart man."

"He was." Her throat bobbed and I knew it was time to change the subject.

I nodded to the stairs. "I could use an extra pair of hands if you have a minute?"

Her brows flew up. "My wrench skills?"

"Actually, yes."

"Squeeze it tight."

"Here?"

"Perfect – wait, a little tighter . . . there." I pushed her hands an inch higher, increasing the pressure.

"Quit manhandling me unless you want my hands around your throat."

"Don't threaten me with a good time, sweetheart." I moved her hand another inch then stepped back, inspecting the position of the toilet bowl she held in place. Too bad I only saw Juniper. On her hands and knees, that tight skirt stretched over her small but perfectly formed arse.

Christ, I started to bite into my fist, realised I was acting like a fucking creep, and forced my brain back to the task at hand, ensuring the base lined up with the clamps I'd drilled into the floor. Slightly off centre, I noted.

Sinking to my knees in the slight space between her calves, I curled my body over hers – the barest gap separating my chest from her back – and slid the heavy porcelain an inch to the left.

She inhaled sharply, making contact. "This all right?" My rough question stirred the hair at her temples.

"So long as you don't move that hand."

I glanced down at the hand in question. It almost grazed her breast. "*Fuck*, sorry."

"Do you often find yourself in these kinds of positions while plumbing?"

"Occasionally. Jealous?"

She scoffed but I didn't miss the flex of her fingers around the bowl.

Picking up the drill, I had little choice but to press fully against her, head curving over her shoulder to line up the large screws perfectly. Her hair tickled my cheek, shoulder curling flawlessly inside mine, like we'd been made just for this. I didn't breathe. Keeping my hips a healthy distance away, I counted to ten, welcoming the whir of the drill that cut through the daze.

"When did you become interested in plumbing?" she asked when it quieted.

"I wouldn't call it an interest in plumbing, exactly. I just like being self-sufficient. When I first bought the practice, the building needed fully renovating. It would have pushed me so far into the red, I'd probably still be clearing the debt now. Why pay someone when I could learn to do it myself?"

"You did it all?"

"Not everything, but I became pretty handy with a sledgehammer – what?" I pressed, noting her smile.

She shrugged. "Nothing, I just didn't realise you were so . . . *guyish*."

136

"Guyish?"

"You know, rough and ready, eats nothing but bran flakes for breakfast, starts a fire with two sticks and some dirt, kind of guy." She was fucking with me.

Ducking beneath her arm so I wouldn't be tempted to deliver a swift slap to that arse, I spread the sealant, holding it in place as it dried. "You're way off with the bran flakes."

"And the rest?" The side of her breast grazed my cheek.

I squeezed my eyes closed, any playfulness fleeing as I ground out, "I'm rough when the mood strikes."

The jovial mood snapped, and we worked in silence after that, her holding the pieces with a steady grip as I bolted the cistern in place and sealed it to the wall.

"That's it?" she asked minutes later, smoothing out the creases in her skirt as she stood.

"That's it." I wiped off my dusty hands, handing the cloth over when she grimaced at the state of her own.

"Do you have a phobia of dirt?" I blurted like an untactful arsehole. I don't know how I hadn't seen it before, but her reaction this morning had been more than simple disgust at animal excrement.

"It isn't the dirt," she replied, gaze never straying from her task. Words clipped enough to issue a *quit while you're ahead* warning.

Push or retreat.

Push or retreat.

My decision flipped like a coin toss. Did I keep this safe semblance of a truce or forge on for more?

I'd never been good at playing it safe.

"Then what is it?" I made a show of collecting up my tools, giving her space. "We agreed a trade, one secret for another," I reminded her. "I answered all your questions about the practice."

"That's hardly a fair trade, I'd have asked better questions if I'd known."

My laugh was a cackle, her teasing feeling like a breakthrough. "Ask whatever you like, harpy, I'll answer." There was nothing she could ask that I wouldn't trust her with.

"Why did you move back to Kinleith?"

Except that.

"You first," I stalled. "Since we're trading."

She blew out a breath, eyes settling over my shoulder as she said, "I hate being an inconvenience. In foster care, the challenging kids are always moved on more quickly. I learned early on it's better not to draw attention to yourself."

Fucking hell.

Just like that, Juniper's entire life unfurled before me like a flip book. No wonder she'd been pissed at my insinuation of knowing her. *Hell*, I might not know her at all, because I finally got it. All the ways she accommodated and made herself smaller. Never pushing her parents or Alistair for more – even her friends on occasion – because love could be withdrawn as easily as it was given. *Fuck*, even the damn cat and the wounds she bore like badges of honour.

I knew my expression was fierce as I dared a step nearer, my self-control crumbling. A slight bend of my knees, that's all it would take for my lips to reacquaint themselves with the taste of her.

They found her forehead instead. Eyes clenching tight, I brushed them back and forth across her skin. "Thank you for telling me." The words felt woefully insignificant. The tip of the iceberg of things I longed to say.

"You're not going to assure me I'm not an inconvenience?"

Keeping her close, I tucked a silken strand of hair back behind her ear, tugging on the end of it until she looked at me. "Striving not to take up space in this world is an impossible long-term goal, sweetheart. I like a little bit of mess."

I should pull away. We were tiptoeing down a dangerous path, with far more than my own heart on the line. But then she relaxed into my hold, letting me stroke over the delicate arch of her ear, and I knew there was no stopping the inevitable.

"You didn't answer my question," she said after a long minute, her voice a little bit drowsy.

"What question?"

"Kinleith." She yawned. "Why did you move back?"

"I wanted my own practice. Property here is cheaper than Edinburgh."

"*Oh.*" I didn't imagine her disappointment. "You don't find it boring?"

"No, sweetheart." My grip on her tightened. "The opposite actually."

14

Juniper

Callum: What did the fast–food worker say to the toilet?
Juniper: Is this a poo joke?
Callum: "Did you order a number two?"
Callum: Get it?
Juniper: A newborn could understand that one, Macabe.

Callum Macabe had kissed me on the forehead and ran away like his shoes were on fire.

He'd stroked my ear.

I don't know why that was the part my brain kept tripping over. Far filthier things had been shared between us. All I knew was the way he'd pinched my earlobe between his thumb and index finger – like he found that tiny scrap of flesh worthy of divine worship – screamed volumes for what he'd do with my clit.

Not *my* clit.

A clit. *A metaphorical clitoris.*

A *gaggle* of clitorises.

No wonder people liked him. A forehead kiss and a

pinch to the earlobe and *Clitoris Ken* had left me weak in the knees.

I might even like him.

And because he'd known exactly what he'd done to me, I'd barely spoken to him the following day.

Or the three days after that.

He arrived at Ivy House at seven p.m. every day, like clockwork. Two steaming mugs of chamomile tea in hand – one for me and one for him – and asked a single question before proceeding up the stairs.

On Tuesday he asked: "What's your favourite *Lord of the Rings* film?"

"*Return of the King*, obviously."

He'd nodded as if suitably satisfied with the answer and handed over a chocolate chip cookie wrapped in a Brown's Café bag.

Wednesday: "How many cats did you foster before Shakespeare?"

"Seven. Some for days at a time. Some for weeks. I looked after a sweet ginger tabby called Oscar for close to a year." The day he got adopted I'd cried in my shower until the water ran cold. I didn't tell Callum that last part.

That earned me a banana muffin Jess served so sparingly, they were akin to gold dust in Kinleith.

On Thursday I'd been giving a sweet couple from Missouri restaurant recommendations and he'd waited until they left to ask: "If you could add one thing to Ivy House what would it be?"

"A wooden gazebo in the wild garden to host summer weddings."

He'd smiled at that. And that smile had spread into his cheeks when he'd caught my attention drifting to his bag, already anticipating the sugar rush. I hadn't even waited for him to disappear up the stairs before swallowing half of the brownie in a single bite.

What the hell was he getting out of this arrangement? How had he so accurately anticipated my early evening sweet tooth? I couldn't make sense of it. The anticipation beating like a trapped bird in my chest as I watched the hand of the clock tick past six fifty-nine had started to feel like a foreign body spreading through my bloodstream. *That's just the extra sugar*, I assured myself.

On Friday, when I'd caught myself putting a little extra effort into my appearance under Shakespeare's contemptuous stare, I'd done what any rational thirty-year-old woman would do when faced with what I feared was a developing crush. I avoided him.

Later that evening my stolen notebook awaited me at the reception desk. A blue Post-it stuck to the black velvet cover.

Made some notes. Hope you don't mind.

And below that.

Shakespeare: try spreading some treats on the floor and lying in the centre with your eyes closed. It's a confidence-building technique.

He had indeed made notes. His messy scrawl scored dozens of brightly coloured Post-its, as though his pen couldn't keep up with his thoughts. He offered insight on what worked and what didn't. Easy changes I could implement now to make Ivy House more energy efficient. Either he knew a lot about green living or he'd researched the topic. That seemed unlikely.

One note, beside my god-awful sketch of a garden compost, had simply said: *Brilliant.* With a little smiley face.

I'd pressed the tip of my finger to that smile—

"I'm thinking of dyeing my hair pink."

"What?" Startled, I almost dropped the bathroom sink I held.

April stood behind me. Bare faced and effortlessly beautiful.

Her words finally registered, and I set down the sink to clutch her wrist. "What did Mal do? I'll end him for you." A dramatic hair change was always the first sign of a romantic crisis.

April laughed. "Want to ease up, killer?"

"Sorry." I released my grip. "Why would you dye your hair pink?"

"I just said it to get your attention, I called your name three times. I haven't heard from you in so long, I was starting to worry you'd killed Murray and gone on the lam."

"I don't think people say that anymore," I pointed out, wiping the sweat from my forehead.

"I'm making a conscious effort to bring it back. It's so *Bonnie and Clyde* – hot-sex-in-a-getaway-car-esque." She touched the short strands of hair slipping from my claw clip. "And you'd look fantastic in a beret."

"I *do* look fantastic in a beret. I have three in my wardrobe." Under a thick layer of dust. I'd made the mistake of wearing one into the village once, I'd barely made it fifty feet from my car before someone shouted, "Where's your baguette?"

No one took the piss quite like the Scottish.

"Because you're wonderfully unique," she replied cheerfully.

I shifted, searching the storage room as her compliment took shape and festered. People liked unique . . . until they didn't. There was a reason people languished in the known, a favourite book read over and over; a movie recited line for line; the same oat and raisin cookie every Monday morning. The familiar held no ugly surprises.

"How's it all going?" April's voice pulled me to the present. "Callum says he's ready to fit the new suite."

I nodded, lifting the sink again and she grasped the other end. "It feels like the drama might finally be over." The day of the flood felt like months ago, when fewer than two weeks had passed. Even with Callum only working a few hours a night, we'd made progress quicker than I anticipated.

"He asked Mal to help with some heavy lifting. That's why we're here."

"He didn't say." Probably because I'd received a singular text from him that morning.

Macabe: Fitting the bathroom in room five today.

That was it. Seven words.

And what did I respond, you might ask?

A thumbs up.

A. Thumbs. Up.

I never used emojis. They were fucking humiliating.

"He also mentioned you planned to paint today, so I wore my best work clothes." Heart a solid lump in my throat, I looked her over again, finally noting the loose denim overalls that somehow managed to hug her curves.

"Oh, you don't need to help." I'd been putting off the job for days now. My heart doing this uncomfortable galloping beat that left me feeling lightheaded whenever I pictured myself making this very permanent change. Sure, I could repaint it if Fiona hated it, but it would never be Alexander's work.

"If I need to bulldoze you, I will, Juniper Ross. I'm here, I'm helping, get used to it." Her hands settled on her hips.

All right then. "Did you just full name me?"

"You left me no choice. You were about to fob me off with some *I can handle it alone* bullshit."

"I *can* handle it alone," I pointed out, leading her from

the storeroom beside the kitchen. Hank didn't even look up from his food prep. *Still ignoring me then.*

"Callum told me not to take no for an answer."

"He said what?" I halted. She kept walking. The sink wobbled between our dual grip. "You know what? Never mind – the man meddles more than Jessica Brown." Desperate to change the subject from anything Callum-related, I asked, "How's things at the distillery?"

"Busy, but good." She adjusted the weight as we approached the stairs. "I think we might need to hire more staff, the orders have more than doubled in the last few months. I found Ewan crying in the dunnage yesterday."

Ewan was Kinleith distillery's youngest employee. A sweet lad if not a little jumpy.

"Actual tears?" She nodded. "Mal can't be *that* grumpy."

"He's not these days." Her smirk was pure female satisfaction. "Ewan cut his hand and felt too bad to leave in the middle of a work day. Mal drove him to the surgery, obviously. And Jacob can't keep up with the workload anymore, though he won't admit it."

"Sounds shit."

Her nose screwed. "There's still so much to do before the ceilidh next month, we might need to consider hiring someone off-island. You're coming to the ceilidh, right?"

"I wouldn't miss it." The distillery's seventieth anniversary was approaching and to celebrate they'd invited half the village for an evening of whisky and live music. April had been organising it for months. "I bet eighteen-year-old April didn't see this in her future." Just a few years ago she'd been walking the red carpet in Cannes, not a denim overall in sight.

Her grin was luminous. "I actually love it, working with Mal every day, being close to you and Heather. Which makes it even more shit that I'm leaving in a few months."

Ordinarily, I'd distance myself with a sarcastic comment, how we wouldn't even notice her absence. But I couldn't bring myself to say it. April's return had changed things around here. Made me and Heather a little more whole, lightening the ancient baggage that lay between us. So instead, I blurted, "Callum stroked my ear."

She almost tripped up the step. "What kind of stroke?"

"Is there more than one kind?" Her pitying expression suggested I'd been sleepwalking for half my life. "*Apparently so*," I muttered. Setting down the sink, I brushed my hands on my jeans. "Let me show you."

Stepping close enough our thighs brushed, April laughed lightly as I twirled one of her stray curls around my finger, just as Callum had done to me. I'd replayed that tiny interaction so many times I had the exact pace and pressure perfected. Her eyes danced but she held still as I tucked the curl behind her ear with tantalising slowness, allowing the tip of my finger to graze the arch of her ear, down the lobe where I pinched once and drew away.

Silence stretched. The smallest flush painted her pale cheeks. Then— "Oh, Juney, you are so fucked."

"What are you guys doing?" We were standing so close, our noses brushed as we turned in unison. Mal waited at the top of the stairs, a wary quirk lifting his brow.

"Telling June how screwed she is," April said.

Mal glanced between us. "How's that?"

"Callum stroked her ear."

He grimaced, coming down the stairs to pick up the sink. "Please tell me that's not a euphemism for something."

"The less you know the better." I continued up the stairs, patting his shoulder as I edged past.

"Thank Christ," I heard him mutter before I turned down the hall.

"*I booked the pitch for five-thirty*—" A low voice rumbled from inside room five. *Callum*. My pulse thundered, as if attuned to the sound of him. I told myself the brief pause on the threshold was simply to catch my breath from the climb. Nothing to do with the man waiting on the other side.

Skin . . .

Pushing the door wide, my brain short-circuited over that singular thought. *Skin. Bare skin. Callum's bare skin. Lots of it. He was shirtless. Completely and utterly bare from the waist up and . . . fucking hell.*

He might have glanced up when I entered. Might have laughed despite the phone pressed to his ear. I didn't care, not as my eyes roved over the sheer majesty of Callum Macabe's chest. I needed an intervention. Needed someone to dig my eyeballs from my skull because I couldn't stop staring. His waist tapered into a magnificent V. His biceps rounded with relaxed power. A light trail of hair led to the band of his jeans, a delicious path it suddenly felt vital to follow all the way to the end. Every inch of him firm and stunning. Real. Not the mass-produced gym bro I'd always suspected lay beneath his clothes. He twisted at the waist, and I choked down my groan at the sight of the navy T-shirt tucked into his waistband.

I needed to get a hold of myself before he noticed. A voice whispered it might already be too late.

Still on the phone, he tipped the receiver away from his mouth long enough to whisper, "I feel like I need a cigarette after that, harpy."

Shit. Cheeks burning like never before, I forced my legs to move, somehow managing to shoulder past him without actually making contact with his skin.

At the small workstation I'd set up last night, I stepped

into the paint-splashed coveralls that had once belonged to Alexander. Ada was covering the reception desk, so I had the entire afternoon to repaint the freshly sanded wood panelling. Forgoing the dark wood stain Fiona picked in the nineties, I opened the can of earthy sage green. My fingers shook as I poured it into the tray. I was fully following my gut on this one, hoping the change would make the room feel bigger. That it would complement the ever-changing skies the large bay window framed like a dramatic oil painting, while also retaining the homey quality guests expected.

The hot prickle spreading throughout my cheeks spoke of Callum's attention on me as I stirred a thick brush into the paint. He was still chatting on his phone and I pretended not to notice, pushing to my feet only to hesitate moments later, the dripping brush mere inches from the wall, as if held back by invisible hands. April and Mal entered, their amiable voices nothing but static in my ears as they dropped off the sink and left again.

"You're staring at that wall like you're holding a grudge, sweetheart." Callum spoke from over my shoulder. I hadn't even heard him hang up the call. "What did it do to piss you off?"

"Nothing." My throat felt like I'd swallowed sand as I forced out a sarcastic comment. "I love my grudges. I tend them like a rose garden."

He said nothing, the silence broken only by the rhythmic drip, drip of paint on the plastic sheet. But I felt his stare like the drag of a finger down my spine. The temperature in the room ticking up and up. *This is too fucking much*. I squeezed my eyes shut, trying to dispel the image of Fiona's disappointed face. She was going to hate it and then she would hate me—

The brush wrenched from my grip and my eyes flew

open, flicking between my empty, paint-soaked fingers and the man now holding it. Callum's shoulder skimmed mine and, without even glancing my way, he set the brush against the wall. "No wait—"

"Too late," he said.

My heart jolted as he worked, wrist flicking in such a way I knew he was writing something. A beat later, he drew back, dipping the brush back into the tray to punctuate the single word with an underline. No, not an underline, an arrow.

Beautiful.

The word was scribbled in block capitals. The arrow beneath pointing straight at me.

"There." He extended the brush. "No going back now."

I took it, words failing me.

"You're staring again." His voice was lower than I'd ever heard it.

"I'll stop staring when you do." Because he *was* staring. The look on his face so intense, I had to fight not to press my thighs together.

His smile turned from playful to wicked. "So *never*?"

I couldn't begin to wrap my head around what he was implying. It was so wrong. The taunting and harmless flirting was one thing, but we were nearing a clifftop. The same one we'd teetered over years ago and managed to scramble back from the edge.

He's Callum. Your ex's brother. I couldn't afford to forget it. "Shirts are mandatory around here, Macabe." I slid a mocking look to that perfect chest. "I can't have you scaring my guests."

"You sure make a lot of rules for someone getting a pretty sweet deal. I'm here, working on a Saturday after all."

"I'll pay anytime you want, just say the word." Drawing

the distinction between a service and a favour would make things a hell of a lot easier.

"Oh, you will pay me." He let the taunt hang. "At the shinty game tonight."

Watching him run around a field all muscular and sweaty and Ken-like? He probably clapped the opposing team when they scored. Who knew good sportsmanship was a kink of mine?

No, I needed to spend *less* time with him, not more. "I have plans."

"Cancel them."

"And if it's a date?" The words shot out before I could stop them.

Seconds ticked by, measured by the pulse in his jaw. "If I believed you, you would of course be welcome to bring this . . . *hypothetical* date along."

"You're coming to the game tonight?" April breezed into the room, Malcolm, Heather and the twins right on her heels. I turned, swiping the paintbrush across the wall before any of them could read it.

"Oh, I'm not—"

"You have to go," Heather cut in as the girls dashed across the room, long braids trailing as they threw themselves at their uncle. Callum scooped one up in each arm, mimicking a vampire snapping his jaw. They both giggled and squealed.

"Again, again," Ava shouted and he spun on the spot.

Something in my gut whooshed and I forced my attention back to Heather. She gave me a bright smile that made my heart swell and said, "I'm dropping the girls off at a sleepover and promised I'd hang around for a while. This way April won't have to stand alone."

"As if. People are tripping over themselves to chat with

Miss Skye 2008," Callum chipped in, slightly sweaty but smiling as he referenced the out-of-date pageant still held at the summer fete every year.

April practically preened at the compliment. Picking up a spare paintbrush, she drew a big heart on the wall, adding a stylised M in the centre. "Y'know, out of all the awards I've won, that might be my greatest accomplishment yet."

"How did I not know about this?" Mal asked.

It was Heather who answered. "It happened during your comic book phase, you were probably sketching in your bedroom."

True to form, April's features melted, as though it were the most adorable thing she'd ever heard, and she threw her boyfriend a flirtatious wink. "I still have the tiara and sash, I'll dig them out later."

He came up behind her, stealing the paintbrush and adding an A right beside the M, so close the edges touched.

"A princess in truth, you kept that one quiet."

April's answering giggle and the loaded look that passed between them hiked the temperature in the room another degree.

The twins let out a joint chorus of "Eww."

Heather coughed, "Children present."

And Mal startled, red-cheeked and grinning.

"How about we actually get some work done?" Callum suggested. "Before Mal pulls a bloody tiara from his pocket and crowns the lass on the spot?"

That earned another round of laughs and a middle finger from Mal. The lightness even getting to me as my friends grouped around, bickering over brush sizes and paint rollers while the brothers withdrew to the bathroom. Amused grunts crept around the door when Mal fitted the sink taps the wrong way around, affixing them so tightly, it took them twenty minutes to correct the mistake.

We drank copious cups of sugary tea and belted out old pop songs that even the twins knew the lyrics to. And much later in the afternoon, when the sun had begun to dip, we stepped back, tired and paint-splattered, to admire our handiwork.

"Don't you like it?" Heather asked after my long silence.

Throat narrow and eyes burning, I could only nod.

"It's perfect," I finally managed. Heather's arm swept around my shoulders, squeezing me like she used to. And it *was* perfect. Not because the green perfectly matched the dark herringbone floor, or because it opened the room up *just right*, but because we'd done it together. Without a word from me, my friends had been here, no questions asked.

And just like that, I understood why my mum had been so hesitant to change a thing.

15

Callum

First rule of shinty: if you didn't bleed, did you even play?

Blood spilled from my nose, the metallic taste filling my mouth and dripping down my chin. I spat, staining the white-painted boundary line red.

"Fuck, Callum – I'm sorry, I didn't see you—" Mal raced to my side on the final whistle, panic staining his sweat-slicked face.

I ran the back of my hand under my chin, catching the flow. "It wasn't your fault."

That honour belonged to the too good-looking Jamie Stewart. I'd always liked the lad, but damn if I didn't want to wipe the smile off his face.

I'd been distracted from the first blow of the whistle. It was the first game back of the season and not only was I out of shape and ill-prepared, but I'd gone and invited Juniper. Despite the crap she'd spewed about having a date, she'd actually shown up as if dressed for one.

Chunky black heeled boots, just thick enough not to sink

into the soft earth of the village green. Bare legs disappearing beneath a calf-length coat that gave the impression of nothing beneath. She looked as if she'd stepped out of a very vivid dream I'd had last night. One that involved me on my knees and those heels buried in my back.

Apparently, Jamie felt the same, because the second the wee prick had been substituted off the field, he'd made a beeline for her. What followed had been an unsettling amount of laughter on Juniper's end. *What the fuck was he saying to her? Knock knock jokes? I'd known him all his life and he'd never made me laugh like that.*

And you've never made her *laugh like that.*

One eye on them, I'd thrown myself into the game, diving into tackles I'd usually be wise enough to avoid. Paying so little attention that when Juniper drew up her coat sleeve and Jamie's fingers drifted over the delicate tattoo on her inner wrist – a small swallow in flight – a roaring filled my head and I'd run nose first into Malcolm's elbow.

There'd been no telltale crunch of bones breaking. And with only five minutes left on the clock, I'd sidestepped Mal's flapping hands accompanied by a string of cursed apologies and thrown myself back into the fray, scoring a final goal before the whistle blew. I wish I could say I hadn't been hoping to impress the wee demon on the sidelines, but I'm man enough to admit my weaknesses.

Pressing one nostril closed, I released a sharp breath, trying to clear the blood as teammates clapped me on the back and strode for the changing rooms. Sweat ran in rivulets down my neck, but a shower would have to wait.

My brother had already reached April and Juniper's little circle, grumbling but clearly delighted when April curled against his chest.

"I stink," I heard him whisper as I closed in.

Her arms looped around his neck. "That's a pity. Now we both need a shower."

Usually seeing my shy brother's face light up felt like a warm hand curled around my heart. But right then, their happiness only entrenched the sting of loneliness settling into my bones.

"Good game, captain." Jamie grinned boyishly, his attention drifting from Juniper long enough to notice my approach.

Fuck off, Jamie.

"Thanks." I kept my voice cool when I felt anything but fucking *cool*. I wanted to push him face first into the mud. I settled for inserting myself between them. The sharp end of my elbow might have been involved, but who could be certain?

In my periphery, Mal and April glanced at me and then each other. April's pointed expression very much saying, *Told you so*. I didn't give a fuck. The in-love busybodies could think what they liked, especially when Juniper looked at me and cupped her hands over her mouth. "Oh my god. What happened?"

Wonderful. I'd taken my brother's very solid elbow to the face, and she hadn't even noticed.

I cleared out my nostril again. "It's nothing."

Pulling a tissue from her bag, April curled it into my palm with a wince. "Is it broken?"

"Nah," I waved off her concern. "Nose injuries always gush like a waterfall."

"You should get it checked out though." Guilt made Mal's voice sterner than I'd ever heard it. "Who's the team's first aider?"

"I am. I'll take care of it at home."

"You can't drive home like that—" he started to argue.

155

"I'm first aid trained, come along." Juniper's tone brooked little argument, already cutting across the pitch like she walked a Paris runway instead of a mud-torn field. And like she held me by the reins, I followed.

I'd follow those legs off a fucking cliff.

"Want to rub my tummy next?" I called after her, my pace languid despite the pounding taking over my face.

"Ha!" It was in no way a real laugh, but I'd take it. "At least we've established who the dog is in this scenario. Do you have a first aid kit?'

"Back of the toilet door." I gestured to the tiny outbuilding attached to the small, moss-covered structure that held two small changing rooms – one for the home team and one for the visiting team. She reached it first, opening the door wide. Noticing the parameters of the cramped cubicle, she held back for me to enter first.

Pulse shifting south of my injured nose and back to my neck where it belonged, I stepped into the dim but thankfully clean space, pulling the small kit from its hook.

Following me inside, she pressed a palm to my chest, forcing me to lean atop the low sink and spread my thighs in order for her to fit. I knew my eyes were huge in my face. Every interaction with Juniper was akin to soothing a skittish animal, you could never be certain if she would soften or strike.

"You neglected to mention we'd basically have to curl around each other to fit." The tops of her coat-covered legs brushed my inner thighs. I bit my lip to hold off a groan.

"All part of the fun, don't you think?"

She laid the first aid kit on the counter beside my hip, flipping the lid and riffling through until she found a gauze and a pair of latex gloves. "If I were a suspicious person, I might think you'd planned all of this."

"To get you alone?"

She raised an eyebrow, the action deceptively casual as she unbuttoned her coat. "*If* I were a suspicious person."

"Harpy." The journey of her fingers over those delicate buttons held me captive. "I would do an extraordinary amount of things to get you alone. But even I draw the line at self-mutilation." No, I couldn't take any credit, but it was working out fucking fantastically.

She twisted to hang it from the back of the door. And this time, I definitely groaned at the first glimpse of her preppy little pinafore dress. A string of white pearls encircled her throat, so prim and proper I longed to replace it with one of my own.

A little demon, I reminded myself. *A maddening, stunning little demon.*

In the taut silence she rolled up her sleeves, pausing long enough to ask, "You're not allergic to latex, are you?"

Fuck. "No." It came out more grunt than word.

She nodded to my team jersey, splattered with a collage of blood, mud and sweat. "Take that off."

"Twice in one day? Perhaps I should accuse you of scheming." The memory of her eyes on my body was enough to make me burn. She might not like me, but this afternoon she'd *wanted* me.

She merely scoffed as I complied, drawing the jersey over my head and dropping it into the sink.

"Want me to remove my shorts, too?" My thumbs were already at my waistband.

"I have zero interest in your sweaty jockstrap, Macabe."

Laughter tore free so suddenly, pain slashed across my face. My hand shot up just in time to catch the fresh trickle of blood. "Thanks for that."

Her eyes flashed and she pulled on the gloves with the

terrifying snap of a Victorian doctor ready to perform an amputation. "It'll teach you to take your eyes off the game." *Not so oblivious after all.* She stepped back into me. Thigh to thigh. My feet bracketing hers. "Tip your head forward and pinch the bridge of your nose."

"Want me to bite down?"

She sighed, but her lips twitched. "Do you ever get tired of being the funny guy?"

"All the time. It's more of a curse, really. That and my good looks."

"*Fucking Macabes,*" she muttered, grasping my chin and dragging it down for a better look. Trapped in close quarters, treating a professional medic and she had no qualms in taking the lead. I could only pray she knew what she was doing, because I'd allow her free rein to do just about anything so long as she kept touching me.

Balling gauze in her palm, she pressed it gently beneath my nostrils. "This is going to leave one hell of a bruise."

"Good job you like bad boys."

She huffed again, creeping closer to that full laugh I craved. "You'll be closer to a labrador that swallowed a bumble bee."

I'd treated enough to easily picture it and chuckled. "Aye . . . you're probably right."

She searched through the box again and I brought my hand to the one still holding the gauze. I'd meant to take it from her, but as soon as I encountered her bare wrist, my fingers caught there instead, brushing once over the bone, just to see if she'd pull away. Her eyes snapped to mine, flaring hotly before she cleared her throat. "It looks like the skin is split."

"That explains the stinging."

"We'll wait for the bleeding to slow and clean it up." She

peeled the gauze back, peeked, then pressed it back into place. "Hopefully it isn't deep enough to need stitches."

I nodded in all the right places, only registering the way her lips moved when she spoke. Every configuration casting a spell over me.

I could meet a thousand women and never discover this energy. *I'd tried.* Date after date after date I'd searched for something even remotely comparable. It only existed here. With this woman I shouldn't want and could never truly have.

Looking everywhere but her face, I said, "You're good at this." She possessed a uniquely tender hand, so at odds with the image she put out to the world. Anyone who thought her an ice queen hadn't truly observed her. An ocean of differences lay between cold and slow to burn. And when Juniper finally burned . . . what a magnificent sight it would be.

"I've had a lot of practice, I was a very self-sufficient child."

"Fiona didn't patch up your grazed knees?"

"She would have if I'd asked, but I didn't need her to." Her attention slid away, as though the confession left her vulnerable. "I took care of myself for years before they adopted me."

I tried to picture her as a child. Scrawny. Scared and alone, but always strong. Holding everyone at arm's length. "And now you take care of your mum?"

Her grip on my chin faltered. "You're giving me a lot of unearned credit."

"Am I? You're here, helping me." I could have easily managed this alone and she knew it. "I might even make the mistake of thinking you like me." My statement hung as she removed the gauze and replaced it with a fresh bundle, her fingers slipping right back into place across my cheek. I knew I should keep quiet – luxuriate in the wonder of

Juniper Ross taking care of me for a few minutes longer –
yet I couldn't stop my mouth from running. "We should
talk about that night in Glasgow."

She stiffened. *Great start.* "Why now?"

*Because I'm dying to know if you replay it as often as I
do?* "It's been long enough, don't you think?"

"I could go another five years."

"*Harpy.*"

"*Callum.*"

Fuck. My hands fisted on my thighs. "If you think flirting
is going to distract me, it won't."

"I said your name."

"*Exactly.* You never say my name." I hadn't been fully
prepared for how it would rattle me. Or the knowledge
from that moment on, it would feel wrong coming from
anyone else.

"Fine," she chimed sweetly, hands falling from my face
to fold across her chest. "If we didn't know each other . . .
if I wasn't *me* that night, would you have fucked me then?"

Rejection. It scoured her features too quickly for her to
hide it. *Absolutely not, I refused to be another person on
that list.* Grasping her crossed arms, I tugged her closer,
securing her body even more tightly to mine so my words
couldn't be misconstrued.

"Allow me to be crystal clear this time." My eyes bounced
between hers. "I wanted to fuck you because you're *you*,
that never changes. But I also knew *why* you wanted me.
I'm not a good man, sweetheart. I've betrayed my brother
in my mind more times than I can count, and I couldn't
have lived with myself if I'd selfishly taken what you offered
when it was little more than pain-fuelled revenge for you."
Biggest regret of my life. Well, second, it sat right below
letting Alistair meet her first.

Silence stretched. "I think that's probably enough for now," she nodded to the gauze.

Stamping down my disappointment, I peeled it away, dropping it onto the pile as she tilted my chin this way, then that. The fabric of her dress brushed my lower abs. I sucked in a breath. I could only hope she didn't glance down at the growing bulge in my shorts. I didn't even have enough brain cells remaining to be embarrassed.

"You played shit by the way," she said, a breath before she swiped an alcohol wipe over the small wound.

"*Shit, that burns.* Your bedside manner could use some work."

Her eyes danced, all humour returning as she wiped at the cut a second time. "I can leave if you like?"

"No. I wouldn't like." Giving into the instinct, I allowed my hand to slide around her waist, bunching the fabric of her dress. "We won, didn't we?"

"No thanks to you."

"So you *were* paying attention."

She shrugged, an unusual gesture for Juniper. She didn't play coy. And was that . . . a blush creeping up her neck? I dropped my head to whisper at her ear, "I was paying attention too. You're very distracting in this little dress." My fingers curved in, pressing grooves into her skin. The other hand falling to graze the short hem.

Her hands slid from my face, nails scraping through my beard, down my throat to where spots of blood had dried. She didn't seem aware of the action.

"*Juniper.*" I squeezed my eyes shut, fighting to keep my oversensitive body at bay. The adrenaline rush after a game always left my body buzzing, and being so close to her – touching her skin – was a rush all its own. I felt like my muscles might shred apart from trying.

Her hands left my body – a flick of latex as she discarded the gloves – and then they were on me once more, cool and soft against my overheated skin. She might look at me with venom, but she didn't touch me that way. Long fingers brushed across my cheekbones, the caress as light as butterfly wings. Then up, up, to the streaks of silver at the temples of my sweat-soaked hair.

I groaned, needing to be the one to kiss *her*. But the way she was looking at me – touching me – she might get there first.

"What are we doing?" she whispered into the scrap of space.

Good question, sweetheart. "Whatever we want."

"Your hands are trembling."

"So they are." I dipped in, brushing my battered nose – barely feeling the bite of pain – then lips over her cheek. She inched back, not retreating but rolling with the movement.

"Juniper," I said again. Her name the only word in the world. She whimpered, head falling into my waiting palm. "You finally going to let me touch you?" I licked her pulse. It pounded beneath my tongue. "Taste you?" I pressed my hips into her, delighting in her frantic nod. "That night at the bar, it's all I could think about. Your thighs hooked over my shoulders – coming on my tongue." The light above us flickered in and out, as if answering the buzz of electricity generating between us. We hadn't technically hit a base yet and I was more aroused than I'd ever been, because this was happening. *It was fucking happening.* No more waiting, no more wondering. Juniper writhed in my arms, curling her leg over my hip. A dream, spinning into reality.

This time, I wouldn't be fucking noble.

This time, she was mine.

16

Juniper

April: June! Code red!!
April: Mini Macabe incoming.
Juniper: A little help! You couldn't intercept her?
April: If the toilet shed's a rockin' don't come a knockin'.
April: Or the Whisky Dunnage ;)
Juniper: And they say romance is dead.

"June?" In my delirium, I confused the voice for Callum's. His fingers speared into my hair, tugging and wrapping. Thumb grazing my jaw, angling my head precisely where he wanted it. Blue eyes blazed, focused on me with an intensity that felt out of place on his carefree features. I could barely breathe beneath that look. *Who needed to breathe anyway?*

Ten seconds. I'd give him ten seconds of calling the shots and then I'd—

"*June?*"

Callum never called me June.

He registered the intrusion at the same moment I did. Balling a fist into my hair, he cursed, low and vicious, but didn't relinquish his hold. If anything, he held me tighter, like a child with a toy he refused to share. Even when I stumbled backwards, he followed, steadying me as the door snapped open.

"Oh, shit. My bad – I was looking for – *June?*"

Callum straightened, his stance widening like if he could just make himself big enough, he might protect me from this.

Too late, my gaze already met Heather's over his shoulder. Her hand locked around the door handle, eyes snapping hopefully between us like a punter at a comedy club, waiting for the punchline. "What are you—" She licked her lips. "What's going on?"

Callum's hands tightened on my neck. His gaze searching mine. I couldn't meet it, too busy falling into despair with only the wall and his hands keeping me on my feet. It was plain to see that Heather already knew, even if she didn't want to believe it.

"Callum?" His name came from her mouth, demanding explanation.

He didn't so much as glance at his sister. "I took an injury. Juniper helped me clean up."

"With her skirt hooked around her waist?"

"*Fuck.*" Callum echoed my singular thought aloud, hands knocking my shaking ones aside as I fumbled to cover myself. He touched me gently, unhurriedly smoothing the material over my thighs. Meanwhile, I could barely hold onto a single train of thought. Heart racing, I stared at my oldest friend in the world and prayed I hadn't given her a reason to abandon me too.

"Bloody hell, you aren't even denying it!" She sneered; the expression too cruel for her pretty face.

Callum finally turned, grabbing his shirt from the sink and dragging it over his head. "What do you want me to

164

say, Heather? You seem to have it all figured out. Want me to treat you like an idiot? Want me to lie?"

"I want you to say a single thing that makes sense!"

His hands went to his hips. Every line of him calm and controlled, completely ready for the argument to come. "No offence, Heather, but at this precise moment, we don't owe you anything."

She laughed. Short and sharp. "Does Alistair know it's *we* now? Of course he doesn't. How about you—" Two pairs of Macabe eyes locked on me. "Anything to say?" My throat worked. She laughed again – this one dismissive – and raced out the door.

The chill hit me before I even realised I'd followed her. Bypassing Callum's reaching hand, I caught up to her quickly.

"Heather – wait." I snagged her wrist, but she flinched away. "Can you please let me just—"

"Was one of my brothers not enough for you?" she hissed quietly. Now it was my turn to flinch. I could feel people beginning to stare, reading the tension even if they couldn't hear us. Jill and her pack of friends where they lingered beside her gas-guzzling Range Rover.

"That's hardly fair."

"What isn't fair is you moving between my brothers like they're a damn selection box. You know what's happening with Dad – the last thing my family needs is *you* causing more tension." *You*, as though I were a stranger she'd encountered for the first time.

"Heather, that's enough – apologise. Now." Callum's voice came from behind me. Fuck, but I wished I'd been the one to say it. The one to demand a little bit more for myself. *There'd been two of us in that bathroom, why the hell do I deserve the brunt of her anger?* But I was too busy choking down the sob creeping up my throat to say anything.

Cheeks flushed, Heather glanced from me to where Callum loomed over my shoulder, then back. Finally, she snorted. "When this all blows up in your face, don't come crying to me."

"Like last time, you mean?" I didn't know where the words were coming from, but I couldn't stop them. Rejection burned like lava through my veins. "When you abandoned me after Alistair ended things then *I* was the one to hold you and your girls together during your divorce."

She winced. The only evidence my words had struck.

"Hey, maybe we should take a beat." Callum's hand curled over my shoulders like it belonged there.

Heather's eyes tracked the ownership of the action. "No, please continue. I'll go." Before I could say another word, Heather's short strides ate up the distance to her car. A concerned-looking April glanced between us, called something to Heather who only shook her head and climbed into her car.

"Just give her a few days, she'll come around," Callum said, turning me to face him. Pulse ringing in my ears, I barely registered his words because he looked . . . *happy?* Blood staining his chin, my coat clutched in one hand, he looked happy. Hopeful.

"Why did you offer to help me?"

"*What?*"

It felt like a veil had been lifted and I was seeing him for the first time. "At Ivy House," I pushed. "Why did you offer to help?"

His throat bobbed. "Because you needed my help."

He's lying, my instinct roared at me. "Don't give me the Community Ken bullshit, tell me why."

"Because I needed it to be me!" His hand dug into his hair. "Despite how fucking busy I am, I needed to be the one helping you – fighting your corner – even if you never knew it."

"What's that supposed to mean?" I knew it was a stupid question before I even asked it aloud. Deep down I'd always felt this . . . invisible thread between us. Like the taut string of an instrument, just waiting for one of us to gather enough courage to pluck it.

He pinched the bridge of his nose, swore, then dropped his hand. "The money. I paid Murray a visit. Made it clear he needed to return every penny he owed you if he wanted to hold onto his licence."

"You—" I broke off, unsure whether I wanted to kiss him or kill him. I settled on the latter. "You had no right. I had it handled, I didn't require your help."

He stepped closer, cutting into my space. "Well, tough shit. You have it. You *always* have my help."

There was something in his voice, an unsteadiness that dragged the question from me. "What . . . what else have you done for me?"

"Juniper—"

"What else?"

He rubbed the back of his neck, as if he were stalling. "The permit. The one you applied for to extend Ivy House's car park two years ago."

"That was you?"

He nodded jerkily. The council on Skye could be notoriously slow. We'd expected to wait weeks, if not months. Instead, the permit for the small extension came through the door in a matter of days.

"It's unlikely they would have rejected it. But Heather told me you needed it in place for the summer season and someone on the board owed me a favour. He pushed it through a little faster, that's all."

Gritting my teeth, I tucked the information away. "What else?"

His eyes squeezed shut. "Coconut milk. I overheard you trying to buy it in the store. Sharon said there wasn't enough demand to bother placing an order. So . . . I have a weekly order too."

"You don't even like coconut."

In all the years I'd known him, I'd never once seen Callum blush. But blush he did. All the way to the tips of his ears. "I've grown used to the taste."

I might have laughed if not for the bats currently taking flight inside my chest. "Anything else?"

He blew out a breath. "How long do you have?"

Silence fell between us, broken only by my ragged breathing. I wanted to chew him out for acting like a high-handed arse. Only that wasn't what came out of my mouth.

"You want me." I spat the words like an accusation.

He didn't even blink. "I never pretended otherwise, sweetheart."

"But . . . you're always nice to everyone but me." The statement sounded about as juvenile as it felt. Even more so after everything he'd confessed.

"You don't like *nice*," he said it with infuriating certainty. *I know you, harpy.*

I raised my chin. "Perhaps I enjoy *nice* sometimes."

"You want nice, harpy, just say the word. I'll be the nicest man you've ever met." The words were a tease against my ear. His hot breath stroking my pulse, sending it soaring.

He wanted me. He'd *always* wanted me. The knowledge was thrilling.

Terrifying.

Forcing my feet to take a step back, that was the feeling I clung to. "You shouldn't say things like that. Not to me."

"Because of Alistair?" I barely nodded before he forged on, lungs heaving more than they had during the shinty match. "Because my idiot brother was too blind to understand he had something spectacular?"

"Stop it!" But he didn't relent, crowding my space until we breathed the same air. Blood still stained his shirt and neck in rusted patches, but it was his barely leashed desire I couldn't look away from.

"You're magnificent like this, did you know that?" His eyes flashed a cold blue, but he looked the opposite of angry. "Did my brother ever tell you? Or were the two of you so damn comfortable together, you never screamed at one another just for an excuse to spend the rest of the night fucking the tension away?"

I was speechless. My heart racing so hard I could feel it in the tips of my fingers.

"I don't know why I enjoy this little game we play so much, but I do know that every time you look at me with that furious little scowl, I want to fuck it right off your face. That's all I've wanted since that day on the train when it took me less than a second to fall completely under your spell." Something ugly snaked through my gut and he caught my chin before I could look away. "One day you're going to tell me exactly what went down between you and Alistair – why you hold onto that damn ring – so I can make sure I never see that doubt in your eyes ever again.

"*Not today*," he reassured me when I started to protest. "I've had a long time to get here, sweetheart. To realise these feelings aren't wrong – that you were never meant to be his."

His eyes traced over my features. Waiting.

He wanted me to say something. To offer a reassurance of my own. But too much had happened tonight. My tongue felt heavy. The panic seizing my chest demanding an outlet. "We . . . we shouldn't do this here. Not now."

Disappointment dragged at his features before he schooled them. "Of course." He nodded stiffly, putting a measure of space between us, though I could tell it was the last thing he wanted. "Will you be okay getting home?"

A sound slipped from me, half laugh, half sob. *I should be the one asking him that.*

I muttered an assurance, accepting my coat without meeting his eye, and stalked away. I didn't once look back, but I felt his attention on me. Even when I tucked myself into bed that night, Shakespeare purring at my feet, I still felt it, with his words ringing in my ears:

That's all I've wanted since that day on the train when it took me less than a second to fall completely under your spell.

17

Callum

Callum: Any luck securing that time off?
Callum: Alistair?
Callum: Are we ignoring each other now?
Alistair: Sorry!!! Long day.
Alistair: I'm still working on it, I'll let you know.

"Is this the last delivery of the morning?" In the car park outside the town hall, I swung down from my brother's ancient Land Rover and opened the back door for Boy. His tail swishing eagerly as his paws met the gravel.

"This and the Sheep's Heid." Bottles clinked as Mal rearranged the crates of whisky stacked three-high, secured in the boot with wide straps.

I had less time to help my brother at the distillery these days, between Dad, Ivy House and the practice. I found time when I could, mainly because it was one of the few ways to spend time with him. My wee brother could be more of a workaholic than me.

He'd never complain but I knew he had a lot on his plate with the anniversary ceilidh only a few weeks away.

Boy's wet nose met my palm, and I brushed it down his neck, kneeling to fuss him. "There's a good lad."

"Don't praise him," Mal groused, meeting us on the path, three very full crates in hand. "He almost refused to get in the truck."

Taking the crates from him, I looked down at the angelic golden retriever I was certain had never done anything wrong in his life. "How does a dog refuse, exactly?"

Mal's fingers rolled anxiously over his other digits as we neared the high street. A familiar gesture I'd seen less and less in recent months. Despite his weekly therapy sessions I knew he attended diligently, he still found it tough to come into the village some days. Rome wasn't built in a day.

"He tucked himself into bed beside April and huffed every time I asked him to move. He didn't want to leave Dudley behind," he explained. "The two of them are attached at the hip these days."

I smiled at the mention of April's feisty, three-legged dachshund. "That's fucking adorable."

"It's a pain in my arse." He could grumble all he liked, I knew he'd do anything for the little family he and April had made for themselves. Even wear a dog sling when Dudley's legs grew tired.

"Will Dudley go with April when her shoot starts?"

The change came over Mal immediately, eyes lowering, shoulders hunching, and I felt like a shit for bringing it up. He'd never admit it aloud, but I knew he felt the time slipping with growing trepidation. Mal was proud of her, but he didn't relish the idea of her being away for months on end.

"He's staying with me, it seemed pointless to go to the effort of getting Dudley a pet passport."

I nudged his shoulder with mine. "That's great, Mal. Let me know if you need any help."

He smiled, though it was small. "I think Ava and Emily have you beat. They begged me to let them dog-sit weeks ago."

I grinned at him over my shoulder, paying little attention as I led us onto the stone path and around the corner. "Luckily I'm their favourite uncle – woah, *harpy*."

"Oh," Juniper gasped, leaping back as we almost collided. Bottles clacked and I held the crates tightly, fighting my first instinct to reach out and steady her. "Sorry, I didn't see you."

I ate up the sight of her, from her heeled boots to her perfectly styled fringe. I'd missed her so much; I swear even my teeth ached from it.

It had been three days since the shinty game. Three days since she'd patched me up in a toilet and, in return, I'd offered up my heart on a butcher's block. Three days of cursing my sister's poor timing and diligently following my own promise to give her space. I'd almost been tempted to ask Mal's advice, but I didn't want to draw him into the mess with Heather. And while my brother had many talents, conversing with women had never been one of them – even he would admit he'd fallen into his relationship through sheer dumb luck.

A fish could tell another fish how to walk, but we'd both still have flippers instead of feet.

Juniper stared back at me impassively, not a single sign of what occurred at the game on her lovely features. My body turned hot, suddenly nervous she might somehow sense every dirty thing I'd imagined over the past days. Namely, her hands pressed to my shower wall. But all she said was, "Nice shiner."

"You should see the other guy."

"It was an accident!" Mal spluttered.

A pretty shade of pink crawled over her cheeks and her eyes flicked to Mal and Boy, like she'd only just noticed their presence. "Hey, Mal." *Fuck*. Would I never grow used to her bashful side? While I adored her viciousness, I enjoyed her blushing even more.

"June." Mal nodded back. And that was the extent of their conversation.

I, for one, wasn't done. Far from it. "Fancy seeing you here." Mal glanced between us. I paid him no mind. If he wanted to ask, he could ask and I'd answer honestly.

I'd been consumed with an addictive weightlessness since word-vomiting my feelings. Even if things never went further, the seal had been ripped off. I was done pretending I wasn't fucking ecstatic every time our paths crossed.

She held up a bundle wrapped in paper. "The fabric came in for room five's new curtains, but they need hemming."

"Excellent," I said, curious about the fabric she'd chosen. "I'll come with you." Somewhere along the way, the refurbish at Ivy House had started to feel like *our* project. Forgotten crates still in hand, I nodded for her to lead the way to the seamstress. Before I made it a step, Mal swooped in, scooping the bottles from my arms with an ease I always envied. "I'll take these. Meet you back here in fifteen."

"You're certain?" I searched his expression.

He rolled his eyes. "I'm a grown man, I think I can handle a single drop-off alone."

I thanked him with a clap to the shoulder. "Want me to grab food from Brown's?"

He shook his head, already backing away with Boy. "April baked lemon muffins."

"*What?*" He'd kept that one fucking quiet when I'd been on his doorstep at five a.m. The prick didn't even have the nerve to answer, simply turned on his heel and disappeared into the stream of people.

With a curse, I turned back to Juniper, only to find her strolling away too. "Hey," I broke into a jog. "Wait up."

She slowed. Marginally. "Why?"

She had to be joking. "So I can walk with you."

"Again. *Why?*"

Stubborn, stubborn woman. Luckily for the both of us, I had the patience of a saint. "Because we're *friends.*" I emphasised the word and that pretty pink covered her cheeks again. *Damn, confessing my feelings might be the best thing I've ever done.* "Friends run errands together sometimes." The smallest of smiles curled her lips as she looked between me and the path, only for it to give a heart-breaking wobble a second later. Up close I could see the skin around her eyes was red and puffy, like she'd been crying. *You're killing me, sweetheart.* I nudged her shoulder with mine. "Did Shakespeare piss in your cereal?"

She gave a wet laugh. "You know, pissy Cheerios would actually be better than the horrific realisation that *you* might be my best friend right now."

My girl knew how to make a man feel special, I'd give her that. "Nah," I said. "Heather's always had a flair for the dramatics, she'll come around." Once I reminded her it was none of her damn business. "And you're forgetting a certain redheaded pageant queen. We'll call it second best."

She clucked her tongue, pretending to think about it. "Make it fifth best."

"Fuck off. I at least want in the top three." I turned, walking backwards so I could see her face when she released the smallest huff of laughter. It made me feel ten feet tall. "So does this friendship come with a bracelet?"

"Absolutely. One of those woven ones with a little charm

hanging from it." Fuck she was cute when she was play-ful. Even cuter when she tried to pretend her eyes weren't roving over me like mine were her.

She came to a stop, that fledgling smile sagging into a frown as something over my shoulder caught her attention. I turned. A handful of tourists and dogs on leads milled about, minding their own business. But there, under the awning of the florist, I noticed Jill Mortimer and two other local women. Huddled in a tight circle, take-out coffee cups in hand, they glanced between us then laughed like schoolgirls.

Noticing my stare, Jill flushed a little and offered a loose-fingered wave. I nodded in acknowledgement, my attention already straying back to Juniper. "Are they above me in the friend ranking?" Other than Heather and April and occasionally Jamie, I didn't see her talk to many people in the village.

She snorted and the short strands of her hair shook. "*No.* I barely know them."

"They're staring at you like they do."

She shook her head again, as though I were an idiot for not cracking the code. "They aren't staring at *me.* Well . . . not just me. They're staring at us."

"*Why?*"

"I don't know. Because they're bored and like to gossip. And this—" She gestured between us. "Is perfect gossip. Jill was at the shinty game, you know."

"Was she?" I still didn't see the point she was making.

"And Freya has always hated me because I dated her husband briefly in high school." She nodded with her chin to the brunette still looking our way. "Because while you might not have noticed as the village golden boy, it's hard to shake a reputation around here."

I was hardly a golden boy, but I got what she was saying.

There was nowhere to hide in a small community. "And what's yours?"

She folded her arms, holding the fabric tighter to her chest. "Troubled youth turned scorned woman and now it probably sits somewhere around Satan's mistress."

"Damn. It's the horns and tail that does it for you, isn't it?" I brushed a hand over my head. "I have an old Halloween costume lying around somewhere, you'll never know the difference."

"Be serious. Ensnaring the venerated village vet pushes me firmly into the scarlet woman category they love squeezing me into."

"Scarlet woman?" I couldn't help laughing at her completely serious expression. "This sounds very high school."

"Some people never grow up."

"At least you got one thing right. This *venerated vet* is completely ensnared." We smiled at one another, only for her face to fall when the group laughed again. Louder this time. And I was able to make out a single sentence. "*With all that black she looks like she works in a mortuary.*"

These fucking people. Ask me six days out of seven and I'd tell you I adored Kinleith and its occupants, that there was no better place on earth to call home. Today, bearing witness to the gradual sinking of Juniper's shoulders and the quiet tension creeping around her mouth, as their immature words struck like bullets, today . . . I wanted to burn it to the ground. How dare they hurt this woman who'd faced more heartache in her short life than many others could survive. No wonder she kept everyone at arm's length. I could force her out of her shell all I wished, but it would never fix the root of the problem.

Fists curling, I cut across the street in the trio's direction. "Macabe." Juniper's hushed shout followed me but I didn't slow. I didn't care what they were saying, what excuses they gave, from now on, they'd keep their poison to themselves. "Macabe, stop." She was at my side, tugging my sleeve. And then she uttered four words that turned my insides to ice. "Is that your dad?"

Stopping dead, my head swivelled as though detached from my body. A hundred yards away, he slowly ambled his way along the uneven cobbles. Alone.

"Dad!" It took thirty seconds to reach him. "What are you doing here?" It was a stupid question. I could already discern from the glazed sheen in his eyes, he didn't recognise me.

Clearly agitated, he shook me off, trying to continue down the path. "I'm going to work . . . I must have got turned around somewhere."

Relenting my hold, I attempted to steer him beneath the awning of the beauty salon as the first smattering of rain began. "I can take you in my car."

"Leave me to it, boy, I'm more than capable." He snarled the nickname with the usual bite of loathing but the tightness in my chest eased some as his gaze settled on me. If it was one of his better days it would be easier to get him home.

"Did you come with Mum?"

"No." He yanked his arm free, wobbling so precariously I lunged to catch him. His thinning hair fell over his forehead in grey wisps as I settled him against the wall. "I drove myself." *He drove himself?* How the hell had this happened? I yanked my phone from my pocket, Mum's number already on the screen. "Don't call her." He slapped it from my hand, I didn't even watch it land. "I don't need you checking up on me. Who raised you, boy? Who clothed you and fed you? It's time you showed me some bloody respect."

How could I ever forget?

The snarl bubbling up my throat melted away when I noticed the front of his trousers, the small but noticeable wet patch staining the dark material.

My chest cracked in two.

For the first time since this man had dropped a terrified sixteen-year-old off at basic training – smaller, weaker and younger than every other recruit – without so much as a *See ya, kid*, I wanted to sink to my knees and sob.

The urge only grew when Juniper appeared at my side. So lost to my grief, I hadn't even heard her approach.

"Hello again, Mr Macabe." Her voice held a softness I couldn't place, all traces of our previous conversation washed away. "Do you remember me?"

It took him a moment. "Juniper Ross. My son's lass."

My son's lass. He spoke of Alistair, and yet the untamed caveman inside roared at me to answer, Yes, *your son's lass. Mine, mine, mine.*

Easily nudging me aside, Juniper offered her arm. "Would you mind escorting me to my car, I'm parked just up the street?" To my surprise, he accepted, allowing Juniper to tuck her arm beneath his, giving the illusion of letting him lead. Struck speechless, I could only follow.

"You're a lot prettier without all that metal in your face." He waved a hand to her profile. "I never understood what my boy saw in you before, but now . . . if I was twenty years younger I might try myself."

He insulted her so casually, like he was reading aloud an article from the newspaper. That was the cruelty of Alzheimer's. It took more than the ability to create and retrieve memories, it stole empathy, and Jim Macabe hadn't been an empathetic man to begin with.

"Dad—" I started to cut in, refusing to see Juniper on the receiving end of his vitriol, while hating myself for feeling embarrassed. But I was. Shame burned me from the inside out.

Juniper waved me off, taking it all in her stride. Somehow that was worse. I slipped forward to intervene when my mother called my name.

Hand waving overhead, open coat flapping in the wind, she broke into a slow run. "There you are," she said to Dad, panting as she drew nearer. I could see the lines of worry etched into the corners of her mouth. "Hi, Juniper. It's lovely to see you."

"Hey, Mrs Macabe." *Fuck.* I couldn't look at her. Couldn't bear to catch a glimpse of what she must be thinking.

"Iris, please. We're still family."

"*Iris,*" Juniper agreed. "Jim was kindly helping me to my car."

"Mum, what happened?" As touching as this little reunion was, I needed answers.

She blew out a breath. "We were in the chemist picking up his prescription. I only turned my back for a minute, and he slipped away from me. He's still as fast as ever."

Was she seriously turning this into a joke? "You should have called me."

"I was just about to."

"You should have called the second you lost him." I hated the chill in my tone, but she needed to stop burying her head in the sand. Pretending everything was fine only put Dad in jeopardy.

"I didn't want to disturb you at work."

I bit down hard on my retort. That I was already disturbed. That it would now fall to me to cancel my afternoon appointments and escort them home. To help bathe him and put him to bed because Mum couldn't – *shouldn't* – do it alone.

That chill spread, encompassing my entire body, because

Juniper was still *here*. Still witnessing this mess. My voice turned hollow when I said without looking at her, "Thanks Juniper, we can take it from here."

"Are you sure? I don't mind—"

"I'm sure." I cut her off, moving in to take her place beside my dad. He leant into me, letting me take his weight. "Find Malcolm and tell him I had an emergency at work if you want to help." *Arse*. Maybe I was the one who'd lost my empathy.

I didn't look back as we strolled away.

"Callum—" Mum started.

I shook my head. "We'll talk at your house."

I'd expected Juniper to be pissed at me.

So pissed, I'd already ranked Brown's array of baked goods on my mental *Earn Juniper's Forgiveness* plan. Brownies took the top spot, she had a real sweet tooth, while my beloved oat and raisin cookies came in last. *Some days it was hard to believe I was in love with such a monster.*

Hours later, I observed her through the break in the trees. For almost ten minutes I'd watched her like a creeper, standing just far enough back so she wouldn't catch sight of my sweaty form as she paced my driveway. Short strides and harsh turns carrying her from one side to the other.

Perhaps she'd come to call me an arsehole to my face. The anticipation made me lightheaded.

The sun disappeared behind the tree line, turning the yellowing leaves a burned gold. I glanced at my watch again, letting the axe I'd been using to rage-split wood fall against my thigh. Make that fifteen minutes.

On her next turn she appeared to come to a decision, steeling her shoulders and murmuring something too indiscernible for me to make out, though I imagined it went a little like, *What the hell am I doing outside this rude fucker's house?*

For that, I had no answer either.

Every muscle in my body clenched at the mere sight of her, demanding I replace all thoughts of this clusterfuck of a day with the exquisite high that sparring with her would grant me. But agitation still left me feeling restless, like a heavy shadow constricting my chest. She was the last person I wanted to take my resentment out on. If she grew the nerve to knock, I'd ignore her—

Her knuckles rapped two light taps. I broke the tree line before I could blink. "Over here." *So much for ignoring her.*

She whirled, eyes raking over me, taking in what I knew were wet patches, sticking my white T-shirt to damp skin. "Nice axe," she said easily, but I didn't miss the bob in her throat. "Are you going to let me in?"

That's a terrible fucking idea, sweetheart. My hand tightened around the wooden handle until it bit into my skin. "Sorry, my mum says I can't play out tonight."

Instead of snarling like I anticipated, she laughed.

"What's so funny?"

"You're scowling. I don't think I've ever seen you scowl before." And then she tried the handle, found it open and strolled inside, kicking her shoes off in the porch like she owned the place. Too busy following her into the living room, I didn't even have time to enjoy the casualness of it.

"Make yourself at home," I called, toeing off my own boots.

She ignored me. "I didn't know you had a rabbit." On her knees beside the log burner, she hovered over a snoozing Simon. Tucked into the patchwork blanket my mother knitted for him, you could just about see his face.

What are you doing here, Juniper?

I remained on the other side of the sofa, fingers digging into the fabric as I used it as a barrier. "He's registered for AAT," I said like that was any kind of explanation.

"What's that?"

"Animal assisted therapy."

One of her fingers stroked lightly down his soft back. "So he's a therapist, not a rabbit?"

I drifted closer, fucking hypnotised by her delicacy. "It's not as complicated as all that. Animal therapy is a proven aid, not a fix to mental health struggles. We visit the primary school once a week with the school therapist present and a small group of children can pet him and feed him. It creates a relaxing space for them to feel safe to talk."

She continued to stroke his back. "What do they talk about?"

"Whatever they want, their home life, their friends, school struggles." I was only there to take care of Simon and observe, but I found myself absorbing every word, so bloody proud of Simon when a kid's tears turned into a grin by the end of a session. Painfully aware of how desperately my six-year-old self, and Mal, could have benefitted from such a scheme.

"Does Simon enjoy it?"

"Yes, he's very good at being handled. And I'm always there to remove him from a situation he won't enjoy."

She stroked him one final time, a single black-tipped finger tracing from his small head to his tail, and then her attention shifted to the glass of whisky I'd abandoned on the coffee table. The alcohol more compelling than the sleeping rabbit, it seemed, because she took a healthy swig, right where my lips had been, and sat down on the low table.

What the hell are you doing here?

Too much of a coward to ask the question quite so directly, I tossed another piece of wood onto the fire and took a seat on the sofa. "Did you interrupt my evening for a reason or simply to steal my booze?"

The glass hung from her fingertips as she held it out to me. "I came to check on you."

Taking it, my eyes dragged over our positioning. How close her knees were to mine. A tug of her wrist and we'd be chest to chest. "As you can see . . . I'm fine."

"Want to talk about it?"

Yes. "Fuck no. I'm piss-poor company tonight."

"I'm always piss-poor company." She stole the glass back, topping it off with the half-empty bottle. "Your dad is worse than Heather suggested."

"We just agreed not to talk about it."

She smiled around the glass. "I was being polite. Answer the question."

"Did you ask one?" The glass slipped from her hand to mine. And the words poured free without me even trying. "The last few months have been a rapid decline, even the doctors didn't predict it would be so sudden."

"And you're keeping it a secret from your siblings?"

"I'm not keeping it a secret, I'm just . . . not letting them carry the burden. Alistair is halfway across the country, Heather's already running herself ragged and Mal—" I broke off, not really sure how to explain it. "My dad was a bastard to all of us, but Mal received the worst of it." My teeth clenched; the fury flamed by my own guilt for not being here to protect him from it. "He owes him nothing." I'd run myself into the ground before this ever became his problem.

"And you do?"

"I'm the oldest."

Her expression was unreadable as she rolled the amber liquid around the glass. She was usually so easy to read, for me, at least, her every thought rolling in her dark eyes. My ignorance made me lash out. "Pitying me, harpy?"

Her head tilted and I couldn't shake the thought she was seeing right through me. "Perhaps I'm seeing you in a new light."

After my behavior today, I doubted it was complimentary.

It had only gotten worse at my parents' house. I'd accused Mum of being selfish. Warned that her desperation to cling to the past would get Dad hurt one day. Even if there was truth to my words, I'd acted like a high-handed prick.

My temples throbbed at the memory of her shattered expression. I bypassed the glass and went for the bottle. "Care to elaborate on that statement?"

"I've always seen you as this frivolous Ken doll."

"A Ken doll?" My imagination conjured up fake muscles and a plastic smile. *Yeah . . . that definitely wasn't a compliment.*

"Like you don't see it." She waved a careless hand at me. "The face, the hair, the body. The way everyone in this village hangs on your every word."

I didn't agree with the hanging on my every word part, but, "I do have all of those things." While I immensely enjoyed Juniper listing all of my attributes, I still didn't get it. "How does that liken me to a children's toy?"

"*Because . . .*" She drew out the word like I was an idiot. "You have an unattainable perfection that people gravitate to. It allows you to say and do whatever the hell you like without the fear of people hating you. I called you disgustingly honest once, but I was wrong . . . you're actually a very skilled liar."

I laughed but it sounded hollow. "I've really ruined what

185

little respect you'd gained for me, haven't I? Though, I can't disagree with that statement."

"Hardly. You only lie when it comes to yourself."

"That's where you're wrong, you're the greatest lie I've ever told."

She froze and I could see the indecision in her eyes, whether to address the statement or ignore it. "While you're taking care of other people, who's taking care of you?"

The question took me by surprise. "I don't need anyone to take care of me." Another lie. I'd let *her* take care of me. And I'd take care of her right back.

She opened her mouth to continue, but I was done with her prying. For years I'd imagined earning her undivided attention, but the reality wasn't exactly playing out like the fantasy. For starters, we both had too many clothes on.

I pulled the glass from her fingers. "You asked your questions. Now it's my turn." What slipped from my mouth next, I would forever attribute to the intoxicating mix of her scent in my nose and the whisky in my veins. I felt too fucking bold. "Who's the last person you fucked?"

18

Callum

Hey speaker, play: "Black Magic Woman" by Fleetwood Mac.

Juniper coughed, whisky staining her lips. "Shit – give me some warning next time."

"Well?" I demanded, too desperate for her answer to be polite.

"No one you know."

My teeth clacked. I didn't know if that made it better or a hundred times worse. A sneaking, jealous part of me expected her to say Jamie Stewart, while another had been terrified she'd say Alistair.

"And you?" A touch of curiosity lilted her tone.

"No one you know," I mirrored. I knew rumours around the village suggested I slept about, but the truth was, a monk had seen more action than I had in recent years. The last time a woman so much as touched me was so long ago, I couldn't even recall her face. Not that I'd tell Juniper that, I had some pride left.

"Well, that was fucking stimulating."

I laughed. The sound felt odd after the depressing as fuck afternoon. "Okay, how about this, why have I never seen you with a boyfriend?"

Her nose wrinkled. "I don't date on the island."

It wasn't exactly an answer, but I let it slide and she nodded that I should respond. I chose my words carefully. "I've never met anyone I wanted to be with."

She paused long enough for me to know she understood my meaning, then didn't look at me when she said, "It's not like you don't have plenty of contenders." I searched her face for the barest hint of jealousy and found it in the tightness around her mouth.

"I suppose the more they try, the less I want it," I teased.

She scoffed, just like I knew she would, and snatched the glass back. "You're such a man."

"Not denying it." Drawn into this game we were playing, I leant closer, knees slotting between hers. "How many men have touched you since that night?"

"Probably fewer than you think."

"That's all you'll give me?" My voice was low. Rough. And if she glanced down at my sweats, well . . . there'd be little hiding what this conversation was doing to me.

She sipped the drink, though it was mainly ice at this point. "It's all you deserve."

"And what we had . . ." I cleared my throat, choking on memories of that night that fucking haunted me. "That's always how you like it?"

I was man enough to admit she'd struck me stupid, following me to my car, tempting me until I could scarcely remember my own name. I'd been half crazed from a single taste. If I'd hoped it would be enough to cure my need for her, I'd been sadly, foolishly mistaken. My balls were still blue five years later. I'd dreamed of it, letting the memory consume me over and over, until I was coming in my own hand before I woke up.

"Sometimes." Her coy shrug said always. "I like to be in charge, I don't see why that's a bad thing."

It wasn't. Fucking hot was what it was. The change in her posture, however, told me she hadn't always been made to feel that way.

I shut the thought down, before the image of my brother and her *together* could surface. Even that wouldn't be enough to make me walk away this time. "And let me guess, these *boys* you grant the privilege of being in your bed, they don't like letting you take the lead?"

When her mouth tightened and she studied the darkened television, I knew I'd hit the nail on the head.

Fucking hell.

Knowing Juniper wasn't getting what she deserved made me all the more desperate to be the one to give it to her.

"Anything you want. I'm game for it," I promised. She jerked, brown eyes almost black in the low light. "Whatever you need, sweetheart . . . I'll let you do whatever you want to me." I shifted closer, breathing in the dizzying lightness of her scent. It wasn't overpowering and clawing like most perfumes. Juniper Ross knew true temptation lay in subtlety. "Do you want me to kiss you?" I asked, just like I had the day in my bathroom.

"No." She didn't shift away.

"You're looking at me like you do."

"There's something in my eye."

There was something in her eye, all right, something that might have scared a lesser man. I imagined it was the same look a siren bestowed upon a sailor at the precise moment they realised they'd fucked up and were dragged to a watery grave.

I inched closer. Testing the boundaries. "You wanted me to kiss you once before."

"A colossal mistake."

"Right now, I'm thinking it might have been the best idea I've ever had." I studied her expression for the slightest give, the slightest hint that she wanted my mouth on her, my hands on her. "What do you want, harpy? Tell me and I'll make you come better than they ever did."

"A bold statement." Her pupils were pinpricks. Words little more than a rasp.

"It's only bold if I can't back it up." I had every intention of doing that and more. I allowed the cocksure smile I knew she hated stretch over my features. A challenge issued.

"Is Simon really a therapy bunny?" Her lips curled inward, as though she hadn't meant to ask the question aloud.

"Yes," I said, doing my best to keep up.

"Ugh! Why do you have to be so kind? It's bloody irritating." Her head fell back, exposing her throat, and I broke, chuckling as my nose found the dip in her collarbone where her pulse thundered.

"Are you turned on by my soft side, sweetheart?"

"Absolutely not!"

"Hmm. Then why are you suddenly all sweet for me?" I licked the skin of her neck and she shivered. "I could show you my other therapy bunny if you like."

"*Shut up*. You're ruining it."

"I joke when I'm nervous." I bit down on her earlobe. "Shutting up now."

She drew my chin away, face lowering to mine. So close, my mouth watered at the prospect of finally tasting her lips again. Just when I thought my heart was about to explode, she stood. "Get on your knees."

I couldn't be sure if my groan was real or imagined, but I followed – I followed with such embarrassing speed, the thud echoed off the walls. "Are we going to play, harpy?" I skimmed my nose over her waistband, gazing up like a love-struck dog at her feet.

"If you can stay quiet long enough."

My tongue brushed the tantalising strip of skin between her shorts and jumper. "I think you like my mouth – in fact, I think you're about to *love* my mouth."

"You're talking a big game, Macabe."

"Perhaps." Her hand brushed over my cheek with surprising gentleness, fingers splitting into my hair where she gripped the roots, snapping my head back. "Take off my shorts."

Fuck.

Like they'd been released from tight constraints, my hands clasped the backs of her calves, curving into the dents behind her knees and up her thighs. Our breaths stuttered in near perfect harmony. When I reached the hem of her shorts, I had to remind myself to go slow, to not fuck this up again. My fingers dipped beneath, and I swore at the first brush of her delicate inner thigh. She might be in charge, but that didn't mean I'd follow her command to the letter. Instead of removing them, I pushed them higher, until the fabric bunched between her legs. There'd be time to play later, right now, I needed to see her. Needed to know if she was as pretty as I—

I paused. Attention arrested by a delicate tattoo, half hidden by the scrap of pink lace. "Well, well, well . . . this is a beautiful fucking surprise." My hand moved with a mind of its own, thumb pushing the silky lace in, baring half of her to me as I read the word in its entirety. I didn't know where to begin. Couldn't form a single thought. The colour. The word, permanently etched onto her skin.

Lucky.

I brushed a thumb over it and felt her tremble.

"*When*—" my voice broke on a hoarse grunt. "When did you get this?"

"I don't know . . . Three years ago, maybe?"

If I hadn't already been on them, relief would have sent me crashing to my knees. Head spinning, I skimmed my nose from her inner thigh to the band of underwear, letting it brush over the neatly etched word I fully planned to worship.

Lucky.

"The clock's ticking," she hummed, though I could feel her muscles turning pliant in my hands. My steady grip the only thing keeping her aloft when my face nestled into the lace between her legs, memorizing her scent.

A possessive rumble built in my chest. "Does this thing have teeth?"

She huffed a laugh. "Only one way to find out."

I licked the word this time and her head dropped back on a low moan. Shedding her shorts, I collected her into my arms, laying her out on the rug before the fire. The light danced off her skin and I drew back to take her in, mouth gaping in awe. Juniper stared back at me, breasts rising and falling with laboured pants. *This is happening. Fuck . . . this is actually happening.* Eyes locked with hers, my shaking fingers grazed from her knee to the little crease at the top of her thigh, where I paused, waited for her nod of consent.

"Touch me," she sighed and pushed the lacy triangle to the side, far enough for me to fully see her.

Swear to god, I fucking whimpered. "The prettiest little cunt I've ever seen, sweetheart." Fingers curled, tugging the fabric tight as my eyes roved her body, from her glistening thighs to her nipples, straining through the knit of her jumper. *This is fucking happening.* I couldn't believe it, even as I hooked her leg over my shoulder. "Still hate me?"

"Absolutely."

I smiled into her skin. "Then let me hear it, harpy."

At the first touch of my tongue she breathed, "I hate you." *Fuck*, I barely even registered the insult, too busy savouring the taste of her on my lips.

"Not very convincing. How about you say my name instead." I licked her again and her nails scraped across my scalp, fisting my hair like reins.

"That's not how this works." Another sharp tug. "I'm in charge, remember?" *And I loved it.*

I never imagined I'd get off on being told what to do, but my cock was hard enough to crack rocks, aching for the slightest touch. With one hand I reached down to rearrange myself, half tempted to slide it inside my sweats and pump until we were both screaming. But I needed this to be all about her.

Long nails clawed at me, and I grinned and grunted at the same time. "I remember, sweetheart . . . but when you come, you better say my fucking name." I dove back in with a mindless ferocity. Trying to categorise every nip that made her shudder, each touch that made her drag me closer. But I was getting swept up in her reactions. In the fact that her panting little moans were the precise tenor I'd imagined them.

"Now stop." Her heel pressed into my shoulder, pushing me away. Breathless and dazed, it took me a moment to catch up, to gather my rattled sanity enough to ask if everything was all right . . . if I'd hurt her somehow. But then she tugged her underwear down her legs, curled them into my palm and drew my head back between her legs.

Holy shit. She was having me edge her.

"Fuck, sweetheart." I grunted against her wet thigh. If perfection existed, it was this woman. This moment. I couldn't get enough.

My tongue found her clit again and her moan shuddered through her slow and long and so fucking sexy I could have come just from the sound of it.

"Look at me," she panted.

"Already am."

I couldn't look away, not as her hips rolled and her eyes fluttered closed with ecstasy. Paying close attention, I caught the rhythm she wanted. Between every few strokes, I returned to that word again – *lucky* – flicking over the raised ink with my tongue while my hands pressed her wider. Giving her the briefest second to steady herself before dragging her higher.

Lucky.

Lucky.

Lucky.

I ate at her like a man possessed. Like a man who knew he had one chance and he better make it count.

Too bad I was fucking greedy. I wanted more than that. I wanted to inject myself into her bloodstream. I wanted her body pining for my tongue and this fucking moment for the rest of her life, even if her mind and heart told her otherwise.

Other than her breathy moans, Juniper remained near silent, teeth clamped down on her lower lip as though, even in the throes of passion, her pleasure belonged to her and her alone. It was the vice grip of her legs around my ears that revealed the truth, so tight they almost muffled my own thunderous groans.

"Don't stop this time," she ordered, her thighs wrapping impossibly tighter.

"Didn't plan to – that's right, fucking suffocate me, Juniper." *What a way to go.*

Her nails dug into my neck. "Can you just shut the fuck up?"

"That's the weirdest thank you I've ever heard." Another lick to her tattoo.

Her back curved, hips lifting in an attempt to follow my tongue. "We aren't arguing now. Either do this or get out."

This didn't feel like the time to remind her this was my house.

"Yes, ma'am." I could tell from the flush of her face that our barbed words raised her blood, made her hotter. *You and me both, sweetheart.*

When she came, she did so quietly, biting her lip and arching her neck. Her coarse inhalations weaving around me like black magic. I drew back to watch, sliding two fingers over her clit to stroke her through the final waves.

With one final tremor, her lower lip slid from between her teeth.

Her mouth looked softer than I'd ever seen it.

Heart ready to burst through my skin, I pressed my forehead against her damp skin, urging my body to settle. A single touch from her and I'd spill in my boxers like a teenager. Not quite ready for that level of shame, I pressed one last, lingering kiss just above her clit that sent another shudder through her. She curled her legs around my neck as though not quite ready to release me.

"That was better than I ever imagined," I whispered.

Fucking understatement.

Her knuckles brushed my hair, weaving the strands between her fingers. Her tone amused when she asked, "Did you just go down on me in front of a roaring fire, Macabe?"

"I'm a romantic." I nibbled on her thigh until she laughed,

no clue how to play what came next. It was entirely her call. If she wanted more, I'd let her use my body in every depraved way we could think up together. If she wanted me gone . . . *well*, I'd find a way to give her that too.

The familiar blaring ringtone made the decision for me. I froze. My only movement the tightening of my fingers on her hips. If I held still perhaps the moment would freeze with me. But it rang again, and reality swept in.

Eyes never straying from her, I snatched my phone from my pocket with sigh. "Hey, Mum." Happily caught in Juniper's snare, I barely registered Mum's words. Some variation of what occurred every night. "I'll be right there," I answered on autopilot.

Juniper watched me unmoving through the short exchange. As soon as I disconnected the call, I pressed my lips to that spot a final time. *Lucky.* And without even trying to disguise the heavy length pushing through my sweats, I stood. "I have to go."

"Can I help?"

"No . . . but thanks." That was the absolute last thing I wanted.

Juniper nodded in understanding but made no move to cover herself. Her thighs glinted in the firelight, slick from my mouth, from how wet she'd been for me. *Fuck*, she was exquisite. I forced myself to look away or I'd never make it out the door.

I could tell she was waiting for me to say something. I *needed* to say something.

How did you encompass almost a decade's worth of want culminating in a single soul-shattering experience?

Thank you for letting me go down on you?

The interruption was probably for the best. It would give her time to wrap her head around what happened without lust fogging her brain. Pulling the blanket from the back of the sofa, I draped it over her, unable to stop my hand from delving between her legs and stroking her a final time. "Don't forget about me."

"Are you talking to me or my pussy?" She hadn't once screamed and yet her voice sounded hoarse.

Laughing, I pressed a kiss to her forehead. "Both." Then I pulled her hand to my mouth, kissing those perfectly manicured nails. "Stay as long as you want." Was it completely delusional to hope I'd find her tucked up in my bed when I returned? Yes, but it didn't stop the image from seeding and growing roots.

The significance of the moment didn't hit until I shut myself inside my truck. When I scrubbed a hand over my mouth and realised I could still taste her there. My hands shook so badly it took me three tries to start the engine, clamming around the wheel as I drove the short distance on muscle memory alone.

Those too short minutes I'd had her beneath me changed everything, while for her, it might have meant nothing at all.

19

Juniper

The Macabe brother rule book: Edited Edition
4. Don't let a Macabe brother go down on you, even when he begs so beautifully.

I set the bowl of cat food down with a flourish, fingers wiggling like a 1950s show girl. "This is the one. I can feel it." Shakespeare took her sweet time, clambering down from the windowsill, stretching her long limbs through the beams of morning sunlight before regarding the offering. Jasmine, the bubbly owner of the village pet store, had assured me that no sane cat would ever turn it down.

Shakespeare edged closer. Sniffed and then tentatively licked, her pink tongue lapping. My breath caught when she paused, head cocked with all the consideration of a critic at a Michelin-starred restaurant . . . then greedily dug in.

Yes! My fist pump was as exuberant as it was silent. Heart in my throat, I watched her for a long moment, hardly daring to believe she was actually eating. Then fled to the bathroom before my presence somehow soured the experience for her.

I grabbed my phone from my bedside table as I brushed my teeth, prepared to read over the daily stream of reminders from Fiona. And almost choked on the toothpaste when I found a text from Callum instead.

Macabe: What colour this morning, sweetheart?

I scoffed, waiting for the simmer of indignation. Only it didn't come.

It *always* came, that's how we worked.

I frowned at my reflection above the sink, looking for the slightest change in my appearance. My fringe had blown out perfectly this morning and my skin was on the glowy side. I looked almost . . . happy. But that wasn't because of Callum. There was no way. I'd had good orgasms before.

Great ones even.

None that made you want to spend the night afterwards. None that tempted you to open your camera and show him precisely what colour underwear you'd picked out this morning.

Not since Alistair.

Shit.

What magic sauce did these Macabe men possess and why did I crave the taste? *Hell*, maybe I should stay away from Mal, what if I got these . . . *feelings* for him next? No. My gut told me that was impossible.

Though my emotions felt as tangled as a string of Christmas tree lights, there was only one Macabe brother my body wanted, and it wasn't the one who'd purchased the ring sitting on my sideboard. Spitting out my toothpaste, I crossed the room in two strides, snatching up the box. The diamond glinted in the sun, sending fractured beams of light in every direction. While objectively beautiful, the square-cut diamond was ugly to me now. Little more than a fucked-up talisman of a hopeless woman too scared to move on with her life. A woman afraid to be hurt again.

Not wanting to look at it a second longer, I shoved the box into the closest drawer like it was the ghost of boyfriends past. Tears dampened my cheeks, and I brushed them away on my sleeve.

If there was a word to sum up an emotion both wonderful and a fucking disaster, it would be appropriate here, because for the first time I wanted to make the healthy decision and get rid of the thing. For the first time, I wanted to make room in my heart for something good. Even if that good was carried on timid wings, not quite certain they were strong enough to make the flight.

I wanted Callum.

I'd need to make things right with Heather before I continued any further down this path – I needed to explain myself properly. Pacing outside his cottage last night, I'd known the second I knocked on his door that I would further cross the line she'd drawn.

I'd also known after the showdown with his dad that Callum needed someone. It was selfish, but I'd wanted that someone to be me.

Then things spiralled and I hadn't been thinking at all.

I looked at myself in the mirror, wondering if Heather would see the truth plastered all over my face. Was it better to go to her straight away and confess everything? Even if it meant she hated me, at least I'd be being honest.

Decision made, I grabbed my keys off the sideboard, deciding I'd pick up coffee and cupcakes from Brown's on the way. You couldn't hate a person who brought cupcakes.

*   *   *

If this morning's little revelation had felt like dangling from a clifftop, Callum on his knees outside the vet practice, a dog's squished little face clutched between his capable hands, might have been enough to plummet me quite willingly to the rocks below.

That was . . . until I saw who he grinned up at.

My stomach sank.

Jill Mortimer. *Satan fucking spare me.* She was nine years my senior, but I swear the woman aged backwards. She had skin like smooth glass and a laugh as lovely and effortless as a beauty queen's right before announcing her singular dream was world peace. But worse than all that superficial crap . . . she never failed to make me feel small.

Callum's mouth moved, his impossibly handsome face partially hidden behind her curves while she giggled with satisfaction, flicking her very long, very glossy hair over her shoulder.

I wanted to gouge my eyes out.

Had the roughness of his laugh always bordered on obscene? And had his lips – lips that sucked my clit last night – always been so captivating? *Jeez, is he going down on her next?*

He should. They looked perfect together. I wrapped my arms around my middle, suddenly feeling silly.

Keeping my head down, I hurried past them, only slowing when I reached the line of customers curling out of Brown's Café and onto the street. The day was crisp and bright, even the chill in the air didn't dissuade customers from occupying the wrought-iron outdoor tables. A group of young backpackers huddled shoulder to shoulder beneath the awning, laughing as they passed around pastries.

"Ouch." The word caressed the hair at my temple, startling me. I didn't turn as Callum slipped casually into the queue. "A bit early in the morning for a brush-off, isn't it?"

Thanks to the extra height from the raised pavement, we stood at exactly eye level, close enough for me to glimpse the light catching the strays of silver hair at his temples. He wore no coat, only deep olive-green scrubs that brought out a tan no Scot had a right to possess.

Sniffing, I straightened my shoulders and indicated the people behind me. "There's a line."

"We'll order together."

Ignoring him, I moved with the line, claiming another inch toward the door.

"Are we back to this, harpy?"

"We aren't back to *anything*."

His expression said I was full of shit. "Then you won't mind buying. I think I'll get one of those expensive cupcakes with the sprinkles on top."

"You hate buttercream icing, it's too sweet." Heat crept up my neck as he grinned, the corners of his eyes crinkling. *Call me Mrs Cellophane, because I'm bloody transparent.*

"Does this count as one of our 'dates'?" I crooked my fingers around the word.

Callum kept pace, moving onto the pavement and letting his shoulder brush mine. "Are we getting a table?"

I didn't have time to grab a table, but that wasn't the reason I scoffed, "Absolutely not."

"Then no."

Why did he get to be the only one to determine the rules of our agreement? "This counts. Take a picture and send it to your mum, tell her we're having a great 'friend date', job done."

He clucked his tongue. "I think we both know this isn't about my mum anymore."

Panic replaced the indignation. Why did he always have to be so honest? "We're sticking to the terms of our agreement," I said more coolly than I'd intended.

"Fine." He shrugged, unbothered. "I'll buy my own coffee."

"Then get to the back of the line." I knew I was acting like a jealous arsehole.

I hated being that girl that blew hot and cold when nothing had really changed since last night – except Jill's fucking giggle playing on a loop in my head. Out of all the women in Kinleith, why did it need to be her?

His head fell back, a half groan half laugh on his lips. "Jesus, sweetheart, are you ever going to stop giving me shit?"

"You've been giving me shit from the moment we met. The other women in your life might enjoy your brand of banter, Macabe, but I don't."

God, stop talking!

"Did you just refer to yourself as a woman in my life?"

"That's what you took from all of that?" I whacked my hand off his bicep. He caught my wrist, running his thumb over the slip of bone there.

"My mind is shockingly single track, I'm afraid."

I rolled my eyes at the honey all but dripping from his tongue. "Don't repeat that to the people of Kinleith who trust you to take care of their pets, you might have a mutiny on your hands. Dennis Foster also happens to be a very skilled veterinarian."

He tugged me closer until I could feel the heat of him through my clothes. Like a true Highlander, even dressed in only thin scrubs, he ran as hot as a furnace. "We discussed your visits to Portree already."

"He comes highly recommended."

If it was possible, he drew me even closer. Until I had no

choice but to look up at him or smoosh my face into his chest. "Obviously I didn't make myself clear enough last night, Juniper. I'm happy to submit to you, any time, any place of your choosing." His fingers danced up my wrist to stroke over my knuckles. "Snap these fingers and I'm yours." His voice turned low. As thick as chimney smoke. I had to take a breath. "But if I find out you've visited that charlatan again, we'll be experimenting with a little role reversal."

My body lit like a furnace. Something hot coiling low and demanding in my stomach. It couldn't be lust. Bossy did *not* turn me on. It never had. "I have no interest in doing *whatever* this is."

He laughed. "Your thighs practically decapitated me last night, harpy. You wanted it just as bad as I did."

"Yeah, no shit. It was cunnilingus, Callum, even when it's bad it's pretty good."

"It was fucking *great*," he ground out. A single look at my face had him groaning. "Fuck, but that face gets me hot. From the moment I laid eyes on you."

Someone behind us coughed and I suddenly became painfully aware of the gazes we were drawing. The group of backpackers watched from over their coffee cups like we were the best show they'd seen all year. "We shouldn't be seen together."

"Worried Jess might guess that I had my tongue inside you last night?" My knees almost buckled. The woman behind us spluttered and covered her child's ears. I barely noticed as Callum's eyes fell to my mouth. He hadn't tried to kiss me last night but looked eager to remedy the mistake now.

"Well, now I am." I laughed, picturing Jess's horror if she ever made that discovery.

He laughed too, his throat working around the sound. "Jess does seem to have her mind in the gutter . . ." Callum kept talking but his words faded as a form I'd have recognised anywhere cut along the street, head and shoulders above everyone else.

Just like his brothers.

"Alistair?" The name felt both familiar and foreign on my tongue.

His head snapped up, purposeful strides wavering as he found me all too easily on the busy street, like he'd done so a thousand times before. An old dance our muscles had memorised long ago, then forgotten to alert our brains when the rhythm changed.

I didn't know why I'd spoken his name, drawn attention to myself. The shock, most likely, because when his feet changed direction, heading right for me, his expression shifting from pensive to elated in a heartbeat, I was certain this was nothing more than a bizarre out-of-body experience. I'd almost forgotten Callum entirely, until his elbow brushed mine and then all I could think about was the scrap of space between us.

"June?" Alistair spoke my name the way you'd address an old friend you hoped to see again but hadn't expected the reunion to happen quite so soon.

From behind round glasses, he ate up the sight of me, calculating the changes from the tips of my thick-soled shoes to my hair that was six inches shorter than it had been the last time we'd spoken. When he'd told me through a video call, guilt-ridden and teary-eyed, that I didn't need to return the engagement ring. As though the four-carat diamond were a suitable consolation prize for losing the man you loved.

His hair was shorter too. Shorter than I'd ever seen it.

His shoulders were broader, ready to burst the seams of his thick navy jumper.

He looked good.

I hated that I noticed and compared, because Callum looked *better*.

Alistair paused an arm's length away, a tentative smile softening the set of his harsh lips. "Hey."

Hey.

Six years of nothing broken with three letters. They weren't even the good ones.

I'd planned for this moment, replaying the imagined back and forth over and over. The ways I'd make him beg. Make him crawl. Now he stood before me and I couldn't utter a single word.

His smile dipped uncertainly, turning into a frown as he glanced to Callum. "Cal, good to see you." If Alistair found our proximity strange, I saw no hint of it as he pulled Callum into a back-slapping hug.

Callum's posture remained a little stiff, but when he drew back, he was smiling, cupping Alistair's cheeks as though he were seven years old. "Why didn't you say you were coming?"

Alistair shifted, eyes cast down, and I remembered why he'd always refused to play cards. He couldn't lie for shit. "I managed to wrangle some time off last minute, figured I'd surprise you."

"You look tired," Callum observed, taking in Alistair's longer than usual facial hair and dark smudges beneath his eyes. And it was with a wash of relief I realised the urge to comfort, to wrap my arms around his middle and kiss the sharp point of his chin no longer existed.

"I'm fine," he lied again. Speaking to Callum but looking at me.

My heart raced.

"Heather's going to die when she sees you, the twins too – wait, where are you staying?"

"I haven't decided. With Mum and Dad most likely . . ."

Their words faded in a hum as a different feeling settled, tight and uncomfortable like a vine curling around my chest. Alistair's eyes kept finding mine, searching for something I didn't know how to give. And Callum . . . Callum didn't look at me once.

My scalp prickled, entire body going hot. My breaths turned choppy. Doubling, until the space of one became two.

You're hyperventilating, the tiny, aware part of my brain warned. Unable to make the connection to my lungs.

I have to get out of here.

Black smudged the edges of my vision. I turned and stumbled – feet heavy as I tripped along the street without a word.

"Juniper!" Callum shouted. I kept going. Clawing at the zip on my jacket. I rounded the corner. Tarmac giving way to gravel. The sandstone village hall stood proud like a proverbial white flag.

Five steps. My car was five steps away.

I dug through my bag, searching for my keys.

Four steps.

Callum skidded to a stop in front of me. Both hands raised as though herding a wounded animal. "Juniper, just wait – are you?" He paled, a muscle in his jaw jumping. "Are you crying?"

Was I? I swiped at my cheeks, stunned to find my hands came away wet. "I'm not bloody crying," I spat, though we could both clearly see the remnants of tears. I hated every stupid one of them.

I hated the pain in his expression when his eyes bounced between mine, then to my car as though he didn't have the faintest idea what to say. *Fine by me.* I tried to slide past him, but he caught me, then held his hands up placatingly when I flinched away from the touch. "You can't drive off like that."

"I'm fine, get out of my way." I desperately searched the other pocket then tore through my bag again. "Where the bloody hell are my keys?"

"They're in your hand. *Shit*, sweetheart." His entire face caved in on itself, devastated for me. "It's okay to be upset about this."

"Don't call me that." I sidestepped him. "And I'm not upset, I'm *pissed*." But that didn't feel right either – it was like an old scar had torn open down my chest, only to discover it had never healed properly in the first place.

"That's fine too."

I choked on a laugh, it sounded pathetic. "Are you a therapist now?"

"*No.* If I were, I wouldn't be fighting the urge to go back there and punch my brother for putting that look on your face."

I dropped my face in my hands. A little of the tightness in my chest easing. "I don't want that. I never wanted—" *Never wanted to come between them.*

His hands curled around my shoulders. "I know."

This was so bloody wrong – all of it – still I gave myself a second to sink into his grip. "This is why last night should never have happened." Backing up, I swiped at my face again. "Between Alistair and Heather, it's too complicated."

"It doesn't have to be." He made it sound so easy.

"Alistair—"

"Alistair is a fucking idiot." He was before me in a

heartbeat, his own breathing erratic as he hissed, "It's what I think now and it's what I told him then. He could have had—" He shook his head, pupils blown as he looked at me with a fierceness that raked like claws across my heart. "He never deserved you."

He never deserved you. How many people uttered those very words? And just like every time before, they rang hollow in my heart.

"If you want to talk to him—"

"I don't want to talk to him. I don't think I should talk to you either."

He swallowed. "Will you let me drive you home? Please?"

I shook my head. "I can manage."

"If that's what you want," he said but it looked as though the words cost him something.

"You don't need to worry about me." I brushed past him this time, without meeting his stare. If I did, I would have given in to anything he offered. To drive me home. To hold me in his arms. I already balanced on a knife's edge.

I reached for the handle. He got there first. "That's an impossible habit to break. Don't ask me to." Slipping the keys from my grip, he held the driver's door wide, waiting for me to climb inside. Once I was behind the wheel, he dropped to his knees, reaching up and around to click the seatbelt into place. Giving a tug to ensure it was secure.

My hands trembled a little in my lap. Callum lifted them and set them on the wheel at ten and two. "Breathe, sweetheart. Take one big breath in." I did, feeling the bite of the seatbelt before I released it. "Again." I complied. "Again." He repeated the word ten more times. Until my tears dried and my grip turned steady. "Will you let me know when you get home?"

I nodded, twisting the keys to start the engine. He finally

pushed to stand. Closing the door with a click, he stepped out of view, waiting, as I backed the car from the spot and drove to the exit. Hitting my indicator left, I glanced in my rearview to find him watching. Hands on his hips, breeze tossing his curls. He waited until my car disappeared from view.

20

Callum

Callum: Get over to Ivy House.
Heather: And why would I do that?
Callum: We can pick up this little fight later. Alistair's home.
Heather: What?? Since when?
Callum: About five minutes ago.
Heather: Shit. Did June see him?
Callum: They bumped into each other on the high street.
Heather: You couldn't distract her until he was gone?
Callum: With what? My juggling skills?

"Is she all right?" Alistair waited as still as a sentry beneath Brown's awning, his features hard as carved marble. Any earlier thoughts of sweet treats long forgotten as I approached.

He looked concerned.

He looked exhausted.

Juniper's devastated expression – her tears – filled my vision and I felt murderous all over again. "A little warning might have been a good idea." I shoved my hands into my pockets, unsure if the rising urge was to strike out or ruffle his hair.

Not that he had much hair left to ruffle.

He grimaced. "I already told you, it was a last-minute decision. I didn't expect to run into her so soon and I didn't think she'd be—" He broke off, running a hand over his jaw in a gesture that reminded me so much of Mal. Alistair's usual polished charm made it easy to forget the similarities between the two of them. But as I stared at him for the first time in almost two years, I found no trace of it.

"You didn't expect her to be upset?" I scoffed, not even trying to leash the fury pounding through me. Or was it envy? Green and selfish and slithering. Juniper had come on *my* tongue last night, a moment so erotic she'd burned every single one of my past encounters to cinders, and twelve hours later she had my brother's name on her lips, tears on her cheeks *he'd* put there. His ring on her sideboard.

Alistair shifted, that hand dragging over his head now, he seemed surprised when he found nothing to grab onto. "What do you want me to say? That a tiny little part of me hoped she'd be happy to see me?" He didn't need to; I'd been an eyewitness to his knee-wobbling relief when he realised it was *Juniper* calling out to him. "Despite everything, I still care for her. I'll always care for her." Each word was a gut punch that caused the stupid, revealing words that came next.

"Did you cheat on her?" I didn't know why the answer mattered so much.

No, I did.

How could I mend a wound without knowing the extent of the injury?

"Of course I didn't." He had the decency to look appalled. "*Christ*, Callum, I might have behaved like a prick, but I'd like to think I'm not completely morally bankrupt – did June say that?"

"No."

He frowned. "Since when did you become Juniper's protector, anyway?"

My muscles locked, the need to tell him so great, as though I'd held the words hostage on the tip of my tongue all these years and they finally sensed an escape.

Actually, it's a funny story, brother, but I fell in love with your girlfriend about six months after you did. And when she became your fiancée, instead of thinking of her as another little sister like I should have, I plotted all the ways I could steal her from you. I thought of her in every depraved way imaginable, how I'd touch her, love her, how I'd make her moan harder than you ever could.

I'd probably leave out that last part.

"I'm not her protector. She doesn't need one," I clipped with certainty. Juniper wouldn't let my idiot brother keep her down for long. And I'd texted Heather the moment Juniper's car had disappeared from view.

"What are you doing here?" He winced at my tone and I immediately felt like shit. I'd been begging him to come back for months. Now he was here and I was behaving like a self-righteous arsehole. "*Fuck*, I'm sorry, I just—"

"I get it. I should have told June I was coming. Guess I was scared she wouldn't care. Or she *would* care and I'd feel like shit all over again."

"You two haven't spoken at all? In six years?" I wished I could say my curiosity was for his sake. Or hers.

He shook his head. "Do you think I should go after her?"

Fuck, no. The sentiment roared in my chest but it was for Juniper I answered, "Give her a day or two." If she wanted to see him eventually that was her right, but right now . . .

she needed time to reinforce her defences. "Have you seen Dad yet?"

"No." He swung a stuffed rucksack over his shoulder. "I just arrived. Figured I'd drop by and see you first."

I clapped him on the shoulder this time, searching for our usual ease. "Perfect. My hotshot baby brother can buy me lunch."

He laughed but it didn't reach his eyes as we stepped into Brown's. All heads turned our way as we shouldered through the narrow door, including Jess's which widened at the sight of Alistair. She was too busy at the till to utter so much as a greeting so we grabbed menus, sitting at the only unoccupied table by the window. I set my phone down on the table, screen up, so I wouldn't miss Juniper's text. "Did you join the army without telling me?"

"What?"

I nodded to his closely shorn hair.

"Oh." He brushed a self-conscious hand over it. "Just fancied a wee change."

"It suits you. How's work going?"

He studied the laminated menu in his hands long enough that an awkwardness curled up like a cat in the middle of the table. "I didn't come here to talk about work."

I frowned. You usually couldn't shut him up about work. Alistair wasn't a narcissist by any means, but he was passionate about medicine. "We can't catch up? We've barely spoken in months."

"Work. . . it's y'know, the same . . ." He fiddled with the cutlery, lining the napkin up against the edge of the table. "*Boring*. There isn't really a lot to say."

"I don't believe that for a minute." Something was going on with him. He had more tells than a dog with a thorn in its paw. "How long are you here for?"

214

"I didn't realise this was an inquisition." I waited, unmoving, until he blew out an agitated breath. "I'm not sure, a few weeks, maybe longer."

Longer? "Oh," I lowered my own menu, really looking at him now. "You'd tell me if something was up, right?"

"*Of course,*" he said quickly.

Too quickly.

My phone buzzed at my elbow and I snatched it up.

Harpy: Home.

The tightness in my chest eased a fraction. One word. But it was enough.

I turned back to ask Alistair just as Jess appeared, far quicker than a woman who refused to use her hospital-issued cane should. "Are my ancient eyes playin' tricks on me, or is that you, Alistair, lad?"

"Jess." His expression flipped from uncertain to charming in an instant. I could almost believe I'd imagined the past ten minutes if it hadn't been for the effortless way that he steered every one of her questions back on her.

"Yer look well lad, you got a sweetheart treatin' you right?"

"No one that compares to you, Jess. How are your daughters?"

"*Ach,*" She waved a hand. "Meddlesome wee shits are on at me to retire. How's life in the city?"

He laughed, sitting back in his chair. "No comparison to Skye. The village is busier than ever, business must be booming."

I ordered on autopilot, fighting the need to shake my brother, find out what was going on with him and fix it. But Juniper's words filtered back. *Who's taking care of you?*

I released my tight hold on the cutlery.

If Alistair needed my help, he'd come to me. Lord knew I had enough on my plate. And it wasn't like I didn't have my own secrets.

So when he asked, "How's Dad?" I told him without a single deviation.

21

Juniper

Alistair: June . . . I'm so sorry about today. It wasn't supposed to go down like that.

"This is why you have your damn rules." I thumped my fist into the pillow, doing a better job of beating it into submission than I was changing the bedsheets.

The guest room was a mess after the oh so charming Mr Lewis had checked out. Dirty towels strewn across the floor, piles of old receipts beside the bed. When I'd stripped off the linens, a crusty-looking tissue had made a little *Ta-da* appearance, as though he'd left it behind as a little departure present. I'd worn the designated "bodily fluids" rubber gloves to dispose of it.

Those gloves saw more action than I was willing to admit.

I usually detested room changeovers, but today I craved the physical work. Turning the music on my headphones up a level, I beat my fist into the pillow again, the image flicking between Callum and Alistair's too handsome faces.

Alistair was back in Kinleith.

It felt as though he'd crossed an invisible boundary line, spinning all my carefully crafted calm out of control. The control that Callum had been chipping away at for weeks now, if I was being honest.

I should have expected it – I *had* expected from the moment Heather had informed me of their father's diagnosis. Alistair would never stay away when he had an ill family member. I'd spent weeks looking over my shoulder every time I set foot in the village. And when he hadn't shown, I'd started to relax.

My own damn fault.

I punched the pillow again, taking pleasure in that resulting *thwack* that reverberated against my hand.

I wasn't certain what had affected me more. Seeing Alistair for the first time since he shattered my heart or his brief head tilt when he'd spotted Callum and I together. I recognised that head tilt. I called it his equation-solving head tilt, when I knew his mind was racing over every possible outcome until he found the most likely. Would he ever guess that his big brother had eaten me out so carnally, I'd thought I might die from the painfully sweet bliss of it?

I hadn't felt this kind of panic since the night Alexander had died and my emotions raged so forcefully, they'd felt too much for my body to contain. Then Alistair had ended things, and I'd just shut it all off. I returned to Skye permanently like a dutiful daughter should and had been going through the motions ever since.

Until last night, a voice taunted. *And that night in Glasgow.*

I hated to admit it, but Callum was right. Some instinct in him just *knew* what I needed, what got me off. It couldn't be a coincidence that the two single times I'd felt anything other than a hollow rage in the last six years, Callum Macabe had a direct line of contact to my clit. I didn't believe in coincidences.

And that was a problem because despite this morning, despite the fact I couldn't stand him half the time – I wanted to feel that rush again. I already knew how good it would be. Only now it was my turn to give him pleasure, and I wanted him out of control and slack-jawed for me as I did so.

I was sliding the pillow into a fresh case when a hand landed my shoulder.

"*Shit*—" I tore out my earbuds. "Heather, you scared the crap out of me!" She was the last person I expected to see.

"I'm sorry." Her expression turned sheepish. "Hank said you'd be up here. He looked about ready to go to war."

I let the pillow fall, sinking down onto the mattress. "Hank did?" He'd given me a once-over when I'd raced through the back door like a bat out of hell, tears crusting my eyes together. I didn't stop to think if he'd put two and two together. "You saw Alistair?" I asked, understanding dawning.

A sympathetic smile twisted her pretty features. "No. Callum told me. He said you were waiting in line at Brown's when he showed up and that you might need someone to talk to."

Damn if that wasn't a little sweet. It made me feel nauseous. "He shouldn't have bothered you, I'm fine." I flopped onto my back, lying diagonally across the bed. If she was here to yell at me again, she could go right ahead. I didn't have the energy to argue.

After a quiet moment, her weight settled beside mine. "This mattress is comfy."

"Thanks. I updated them to memory foam last year."

We lay like that for a few minutes, watching the interspersed cloud cover lighten and darken the room before she said, "Want to know who you remind me of?"

"Morticia Addams?" I asked hopefully.

She snorted. "*Yes* – but no. You remind me of Malcolm."

Horrified, I tilted my head to look at her. "Your brother Malcolm?"

"Don't look like that, Mal is amazing."

I agreed but, "Mal is . . . *soft*. Sickeningly sweet some-times, I'm none of those things." *Shit*. Did other people think that?

She laughed at my description of her brother. "He is all of those things, but for so long he didn't know how to show it. He kept all his emotions buried inside and everyone who loved him at arm's length."

"You think that's what I'm doing?"

Her face twisted, blonde hair like a halo around her head. "Will you be mad if I say yes?"

I bit my lip. "I wouldn't be mad. But I would tell you that you're searching for a problem that isn't there." Keeping my emotions to myself didn't make me repressed. I just pre-ferred to handle my shit alone, like I always had.

I glanced again to discover her already watching me, Macabe eyes roving gently over my face as though, after twenty-five years of friendship, she was seeing me for the first time and was disappointed in what she found. "All right, June." She faced the ceiling. I thought she was about to leave until— "I'm sorry."

I swallowed, fingers locking around the pillow I clutched against my chest. "Why are you apologising?"

"Because I've behaved like a massive dick. I shouldn't have jumped down your throat the other night—"

"You had every right to—"

"No, I didn't. You and Callum are adults and free to do whatever the hell you like, it just surprised me, and I reacted badly. Just like I did when Alistair called things off." She took a breath. "You were so mad at him . . . and I didn't

220

know how to be there for you while still loving my brother. I felt like I had to choose. It's a shitty excuse, I know – I should have been on your side."

I thought back to the biggest argument we'd ever had. How we'd screamed at each other in her kitchen when she refused to hear a word spoken against him. We didn't talk for months after that, the longest I'd ever gone without her in my life. And even when we made up – we'd lost the ease I'd always taken for granted.

"He's your brother." I'd been hurt, but truthfully never blamed her. *Of course she'd pick her family over me.*

"He is. But you're my sister – a sister I chose for myself. He broke your heart and I should have been in your corner . . . god, I was so naive." Her voice broke, eyes shining with unshed tears. "I didn't understand how it feels when the person who promised to love you above all else, actively *chooses* to leave. How it completely resets everything you thought you knew about yourself. Y'know, I thought, *He's just a man, she'll get over it.* But it's not about the man in the end, is it? It's about who the heartbreak turns you into. The shattered confidence, the whispers and the knowing glances in the village that make you question if everyone else saw it coming and you were just too damn blind to see it. And if they did know, then why the hell didn't they warn you? The questions you replay over and over: *What's so wrong with me that I couldn't make him stay? How long until everybody else sees it and leaves too?*" I reached for her but she held up a hand, batting away the tears that fell. "All I mean is, I'm really bloody sorry Juniper, I wouldn't have gotten through those first few months after Mike left without you. Now it's my turn. Whatever you need while he's here, it's yours."

She was choosing me. That was what she was trying to say.

My own tears welled, so thick I was sure I wouldn't be able to speak. Scooching closer, I placed my head on her shoulder. We lay in silence for a long moment.

"Shit . . . I think I'm coming down with something." The back of my throat had felt scratchy ever since seeing Alistair. Then there was all the bloody crying.

"So . . . are you like, dating Callum now?"

"No." The word burst from me but didn't feel quite right. "Not exactly . . . we, well . . . it's complicated."

"Ugh." She groaned. "I need to find new friends who aren't into my brothers. It's gross."

I laughed and she stroked my hair back in a way only a mother could. Then I remembered, "Heather . . . I think a guy jerked off in these sheets."

Heather shrieked in horror, and we leapt to our feet, brushing at our clothes as though we'd had front row seats to the semen party. Then we were laughing. So hard I had to swipe away a different set of tears.

Anger was a release. But I'd forgotten that laughter could be one too.

"June! You okay?" Hours later, April's door swung wide. Her eyes were wide, every freckle standing out on her stark features.

"Can I come in?" I asked but she was already stepping aside, making room for me as I barrelled into the small but homey cottage she and Mal shared. Mal gave me a small nod from his spot on the sofa. He held a book in one hand, the other stroked lazy lines down Dudley's back.

"I was just about to call you," she said, following me into the kitchen and picking up a mug. "Mal told me about Alistair, want to talk about it?"

"That isn't actually why I came." I shot one nervous look

at Mal then thought, *Fuck it, he's a part this now.* "Callum went down on me."

April spluttered, droplets of coffee staining her shirt. "*He what?*"

"*Bloody hell.*" Mal stood, swiping a hand over his jaw. Dudley popped his head up, whining at the sudden lack of stroking taking place. "I can't know about this. I'm seeing Alistair in an hour."

April scoffed indignantly. "This has nothing to do with Alistair."

"I'll be with *both* of them and I'm terrible at keeping secrets. The last time I broke out in hives."

"All right, enough of this." I waved a hand as April settled on the sofa and tucked her feet beneath her.

"Was it good? With Callum, I mean," she said.

"Do you even need to ask? You've seen the man." He had a mouth made for sin.

"Leaving now," Mal declared, tucking his book beneath his arm and pressing a kiss to April's forehead.

"It was so good, April," I moaned, covering my face with my hands the instant the front door closed behind Mal. "Like, the hottest moment of my life, and now I'm fucked."

"Why?"

"Because I want to do it again. And again and again." I wanted him so badly that even Alistair's return hadn't curbed the hunger for long.

"*That* good?" I flicked up a brow and she grinned. "*Shit.* It changes everything, doesn't it? When someone just knows what you need and how to give it to you."

"It can't."

"Why?"

"Because it can't go anywhere." And the longer it went on, the more dangerous a game we were playing.

April folded her arms. "At the threat of sounding repetitive, but again, *why*?"

"Alistair! They all have so much going on right now with Jim, I'm an extra problem they don't need."

"Alistair gets zero say in your love life. And I've seen the way Callum looks at you, you're the furthest thing from a problem for him."

"How does he look at me?" I cringed as soon as I said it. Like some love-struck sixteen-year-old begging for her crush to finally notice her.

Pathetic.

She smiled softly. "I asked Heather that exact question about Mal once."

"What did she say?"

"She said he looks at me like I'm a revelation." My heart squeezed at the gentle love in her eyes. That's exactly how he looked at her.

"And you think Callum looks at me that way?"

"Absolutely not." She laughed. "He looks at you like the world's about to catch on fire and you're the only person he'll save. I don't know how he's hidden it so long . . ." She trailed off, catching my dazed expression. Her words reverberated through me on a loop, as did the image of Callum on his knees, tongue working my clit, a frantic fervency in his eyes as he watched me come, like it was the most important task he'd ever been given.

"It's okay to like him," April said after a moment.

"I don't like him," I lied. Not quite ready to admit my feelings aloud. She rolled her eyes. "What? What's that look for?"

She shrugged. "The lady doth protest too much, methinks."

"Please don't bring my cat into this." I groaned. "And the lady protests the perfect amount!"

22

Callum

Callum: Can you take Dad to his appointment this morning? I have some errands in Portree.
Callum: There's a timed daily routine taped to the fridge. Stick to it to the letter, it helps ease his anxiety. I can talk you through it.
Alistair: I think I'll manage.
Callum: Sorry, sorry, I forgot we had *Dr Macabe* on the island.
Alistair: I can't take the insult. I'm packing my bags as I type.

"No wonder you haven't laughed in years if this is the music you listen to, harpy. It's depressing as fuck." The man's melancholy voice droned on as I observed Juniper from the doorway of Ivy House's small kitchen. For a moment I was afraid I'd gone too far. And then she glanced up from the mixing bowl she stirred with a large wooden spoon. Her wicked smile filled with enough electricity to restart my heart.

"I can put on some Phil Collins if you prefer?"

225

There she is. Always right back in the saddle.

"How old do you think I am exactly?" Easing closer, I laid my hands on the stainless-steel counter.

"Old enough you should consider getting one of those little chains to attach your wallet to your trousers."

"Feeling snarky this morning, sweetheart?" I should take her over my knee for that one. Admittedly, if one of us were to get our arse reddened, it was more likely to be me.

"Seems like it."

I finally looked her over. In leggings and a baggy T-shirt, she was more dressed down than I'd ever seen her. Still, she made my breath catch. It was fucking witchcraft, I swear.

That was the difference between infatuation and love. Juniper would always be the most stunning woman I'd ever laid eyes on, that was an indisputable fact, but what made her *beautiful* to me in that moment was her strength. Her eyes were still slightly puffy, her nose red from the emotional blow Alistair had inflicted and yet, here she was, just as I'd predicted.

Her eyes flicked up from the bowl again. "You shouldn't be back here."

"Morning to you too, sunshine. We're leaving in ten minutes, change into something warm." Surprise stole across her face. "You said you wanted to stick to our bargain. I still have three dates, remember?"

"I'm ill."

"You don't look ill." I looked pointedly to the finger she was currently licking batter from.

She paused; finger caught between her lips. "It isn't contagious."

"Great." I clapped my hands together. "Let's go." *Come on*, I silently urged. *Come with me, sweetheart. Don't let this change things.*

226

"No."

"No?" Hank's rough voice filtered through the door a second before the gruff man appeared, already buttoning his chef whites over his wide chest. "What are you doing in my kitchen?"

"*Helping.* I already started on the oatcakes."

Batting her hands away, he took the bowl and stuck his little finger in the batter and tasted it. Cringing, he added another sprinkle of sugar. "I dinnae need your help. You may as well take the lad up on his offer."

"See?" I winked at Hank. He glowered back. "We can go back and forth all day, harpy, but this ends with your arse in my front seat."

Ignoring me completely, she rounded on Hank. "Who's going to run the breakfast service?"

"Ada, she's already in reception."

Juniper's eyebrows lifted. "You came in together?"

I didn't think it was possible, but the man actually blushed. "It's not like *that*, she got a flat tyre yesterday. I offered her a ride," he muttered. Juniper looked so delighted, my own lips curled into a smile.

"Can you survive without her?" I asked Hank, slipping around the counter to cover Juniper's mouth with my hand before she could protest.

His moustache twitched. "Aye."

"Then it's settled." With a slight pressure on her shoulder, I steered her out the door. "*Fuck.*" I flinched away as pain seared through the fleshy part of my palm. "You bit me."

"Hands off," she hissed while I marvelled at the tiny little teeth marks.

"Would it be weird to get these tattooed?" I held my hand out for her to see.

Her lips twitched just as I'd hoped. "You're a strange man, Callum Macabe."

I kissed her cheek in lieu of a response, already backing down the hall. "I'll be in the car, you have ten minutes. Oh, and remember a swimsuit . . . Or don't."

She flipped her middle finger.

I flipped mine right back.

Alistair: Do you know where Dad's medical notes are? Mum can't find them.

The text from Alistair was time stamped five minutes ago.

Callum: Top drawer of the desk.

Alistair: That was quick. Thought you were headed to Portree?

Shit.

Callum: Fuel stop.

I hated lying. It didn't come easily to me, even with the screaming voice that told me lying was the safest course of action for now, given the tangled history. I felt especially bad using the time having Alistair home freed up to spend with Juniper.

Callum: I left some leaflets in the kitchen for daycare facilities and carer support groups, can you ask Mum to look at them? I think it will help coming from you.

Alistair: Leave it with me.

The car door opened and I dropped my phone into the cup holder. All thoughts of my dad and Alistair melting away as Juniper slid into the passenger seat. The beanie I'd bought slipping low on her forehead, sunglasses so dark you might mistake her for a funeral attendant balanced on her slightly upturned nose.

"Worried you might be seen with me?"

"Aren't you?"

"No." I held out a Brown's takeaway cup and started the engine.

"You brought me coffee?"

"Nope, it's empty. I know how much you like collecting the little cups."

"You're extra funny in the mornings, Macabe." Her words dripped with sarcasm. "I meant . . . you live right next door." She pointed at the tree line. "Why drive all the way into the village just to get coffee?"

Because I know you love Jess's coffee. Cheeks threatening to heat, I shoved the cup into her hand. "Enough questions. Just drink it."

She took a sip and grimaced. "It's cold."

"Yeah . . ." I winced, choking down another long sip of my own. "It would have been warm if you'd been ready on time. Now we both have to suffer." Starting the engine, I gestured to the centre console. "It's a bit of a drive, put on that sad music you love so much."

23

Juniper

Isle of Skye Guidebook
   The Fairy Pools
   Distance: 8km.
   Time: 3 hrs.
   Terrain: Rough moorland path. Narrow bridges between
   pools. Undulating hills.
   Visitors can enjoy the stunning walk bordered with
   flowering heather and peat. Follow the crystal-clear
   burn in the shadow of the Cullin mountains. Pause to
   explore the many enchanting pools and waterfalls, those
   who feel brave enough can even enter the icy water.

"You didn't say we'd be hiking." The stupid trainers I'd
chosen, built purely for aesthetic purposes, slipped on flat
rock, tossing my weight.

Callum caught my elbow, steadying me before we continued. "We can still see the car."

I glanced back over my shoulder and . . . yep, there it
was. "Only because it's on a hill," I shot back, manoeuvring

slowly down the steep decline. Well, *I* was slow. Macabe appeared to be floating; even with his hiking boots partially laced, he strolled down the hill like he walked on water.

"Forget about the hike for a minute and look at all of this." He drew us to a stop, gesturing with both hands to the mountain range in the distance, their vast snowy peaks cutting into the crisp sky like something out of a *Lord of the Rings* movie.

This was the Cullin mountain range, or so he'd told me in the car after narrowly avoiding a head-on collision at the discovery of my *criminal lack of knowledge of the land I was raised in.* Or something to that effect. I'd been too distracted by the stretch of his cable-knit jumper over his wide shoulders.

"It's nice, I guess." I kept my tone bored, just to piss him off, but it was an effort to disguise my wonder. Off the narrow stone pathway, water trickled in narrow burns, dancing and diving where it cut like glass through the primaeval rock, branching off like a sea of spiderwebs until the streams culminated in dozens of small waterfalls, spilling over into shallow turquoise pools. Boulders coated in moss of the brightest green lined the pathway, so large they could only have been placed there by giants.

Callum, obviously seeing straight through my disinterest, said, "I felt overwhelmed on my first visit, too."

I understood now why this place was named the fairy pools. We'd ventured no more than ten minutes from the car, and I felt as though I'd tripped and fallen into another world. How had I sent so many tourists here and never visited myself?

"There's an old legend that goes with this land," Callum started, his voice holding the deep baritone of a natural-born storyteller. "The story says this is the site of one of Scotland's bloodiest battles, Coire na Creiche, between the MacLeods of Dunvegan and the MacDonalds of Sleat." He turned back at a particularly steep step to take hold of my hand and help me down. I could have told him my legs were almost as long as his were. *Could have* but didn't. And when he kept our fingers loosely tangled, I didn't object to that either.

"What did they go to war over?"

"Why does anyone go to war? Money, land, resources. A woman, most likely." He tapped his shoulder against mine. "Anyway, it was the MacDonalds who eventually claimed the victory after many days of battle so bloody it's said the pools ran red with it. So much death and destruction to the land, they vowed it could never be repeated again. True to their word, it was the last clan war of Skye."

Letting the fingers of my free hand dance over the long grass, it was impossible to imagine this peaceful place as Callum described it. "That's a good story."

"I thought you'd like it, bloodthirsty demon."

I flashed my teeth and he laughed.

"Did you like being in the army?" All ease disappeared and it was my turn to right him as he actually stumbled. "I'm sorry, you don't need to—"

"No. It's fine, it took me by surprise, that's all. People are always curious about my time overseas but no one ever asks how I felt about it."

I lapsed into silence, giving him room to change the subject. I should have known Callum wouldn't shy away.

"I hated it."

"What part?"

"All of it. The training, the deployment, the things I saw that will haunt me for the rest of my life." His voice held more bitterness than I ever thought him capable of. "For as long as I can remember my mum called me her *sensitive wee boy*. I don't think I was more sensitive than any other, but I was drawn to art, like my mum, and loved animals. And she nurtured that side of me. But the older I got, the more obvious it became that he . . . *he* hated all the parts of me she loved." I didn't need to ask who *he* was. "He wanted his boys to be men and as the oldest it was up to me to set an example. I grew to hate that nickname and the gentler parts of myself . . . until I found myself halfway around the world, just another body in a war I couldn't stand, holding my friends – too young to truly understand what they'd signed up for – as they died. Doing what I could to aid innocent civilians we were *supposed* to be helping, and all I could think was: if this was living up to my father's expectations," he shook his head roughly, emotion clogging his voice, "I wanted no part in it."

Something sharp lodged in my throat. I couldn't talk around it. So I squeezed his fingers. He squeezed right back, bringing his other hand around to cover my knuckles, holding on like I was a lifeline. I'd never been that for *anyone*. For my entire relationship with Alistair, he'd been the epitome of a stiff upper lip. Always in control. Rarely brought his work home with him. Never once needed to lean on me. It was for that alone I said, "I can't believe I didn't see it before."

He glanced at me as we walked. "What?"

"You and me. I always thought we were complete opposites, when in truth – it's like looking in a mirror. At a much more put-together version of myself, but—" I felt my cheeks heat, realising I was completely jumbling this. "All I mean is, I get it. Trying to live up to expectations."

He said nothing for a long moment. "Whose?"

"Everyone's." The word was barely audible over the rush

of water, and yet it felt like I'd stood atop a cliff and screamed it. "Have you ever noticed the first thing new parents always say is how they'd never known real love until the moment they held their child in their arms? Well, my birth parents never loved me." I shrugged as though the knowledge hadn't torn me to shreds over and over. "I failed at the very first test. I guess, I've been playing catch-up ever since."

"What test?" *Good bloody question.* When it became apparent I wouldn't answer he asked another. "Why don't you call Fiona Mum?" Of all the things he might say, I didn't expect that.

I kicked a stone. "She didn't ask me to."

"You think she wouldn't want you to?"

"No . . . I'm sure she wouldn't mind. But it's always been easier to keep that separation. Just in case . . ." I trailed off, unsure how to give voice to my worst fear. "I was seven years old the first time I met Fiona and Alexander, living with a foster family near Inverness that had three young children of their own. I remember Fiona's voice trembling as she handed me this stuffed rabbit I was too old for and said, 'Hi Juniper, you're going to come and live with us if that's all right?' And I asked, 'How long am I staying?'"

His expression splintered and I knew he understood. "The people who are meant to be in your life won't reject you for not being perfect, Juniper. If they do, they were never *your* people."

"Knowing that doesn't take away the fear." I lived in perpetual fear. Curled up and made a comfy little home out of it. "Give it a few weeks and you'll be sick of me, too."

"That's impossible." He drew me to a stop, fierce determination lining his face. "You remember what I told you the other day, about my feelings for you?" Heart thundering, I nodded. "I'm not going to push you to answer with everything going on but I need you to know – I feel like I've been sleepwalking through my life these past few years. The only bright spots in my day were you . . . I'd see that smirk and something dormant inside me sparked back to life, daring me to try and win another one."

Pausing on the path, he tenderly clutched my face between his big hands. "At the risk of sounding disgustingly cheesy, sweetheart, but even if I did grow tired of you? So what? You say a giant *fuck you* and move that gorgeous arse on to something better. *Juniper Ross* doesn't beg for anyone's love."

His forehead fell to mine. "I also know those words mean nothing if you can't see it. You need to see yourself and advocate for yourself, only then will you not give a shit when someone who isn't worth an ounce of the breath in your lungs decides they don't want to be in your life."

His words made my heart pound. "Advocate for myself like you do?" I said and he squinted, trying not to laugh. "You take responsibility for everyone around you, like it's your job to put everyone first . . . including me." *I see straight through your bullshit*, I said silently, *like you see through mine.*

His smile was so slight, so unlike his Community Ken smile, I felt like I'd earned it. "We can be a work in progress together."

I didn't know exactly what he meant by that, but I had to admit, it sounded nice. "I think I might like you, Macabe."

Forehead still pressed to mine, he laughed again. "Need a sick bag?"

I punched his shoulder. "And just like that, I'm cured."

Slinging an arm around my shoulders, he tucked me close, steering me down the path, "No takebacks, sweetheart. You. Like. Me."

I did. It was a huge fucking problem.

* * *

"I'm not getting in."

"Yes, you are."

Standing on a flat rock, I shivered and tucked my coat more tightly around me, the two-piece I'd grabbed suddenly feeling like a stupid idea. "The water looks dirty." The clear blue waves chose that moment to lap over my bare toes, calling me a liar.

"Harpy, my balls are trying to claw their way back inside my body, so do us both a favour and get that sweet arse in here." Standing at waist height in the pool, Callum slapped the water's surface to punctuate his point.

The freezing wind did a good job at distracting me from the heat his shirtless form inspired. Not to pass up an opportunity, my eyes flicked down his chest, to those ridiculous blue swim shorts and the tiny, tiny bananas. "Sounds like a *you* problem."

"Five minutes. That's all I'm asking."

Shit. I hated when he used that tone, all demanding but hopeful, like this was something he *needed* to share with me.

"Fine." I wrenched down the zip of my coat. "Don't look at me."

"Wouldn't dream of it."

I waited until he placed a hand over his eyes, took a single second to note the way the mirrored surface reflected Callum's stacked abs, admiring all twelve of them, and threw my coat over the closest rock with the rest of my clothes.

At the first curl of water around my ankle, I hissed. Callum's fingers split and he let out a low, appreciative whistle.

"You said you wouldn't look!"

"I lied." His hot gaze roamed. "Are you trying to kill me? Who wears that for wild swimming?"

The simple but stringy black bikini left very little to the imagination. "It's the only suit I have." He only grunted and I stepped in up to my calves, arms curling to conceal my small chest. "It's freezing."

"Ten more steps and I'll warm you up." He said it like the sweetest threat and damn it, I quickened my pace, cutting through the water until I was close enough to see my reflection in his eyes.

"Now what?" My teeth chattered.

"Whatever you want, that's the beauty of this place." He held his nose and ducked beneath the surface, disappearing for a heartbeat before his hand curled around my ankle and tugged. Losing my footing, I screamed, my entire body jerking from the cold as water surged over my head. Bubbles pouring from between my lips, I struck out at the first patch of skin I could find—his ribs—and resurfaced to the sound of boyish laughter. It dragged me back eight years to a night we shared pizza on Alistair's sofa and I couldn't stop myself from staring at the most carefree man I'd ever met.

I pushed matted hair from my face. "I hate you."

He traced a thumb along my lower lip. "Your nipples say otherwise, sweetheart." His attention consumed by the action, he pulled my lip down and watched it bounce back into place. It was so erotic, a little moan escaped me, and his eyes shot to mine, confirming my arousal. "I'm going to kiss you now, all right?"

"Yes." The word was a whimper.

There was no slow build-up. No customary graze of noses before the tentative learning of lips.

Seizing my cheeks, Callum's mouth enveloped mine, his fresh stubble scratching exquisitely over my skin. Wet skin slid together, my legs brushed his, lips parting to drag his tongue into my mouth, sucking on it to savour the final remnants of his laughter.

"*Fuck*," he murmured into my mouth, then dove in for another, kissing me as though he wanted to tattoo the taste of me onto his lips. "This isn't why I brought you here."

"No?"

"*No.*" He squeezed my waist. "I brought you to cheer you up."

"Mission accomplished."

"Yeah?" *Shit*, if that smile wasn't hopeful.

I nodded and his nose ran down the side of mine, ending in another toe-curling kiss, punctuated by his moan in my mouth. "I'll never get enough of this."

My arms wound around his neck, fingers fisting his hair as I said, "Good, I don't want you to." Beneath the water, his hands circled my thighs, hoisting them up and around his waist. And then we were moving, slicing through the water until my back met stone. A rushing sound filled my ears, and I had just enough of my senses left to register that he'd partially hidden us behind the waterfall, white foam rippling about our waists.

"*Juniper.*" He pulled back, eyes darting between my face and the slow, almost imperceptible roll of our hips. He shook his head, trying to snap himself free of the frenzy.

"Don't stop," I begged him, tugging on his hair, addicted to the sensation of his thick cock against my thigh.

A hand left my hip, reverently coasting over my stomach to settle beneath my breast. "So soft . . . I fucking love your skin, I've imagined telling you so many times."

"Tell me now."

He explored further, starting at the point of my chin, dragging down my throat to the little hollow there. "Your skin is perfect. Softer than silk. And you smell fucking

238

incredible, it's all I can think about when I'm near you." The words were half slurred as he fiddled with the little strap tied behind my neck.

"Undo it," I begged, head falling back against the stone.

"Don't fucking tempt me, not here." He cursed into my neck, inhaling deeply then following it up with an open-mouth kiss, his thumb brushing my nipple over the fabric.

"Please." The embarrassing plea tore from me as my hips snapped against his.

But it was his turn to moan, his forehead falling against mine. "Jesus . . . Is that what I think it is?" Too lost in the sensation, I had no idea what he was talking about until his nose brushed over the painfully tight bud. My breath caught and he slid the triangles to the side, exposing me completely.

Then he just stared at me. His expression somewhere between awed and tortured.

I knew what he was seeing. Two delicate gold bars pierced my nipples, a dainty little diamond on each end. "*Fucking hell*." His free hand scrubbed over his jaw. "When?"

I knew what he meant. "A few months after I moved back to Skye." I'd cut my hair short, but the transformation hadn't felt like enough.

"Can I touch them?"

"You better."

Air punched from my lungs as the rough pad of his finger traced one bar, then the next. His eyes – pupils swallowing the blue entirely – fixed on my face, utterly obsessed with my every breath and groan. "You're so beautiful . . . I can barely stand it." His hand trembled, thumb running along the crease where my breast met my ribs, where a string of flowers marked my skin. "And this?"

It took me a moment to answer, "That one is older . . .

239

Six or seven years." Alistair had accompanied me to the tattoo shop, wanting to hold my hand though I was an old pro at that point.

Callum exhaled, his expression was like nothing I'd ever seen on him. Serious. Filled with intent. And then his tongue was there, brushing over the raised peak in a burning sweep, pulling the bar into his mouth.

"Are they sensitive?" he husked against my skin.

"*Yes*." My eyes squeezed shut.

"I swear to god, sweetheart, the hottest thing I've seen in my entire life. Can I put my fingers in you?"

I nodded frantically, hips rolling on their own volition. How did he always know the exact right thing to say? The exact way I was feeling? Men had told me I was hot before . . . in every variation a woman could think of. But not a single one had looked at me like Callum while saying it. Like I was a goddess worthy of worship. As though the words had lived on the tip of his tongue all these years and finally speaking them aloud was the ultimate relief.

"I need you higher," he grunted, biceps curling beneath my arse. Dazed, I was slow to tuck my thighs at his ribs, bracing my back against the wall while he licked up my sternum. "So perfect."

Why was he the only one doing the touching?

Reaching around my thigh, I had to strain to palm his incredible length through his shorts. I managed a single glide of my hand before he nudged me away. "Shit! No . . . no. You can't do that." He sounded so lust-drunk, I couldn't believe he didn't want it. "We're just . . . *fuck*, we're not having sex, we're just fooling around."

"This seems very one-sided."

His hand found the band below my belly button and

traced down over the fabric. "I'll go off the second you touch me, sweetheart."

My answer was cut off by his appreciative, rumbling groan when his thumb brushed my tattoo again. "Lucky," he murmured, those clever fingers prickling like electricity over my inner thigh, then lower. I whimpered, high and loud at the first stroke of my clit.

"Touch me properly." I wanted him to pull my hair and hold me down until I screamed.

"*No*. Today we're doing this soft and sweet," he answered, gifting me with a torturous back and forth slide over the wet fabric. I bowed into the touch, pleasure skittering up my spine. "Look at me, Juniper, I've been dreaming of this for so long, I want your eyes when you come on my fingers."

The words caught on something ragged in my chest, not smoothing, but soothing. A gentle balm to an old wound. He'd thought of me. For *years* he'd thought of me. My lids cracked and I watched him, eyes all over me, damp hair falling across his forehead. He looked like a dream, blocking out the morning sun with his wide shoulders, his rock-hard length rolling against my thigh as his finger slipped beneath the bikini bottoms and inside me.

I bucked.

"I've got you," he whispered against my ear, drawing a slow circle around me before adding a second finger. Pressing deep and withdrawing at a slow, maddening pace. My body came alive beneath his, sensation flooding me until I was writhing, trapped between him and the stone.

"I'm . . . I'm close," I gasped less than a minute later. My words were laced with panic as the sensation snuck up on me.

"*Fuck*, that's it . . . that's it." His attention was wrapped to the place between my thighs where I moved on him. "Trust me, sweetheart. I've got you, I'll give you whatever you need."

It should have taken an age for me to come this way, with nothing more than his mouth on my breast, his two fingers only teasing. But the sensation of water hitting every point of my sensitive skin had me exploding with small jerks and pealing moans, my body shuddering over and over as he continued to stroke me. I couldn't be sure if I came more than once, one orgasm simply rolling into another and another, or if whatever magic he crafted with his fingers suspended time, holding me in that bliss until I was certain death waited on the other side of it.

When I finally collapsed against his chest, spent and panting, I asked the most stupid question to ever pass my lips. "Do you need to come?" Of course he did, his teeth were gritted, his entire body trembling with the force of holding back.

He nodded desperately, hands opening and closing on my hips. "Can I?"

Consumed with the need to see him lose control, I tore at the ties of his shorts. "You said you think of me, show me how."

With a barked curse, his urgent fingers joined mine and he swore again as we knotted the strings tighter.

"Fuck it." He yanked the waistband down enough so only his gorgeous cock slid free, standing proud and hard against his stomach. I didn't even manage to drag my thumb across the tip before he snatched my hand away with a shudder. The tips of his cheeks stained red and he shook his head, like his eagerness embarrassed him. "I'm losing my mind. If I get inside you this is over, I'm not wasting our first fuck on this."

"But I want to—"

"Not this time. I just want to look at you." Scooping both of my hands in one of his, he held them above my head. The other he curled over my breast, thumb flicking over the piercing until it was almost raw as he pressed between my spread thighs and lodged his cock against my clit. "I've had a long time to think about it, have so many plans for our first time, sweetheart." He rolled his hips, words sharpening into grunts. "Every one includes fucking you so long and slow, you can't remember your own name."

Despite the desperate tremor to his voice, every slide of his body against mine was unhurried. Measured. His mouth dropped open, leaving him slack-jawed as his attention pinged from my face to my breasts to my half-concealed pussy.

"Fuck . . . that feels unreal. All this time I knew you'd have the hottest little body, harpy. But you're something else—" Unable to hold back my whimper, I arched my back, letting him see all of it. "Keep your eyes on me and bite your lower lip, give me that pissed off expression that gets me off."

I complied, glancing up at him with a little smirk. His arms tensed around me.

"*Fuck*, yes. Just like that," he choked, pace faltering then picking up speed as he slid over my pussy again and again.

He was using my body to get himself off and it was the hottest thing I'd ever encountered. I found myself moaning, thrusting every time he did, driving him higher and higher. The fact I wasn't even touching him only made me feel more powerful. Control wore many faces – and I knew without a doubt I controlled every moment of this.

He looked like a man possessed, gasping and snarling, thrusting against my body like he owned it. He'd gone from seeing to *my* every need to selfishly taking his. "Juniper . . . Juniper. *Fuck* – can I come on your stomach?"

I nodded eagerly, barely hissing my agreement when he did exactly that.

He mouthed my name while he came. Wide, glassy eyes finding mine, as though the pleasure took him by surprise and he needed to be sure I was right there with him.

And I knew then, this went far beyond *fooling around*.

This was the promise of him and me. The promise of something more. And though I didn't quite know what that *more* looked like, I broke his hold to wrap my arms around his neck and held on for dear life.

24

Callum

Google search: Does defiling a historic site come with prison time?

Just as it had in biblical times (probably), the second my cum cooled against her skin, the rain started. It disturbed the pool's glassy surface, turning it from a clear blue to grey as it lashed in icy sheets. Juniper half screamed, half laughed, her body squirming and sticking to my chest as she fought to escape the chill.

Breathless and dazed, I pressed a kiss to her sweaty forehead, dragging her bikini top back into place. All but pouting at the loss as I swiped a wet hand down her stomach to wash away the stringy white mess.

"I'm fairly sure what we just did counts as sacrilege." She shivered and bit her lip.

"Aye." It was the closest thing to a religious experience I'd ever encountered. I could barely even speak as I dragged her from the water, half expecting to find felled trees and crumbling stone. *Did that really just happen?* It seemed unlikely, and yet my half-sated cock was admirably fighting against the cold, begging for another round.

Wrapping the thick towel around her shoulders, I chafed her arms until her teeth eased chattering. The rain poured, no sign of letting up. "Get dressed. We'll have to run for the car."

She nodded, saying no more as she shoved her legs into her jeans without removing her bikini. I hurried too, clothes sticking and chafing in all the worst places. Forgoing my thick, knitted scarf, I wrapped it around Juniper's waist, using it to lasso her closer before tucking it around the dripping ends of her hair and knotting it below her chin. *Fuck*, her lips were turning blue. "Ready? Careful on the rocks, they'll be slick."

She nodded hastily, accepting my outstretched hand as I slung both our bags over my shoulder and urged her onto the path, lifting her over a burn that had broken its bank and up the hill.

"What the hell is happening?" Juniper yelled over the roar of water, eyes on her feet as we picked our way between slippery rocks. The clouds had gone from grey to a menacing black. The waterfalls rushed as though trying to escape an enemy, spitting white foam. "Did you know there was a storm coming?"

The weather on Skye could turn at the drop of a hat, sometimes offering up four seasons in a single day. *This* was another beast entirely. "No." Not that I'd actually bothered to check, I'd been too eager to get a few hours alone with her. I was no better than a damn tourist, ill-prepared for Scotland's wild nature.

I gripped her hand tighter. "Almost there, I can see the car." The single vehicle in the large car park sat like a lighthouse in a stormy sea.

I unlocked the car before we reached it, yanking open the passenger door and lifting Juniper inside by the waist then racing around to the driver's side. "Are you all right?" Throwing myself in, I cranked the heat until it blasted from every vent.

Water gathered on her eyelashes before snaking down her cheeks. "I might lose my fingers, but otherwise fine." Laughing, she held her red digits aloft. I brought them to the vent, rubbing my own stiff fingers over them while she winced.

I felt like shit. "It would have been a fine idea to check the weather."

"Probably." But her tone was light and there was a flush to her cheeks, a thrill sparkling in her eyes. "You seem to have a knack for leaving me soaking wet."

I spluttered. These dates always seemed to end in disaster. If I'd hoped to impress her, I'd failed spectacularly. "I wish I could say it was always intentional."

"But fun nonetheless." Surprised, my attention shot from her elegant fingers, still clasped in mine, to her face, her lips. A part of me expected her to regret what happened in the pool, explaining it away as a moment of madness.

"Can I kiss you again?" she asked shyly. My stomach just about dropped out my arse. After all that had happened, hearing that from her felt like diving off a cliff edge.

I nodded mutely and she moved, relief making the moment that much sweeter as her fingers sank into my wet hair. And all I could think was, *Please don't break my heart*.

Her lips were thorough, moving with surprising gentleness, like she was drinking from my mouth. It took me a moment to catch up, but when I did, I pushed for more. Nibbling and then biting down on her bottom lip hard enough to make her hiss.

I could have had her here. Beneath the blanket of rain, no one would ever know. But she shivered and I choked down my desire. "We should get you home."

* * *

"You're acting weird."

I frowned at the marble counter in my kitchen, pushing the mug of tea to where Juniper sat on the stool on the other side. Her hair had dried in chaotic curls by the time we'd pulled up outside my cottage. She'd cringed at the sight in my hall mirror, attempting to finger comb them into submission until I told her in no uncertain terms, "*I fucking love your hair like that.*"

She'd flipped me the finger, but I'd also noticed she'd ceased taming the ringlets. That was good with me. A little imperfection suited Juniper just fine.

"I might be acting a little weird," I conceded, filling my own mug with boiling water. I was pushing my luck, was what I was doing. Somehow during the thirty-minute drive back to Kinleith I'd managed to tempt her into my cottage for a drink before her afternoon shift at Ivy House.

Tea.

That would be the extent of it, I'd promised myself. Tea and conversation.

Juniper had the startling ability to make me lose all common sense the moment I got within ten feet of her. She'd given me free rein of her body back at the fairy pools, I knew it cost her something to trust I would give us *both* what we needed. But I wanted more than trust over her pleasure.

I wanted her to trust me with her heart.

Trust that every cheesy word out of my mouth was more than lines to get her into bed.

So . . . Tea. That trust would begin with tea.

"Do you have a favourite movie?"

She looked at me like I'd grown a second head. "Not really."

Great start. "Season?"

"Spring."

"Sport?"

She blew on her tea. "I hate sports."

Yeah. I'd known that one. "Dream job as a kid?"

"Vampire." Her brow flicked up. "Do these questions have a purpose beyond hacking my online banking?"

I sighed. "We're getting to know each other."

"Oh, then please continue." She swung a knee over the other, settling in. "I can't wait to tell you my favourite sexual position."

Struck stupid. My mouth opened then closed. "What's your favourite— *No*—" I held up my hands, backing away until my hip hit the counter. "I don't want to know. This is a non-sexual discussion."

Her teeth flashed. "It's a good one."

Fuck. I broke like a twig beneath her boot. Rounding the kitchen island to haul her into my arms. "Tell me."

The command had barely passed my lips when my phone lit up. The camera at the front door picking up movement. I flicked open the app and Alistair's face filled the screen. Hood up, water ran off his dark green raincoat in rivulets.

My breath caught. Bringing a finger to my lips, I turned the phone for Juniper to see. The widening of her dark eyes was her only outward reaction. The tip of the iceberg, I knew.

Alistair knocked. "Callum, open up! It's pissing down." His voice filtered down the hall.

I'd left the door unlocked. We had mere seconds until he

discovered that for himself. Still clasped together, we stared one another out, like a fucking game of chicken.

The handle rattled.

Neither of us blinked.

The door creaked.

Juniper smirked.

Boots hit the tile in the porch.

My fingers dug into her arse.

"Callum?"

I broke. Scooping her into my arms, I threw her over my shoulder, striding quickly through the door at the back of the kitchen, leading to my bedroom and home office. Her victorious laugh was muffled, teasing and hot against my neck. Inside my bedroom, I set her down, pressing her to the wall beside the door. "Think you can keep quiet, harpy?"

"Cal?" His voice came from the kitchen.

"If given the right motivation." *This woman.* No matter how messy the situation, those words sent a thrill straight to my cock. My hand hit the wall, lips crashing to hers, tasting her like it might be the last time. She met me with near startling urgency. Tongue delved between my lips, caressing, until my hands tangled beneath her shirt.

No more than a second could have passed when she urged me away. "You have to go."

"Aye." I kissed her again.

She laughed into my mouth. "*Go.*"

"Stay here." Tucking my raging erection against my fly, I kissed her forehead one last time then slapped her arse, urging her toward my bed. "Go roll around in my sheets, I want them to smell like you."

25

Juniper

Surprise. I didn't wait there.

Back pressed to the wall beside a series of black and white prints of Skye's moody landscape that I'd very much like to hang in my own home, I listened to the brothers move about the kitchen.

"Sorry." Callum sounded out of breath. "I was . . . just about to climb in the shower when I heard you." I cringed at his words. How it would pain him to lie to his brother.

"Why are you all wet?" Alistair's familiar clip cut straight to the point.

"I went for a hike this morning. Got caught in the downpour." Cups clacked and I knew Callum was tidying away the evidence of my visit.

"I thought you were going to Portree," Alistair said and I could picture the little "problem-solving" indent he always got between his brows.

"I did. And then I went for a hike. What are you doing here?"

"I dropped by to see Juniper." My heart stalled, one beat

stretching into another. As did the silence from the next room.

"*Oh?*" Callum reached for casual and failed. "She wasn't in?" *Bloody hell.* Hadn't I accused him of being a very skilled liar only days ago? I might as well have opened the door and announced myself.

"Ada said she'd be back this afternoon." *Damn Ada.* I need to have a word with her about handing out that kind of information.

"I thought you were giving her time." Tension oozed in Callum's words. He almost sounded jealous.

"*I did.*"

I couldn't contain my snort. *One bloody day.*

"One day hardly signifies." My thoughts and Callum's biting words went hand in hand. "You wait for her to come to you. I mean it, Alistair. She's earned that right." Trying to picture the menacing look on Callum's face, I let my eyes flutter shut, fingers flying to my racing heart. *Calm down, heart*, I warned the cold, shrivelled organ threatening to take flight beneath my ribs. *Don't be hasty.*

The only bright spots in my day were you. The memory of those words only made my heart beat more furiously, like a warm fist had wrapped around it, melting it's icy shell.

My back slid down the wall.

Juniper Ross does not beg for anyone's love. But I might. One more hour in his sunshine presence and I might just beg for his.

Tucking my knees to my chest, the words, *Danger! Danger!*, flashed like sirens behind my lids.

Loving Alistair had been easy. And still it had broken me. I'd *allowed* it to break me.

I'd turned him into a monster in my head. An ogre to blame all my unhappiness upon. I still wasn't ready to forgive him, but I was clear-sighted enough to see that the blame didn't lie *entirely* at his door.

This thing with Callum wasn't love . . . not yet. It was worse – it was hope.

Shit.

I scrubbed my hands through my still damp hair, a memory rising of Alexander – my dad – in the last days of his life. *It's all pain in the end, wee one, might as well make the journey worth it.*

Even back then he'd been trying to warn me, as if he could see the wall I'd erected around myself. Knowing his death would lay the final brick.

"How's Dad today?" Callum's voice filtered through the crack in the doorway and I knew it was time to remove myself. Rising on shaky legs, I scrawled a note, placed it atop his pillow and climbed out his bedroom window.

26

Juniper

Juniper: Left my bra under your pillow. It's green today.
Callum: Did you really?
Voice note from Callum: You're a fucking tease, harpy.
Juniper: Ha! Not even thirty seconds between messages.
Did you run?
Callum: I'm fast when properly motivated.
Juniper: I know ;)

"What did you do to my cat?" Toothbrush in hand, I watched Shakespeare and Callum from my bathroom doorway. Shakespeare, sensing the attention, flipped onto her back and stretched out her demon legs, allowing his unscathed fingers to coast down her belly. *Outrageous.* Where was the hissing? The bloodshed? "She looks high!"

"I've been known to have that effect on the ladies," he said at the same moment Shakespeare purred, further proving his point.

"She makes that sound after I give her catnip."

"No drugging necessary, some women actually enjoy my company." He shot me a lazy smile, his hair slightly flattened at the back from where it had squished against the sofa cushions. Other than a couple of flirty texts, we hadn't spoken all day after our interruption from Alistair, unusual for Callum whose text messages, I was coming to learn, usually came as thick and fast as his thoughts.

I'd grown so twitchy Ada started to fret over the woodworm "infestation" again. I'd eventually shoved my phone in the desk drawer and vowed not to think of his irritatingly handsome face for the rest of the day.

The reinstation of the Macabe brother rule book only lasted a few hours because, at the end of my shift, as I slipped out the back door to walk the fifty yards to my cottage, a husky voice whispered, "Can I walk you home?"

It was late, but I invited Callum in to watch a movie anyway. Though he had an early start at the surgery, he said yes.

Curled beneath a blanket, Shakespeare forming a dangerous wedge between us, we'd watched a nineties action film in companionable silence, Callum's breaths coming so steadily I thought he'd fallen asleep until he reached over and laced his fingers with mine, pulling them beneath the blanket to rest atop his thigh.

It was past midnight now, the credits rolling silently on the screen. Callum had made no move to leave and though I knew what this thing between us was building to – what I wanted it to build to – I hesitated, taking time to layer on almost every toner, moisturiser and night cream I owned until my face looked like I'd done an hour of hot yoga. I'd break out tomorrow and it would be my own cowardly fault.

"You've been in there a long time," he said, turning my

favourite skull-shaped mug in his hands. His smile a lovely line between charming and timid.

"I . . . *uh*. I have a very thorough flossing routine."

One brow rose at my utter stupidity. "Is that so? Talk me through it."

"It's a whole thing," I waved a hand as he stood. "It doesn't matter."

"But I'm fascinated."

"By my floss routine?"

"By everything." He came a step closer, halting when I mirrored the action and bumped into the bathroom door. "*You're nervous*." He said it like an impossibility. The way a person might say, *Renesmee is an amazing choice for a baby name*.

"This is new territory for me." I admitted.

He nodded, grasping what I meant without explanation. "Me too."

The confession only managed to thicken the tension so I beelined for the bed, more than ready for the release we both needed. "Bathroom's yours."

He returned before I'd even fully unbuttoned my shirt. Kneeling above me, he caught my wrists, pinning them to my sides. "*What are you doing?*"

"Taking my shirt off. Isn't that why you came here?"

"No." Eyes screwed tight, his head fell to my shoulder. "*Fuck no.*"

"Umm . . . *ouch?*"

"I didn't mean it like that and you know it." Pulling back, his gaze roamed me hungrily. Hands still secured in his, my shirt agape, barely covering my nipples. "*Fuck*, Juniper." He released me, rebuttoning it with clumsy fingers. "I came here to tell you we should take things slow . . . but I didn't know you'd look like *this*."

256

"I'm wearing pyjamas."

"Exactly." A muscle in his jaw jumped. "I've never seen you this way. It's doing all sorts of things for my domestic fantasies."

Domestic fantasies? I laughed, "Do I even want to know?"

Falling back onto his heels, he scrubbed a hand over his bristled jaw. "On the threat of you discovering how thoroughly I'm obsessed with you? Probably not."

"Now you *have* to tell me . . . my brain's conjuring up all sorts of *Stepford-Wives*-esque movie montages." I mock shuddered. "It's all '*Have a good day at work, dear*' and floral dresses . . . I look terrible in florals. Do you want me to meet you at the door at five p.m. with a plate of freshly baked mini muffins? Because that's where I draw the line." When he didn't even laugh, I poked him with my bare foot. He caught it, pulling it into his lap. "Tell me."

"You're a bloody menace, woman." He sighed. "Lie on your side, I'll show you." I complied, flicking a saucy look over my shoulder when he settled behind me. "Mind out of the gutter, harpy. Look at the wall."

"Bossy," I said, even as a little thrill shot through me at this side of him I didn't glimpse often.

"For tonight, I'm in charge." Scooching in, his front met my back, my arse curling into his lap and *hello* . . . a very thick, very hard cock pressed back. I wriggled against it, unable to stem the instinct. Callum only curled his arm around my waist, clutching me to him until our chests rose and fell together. "*This*," he whispered into my hair, voice so damn rough. "This is my favourite fantasy – where I just hold you."

"Nothing else?" My tone called bullshit.

"*Nothing else.*"

"Why?" I practically exhaled the word, his meaning

entirely lost on me. Men never wanted to go slow with me. Usually they hit fast forward to the ending.

"Because when something matters, you take your time with it."

His meaning scorched through my veins: *You matter, Juniper.* "So we're not having sex?"

His soft kiss to the back of my neck made my eyes burn. "Not yet, sweetheart."

"When?"

I expected him to laugh. Instead, he kissed my pulse. "When you trust that I'm in this." A squeeze at my hip. "When I'm certain you're comfortable with the idea of us."

Us. We were an *us.*

Us hadn't worked out well for me, not ever.

Suddenly feeling like an exposed nerve ending, I closed my eyes, brain resetting to fight or flight mode as I reached for the cold pillow. "You shouldn't stay the night."

"I don't remember setting those parameters." Before I could argue further he flipped me onto my front, his muscled arm curling between my legs, cupping an entire cheek of arse and leveraging me half onto his chest like I was a five-pound cat and not a fully grown human.

Getting comfortable, strong arms banded around me, his nose pressing into my hair and breathing deep. *He's snuggling me.* Deep down, in a dusty little part of my heart I'd locked away, was a woman who craved being cherished and somehow he'd figured that out.

If only I could turn my brain off. "Are you taking things slow because of Alistair?"

He cupped the back of my neck, thumb rubbing in a slow circle. "No." Another circle. "I hate keeping secrets, so I'd prefer to tell him. But you're in charge here. We tell him when you're ready."

"Why am I in charge? You should get a say, too."

"Because I'm already there, Juniper. I'm sorry if that freaks you out, but, *hell* – one word from you and I'll announce it with a bell on the high street like the fucking town crier."

"A bell?" Smiling into his T-shirt, I snuggled in a little bit more.

"*Yes*, a bell," he snarled, the un-Callum-like sound reverberating in his chest as he released me only long enough to turn off the lamp. "Now go to sleep before my self-control completely shreds to pieces."

"Yes, sir." He slapped my arse, so I pinched his nipple, making him grunt. "Callum?"

"Aye?" His hand rubbed up and down my back.

"I like you." I held my breath while his body pulled taut then softened beneath mine.

"I like you too, sweetheart."

27

Callum

"It's me!" I called. Kicking off my boots in Juniper's hall-way. I lined them neatly beside her heeled ones, as I had every day for the past two weeks since our date at the fairy pools – since we decided to take things slow – and followed the scent of burned toast until I found her in the kitchen. Her fringe fell into her eyes as she scowled at a sizzling saucepan. Condiments and open jars lined every inch of the countertop. "Everything okay?"

She looked fucking pretty today, a tight T-shirt tucked into jeans that made her legs look a mile long. Gold clips held back the top half of her hair. "I'm cooking for you." Sauce spat and smoked. "*Shit*." She whirled, flipping down the heat. Her nose wrinkled. "Attempting to, anyway – this is a bloody mess."

If I'd thought it impossible to be any more addicted to Juniper Ross, I was wrong. After holding her in my arms almost every night for two weeks, I'd become utterly obsessed.

Consumed.

She was officially, unofficially, mine. Not that I'd ever say those words aloud to Juniper. I could wait for her to come to that conclusion all by herself. She would . . . *eventually*, and I'd be right there to comfort her then remind her how incredible we were together. Because we were fucking *incredible* together. Cloistered away in her cottage, a perfect little bubble that threatened to burst every day we kept this from Alistair.

A weird taste filled my mouth every time I considered it.

It wasn't guilt, the flavour was far too sweet for that. It was more like . . . unease.

Jealousy.

Every time he asked about her or his name appeared on her phone, it grew.

Juniper and Alistair's history dictated he deserved to hear it from me, but Juniper held every scrap of my loyalty. Until she gave me the green light, my lips were sealed. When Alistair learned the truth, I'd take the full brunt of his anger and then happily remind him he didn't get to have it both ways. He couldn't break things off only to have a say who she moved on with.

Until then I'd continue to be selfish with her, seizing any scrap of time she offered.

True to my word, we'd kept things purely PG. Making out on her sofa like teenagers with Meg Ryan's full filmography playing in the background. There was that one time I made her come on my thigh. It had been glorious and purely accidental. Juniper had been just as stunned as me as she screamed out her release. Turned on to the point of no return, I'd swiftly excused myself to stroke one out in her bathroom, surrounded by bottles of perfume and body lotion that smelled just like her.

Well aware of my crisis, Juniper had hovered outside

the door, teasingly offering encouragement. Barely uttering the words, "*Want me to choke on it, big boy?*" before I exploded with a hoarse cry.

Quickly setting myself to rights, I'd wrenched open the door to find her biting her lip, a playful gleam in her eyes. "Never call me *big boy* again," I'd growled, carrying her back to the sofa, past the tempting bed only feet away.

When things got hot between us, I didn't stray from that sofa. If I got her beneath me on a bed, I'd be fucking done for.

Curling an arm around her waist, I glanced over her shoulder at the brown mushy concoction and asked hesitantly, "What is it?"

The spoon clattered as she threw it down. "It was supposed to be falafel."

"It looks more like haggis." I teased. Her scowl deepened and I eased the pan from her grip, gave it a stir before adding a little more oil. "Why the sudden urge to cook?" She'd eat cereal for every meal if she could get away with it.

"Because you've cooked for me every night this week."

I set the pot back on the burner, lowering the heat. "Because I like cooking for you."

Her hands flew to her hips. "Maybe I was enjoying cooking for you."

"Were you?"

"*No!* I bloody hate it." She rubbed at her temples.

Laughing – I was doing that a lot these days – I lifted her by the hips – something I'd discovered she loved because it made her feel delicate – and set her down on the counter amongst the condiments. Like this, she was a head taller than me. "Then don't cook. We'll order pizza."

Not needing to be told twice, she pulled up the only pizza place in the village on her phone. "Where did you learn to cook, anyway?"

"The army, they train you to be pretty self-sufficient. Not the . . . what was it you called me? *A man baby who hires help to do their laundry.*"

"That was like, seven years ago. I can't believe you remember that."

I pinched her waist. "I remember everything you say."

Her dark eyes scanned my face, weighing the words. When she didn't say anything, I brushed a finger along the crease of her elbow, frowning at the fresh welt from Shakespeare. "Did you wash this out?"

She nodded as I pressed my lips to the sore spot. Her hand raked into my hair, so fucking tender, I swore I'd spent the last weeks in the twilight zone. That was the only explanation. No one got this lucky.

Planting a hand on the counter, I noticed a pile of haphazardly stacked books. Expecting cookery recipes, I slid the spines to face me.

The Truth About Dementia
What No One Tells You About Dementia
How to Support a Caregiver

I read the titles three times, feeling like someone just punched a hole through my chest. "Where did you get these?"

"The library."

"Why?" Deep down, I think I knew why. I needed to hear it anyway.

Her eyes bounced between mine, evaluating the precipice her next words might pitch her over. "Because I want to be there for you."

What else was there to say?

I spoke my thanks onto her lips, making certain she tasted every shred of gratitude before I dipped to her jaw. Her throat. I couldn't resist hiking her T-shirt up and pressing my lips to the curling tattoo on her rib cage. *Too good for me*, I thought, *Too sweet*.

I was about to speak the sentiment out loud when her fingers tugged my hair. "We need to take the pizza to go, I have a surprise for you."

28

Juniper

Juniper: Enough about work, tell me about the cruise. How's the weather?

Juniper: Actually, screw the weather. I want to know about the men . . . Is there anyone you like? Are you finally getting some?

Fiona: You're as bad as your aunt.

Juniper: Sylvia knows how to have fun. Don't avoid the question!

Fiona: A lady doesn't kiss and tell.

Juniper: That means yes.

"Is the shower leaking again?" Callum's fingers clasped tightly in mine as we crept up the stairs of Ivy House. In the other he held the steaming pizza box.

"Nope. It seems you actually do great work . . . for a cowboy."

"You're a cruel woman, harpy." That hand went to my waist, halting my first step on the landing, voice curling at my ear. "Turnabout will be fair play once I get you riding me."

Jesus. I didn't know how we'd lasted this long. I hadn't so much as touched a man for almost a year before this thing with Callum and I'd been fine. A little *tightly wound*, but fine.

Suddenly sex – *sex with him* – I couldn't think of anything else.

Slow. I repeated the word to myself. The word that had become akin to a talisman to Callum this week, whenever things progressed just a little too close to the point of no return.

It was his boundary, and I respected it.

"When I'm riding you, *Macabe*, this little argument will be the furthest thing from your mind. Now shut up before you wake someone." I unlocked room five, not bothering to flick on the light.

He made it two steps inside. Then stopped. "What's all this?"

I closed the door behind us, so only the spill of moonlight from the open curtains and the golden warmth of the fairy lights I'd dug out of the Christmas box shone between us. "I thought it was about time I took you on a date."

I suddenly felt silly, as he quietly tracked my efforts at a romantic gesture, from the neatly made bed to the mound of plaids circled by unlit candles on the floor before the window. Seemingly forgetting the pizza, his arms went limp at his sides and the slices slid across the box with a wet scratch.

He hated it.

"I meant to come up and light the candles but you distracted me," I said quickly. "And I can grab more blankets if it's not warm enough." His throat only bobbed so I kicked off my shoes, stepping onto the soft plaids. "Look, we can do something else if this is terrible—"

"It's not." His eyes shone. "I just – I have the stupidest urge to cry."

My heart thumped, tasting the sweetness of this moment I would return to over and over until the edges began to smudge, when Callum Macabe looked at me as if I were made of starlight. "Then cry."

Eyes shining, he, nodding to my socked feet burrowing into the blanket. "That's something I always liked about you, you know."

"My ability to plan a cheap date?" I waited for him to sit then spread another blanket over our laps.

"*No*. That one of the first things you do anywhere is take your shoes off." It was a quirk few people noticed. Alexander always said it was because I could make myself at home anywhere, but I always felt it was the opposite, that it helped curb my desire to run.

Beneath the blanket, Callum tugged my legs over his lap, running a thumb along the arch of my foot again with exquisite pressure. "For a woman who apparently hates nature you're definitely the bare-feet-in-the-grass type." He repeated the action, and I couldn't hold back my moan. "Every time I'd see these black-painted little toes, I had to fight the urge to bite every single one of them."

"A foot fetish? I didn't peg you as a deviant."

"More like a Juniper Ross fetish." His head tipped, and he nipped at my jaw, nose skimming until it rested at the small birthmark at the base of my neck. "This little mark I only ever got to see when the weather was warm enough for you to wear a strappy little top. Did you never catch me searching for it?" I shook my head. "How about your mouth?" His fingers traced my lips and they tingled as though touched by electricity. "Every time you spoke; ate;

smiled; you had me, sweetheart, you had me right in the palm of your hand and I didn't even try to hide it."

The confession blew me apart, I needed him to kiss me, needed him under me and – and because he could read me like a book – he went right back to rubbing my feet. Torturing me with every touch.

I flopped back into the cushions.

"Are you going to tell me what's been going on with you?" My eyes sprang open and he continued, "You were quiet this morning. And last night."

"Lubing me up with foot rubs is coercion."

His nose wrinkled. "Please never use the term 'lubing me up' out of the house."

"Too graphic?" I grinned.

"What do you think?" He tugged my foot further into his lap so I could feel just how graphic he found it. "Now tell me."

I hesitated, biting my lip. "It seems stupid."

"If it's upsetting you, it isn't stupid."

I blew out a breath, "Fiona hasn't called in over a week, she always calls."

His thumbs didn't stop their ministrations. "Why don't you phone her?"

"Because as soon as I talk to her I'll have to confess everything. I guess it's finally dawning on me that she'll be back soon, and she might not be happy with what she finds."

"Have you considered that maybe she hasn't called because, instead of worrying, she's using her time away to let loose, exactly like you hoped she would?"

"You think?"

He shrugged, hands tightening around my foot. "As much as you needed to know that you can manage this place alone, she probably needs to discover that there's still a life for her outside of Ivy House."

We lapsed into silence as I pondered that. I'd spent so long thinking of the inn and Kinleith as some kind of self-exiled prison, I'd never once stopped to consider if Fiona felt the same. Was she clinging to the past so tightly because she feared letting go without the promise of something to catch her?

"I don't know her like you do, sweetheart. But I *do* know that you were really fucking brave, you took a risk and worked your arse off to make it happen. There isn't a chance in hell Fiona will walk into this room and not see the love and dedication you've poured into every inch of it."

"*Bloody hell.* You're irritatingly sweet sometimes. No wonder every woman on this island melts for you."

He laughed, sinking down beside me until we were eye level. "Melts for me? Who might that be?"

"Who do you think? Jill Mortimer." My nose screwed. "Just the thought of her curves and all that blonde hair makes *me* want to date her."

Callum looked delighted. "*Oh*, I get it now."

"What?"

"This . . ." He waved a hand. "Seeing you jealous is a lot of fun."

"I'm not jealous!"

Eyes dancing, he crawled over me. "You are so fucking jealous. It's cute. If it makes you feel better, I've been there . . . a lot."

I bypassed that little confession and said, "A man hasn't called me cute in my entire life."

"Idiots. The lot of them." He parted my thighs with a knee and lowered between them. "You're exceedingly cute. *Especially* when you're jealous."

"*I'm not jealous.*"

He pecked a kiss to my throat, then a second to my pulse. "Did you write about it in your diary? Burn pictures of my face on a blood moon?"

"*Fuck off*, Macabe."

He barked a laugh. "Back to Macabe, are we?"

"Yes!" Feeling way too vulnerable, I folded my arms over my face, shielding my expression.

"Juniper, sweetheart . . ." His face burrowed into my chest, allowing me the privacy I needed. "Nothing ever happened with Jill. Unless you count a drunken kiss when I was sixteen . . . which I don't."

My body, just on the cusp of relaxing, stiffened all over again and I was glad I couldn't see his face as I spat, "That counts."

His fingers brushed up my waist. "Then I feel pretty shitty because it was my first kiss and I'd downed an entire bottle of cheap cider five minutes earlier, which I proceeded to throw up all over her shoes the second it ended. Not exactly my finest moment."

I dropped my hands, meeting his steady gaze. "I'm sorry. I'm a child."

"You're human. You think I don't want to tear the balls from every man you've ever been with? Because I do. And I've had copious amounts of time to imagine exactly how I'd do it."

"How?"

He bared his teeth. "*Viciously.*"

"Painfully?" My legs tightened around his hips.

"*Jesus*, you're a bloodthirsty little demon, anyone ever tell you that?"

"Frequently."

His hands dove into my hair, forcing me to hold his stare.

"And just so we're crystal fucking clear. There's been no one else . . . not since I broke up with Beth."

Beth. I remembered the kind brunette. A school teacher he'd dated for a few brief months after Alistair and I got engaged. "Why?"

"There's nothing more lonely than a relationship with the wrong person."

My chest tightened. "So you're saying you want the full Juniper Ross experience?"

He brushed my hair back, eyes dancing. "Unequivocally. What does that entail exactly?"

"Well . . ." My hands flicked nervously over the blanket's trim. "Demon cats to start with."

"Perfect." His thumb stroked my earlobe. "What else?"

"Mercurial moods," I said.

"Mercurial moods happen to be my favourite kind of moods."

"How long?" I asked.

I knew he understood my vague question, because his fingers stilled. Then he rolled onto his side, drawing me after him until my back was to his chest, pulling the blanket over us until only our heads poked out the top, like we needed to be comfortable for this confession. "From the very start. The first moment I saw you on the station platform."

"*Wait* . . . the platform. You mean on the train?"

"No. I noticed you through the window while I was running down the platform. I couldn't say why at the time, but something pulled me to you before my brain could even catch up."

I stroked the back of his arm, enjoying the picture he painted. "What did you think when you sat down?"

I felt his chuckle against my back. "That you were too young for me."

"Still true."

He pinched my waist. "I thought . . . you were beautiful and brilliant and so damn intriguing I couldn't let you walk away from me at the other end."

It was fucked up. But I heard his sweet words and didn't know how to associate myself with the picture he painted.

"What?" he asked eventually, my silence bringing his head up.

"I don't know . . . It's just hard for me to believe, I guess."

"That someone would think that about you?"

"*Yes.*" The admission felt loud in the quiet room. "You just seemed so flirty and confident, I thought it was all a joke to you. That's why I didn't tell you who I was right away, I wanted to beat you at your own game."

He groaned, pressing rapid kisses to my neck. "What you must have thought of me."

I tipped my head back. "I thought you were funny and too attractive. Even if I was in love with your brother." He stiffened and I grabbed his arm before he could pull away. "I'm sorry—" We hadn't discussed Alistair since that first night. Like a coward, I was waiting for him to broach the subject.

"Don't apologise." I felt his slow sigh. "I never blamed you for loving Alistair. I was jealous as hell, but I never blamed you. And when it ended . . . I blamed *him.*"

I picked at a loose thread on the blanket. "I thought you were happy because I wasn't good enough for him."

"You are *everything*, Juniper. I can't believe I'm going to say this, because it's in my interest *not* to . . . I hate even thinking it, but, it was real for him, sweetheart. I don't know all the gory details of what went down between you, but however it ended, his heart broke too." The knowledge was a balm I hadn't known I needed. And yet I felt nothing but an absent sort of ache for Alistair as another truth locked firmly into place. A far scarier one because it meant putting my heart on the line all over again.

His hands tightened around me, like he intended to keep me. "I was thinking. The ceilidh at the distillery next week . . . Maybe we could use it as a soft launch."

"What's a soft launch?"

He played with the ends of my hair, the only sign that he was nervous. "We share a few dances, let people see us talking – I obviously won't be able to take my eyes off you – a soft launch."

"So we'd let people know we're together. Like together, *together*?"

"Yes, together, together. I can ask on a slip of paper if you like, circle A for yes, B for no."

"Arse." I reached back to pinch his thigh. He flinched, laughing hard against my nape. "Now I'm definitely not going."

"You offered the full Juniper Ross experience and I'm cashing it in."

"People will gossip," I reminded him, more nervous for him than for me, he had far more to lose and not just with his family. Some people in Kinleith had old-fashioned views; dating his brother's ex-fiancée hardly gave off the "respected member of the community" vibes he'd perfected.

"I couldn't give a shit. We tell the people who matter, everyone else can go to hell."

His steely resolve made my chest loosen. "Fine."

"*Fine*? That's all I get? Fine? I'm glad time spent with me is so appealing."

"I can still change my mind."

"Nope. No take-backs." He pulled me tight to him, humming his pleasure.

We were doing this. I suddenly felt ill.

"We need to tell Alistair," I said. I'd known we couldn't stay in this little bubble forever, but I'd hoped we'd get a few more weeks.

I tried to imagine Callum and I holding hands as we walked down the high street. Sitting across from Alistair at Macabe family dinners. A dream that still felt out of reach.

It was the green light he'd been waiting for, but his pause felt hesitant. "I know. I don't want to ruin Mal and April's night, so I'll tell him after the party. He should hear it from me."

I batted the worry to the back of my mind, settling against the crook of his arm as we stared at the glittering sky outside the large open window and said, "Is this why you brought me up here? A smart move on your part. A target is more vulnerable half frozen to death."

"Evil wee harpy," he tsked, but rearranged our bodies until his leg hooked over mine. "You brought me here, remember? And I didn't even get to eat the pizza . . . I'm beginning to think it's so you could have your wicked way with me."

Very tempting, but that wasn't why I'd planned this. "Be patient, you'll see."

We didn't have to wait long.

29

Callum

Isle of Skye Guidebook

In Scottish Gaelic folklore, the Northern Lights are known as *Na Fir Chlis* – "The nimble men". On the Isles you might hear them referred to as the "Mirrie Dancers", for the amazing natural phenomenon appears to dance across the sky. The best months to spot the Northern Lights on Skye are around the equinoxes: March, September and October.

"There it is, look—" Juniper gently shook my shoulder just as I started to nod off.

Blinking, I pushed onto an elbow. "Is that—"

"Yep."

The thin curtains billowed in the slight breeze and we both stared in wonder. As if the late hour had thinned a veil between this world and the next. An ethereal pathway suddenly winked across the sky. Light branching off in a hundred different directions. Bold greens and pinks and purples seemed to shimmer, so close Juniper reached out a hand, tracing the dazzling shapes as if to touch them.

"This is . . ." My voice was as embarrassingly wet as my eyes. "For the first time in my life I have no words."

"Me neither." She sounded small. Humbled.

"How did you know about this?"

"Ada has an Aurora Borealis app. She got an alert this afternoon."

Skye had such little light pollution I'd been lucky enough to see them a few times before . . . but never with another person. *The* person.

After a minute Juniper pinched my chin, urging me to face her. I couldn't have dragged my eyes away for anyone else. And when she kissed me, I groaned into it, like she'd reached into my chest and wrapped a fist around my heart. I clasped her cheeks. "Thank you for showing me this."

"Anytime, Macabe."

We stared at the light display for an age before I gave into the urge to touch her, divesting her of that thick fleece and pulling her into my lap, desperate to touch her in this moment. Beneath *this* sky. Her T-shirt was next to go and I groaned in appreciation. "Baby blue might be my favourite yet."

Her nipples peaked through the scallop-edged lace, practically begging for my mouth. "Good. Because I wore it for you."

Fuck, sweetheart. My hands fumbled, too eager as I lifted her breasts to my mouth, dragging a wet kiss over the perfect curves. "Careful, harpy. If you keep being sweet to me, I might get used to it."

She arched into the touch, urging my mouth, my tongue, lower, until it soaked the lace. "*Good.*" Holding my head to her chest, she writhed, her legging-covered centre riding the hardness in my jeans. "You deserve a little sweetness." Her arms circled my neck, a little clumsy and a little desperate.

My heart thundered.

I love this woman. I love her in a way that makes me understand why people would so willingly die for it.

Fuck slow, an earthquake couldn't have stopped me from watching her fall apart in my arms. "Touch yourself," I rasped. Fingers gripping her waist, I laid back against the cushions. "Sit on my chest . . . Show me how you stroke your clit in the shower, imagining it's me."

"You're certain?"

I couldn't hold back my pained laugh. "Yes, I'm fucking certain. We still aren't having sex, but I want this . . . if you do?"

She nodded eagerly and I gave her room to kneel, holding out a hand to steady her as she tugged her leggings and underwear down her legs. I removed my own shirt, my cock ready to tear through my fly by the time she straddled me.

The plaid pooled around her waist, and I tugged it back with shaking fingers, pressing her thighs open, staring at her, hot and bare against my stomach. *Fucking mine*, the beast in my chest wanted to snarl.

"You're drenched, sweetheart." We were both breathing hard, our chests playing a game of call and answer. "Have you been like this all night?"

She nodded. And that beast roared again, promising to erase all memories of my brother from her mind until there was nothing left but me. "Touch yourself . . . *Fuck*, Juniper, let me see you."

My words seemed to wake her, lips switching from slackened to sinful in a single breath. "In a minute." She unclipped her bra, dragging the straps down her arms. I barely had time to take in the swells of those pretty tits before she kissed me. A delicious little humming noise vibrated up her throat and she pushed the sound into my mouth with her tongue. Her graceful hands curved over my shoulders and the action had me hissing as her nails dug in rather *ungracefully*.

It was hot and so fucking primal that I bucked beneath her.

"How are you so fucking perfect?" She was a dream . . . *better* than any dream. In the early days she'd become a paragon in my mind. Beautiful, sarcastic but caustic. The face of an angel and a tenderness for those she cherished and *fuck*, how I'd longed to be one of the select few.

The flesh and blood woman in my arms was *real*.

"Maybe I'm only perfect for you." Her words, combined with the tight press of her against my cock, had me groaning, eyes squeezing and praying for a strength I didn't possess.

"Fuck, sweetheart . . . Don't move or I'm going to fucking blow."

"I thought you wanted me to touch myself." Her hand was *there*, her fingertips no more than a graze over sensitised flesh as she worked herself. She moaned and I lifted my head, needing to see, even if it meant humiliating myself by blowing like a teenager.

I didn't move, didn't breathe as I watched her slip two fingers between us, positioning them so one touched her clit and her knuckles grazed my length every time they slid through her folds. The other went to her breast, rolling and flicking. "Fuck, sweetheart, *fuck*, that's it, press them inside, pretend they're mine."

Moaning, her hips began to roll. Unable to tear my gaze from the junction between her thighs, I moved with her, clutching her hips between desperate hands, spellbound as she rode me like the darkest kind of goddess. "*Callum*—"

I pushed to sit, holding her against my chest. "What do you need?"

Her eyes bounced between mine, as dark as world eaters edged with a panic I didn't understand. "Just . . . stay with me, please stay with me."

"Take what you need. I'm not going anywhere." I bit her ear and licked her jaw. Nibbled on the proud little point of her chin and then kissed it. Her tits got the full attention they deserved, dividing my attention between the two, sucking until they were swollen and glistening. All the while she moved for the two of us. "You going to say my name when you come, Juniper?"

She nodded frantically and I knew I wouldn't last long. I counted to ten in my head. I made it to nine. "Now, Juniper." I batted her hand away, dragging it around my neck, and replaced it with my own, sliding my finger over her slick clit like I owned it. "Dig those claws in and come for me." My body ached as I held back my own release, thighs burning, every inch of me sticky with sweat.

Juniper's lashes lifted as her nails dug into my back, tugging me flush against her until I felt the imprint of those gold bars on my chest, sighing my name exactly the way I dreamed it. And just when I thought I couldn't ask for anything more . . . she screamed it, trembling in my arms, every perfect line of her taut with pleasure. *My* pleasure.

I owned it now.

My name on her lips was the final shove and I went off like a fucking gunshot, bucking wildly through every rendering pull.

I love you.

I love you.

I silently repeated the word with my every groan into her throat.

This woman had broken me a long, long time ago. Hairline fractures that could be patched and melded.

279

Covered with grins and charm until I resembled something semi-functional. But now . . . she'd completely and utterly ruined me.

Ignoring the cum cooling in my boxers, my groans turned to kisses. "That was perfect. *You're* perfect." I said. My hands unlatched from her hips, lacing into her hair to hold her to me. "You own me, sweetheart. Entirely."

She brushed a stray curl away from my sweaty forehead. "You might own me a little bit too."

30

Callum

Heather: Alistair came by my house to ask why you're
acting so weird. You need to tell him!
Callum: Planning on it.
Callum: And, he thinks I'm acting weird? I saw him this
morning and barely got a word out of him.
Heather: I assumed he was brooding because Juniper
won't take his calls.
Callum: How many times has he called her exactly?
Heather: God, I hope for his sake no more than twice.

"Are you certain tonight is a good idea?"

"It's a perfect idea." Given my current view from where
I lounged on Juniper's bed, it might have been the best idea
I'd ever had.

Arse in the air, scarves and shoes flew over her head
as she rummaged through her messy wardrobe. "I know
they're here somewhere . . . aha!" She spun on bare knees,
holding the black shoes – which looked exactly the same as
every pair of shoes she owned – triumphantly.

Her glee was short-lived because she scowled at where Shakespeare had curled up on my lap. "I hate you both."

She stomped over to the table, and I followed, scooping Shakespeare into my arms. The cat had certainly grown attached in the past few weeks, much to Juniper's ever-growing annoyance.

"You're being cute again."

"*You're being cute again*," she mocked, proving my point as her voice dropped into what I assumed was a derogatory impersonation of me, but only reminded me of the rasp of her voice right before she came.

I wasn't surprised to discover everything about Juniper appealed to me. From the way she ate her breakfast cereal, taking one spoonful of milk to every crunch of the sugary hoops, to her fifty-seven-step nighttime routine.

She dropped the shoes with a shaky exhale. I set down Shakespeare, moving to clutch her hands. "Maybe we should stay in tonight, they won't miss us," I said carefully, worry starting to gnaw at my gut. It was a Saturday, so I had an afternoon shinty game before the ceilidh tonight. We'd agreed to arrive separately so as not to rouse suspicion, meaning I wouldn't even have a chance to check in on her before it started.

My tone must have given me away because she finally looked at me, teeth gnawing her full lower lip. "Have you changed your mind about telling Alistair?"

I smoothed my thumb over the small dent she'd made. "Of course not."

And I hadn't.

Me and Juniper together. *For real.* That was all I'd ever wanted. But now I had her, the fear of losing her had become a physical weight that kept me up at night. If someone asked me a month ago, I would have replied with arrogant certainty that I'd accept all or nothing when it came to Juniper Ross. But now, I knew I'd deceive everyone I cared about for the rest of my life if it meant keeping this slice of perfection with her.

That *she* was willing to take this chance humbled me. I kissed her forehead. Her nose. Her lips. "I haven't changed my mind."

No matter how badly I wanted to update my relationship status with a text alert to every person in Scotland, I'd promised Juniper a soft launch and that's what she'd get. She hadn't confessed to any deep or lingering feelings yet. But she'd agreed to give this a real shot. Publicly. That was enough for now.

"Good. Then we are going?"

With a sense of foreboding that I wrote off as pre-match nerves, I folded her into my chest. "We're going."

"Save a dance for me?" she whispered.

"They all belong to you."

* * *

I arrived at the ceilidh early and it was fair to say I was in a foul fucking mood.

Ribs still screaming from the knock I'd taken in the opening twenty minutes of the game from the literal child marking me on the Inverness team. I should have admitted defeat and subbed out like I'd have forced any of my teammates to do, but the wee prick's sarcastic, "*Give up, old man*," had kept me in the game to the bitter end. I'd seen enough broken ribs in my life to know mine were only bruised, so hadn't paused after the game to ice them, heading straight to my parents' house to find Alistair had already left to help Mal set up. From there I'd barely had time to race home and change if I wanted to arrive before Juniper.

In the tasting room, while April, Mal and Heather buzzed about, laying out food, helping the musicians with their gear then greeting the arriving villagers, I'd been content to let the bar April's late grandfather had so lovingly crafted hold me aloft, pretending to nurse a glass of whisky, one eye firmly on the door as the minutes stretched into an hour.

She was late.

Lost in his own thoughts, Alistair stood silently beside me, looking every bit the handsome Scot in his kilt, the same dark green and purple weave as my own.

His coiling agitation was also a twin to mine. His fingers drummed atop the bar, foot beating an unsteady rhythm into the floor, out of time to the music. Ordinarily, I would have needled my baby brother with questions until he confessed to whatever was eating at him. But not today, not when I suspected the answer lay in the reason for my own sweaty palms.

With every new arrival, laughter and the subtle scent of sweat pressed in. My head spun and I rubbed at my tightening chest, imagining the flash of Juniper's dark hair and wicked smile, the silent confirmation she hadn't changed her mind.

Is this how Mal feels all the time? Bloody hell. The strength it must take him just to step foot out his front door every morning.

I was one more fiddle solo away from ordering another drink when the back of my neck prickled, and I knew Juniper had arrived. I glanced over my shoulder and the entire room blinked out of focus, every other person dulling to the greyscale of a black and white movie while she'd been painted over in intricately textured impasto strokes.

I'd seen her dressed to kill a hundred times before. The woman wore clothes the way a medieval knight wielded a weapon. So I shouldn't have been so awed I almost swallowed my own tongue as I took in the figure-hugging dress that had nearly brought me to my knees once before. At her engagement party.

Finally. I must have spoken it aloud, because the word rumbled like an expletive. Dropping my drink on the bar, I started to go to her. But, *wait* – that voice didn't belong to me. Those weren't *my* shoulders slicing intentionally through the crowd.

Juniper's wide eyes found mine as Alistair approached, a question mark visible in the dark depths.

I shook my head roughly. *No. I haven't told him. I haven't broken our agreement.*

Her smile wobbled in relief. I scrubbed a hand into my hair, unable to do anything but watch as he said, "Hey." They stood thirty feet away in the middle of the dance floor, no way I could hear his words, but I was so attuned to her, he may as well have bellowed them down a long corridor. "Will you kick me if I ask you to dance?"

Did he even recognise the dress?

Juniper's gaze found mine over his shoulder and I met it with unflinching intensity. *Yes, you got me, harpy. I'm beyond fucking jealous. Come here to me before I drop to my knees and start begging.*

Her brows rose at whatever she found on my face, posture stiffening as she finally noted every person in the room drinking in their interaction.

Noticing too, Alistair winced but extended a hand, saying something that made her lips tip down before . . . *Fuck*, Duncan from the hardware store stepped in front of me, his too large head cutting off my view.

Fucking Duncan.

I strained my neck, clutching my ribs as the action pulled at the injury, just in time to see her place her hand in Alistair's.

31

Juniper

Isle of Skye Guidebook
Ceilidh: (pronounced kay–lee) descended from the Gaelic word *céilidhe* to "visit". Historically, this referred to any type of social gathering. In modern times it's a good excuse for a fun-filled evening of traditional dancing and music. Don't worry, you don't need to know the steps to join in!

The song was far too quick for the awkward two-step Alistair and I fell into, the fiddle and piper feeding off one another's energy in a tantalising chase from the small, hastily erected stage in the corner of the tasting room. From every side, hands clapped and feet pounded, the vibrations forcing us closer together.

"This place is really nice." Alistair eventually spoke over the thrum, chattering nervously as though I were a complete stranger and not the woman who'd once applied a daily ointment to his backside during an allergy flare-up. "I wonder why Kier hid it away all those years? I worked here for a summer as a teenager, I didn't even know this room existed."

Heather shot me a worried look from where she manned the bar. "*Need help?*" she mouthed. I shook my head. Better to get this over with.

Clasping a hand loosely over his shoulder, I turned my back to the room and the cool blue eyes scorching a line down my body, staring at the knot in Alistair's tie. "Should we cut straight to it?"

"You didn't answer my calls." A self-deprecating smile cutting over his bristled jaw. "I should have known you wouldn't take it easy on me." His tone was as dry as his grin, but it still managed to piss me off. I could feel the stares. Hear the whispers. My name would be all over the village by morning, so no, if he wanted to do this with an audience, I wouldn't take it easy.

"It's no more than you deserve."

The hand at my waist clutched tighter, like he worried I might turn into smoke and disappear before he could say his piece. "I know. I'm sorry for the rambling . . . and ambushing you the second you walked through the door. That wasn't cool. I've dropped by the inn a few times – Ada said you were out."

My head cocked. I might not have seen him in six years, but I knew Alistair in a way many didn't. He was always so . . . unflustered. Beneath his put-together smile was a layer of something I couldn't quite put my finger on. Panic, perhaps? *Desperation.*

Not my business.

"Why? Kinleith is big enough for us to avoid one another." It wouldn't be quite that easy with me technically dating his brother. *Wait, was I dating his brother?* That's what tonight was supposed to be about, but Callum hadn't made a single move across the room to me.

"I wanted to put things right between us and you wouldn't answer my texts so—"

"I don't owe you an answer." I pushed down the urge to stomp my pointy heel onto his foot as he pushed me away, spinning me, then drawing me back in. "You ended things over a bloody video call, Alistair," I hissed, glancing around to make sure no one overheard us. "You said I was the love of your life, got down on one knee and asked me to marry you, then only six months later – *just after my dad had died, no less* – you broke up with me in a *two-minute* conversation. Why does it suddenly matter now?" The guitarist pounded his foot as the short, crisp notes gained speed. A woman nearby threw her arms up with a cheer. Alistair adeptly twisted us, avoiding the collision.

"I should have come home earlier." His throat bobbed. "I'm a coward."

"Coward is putting it kindly."

He nodded like a bobblehead, adeptly leading me into a new rhythm while keeping a respectable distance between our bodies. He'd always been a capable dancer. "When it all went down, I thought a clean break would be better for both of us. Even then I knew I'd behaved like a bastard, but I convinced myself you wouldn't want to hear from me." He shook his head roughly, looking so damn apologetic. "Callum tried to warn me otherwise . . . and with every day that passed it only got harder to cross that line."

"You acted like a bloody scared little boy, running the moment things got tough." My voice whipped. For years I'd imagined throwing those words at him, now I'd gotten the chance and didn't feel an ounce of satisfaction.

His lips pinched. "I deserved that."

"And you were selfish."

"Yes." His eyes held mine, head dipping as he said, "I deserve every single one of those insults, and if you want me to stand here all evening while you scream at me, I'll do it."

I didn't dare say I'd barely even gotten started should it unleash the dragon fire I'd been swallowing down for over half a decade.

"Back then, climbing the professional ladder meant everything to me. I was so self-centred; I couldn't see past my fear of losing everything I'd worked for. The prospect of moving back to Skye felt like a step backwards on that ladder . . . several rungs, if I'm being honest."

I reached for that fire now, surprised to find the well in my belly only half full. "I never asked you to come back to Skye."

"*June*." My name was a gravelled sigh, like he'd been holding it in since our last conversation. "You're still living here and I'm still in Glasgow. One of us would have made the decision to end it eventually."

"*Oh* . . . so you did me a kindness?"

"No." The word cut like a blade as he spun us again, just enough for me to catch a glimpse of the bar from the corner of my eye. Callum was standing in exactly the same spot and I couldn't help drinking him in. Almost as tall as the low-hanging pendant lights, his head cut above every other man, bar Mal, in his vicinity. He'd kept his curls unstyled. A little messy. I hadn't had a chance to see all of him yet, but I knew from previous experience how well he filled out that kilt.

I wanted this to be over, I wanted to be in his arms where everything felt better.

Callum smiled and my heart swelled, his fingers playing with the frosted glass in his grip, only . . . it wasn't at me but the pint-sized blonde at his side. *Jill Mortimer*. The woman was as persistent as black mould but admittedly far more appealing.

They looked really bloody good together.

Alistair's voice jolted me back to our conversation. "I'm trying to say I was an arrogant wee shit back then. Even if we hadn't worked out, I should have been there for you, like you would have for me in a heartbeat. We were more than a couple, June, we were best friends. I failed at that."

I felt like I'd been blasted onto another planet. If there was one thing Alistair could be relied upon for it was his absolute certainty on being right, and nine-point-five times out of ten, he *was*. His intelligence and confidence had been a big part of my initial attraction. Now he stood in front of me, not only admitting to being *wrong* but apologising for it. That frankness smothered any fire I had left. Like hot coals tossed into snow, I practically sizzled under his stare.

Wilting beneath the urge to just let all of this go.

I kept moving for a few moments – feet shuffling from side to side as one song bled into the next – considering the two possible paths before me. One where I remained cocooned safely in my bitterness for another six years and the second . . . I didn't know that I was brave enough to take it. I'd let this grudge mould me for so long, I didn't know who to be without it.

"If I decided to forgive you, what happens then?"

His smile sat right on the cusp of hopeful. "Then, I suppose we'd be friends again . . . Only if that's something you're ready for."

"I'm not sure." My shoulder brushed his chest as he spun me beneath his arm.

"I'm not asking you to forgive me. I don't expect you to." When I came back to face him, the bleakness in his expression caught me off guard. "I know I don't have the right to ask you for anything but . . . I feel like there's this gaping hole in my chest and you're the only person who can fill it."

"Alistair . . . I'm not . . ." *Shit*, I couldn't believe I had to say this. "I'm not in love with you anymore, I haven't been for a long time." I'd been hurt that his actions left me feeling small and unwanted. That wasn't love. It was exactly what Heather had said, the loss of my own self-worth.

"I know that," he said, a little hollowly. "I told you, I want to spend time with you. To be . . . friends." His eyes, almost identical to Callum's, flicked away as he spoke. Flustered. Hesitant. "Do you think it's possible?" So damn hopeful.

Shit. We couldn't tell him tonight.

My attention shifted as we swayed, searching for Callum. Would he understand a blinked SOS code?

"If I say yes, will you take the ring back?" I asked Alistair.

His rhythm faltered and I knew I'd surprised him. "Deal." But the word was heavy. Like a rock dropped into water.

32

Callum

Callum: Want me to swing by the house later?
Mum: New meds seem to be working; he's fallen asleep in front of the TV. Don't worry yourself, have some fun.
Callum: I always worry.
Mum: Who's the parent here?
Callum: Hard to say. Mrs Brodie used to say the Macabe brood were raised by wolves.
Mum: She was always an old grump, that's why the school fired her.
Callum: I think she retired after Heather filled her desk drawer with worms and called it a science project.
Mum: She was a very inventive seven-year-old.

"So I said to him, Marcus, if you want my grandmother's china set, you're going to have to talk to my lawyer." Jill Mortimer finally paused to take a breath. Sucking obscenely loudly through her straw. "Can you believe the audacity of the man?"

"It sounds like a bad situation." Head pounding from

music and the little fact of my brother currently spinning the love of my life in his all too capable arms, I was scraping the bottom of the barrel for my diplomacy.

Jill scoffed and signalled to April who lingered behind the bar for a refill. April topped up Jill's glass without a word, her moss-green eyes sliding to me as she punched the soda gun a little harder than necessary. I cocked a brow in question, and her eyes narrowed. Never one to take a hint, I stuck out my tongue, fully committed to this silent conversation without the faintest idea of what was actually passing between us. Sweet little April could have been communicating anything from, *Stop acting like a maudlin prick*, to, *Your kilt's tucked up at the back and your arse is on display to the entire village.*

I patted a hand down my backside, finding the plaid hanging exactly as it should be. It wouldn't be the first time I'd been caught unawares. Wearing a kilt wasn't for the faint-hearted.

With a final glare, April cut down the bar to the next patron and Jill pulled a silver hip flask from between her breasts. Averting my gaze to confirm that Juniper and Alistair were in fact still dancing, I said a little too bitterly, "You brought your own whisky?"

"Heavens no." She unscrewed the cap, adding a very generous glug of a clear liquid to her glass. "It's gin. I might be forced to give up my Scottish citizenship, but I can't stand the stuff."

"Then why did you come?"

The curl of her hand around my bicep made me jump and I realised I was still staring at Juniper. Her blunt bob was as sharp as a knife's edge, one side tucked behind her ear as she leant in to better hear Alistair, displaying the row of tiny little gold hoops I'd traced with my tongue this morning.

It felt like punishment for being a coward. *I should have told him how I felt weeks ago. Years ago. She'd be in my arms right now.*

How did anyone fumble the bag quite this spectacularly?

"I hoped I'd get a chance to talk to you." Jill's fingers slid from my bicep to my forearm.

"*Jill*—" I started to draw away.

"Later." With a sly little wink, she pressed her back to the bar beside my elbow, gazing at the dance floor as she sipped her drink. "Oh, look," she nudged me. "Your brother and Juniper Ross are looking very cosy." I couldn't tell if she was purposely trying to provoke me. But that ugly feeling racked higher and I curled my fingers, anchoring myself to the bar. Either Jill possessed the uncanny ability to read the tension pouring from me or it was total ignorance that made her continue, "*Poor girl*, it will never last."

She didn't sound the least bit sorry.

Remembering the embarrassment on Juniper's face when we'd overheard Jill and her friends gossiping in the village, I bit out, "And why's that?"

Jill tutted, resigned to being the only person capable of reading between the invisible lines. "Well, Alistair's a doctor. If he's to be respected in the village, he'll need a good woman on his arm, not a snake-tongued lass who's slept with half the island and dresses as though she's eager to take on the rest."

Indignation rattled through me, so acute I felt my bones quake. Instead of rising to her transparent attempt to bait me, I released a low, appreciative whistle. "I'm impressed she finds the time to bed hop while running a successful business."

Jill scoffed, "That's a generous assessment of that rundown little inn. Don't play with me, Callum, you can't seriously think she's a suitable match for you . . . *your* brother." She fumbled to finish. It was too late. I'd caught her slip.

I took in her flushed cheeks. The way her eyes bounced between my face and the glass in her hand. *If he's to be respected in the village, he'll need a good woman on his arm.*

Alistair didn't even live in Kinleith.

Her dislike of Juniper had nothing to do with Alistair or even who Juniper chose to spend her nights with . . . all she cared about was that it wasn't me.

Just like that, I was done.

Bending, I fixed my gaze on Jill's, removing any possible chance of misinterpretation. "I'm only going to say this once and I expect you to heed my warning. From now on, you don't say another ill word about Juniper. Scratch that – don't even say her name. Understand?"

Her mouth gaped but she covered her shock with a laugh. "Callum, I didn't mean to upset—"

"Yes you did. You knew exactly what you were doing. Juniper doesn't need me to defend her, but I refuse to listen to another second of your vile shit. Tell me you understand," I demanded, eager to get to the only person I truly wanted to spend this night with.

Still swaying horrendously out of time, every moment Juniper danced with someone who wasn't me had the red mist rising higher. Brother or a fucking stranger off the street, it didn't matter. *Those should be my toes she's massacring.*

"Callum—" Jill reached for me. I retreated, never wanting those hands on me again. "What's wrong?" Her eyes searched mine and I saw the precise moment she found her answer. "*You and her?*" she hissed. "I knew it. I didn't want to believe it, but I *knew*."

The envy in her tone left me twitching, it was like look-ing in a fucking mirror. For that reason alone, I tried to soften my voice. "I'm sorry for my part, I should have been upfront from the very beginning. Regardless of my feelings for Juniper, nothing would have happened between us. I'm still happy to be your vet with the presence of Kelly in the surgery. Otherwise, I can make some recommendations—"

"Fuck yourself, Callum." Her lips bared in a snarl. "Are you honestly delusional enough to think you stand a chance there? Wake up! It couldn't be more obvious that she's still in love with him." Setting her glass down with a careless smack, she snatched up her purse and beelined for the door.

Like a true glutton for punishment, I instantly sought out Juniper. Still dancing with my brother, they were chatting almost amicably through a slow number. Alistair gazed at her like she'd hung the fucking moon, eating up every word from her lips. I didn't know what I'd expected when the two of them finally spoke again, but it sure as shit wasn't whispered words and pleasing smiles. Signalling for a refill from April, my brain took a tortuous journey back to another night, that very same dress, a glass of whisky in my hand while I lurked at the bar and watched them dance at a distance, my jealousy almost eating me alive.

Tonight, they couldn't have danced more than two songs together, yet it was long enough to unearth every contempt-ible thought I'd ever had. I wasn't particularly proud of this side of myself, the covetous beast that rattled the bars of its enclosure any time Alistair got within an inch of her, but it was there all the same.

"That went well." Mal's low rumble cut in just in time to stop me doing something stupid.

"About as well as to be expected," I shot back with a bluntness that didn't invite him to linger. Being a stubborn bastard, he waited, hands drumming on his folded arms. Why of all times did he choose now to take an interest? "Go on then."

"What?" He feigned casualness. A good job April was the actor in this pairing.

"Cut the crap, Malcolm, I know when you have something to say. You're far too fucking obvious."

"Fine! I've known about . . ." Reddening from the collar of his shirt to the tips of his ears, he wiggled a finger in Juniper's direction. "The entire time."

What the fuck? "How?"

"Juniper told April. I overheard." His grimace was enough to make me laugh. "It's not funny. She made me an accomplice."

I laughed louder, drawing stares. "Why didn't you say anything?"

"Because I'm keeping my nose firmly out of it." Turning, he planted a hand on the bar. "If Alistair has a problem with it are you going to stop?"

"Thought you were keeping your nose out of it?"

"Answer the question." He shot back.

"No." I barked. "I'll be Juniper's for as long as she wants me. End of discussion."

"*Shit*." He cut a dark look to the dance floor. "I hope you know what you're doing."

I didn't. Being with Juniper was the only time in my life when I felt out of control. Not going through the motions, day after day. *Fucking Community Ken*, she called me, always doing exactly what was expected of me. With her . . . I felt reckless. Not the crash and burn kind of reckless but the desire for her to keep me on my toes for the rest of my life kind of reckless.

"Tell me, would you have done anything differently if

it were April?" I bit out. "If she'd been mine first? Would it have stopped you, or would you have taken whatever scraps she deigned to offer and be fucking thankful for it? Look me in the eye and tell me you wouldn't have lied and betrayed every single person in your life for a single night with her. Knowing you might never get another." He didn't need to answer. The violent thrumming of his jaw was enough. "Think less of me if you must, but don't ask me to stop because I won't."

In my periphery, April hovered on the other side of the bar. "You might as well say your piece too, Sinclair."

She didn't hesitate. "Are you in love with my best friend?"

"Yes." I hated not saying it to Juniper first.

"How long?"

"Years," I said and April smiled. "What?"

She shrugged, laying out a row of glasses on a tray. "Just . . . Juniper deserves that kind of love." She nodded to the dance floor. "Perhaps you should tell her that yourself."

My gaze snapped up in time to see Alistair's head descending toward hers. Whispering in her ear. I moved without thought, the way I should have the instant she arrived. The instant I saw her on that train. Wielding my elbows like weapons, I barged through the throng. Someone shouted in protest, a foot squished beneath mine, but I paid no attention. My eyes too focused on Alistair's hand on Juniper's bare back where her dress dipped, steering her off the dance floor. Tucking her hair behind her ear, Juniper laughed, the sound like a strike of lightning in my veins, scorching me from the inside out. Obliterating every sensible thought in my brain that didn't end with me ruining this cosy little moment.

Four steps, that was all it took to reach them. For me to curl my hand around her bicep and draw her to my side.

"Callum—" Alistair sounded almost jovial, like he'd finally shifted the heavy weight he'd been carrying.

"What are you doing?" Paling, Juniper tugged her arm free. But I was over standing on the sidelines, over choking down the words I wanted to say to keep other people happy.

"Callum—"

Ignoring her, I looked Alistair straight in the eye and said, "I'm dating Juniper. Sorry if that's weird for you."

The confession left my tongue like a hand grenade, but he didn't so much as flinch.

For the space of two heartbeats, he just stared at me.

The band kept playing but the three of us held the attention of every person in the room. I couldn't give a fuck.

"Well?" I urged. "If you want to hit me, I won't blame you."

"I'm not going to hit you," he replied, stone-faced, his tone so level I might have believed he'd gone through basic training himself. "Is it true?" He asked Juniper.

She was frozen at my side, chin raised, eyes burning in defiance. "We should talk about this outside," she answered, voice coated in hoarfrost. The ice queen I'd once accused her of being. I wanted to draw her into me, breathe in her sugar and spice scent and melt her with my tongue, but I knew right away I'd fucked up.

Knew it before I opened my damn mouth if I was being completely honest.

Alistair's gaze bounced behind us, and then to the eager-eyed villagers as if noticing them for the first time. "Very well." A tight nod and he spun on his heel. Juniper followed, her gait slow, the sway in her hips a pretty pretense at appearing unbothered.

I clenched my fists, the only thing I could do to stop

myself reaching for her as I trailed after them like the fucking odd man out, catching the door when she let it slam
in my face. My laugh was bitter, in harmony with the cold
night air stinging my overheated skin.

"Fucking touché, harpy."

"Just stop talking." Rounding on me, she poked a dag-
ger-tipped finger in my chest. Nostrils flared, gloriously
furious, she looked like a goddess, backlit by the moonlight.
"I think you've said more than enough tonight."

"We agreed we were going to tell him," I said calmly,
very aware of Alistair two paces away, hands on his hips as
though he needed to witness Juniper and me in real time to
believe it. "I thought that's what you wanted."

"Don't pretend a single moment of that was about us!"
she yelled, every line of her taut with fury. "What happened
to a soft launch? Those were your words and then you just
claimed me like used furniture at a flea market. That was
all about you and your own fragile pride!" With a disgusted
shake of her head, she spun away, like she couldn't even be
bothered to look at me.

Hell no, sweetheart.

I followed her – like I always would – but Alistair was
quicker. So fast, I didn't even see it coming.

One second I was on my feet, panic stealing the breath
from my lungs as I watched her walk away, the next I was
flat on my back, fire lashing from my cheek to my lip, my
wee brother's forbidding face blacking out the stars.

33

Juniper

April: Need help burying a body?
Juniper: Not yet but stay on standby.
April: Yes ma'am. I'm great with a shovel.
Juniper: I hope that's under special skills on your résumé.

Three things happened at once.

I screamed.

Alistair roared like a wounded animal, shaking out his hand.

Callum's body stiffened and hit the ground with all the force of a car hitting a tree. It might have been comical if I weren't the proverbial rag doll in the centre of it all.

"Whoa, whoa, whoa." I tried to rush toward them, but my heels sank in the gravel, slowing me down. "What the hell are you doing?"

Mal got there first, I hadn't even noticed him follow until his arms circled Alistair's chest. "*Calm the fuck down,*" he was saying. I barely heard him, dropping to my knees beside Callum as he pushed onto an elbow.

"Thought you weren't going to hit me," he said, blood trickling from a small cut on his lip as he turned his head to spit.

Alistair flexed his fingers. "I changed my mind."

"Feel better?" Callum asked, wiping the blood from his chin.

Alistair bared his teeth. "Not even close."

Callum nodded, like he expected as much, then looked to the hand Alistair cradled. "You tucked your thumb; you've probably broken it."

"*Bloody prick.*" Alistair charged again, making it a step before Mal hauled him back, muttering rushed words to try and defuse the situation. "How long have you been fucking her?"

"*Watch your tone.*" Callum's voice was pure venom. Nostrils flaring like a dragon woken from a century-long sleep.

"Why? It's true, isn't it? I bet you've been planning this for years behind my back." His eyes shot to me, wilder than I'd ever seen them. "Or maybe it was all your idea to get back at me."

And so what if it was? I wanted to yell. The ridiculous display of testosterone making me want to lash out. Act as childishly as they were. But fury was pouring from Callum, promising more than a single punch.

"Go inside and calm the hell down," I said to Alistair. "The victim complex is starting to look pathetic." My words probably made things worse, but I didn't care. For weeks I'd resisted Callum for this very reason, explicitly telling him I didn't want any conflict. Then he'd had the gall to go and cause a scene in the middle of April and Mal's party.

Giving Callum another quick once-over to be certain he wasn't about to drop dead, I stood. "Sorry, Mal." I couldn't meet his eyes. "Will you tell April I'm sorry I ruined your night?"

"You didn't ruin anything," he promised. "Let me get her, she'll drive you home—"

"I prefer to walk, thanks." Chin high, I slipped a bored expression firmly into place and started down the long driveway.

I made it five steps before I sensed Callum behind me. "We need to talk about this, just the two of us."

"Oh, so now you want privacy? Why don't you invite him to watch us fighting like a *real* couple? Hell, why not fuck me while he watches too?" The words were hot and vicious, angry butterflies taking flight in my stomach.

"Don't fucking tempt me," he growled as he rushed ahead, stopping me in my tracks. Beads of moisture danced in the air, doing little to cool the fervent frenzy beginning to spiral between us. This was always where we'd existed, in the murky middle of a Venn diagram made up of lust and loathing. If he got a step closer, the scales would tip and I'd beg him to fuck me up against the nearest tree.

"Touch me and you'll regret it," I warned, loathing winning out as the memory of his betrayal sank its claws into my chest.

"That so? I think you're a liar, harpy. A pretty little liar." But he didn't touch me. Just curled his fingers into fists and let me pass. Thankful for my skill in heels, I continued down the uneven path without so much as a wobble.

"Are we walking?" he called after a moment.

I kept my focus on the streetlights ahead. "This is stalking."

"How'd you figure that? I'm going home. It just so happens we live a hundred yards apart. Besides . . . my current view is impeccable; can you blame me for following like a stray dog?"

"Don't!" I snarled, spinning to poke him in the chest,

right in the spot that my own heart was cracking. "You don't get to pull that bullshit back there then joke and flirt as though it hasn't changed everything."

His hand circled my finger, keeping me there. "This changes nothing between us, harpy." Back to harpy, just like that. I tried not to let the wound show on my face. "Aye, I shouldn't have said it like that, I fucked up. I fucked up because I'm so out of my mind for you, I can't think straight half the time—"

"Don't try and blame this on me!" *Screw him.*

"I'm not blaming you! What I'm doing is a terrible job of explaining that I can't hide this anymore. I thought I could play it cool and keep my cards close to my chest. I asked you to soft launch, for fuck's sake! How the hell am I supposed to soft launch when there's nothing remotely soft about the way I feel for you?" He raked a hand through his hair, eyes wild in the moonlight. "I know exactly what I want from you, Juniper – what I've *always* wanted. Can you say the same?"

There's nothing remotely soft about the way I feel for you. What was I supposed to say to that?

My mouth went dry, any reply catching in my throat when music from the distillery sounded from further down the road. A flash of light as the door opened and closed, then an engine roaring to life.

"We shouldn't talk about this here." I swallowed, starting back up the road.

"Right." He chuckled, voice suddenly smooth, as though we hadn't been screaming at each other thirty seconds before. "Wouldn't want the thistles to overhear our argument, they're notorious gossips."

Jesus, it was like he had multiple personality disorder. Playful Callum had entered the chat, but there was an edge to his exuberant exterior. He teemed with restless energy, his hands flexed at his sides, opening and closing as we walked.

He was making my head spin.

So like any well-adjusted adult, I held my fury close, stoking the flame as I ignored him the entire way home.

How had this night veered so off course? Only this morning we'd been joking and kissing in my kitchen, daring to imagine our life with our relationship out in the open. I'd been afraid in the best possible way. Observing with a quiet, tentative hope that not only was my life beginning to write itself beyond the blank page I'd been toiling over for years, but it would be bursting with intensifiers and interjections, dog-eared corners and doodles in the margins. Full, messy and quite possibly worth rereading.

And now . . . we were back at the starting line, a single snide remark away from a cheap hate fuck.

By the time we reached my cottage, I'd fallen back into my safe defensive bubble.

How dare he force his way into my life and mess things up with his kind eyes, dirty laugh and even dirtier words. The old Juniper knew better than to let a man tangle her up in knots.

"You're not coming in," I threw over my shoulder, digging through my bag for my keys.

Callum clearly had other ideas because one hand found my waist as he stole the keys from my fingers. "Yes I am."

"Don't manhandle me."

"Keep pressing that arse against me and we'll discover just how much you enjoy my manhandling." He punctuated the point with a slow caress of my arse.

I couldn't contain my moan, even as I knew how pathetic I was for almost giving in. He'd humiliated me back there, then a few tempting words and he had me almost panting against my front door. "I hate you."

"*Oh yeah?*" He reached around me, unlocking the door but holding me against him on the threshold. "Sometimes I think I hate you too." His voice was gruffer than I'd ever heard it. "The power you hold over me, I don't think you even realise how dangerously you could wield it."

Fuck him. Fuck him and that gravelled tone.

Barging through the door, I sped down the hallway and into the living room, tossing my purse onto the sofa. Upon seeing us, Shakespeare paused her licking, hissed, then dove into the safety of my closet.

I felt him pause on the threshold, the ticking of my clock our only companion as the tension thickened. Refusing to be the one to speak first, I kept my back to him, staring through the large window. Total darkness stared back.

"If you want to scream at me, now's your chance, sweetheart."

It was the endearment that finally broke me. The way he chopped and changed as if I were two different people. I whirled. "Don't call me that."

"Why?"

"Because it gives mixed messages. One minute, I'm Juniper or sweetheart and I feel . . ." I *feel*. My laugh turned acrid. "Forget it."

"Fuck that. We are years past forgetting it!" He cut across the room until he filled my vision. Sharp cheeks, heavy brows, that beautiful straight nose and bloodstained scruff. Bright blue eyes filled with more fury than he'd ever directed at me. "If for even a second you think I don't want to know every single thought inside that head of yours, what the hell have we been doing here?"

"Exactly that! You call me sweetheart and say wildly

romantic things and then the second I'm not the perfect person you've built up in your head, I'm right back to being harpy, the ice queen you can't stand."

"You think I don't know exactly who you are? That I haven't always seen you, even when you didn't want me to? I know you . . . And despite what your name suggests, I know you'll never hold the easy warmth of summer." His hands swept around my face, refusing to let me turn from him. "You . . . sweetheart . . . harpy, are the wild moors of this island. You're like your damn demon cat, claws in my back and blood on my lips. But there isn't a single day that I won't welcome that sweet bite of pain." Both of our chests rattling, he glanced between my eyes, smoothing back the hair that had tangled in his fingers.

"If any of that is true, why the hell did you pull that shit back there?"

"Because I was jealous!" he roared. "Because you were in his arms, in this dress, when it should have been mine. Because he couldn't take his eyes off you. If you wore *this* dress to torture him, I don't think it worked on the right brother. Did he even recognise it?"

"No, he didn't," was my blunt answer. And that wasn't why I'd worn it, but I hadn't counted on Callum recognising it.

He grunted again, as if the sound made up a complete sentence. "If I put my hand beneath that dress, would I find you wet, harpy?" I said nothing but my traitorous fingers curled into his shirt. "*Yes*," he hummed for me. "I think I so. But would you be wet for *me* or Alistair?"

"Fuck you." But the curse became embarrassingly invalidated by my thighs clenching.

His big hand gripped my waist. "Later. You didn't answer me."

"What was the question again?"

"About Alistair." His head tilted, dark hair falling over his brow. "When I said he couldn't take his eyes off you."

"That's not a question."

His eyes burned as he continued. "I heard the two of you fucking once, did you know that?"

What?

"You visited Edinburgh right before Christmas, a year or so after you started dating. He surprised you with dinner and a show to celebrate your anniversary, but the hotel reservation fell through, so you spent the night at my place." I remembered, *shit*, I remembered. Callum's stylish New Town flat. The creaky bed in his spare room. "You tried to be quiet . . . but you were a little drunk, stifling your moans while he went down on you on the other side of my wall." He sounded tortured, fingers knotting into my hair, tipping my forehead against his. "That's when I first learned the addictive noises you make. You sighed his name, over and over and over. I thought I'd go insane from the sound of it."

His words . . . they shouldn't have been so bloody hot. Every limb trembled by the time his mouth reached my ear, fingers curling around the hem of my dress. "Are you going to sigh my name, Juniper?"

How many times had he asked me that very question? And all this time he'd been trying to rewrite history.

My eyes flew open. No. *No.*

I wanted him so badly my body tingled with it, like a loose live wire. But not like this. Not in reaction to Alistair. I shoved at his chest, and he released me at once, fingers uncurling one digit at a time. "I have no interest in doing . . . whatever this is."

A muscle in his neck jumped and he tugged at his tie. "Fine. Then tell me honestly, are you still in love with him?"

34

Juniper

The question hit me like a slap.

"Are you joking?" The distance left me cold, but I stumbled around the coffee table, taking some much-needed space.

"You look like a fucking queen in *his* dress. You keep *his* ring on your sideboard like a goddamned trophy, what am I supposed to think, Juniper? I told myself over and over again that it didn't matter, so long as I got to keep you." Callum stared at me with an honesty no other man had ever offered, like he'd placed his aching soul on the butcher's block and handed me the knife. "But it *does* matter, with you, everything matters. Every emotion is amplified, bigger than they have any right to be." His Adam's apple bobbed. "Before, I thought the torture of wanting you but never having you would be enough to kill me and now, fuck . . . I haven't even had you, not really, and you've ruined me." His hand scrubbed across his ruined lip. I wasn't certain he even felt the pain. "If I'm in your bed, sweetheart, I need to know exactly why I'm there or – or I'm out."

My brows pinged up, unable to hold back my surprise. "Is that an ultimatum?"

He nodded choppily, as though stunned the words had passed his lips. "*Yeah* – yes. I guess so."

I should have told him to screw his ultimatum. Sent him out into the night and carried on with my lonely little life like he hadn't left an irreparable Community-Ken-shaped hole in it . . . because I knew, without a doubt, Callum Macabe had the power to ruin me too.

But deep down, I knew I craved the rebuilding that could only come after total destruction.

"You've got some fucking balls, Macabe." I continued my slow journey around the table, enjoying the way he tracked my every move. He'd been honest with me, and he deserved my honesty in return, so I said, "The only reason I wore this dress is because I look phenomenal in it and thanks to you I've finally reached a point where I don't look at it and feel terrible about myself. I didn't think you'd even recognise it."

His teeth flashed and I knew he wanted to reach for me. "The way you look in that dress is a particular fantasy of mine."

Every part of me heated, from my fingers to my breasts and down to my toes, but I forged on. "I danced with Alistair tonight to hear him out. So I could put the past behind me and start *us* on a clean slate. He apologised and I accepted – though it's probably null and void at this point – so long as he agreed to take the ring back." I blew out a breath, steeling myself for the next omission. "You weren't exactly wrong when you said I kept it like a trophy, just not for the reasons you think."

"Tell me," he urged softly. "You can tell me anything, even if it's something I don't want to hear."

"The past few weeks have helped me realise—" I cut off, nervously licking at my lips. "Screw that – *you* have helped me realise that I've been using it as a kind of physical representation of how unlovable I am."

If it were possible to see a heart break in someone's eyes, Callum's did exactly that. "*Sweetheart*—"

"Just hear me out, please?" Though it looked like it pained him to do it, he nodded, his taut muscles telling me he was physically holding himself in place. "All this time I've been viewing Alistair, even my birth parents, as the villains in my life. Evil masterminds twirling their moustaches while they plotted the most painful methods to wreck me. I can see now that I've been giving them too much credit, because the truth is . . ." The words wobbled past trembling lips. But I had to get this out, needed him to understand all the ways he'd helped me heal. "The truth is . . . they just didn't love me enough."

"*Fuck* . . . love." He met me in two strides. Strong arms gathering me until I felt his pounding heart. I instantly felt stronger. "They didn't deserve you. Not for a single second—"

"It's okay." My hand brushed his chest, luxuriating in the heat of him. "That's what I'm saying. This isn't a movie. This is real life, full of fucked-up, messy decisions. Their actions weren't calculated or malicious, they were just . . . life." I swiped at the wet beneath my eyes. "It wasn't right. But because of that, I found my family . . . I found you."

"Nothing will ever stop me from fighting for you," he promised, the words a whisper on my lips. Then as if he couldn't hold back a second longer, my back hit the wall. He tilted my chin up, nothing but wonder in his expression. "I love you. Even when it hurt, I loved you." For just a glimpse I saw the hopeless, desperate man hiding beneath all that charm. "I love you so much I'm not sure those words truly mean anything."

"They mean everything."

His lips traced my brow. "I've had a lot of time to think of alternative ones."

I started to reply, but he pressed a finger to my lips. "It's my turn, okay? I've been waiting a long time to speak these words to you." He waited for my nod, that hand sliding around to cup my cheek. "I've loved you from the moment I set eyes on you, but it was the night in Glasgow that solidified it for me, when I knew I needed to be more than a placeholder for your revenge." When I winced, he pecked a kiss to my nose. "I wanted your friendship and your time, as much as you would give me." He kissed my neck. "I wanted to be familiar with you; your mind *and* your body. I wanted to learn the songs you sing in the shower and the shit TV shows you watch when no one's around."

His lips brushed mine, there and gone so quickly, I chased them. "Questions of you kept me awake at night. What books were on your bedside table? How did the precise beat of your heart sound? What would the touch of your tongue around my cock feel like?"

It was a travesty I hadn't tasted him yet.

"I wanted to hear you sigh my name and then scream it. I've ticked a few of those off the list, but I'm so fucking selfish when it comes to you, I need more. I want my voice to be your favourite sound in the entire world. I want you to be as addicted to my taste as I am yours. I want to take you on an actual date and watch you go sweet for me, and when we get home, I want you to give me shit and pull my hair, right before you crawl for me. And if you can't give me that, you can be damn sure I'm desperate enough to accept your friendship . . . but I'm going to need a minute to get there."

He finished and the silence hung, thick, tangible and oppressive. His chest labouring like he'd spent years running to this very moment. The words were too perfect, every alarm bell told me not to believe them.

But this was Callum.

So I tilted my head and said, "You want me to crawl?"

His jaw pulsed, like he was worried he'd said too much. "On occasion."

"And when I'm not on my hands and knees?"

"Then I'll be the one crawling."

My pulse pounded in my ears, the moment sliding from sweet to sensual in a single heartbeat. "Prove it."

His nostrils flared but he offered no complaint as he held his ribs and slowly lowered to his knees, eyes on mine. I got off on every moment of it, the knowledge no other woman had ever had him this way.

"Did you hurt yourself?" I nodded to his hand.

"I took a tumble during the game." He lifted my foot to his chest and unbuckled the strap. One then the other. "Don't worry, I'll keep up just fine." My shoes hit the floor with a clack and he drew back, awaiting my next move.

Fighting to keep my breathing even, I brushed his thick hair back from his forehead, marvelling at the carnal grunt that punched from him at the slight touch.

He wanted me.

He'd been telling me so for weeks, but the truth of it was finally sinking in: this kind, generous man wanted only me.

"I wreck everything," I whispered, uncertain if it was honesty or a final effort to scare him away. "It was partly my fault things broke down with Alistair . . . After my dad died, I shut down. Stopped communicating. He got tired of caring. I might wreck this too."

His hands dragged up the backs of my legs and squeezed, steady and sure. "Then wreck me. Just don't leave me."

"Take off your shirt," I said roughly.

He heard the promise in the statement because he tore off his jacket before I even got the words out. His shirt and tie came off next, releasing it from the waist of his kilt, he wadded the fabric and tossed it aside. I almost swore at the sight of his bare chest. He was a work of art, hard lines and roped muscle. I let myself stare, leaving no patch of skin untouched. I'd accused him not too long ago of being a pretty boy. That couldn't have been further from the truth. The tapered V at his hips pointing to the trail of hair below his belly button was pure male. There was no other word to describe him. Especially with the dark bruise spreading across his rib cage, matching the cut on his lip.

"That looks painful," I noted, tracing my nails across the edge of it. "I can't believe Alistair hit you."

"Worth it." He voice was thick as he nodded to me with eager eyes. "Take off your underwear."

Fisting his hair, just as he'd asked me to, I dragged his head closer. He grinned up at me and, for once, it was a little savage. Both sexy and feral.

"You seem to be mistaken, Macabe. I'm in charge, remember?"

"You're in charge," he agreed. Yet his hands roughly palmed the backs of my thighs, creeping up to cup the globes of my arse.

"Good, up on the bed." I stepped out of his reach and he stood, not taking his eyes off me for a second as he backed up, palmed his bruised ribs and lowered himself to the end of the mattress.

"You might need to go on top."

"I promise to be gentle with you," I cooed, grazing my

nails across his nipple, just hard enough to make him wince and then shudder.

"Or don't." His teeth gritted, gaze dragging down my body. "Dress. Take it off." When I made no move to comply, he fingered the hem, pulling the fabric taut. "I'm all about give and take and, so far, wee harpy, I've done a fuckload of giving. It's my turn and I can't stand to see you in another man's dress for another damn second." Another tug, this one rough. "Take it off or I tear it, your choice."

I considered this just long enough to torture him, then retreated out of his reach. Taking my sweet time as I found the zip along the side and languidly inched it down. He didn't breathe. Watching with enough heat in his eyes to set the dress aflame as he waited for what came next.

"*Red*," he groaned, as the dress dropped below my bra, scrubbing a distracted hand over his mouth. The fabric pooled at my waist, then hit the floor with a soft sigh. "Fuck . . . you look so fucking pretty like this. Spin for me."

I didn't, biting my lip instead.

His fists clenched and I knew it was with the effort of staying seated. "Are you going to be trouble, Juniper? Please say yes." We shared a charged look, remembering that night in Glasgow.

"Undoubtedly." Giving in to the urge to touch him, I crept close enough to grasp his shoulders. His thighs split automatically and I climbed over him, settling against his cock that pressed through his kilt. "No touching . . . not yet."

Like snapped rubber bands, his hands pinged around my hips. I laughed, pushing them back to the mattress. "You don't follow instructions very well for an army man."

"Harpy, I'm close to blowing just looking at you, I can't even remember my name right now, let alone follow instructions." His assessment sent a delicious curl through my lower stomach. I was going to devour this amazing man, but I wasn't through playing quite yet. Sliding from his lap, I returned to his pile of clothes and collected his tie. Lowering to my knees between his muscled thighs, I gathered his hands behind his back, looped the material around them once and paused, waiting for his reaction.

His startled eyes shot to mine at the same moment his nostrils flared in such obvious arousal, I had to squeeze my legs together.

"Problem?"

He shook his head, seemingly incapable of words. That wouldn't do. I traced a finger around his wrist.

"I need to hear you're all right with this, Callum."

His nod was rapid, eager. "I'm good – *more* than good." By his reaction I assumed he didn't have a safe word. I asked anyway. "*No*. Should I?"

Looping the fabric twice around his wrists, I tied a comfortable bow, all the while placing soft kisses between his pecs. "Say *stop* and I'll untie you immediately. Or you can pick something else . . . anything you like."

While he deliberated, I slid a finger between his skin and the fabric, testing it wouldn't pinch.

"*Ivy*." His thighs tightened around my hips.

"Perfect." I trailed my fingers down his abs, and he sucked in a breath. "Lean back on your elbows." He watched me with hunger that almost beat my own and I flicked up the hem of kilt, almost losing an eye when his cock sprang free from the weight of the plaid, the tip already swollen and glistening. Looking up at him beneath my lashes, I quirked a smile. "A true Scot, Macabe. I like that." And then I closed my mouth around him.

"*Juniper*." His eyes squeezed shut and hips snapped,

filling my mouth more thoroughly than I'd anticipated. I choked a little and moaned, curling my fist around what was left of his magnificent length. So thick, my fingers didn't meet around the middle.

I dragged him all the way to the back of my throat, getting off on the way his breath rattled, and his fingers twisted in the sheets. "You have a gorgeous cock, Macabe," I mumbled around the tip, mouth stuffed full.

"You're making me blush." A single glance at his face confirmed he spoke the truth. Nails dragging up his thighs, I hummed around him, and his thrusts stuttered, stomach flexing as he fought to regain some kind of control. I curled my lips in, making sure to leave the red stain of my lipstick behind. "*Fuck* . . . look at me when you do that, Juniper – fuck, *slow* . . ." he begged. "I need you to go slow." He collapsed back on the bed, barely seeming to notice his arms crushed beneath him. He was coming apart, his chanted, "*Fuck*, *fuck*, *fuck*," bordering on delirious. I soaked it all in, working him as torturously slowly as he'd requested until his back bowed.

"Harpy . . . Get that sweet arse up here, I need to taste that tattoo again."

I hummed around him. "I'm having too much fun here."

"*Fuck* . . . it's too good. I'm going to lose it." His thighs squeezed me tightly. "I can't come yet."

"Why?"

"Because there's no fucking plane of existence where I'd allow myself to come before you do."

I laughed, licking all the way up his length one final time. "Male pride is a beautiful thing." Pressing my thighs together as the throb between my legs bellowed in agreement, I kept right on teasing him. "Ask me."

"*What?*" His head shot up. Still on my knees, I kissed

the inside of his muscled thigh sweetly, a dichotomy to my devilish command.

"I said, ask me." Another kiss. "If you want to be inside me, beg for it."

"Please." The word tore from him without ego. "Get up here and let me inside you, let me touch you, let me . . . let me make you feel good too."

My legs were shaky as I stood, clutched his shoulders for support and hiked one leg over his waist, utterly transfixed by that full masculine mouth as he pleaded for what only I could give him. I locked my ankles around his back, goosebumps rising at the caress of his bound hands on my calves. Calloused fingers brushing the tops of my feet. "Still doing all right?"

"Yes." His thundering chest brushed mine. "That answer might change if I don't get inside you in the next five seconds."

I cupped the back of his head, capturing his lips with mine, savouring the drag of his stubble against my skin. "You are doing so well, baby." I shifted in his lap, letting his cock lodge against my clit, only damp lace separating us.

"Need to fuck you, harpy."

My fingers dragged over his nipples. "Beg me one more time. I think you can do better."

"Please." The groan was unlike any sound I'd ever heard from him. If I hadn't trusted before that he belonged to me entirely, I did now.

Bending, I riffled through the bedside drawer for the box of condoms I so rarely used, tore open one with my teeth and pressed his kilt against his stomach with one hand, rolling the condom down him with the other. He was trembling, head hanging between us to watch every movement.

"You look so good beneath me," I said, dragging my

underwear down. I knelt far enough back to admire his form.

"I'll look even better inside you." He licked his lips. "Get on with it."

"Who's in charge here?"

He tugged at his bound wrists as he lined us up. "I'm the one tied up, sweetheart. Now fucking ride my cock, I know you're as desperate for it as I am."

We both groaned as the first inch disappeared. He felt so big, so perfect, in this position it took three slow thrusts to seat him fully.

"*Juniper*," he sighed. "Fucking made for me."

When I fully sank down, I pressed a soft, *Hello* kiss, to his lips, along with a little nice to meet you wiggle.

"*At fucking last*," he growled right back, pressing a kiss to the centre of my chest.

Too far gone, I could only wrap my arms around his neck as I rode him with languid rolls of my hips, moaning at the hot throb of him deep inside me. *Fucking made for me*, the words echoed, and my heart ached with them. This man who took care of everyone else and took so little for himself.

Unable to use his hands, Callum sat straighter and bent his knees, firmly situating me in his lap, taking me as hard as his constraints allowed.

"Take that off." He nodded to my bra. "I want your nipples in my mouth." I snapped it open, gasping and clutching his head as he followed through, sucking my nipple between his teeth and curling his tongue around the bar. Loving my breasts as thoroughly as he loved every inch of me.

"So fucking perfect." He whispered the words against my skin, like they weren't for my ears but a prayer of thanks. "How is this so perfect?"

"Because we're us and that's everything." I dropped my head to his, quickly losing control of this ride. It was near impossible when he worshipped me with his mouth. But when he did it with his words . . . it became unthinkable to hold back even the tiniest piece of myself.

"I want that vicious little tongue next."

I didn't hesitate, crushing my lips to his. Loving the clack of his teeth against mine, the claiming onslaught as he left no spot in my mouth undiscovered. He kissed me like he wanted to fuse our souls together.

I met him stroke for stroke, feeling no guilt in our shared pleasure as I angled my hips to take him deeper.

"Say my name, sweetheart."

"Callum," I sighed at once.

"Touch yourself, let me see it."

My hand started its descent, making it all the way to my trembling stomach when I realised it wasn't my own hand I craved. "I need you to touch me."

All it took was a single tug at the tie and I was flat on my back. The pain in his ribs second to this pleasure apparently because his hands were everywhere, in my hair, between my legs, dipping into the curve of my waist, strumming my nipples like his favourite instrument. I answered every touch, writhing against the sheets as he dragged in and out of me, pulling my thighs around his hips until I felt that elusive pressure against my G-spot.

My hoarse cry made him grin wolfishly, then find that spot again and again. "Callum," I whimpered his name like a question, not even sure what I was asking for.

But he knew. He *always* knew.

"You're so close." His breath was hot against my ear, his body finally pressing mine into the mattress. The weight of him threatened to crush me but I clutched him tighter, locking my legs around his waist. "I can feel you tightening around my cock, sweetheart, it's fucking heaven, I've never felt anything like it." Goosebumps rose everywhere his lips touched as he talked me right up to the cliff edge. "You're perfect. So fucking pretty." His hand grasped my thigh, pushing it higher, spreading me open for him as he took me over and over. "You act like a bad girl, but I know your little secret . . . you are so," he kissed my jaw. "Fucking." His lips fluttered over my nose and my back bowed. "Sweet."

"Callum."

"That's it . . . that's it, sweetheart. Roll your hips, take whatever you need. I'm yours. I'm going to get you there . . . I'm always going to get you there." My eyes squeezed shut, hearing only his voice as it caressed every single one of my nerve endings. "No one's ever made me hard like this, gotten me off like you do. A single look and I'm fucking gone."

I whimpered. It might have been his name. It didn't matter, I was too busy floating away.

He didn't even have his fingers between my legs. It was just his words and his cock. I'd never gotten off from penetrative sex alone . . . but this, he was talking me through it, *loving* me through it.

"I'm close . . . I'm so close, Callum."

"I know . . . I've got you. I fucking love you, Juniper." Hand tightening beneath my back, his voice turned strained, fighting not to come first. "My Juniper . . . *mine*. I'm going to keep you. Keep on loving you. Now come for me, keep swallowing my cock and come for me. Come for me."

The words crumbled to staccato syllables, followed by mindless ramblings that echoed only in my head as I joined my lips to his, my orgasm rolling through me like an ocean swell. Slow to build and slow to release. It caught me in its clutches, holding me right above the precipice as Callum's lips tore free and his harsh curse melded with my cries. Our hips refused to slow, his kilt dragging over my rib cage as he fucked me over and over, still impossibly hard inside me.

"What the fuck . . . what the fuck . . . *Juniper*."

"Don't stop."

"Fuck . . . Fuck, fuck, fuck." Both of his hands planted either side of my head. His eyes wide with disbelief as he matched my pace through the final throes of pleasure.

Only when my body turned pliant did he collapse on top of me, then immediately roll onto his back, dragging me with him until I sprawled over his chest.

I slumped against him, my ear to his racing heart as we clung to one another like survivors of an apocalypse who'd just discovered they were the last two people on earth.

35

Callum

Heather: Where did Alistair and Callum run off to? We didn't even get a chance to chat.
Mal: I don't know anything!
Heather: Guys?
Alistair: I suddenly felt sick so I'm heading home. I think Callum is otherwise engaged.
Mal: Maybe Callum's sick too. He definitely looked a little peaky.
Alistair: Thought you didn't know anything?
Heather: What the hell is going on?

"Are you okay?" I asked Juniper the second I was able. The smile on my face likely visible from outer space.

She laughed, her entire body soft and trembling. "What the fuck was that?"

"I was hoping you could tell me." I kissed her sweaty forehead, brushing my lips back and forth. "You just sucked my cock so well I thought I was having an exorcism."

"The power of Christ compels you." She giggled again,

the sound music to my ears. Her legs split over my waist, and I groaned, my cock still buried in its favourite spot, deep inside her. "And I can't explain it." She pillowed her chin on her hands, looking so fucking content splayed out across my chest, I shook my head in disbelief. "That's never happened before."

I assumed she didn't mean the orgasm as I'd made her come multiple times by now. Or the hand tying. She'd been in control to a point it felt safer for my sanity not to analyse it.

"Elaborate."

She licked my nipple and I grinned, the little demon loved my nipples almost as much as I loved hers.

"You made me come without even touching my clit."

Surprised, I tried to think back and regrettably failed. The best sex of my fucking life but from the moment she'd smeared her lipstick on my cock it had all felt like an out-of-body experience. Regardless, I had the urge to beat my chest like a caveman for putting that satisfied smile on her face.

Though it caused my cock to slide rather unceremoniously from her, I caught her beneath the arms – chuckling as she squealed – and dragged her up my chest. I needed to look her in the eye for this. "Did you, Juniper '*Callum shut the fuck up*' Ross, just come to the sound of my voice?"

"I don't think you're giving enough credit to the baseball bat between your legs."

I grinned like an absolute fool. "I knew it. This whole time you've been getting hot when I talk to you, sweetheart."

"I wouldn't say the whole time—"

I squeezed her hips, delighting in the realisation I could now have her laughing beneath me whenever I pleased.

Attempting to get away, she rolled off me and onto the twisted sheets.

I followed, ignoring the twinge in my bruised ribs, and pinned her arms above her head. "Admit that you like it."

Her smile was wide and stupid and so damn pretty I couldn't resist kissing it. "I might not hate it."

"Liar." I clicked my tongue. "In fact . . . I think you *love* the sound of my voice."

"Are you attempting to trick a love confession out of me?" Her long legs swept my thighs. I groaned, falling into the cradle of her hips when holding myself aloft suddenly became impossible. I was so weak for this woman. Pathetically so.

"Maybe." That's exactly what I was doing.

"*Damn.* Now I definitely can't say it back."

"Minx." I bit her neck and she laughed throatily. "Say it."

"Nope."

"*Say it.*" I punctuated the point with a flick of the bar through her nipple.

She gasped but still managed to lift a single perfect brow in challenge. "Make me."

Oh, fucking gladly.

Rising first, I dragged her after me, delivering a swift slap to her perfect behind. "In the shower. Now."

Turning on the spot, she curled her arms around my neck, pressing a kiss to my lips that swept me away. I would never get enough of her. My hands fell back to her thighs, half lifting her as I stumbled through the dark to the bathroom door.

Reaching around her, I flipped on the light, laughing into her mouth when she cried out at the cold tile on her bare toes. "It's bloody freezing."

"Aye." It was, now that she mentioned it. Our body temperatures must have dropped some. "Get in, I'll warm you up."

She barely had the shower door open when a crash sounded from the other room. We frowned at each other. "It's probably Shakespeare destroying my shoe collection again," she said.

I flipped on the water as another crash followed. *Bloody cat.*

Staring at Juniper's very naked, very wet body, I could have wept. "Warm up, I'll be back in a second." I kissed her forehead and closed the shower door, walking back into the open-plan space. Clothes and shoes were scattered from the bed to the living room, like a reverse treasure hunt.

I flipped on the wardrobe light, shifting the clothes on the lower rails, searching for Shakespeare. Nothing. Retracing my steps, I tried the kitchen next. She liked to sit on top of the refrigerator sometimes, she might have fallen down the back.

Crash.

I halted, head tilting to the front door. My feet were already moving down the narrow hallway, growing colder with every step. I found the front door ajar, creaking in the frame as the wind blew it back and forth.

Giving zero fucks for my current state of undress, I poked my head out, glancing over the small, sleepy front garden. Finding all well, I closed and latched it then hurried back to the bathroom. Juniper was washing suds from her hair when I slid the fogged glass back. I followed the trail all the way down to her toes.

"Everything all right?"

Hands immediately seeking the closest scrap of her skin, I crowded her into the far corner, joining her under the hot spray. "The front door was ajar, we must have forgotten to close it earlier."

She nodded contentedly. Then wide eyes flew to mine. "Shakespeare! Did you see her?"

I shook my head. "She doesn't go outside?"

"*No*." Scrambling around me, she flung herself from the shower, almost slipping as she snatched a towel from the hook. "Kelly advised against it until she was fully settled."

"*Shit*." I followed right on her heels. "Don't worry, we'll find her." Drying myself off with quick, rough swipes, I had little choice but to re-don my kilt and shirt or waste time going next door to change. Maybe I should move a few belongings over here, or Juniper could move her stuff into my place . . . *Not the time.*

Juniper disappeared inside her wardrobe while I dressed, cursing and banging as she hurried. Worry strained her face when she returned, suds-soaked hair dripping onto her knitted jumper. I went to her side, cupping her shoulders.

"You can't go out there like that, you'll freeze to death." She didn't even have matching shoes on. It didn't feel like the time to point it out.

"I have to." She clutched my shirt. Tears lined her eyes as she screwed the fabric between desperate hands. "She could be anywhere by now. She must be so scared; I have to find her."

"Sweetheart, cats are resourceful, she's going to be fine." I squeezed the ends of her hair to get rid of some of the moisture then tucked it behind her ears. "At least put a hat on so I don't need to worry about you too."

"Fine." She grabbed the beanie I'd bought for her while I dug out a couple of torches. Then hand in hand, we went out into the night.

* * *

"Shakespeare!"

"Shakespeare!"

Juniper's shouts had turned to panicked cries long ago, tearing through the trees and hedge growth surrounding our properties with a singular focus. I'd taken a more *methodical* approach, leaving no stone unturned, searching every nook and cranny a terrified cat may think to hide.

Through every moment, logic screamed at me, the words I'd tell any pet owner as a veterinarian: cats have a canny ability of finding their way back home, days or weeks, sometimes months after going missing. But Juniper wasn't *any* pet owner and Shakespeare wasn't *any* cat. She was nervous and slow to trust. Would she even think of this place as home yet? I didn't have the heart to raise the question aloud.

"Anything?" The light of Juniper's torch bounced as she jogged to meet me.

I shook my head. "Sorry, sweetheart." Her crushed expression killed me. Her teeth were chattering, and I pulled her against my chest, chafing her arms. "We're not giving up. I promise you, she'll be back by morning, the same wee pain in the arse she's always been."

"What if she isn't, Callum? She literally ran away at the first opportunity presented to her. And I was so distracted I didn't even notice. It was cruel to bring her home in the first place when she clearly hates me. I should have left her with Kelly . . . or a shelter, at least she'd be safe right now." Her tears soaked my neck, and I rocked her, pressing my lips to her hat, kissing her even if she couldn't feel it. "She hates me," she repeated, sounding so young and lost all of a sudden tears unexpectedly burned my own eyes. "I don't even blame her."

They just didn't love me enough.

This was about so much more than a cat. If Shakespeare never returned would she see it as just another being she loved abandoning her? Understanding came a long time before acceptance. Deep down she might understand another person's love didn't equal the value of your self-worth, but how long would it take her to accept it? To not blame and hate herself for every small rejection?

"Impossible," I said fiercely. Wishing I could imprint the sentiment onto her soul. "It would quite literally be easier to tear my own heart from my chest than hate you."

"Look at how quickly she bonded with you. I've tried everything I can think of . . . for months and—" Tears glistened on her pale cheeks. "I wouldn't come back to me either."

Fuck.

Clasping her cheeks, I glanced between those eyes that had always consumed me. World eaters, I'd once called them, when I should have said: *my entire world.*

"We're getting her back. Do you trust me?" I'd search every inch of this damn island if that's what it took. She nodded weakly and the tightness in my chest eased marginally. "We need to stay calm and form a plan, coming at this half-baked won't get us anywhere. First thing, I assume she's chipped?" Juniper nodded. "That's good, if anyone picks her up, they'll likely bring her straight to the practice anyway. I have a humane trap stored in my office. I'll drive into the village—" The crunch of tyres cut me off and we both turned as headlights shone down the lane, too bright to make out the driver. It was almost two in the morning, who the hell would be visiting at this hour?

Shielding my eyes, I shifted, blocking Juniper from sight.

We didn't have to wait long. The window lowered and Mal's voice cut through the quiet. "Thought we'd find you here. I've been phoning you for the past thirty minutes."

I patted down my chest, pulling my phone from my jacket pocket. Five missed calls flashed on the screen. "I must have switched it to silent," I said. Ducking my head, I glanced inside the car, finding Mal still dressed in his traditional garb, April beside him, looking more than a little rumpled in her dark green dress. "What's going on?"

He grimaced. "It's Dad, he's had a fall—" The rest of the sentence faded to white noise, my brain fighting to compute what I was hearing. That Alistair had found Dad lying by the side of the road almost a mile away from our parents' house on his way back from the party, a gaping gash to his forehead. That Dad had snuck out of the house while Mum slept. I barely even felt Juniper's hands urging me toward the car until she spoke my name, her voice the ring of a bell I'd always respond to.

She kissed my chilled fingers. "Callum, you have to go."

My throat felt too tight to form words. "But . . . Shakespeare—"

Juniper's tear-streaked face softened, even as her lower lip wobbled. "Don't worry about that for now."

"What happened to Shakespeare?" April bent over the centre console.

"She slipped out earlier this evening, we can't find her," I said.

"Shit, June, I'm sorry. I'll stay and help look." April started to unbuckle her seatbelt, but Juniper shook her head.

"You guys need to get to the surgery, Iris and Jim need you. I can keep looking."

"Alone? *Fuck no*." I needed to go, logically I knew that. Mum would be beside herself, so would Heather and the twins. The weight of responsibility slumped heavily around my neck, the sweet perfection I'd found in Juniper's bed only an hour ago already feeling like a distant memory.

My family needed me, but Juniper had become my family too, mine to take care of, she deserved to be someone's first priority. Torn in two, I pulled her aside, staring down into her resigned face. "I'll stay."

"Don't be stupid, this isn't important—"

"Of course it is." My hands tightened around hers. "You aren't doing this alone. I won't let you." Just the thought of her searching through the night by herself, feeling alone and unloved, made me want to break something. *Fuck*, the first time she needed me and I was failing at the first hurdle.

Scrubbing a hand down my face, I wracked my brain for a way around it. "You could come with us, we'll check in on my dad and come straight back."

"No." She made the decision for me, pushing me toward the car. "You know my presence will make things more complicated with Alistair. You need to go and be with your family, you'll hate yourself if you don't."

Fuck, but she was right. Still, I hesitated, dropping my forehead to hers. "I'll take my phone, keep me updated. Give it no more than an hour and if you haven't found her, leave some food out and go inside to warm up." I cupped her cheek, forcing her to look at me. "Promise me?"

"I promise." Despite all her bluster, Juniper couldn't lie for shit.

I kissed her deeply, dragging her bottom lip into my mouth. "I love you. Do you believe me?" If she didn't believe I was coming straight back to her, there was no way I could force myself into that car.

"Aye." Her smile was timid but real. My knees almost buckled at the relief of it.

Even with our audience, I kissed her again. I couldn't help it. "When I get home, I expect to hear you say it back." Another kiss. Slow and deep, to say I'd see her soon. "Be careful."

* * *

"I think you like keeping me on my toes, Jim." A sweet-sound-
ing Lowlands voice sliced through the tense surgery room
like bagpipes at a fucking funeral.

"I didn't expect to see you here, Dr Redford." I climbed
to my feet to shake hands with Dad's usual doctor. She
looked tired, her scrubs a little creased, her blonde hair
beginning to slip from her top-knot. But her smile was as
kind as ever. She possessed a rare gentle hand that managed
to calm Dad.

"I volunteer every second Saturday." She folded both
hands around her clipboard as she glanced around the
room. "A full house today."

Heather was on her way with the girls. But every other
Macabe had poured into two cars and currently took up
most of the three-foot-square cubicle of the Isle of Skye
Minor Injuries unit. The hour drive from Kinleith to Portree had passed in an agonising, knee-bouncing crawl, my
thoughts spinning from Dad to Juniper then back again.
I'd made Mal relay Alistair's message, word for word, too
many times to count, that Dad was okay, a little banged up,
but conscious. I hadn't truly believed it until I saw him with
my own eyes, lying on the narrow bed, his hand clasped
between Mum's. Quiet, but alert, despite the long cut to his
forehead. A nurse had looked him over initially but called
a doctor to determine if he had a concussion and to stitch
him up. That had been hours ago.

Dr Redford approached his side, giving Mum's shoulder
a reassuring squeeze. "Looks like you've had an accident
there, Jim. Line dancing again, were you?"

Dad didn't answer and Alistair pushed to his feet,
towering over the young doctor. "I'm able to stitch the

wound myself if given access to a room and the necessary equipment."

I scowled where I reclined against the wall. Alistair hadn't spoken a single word to me, not that I exactly blamed him. Juniper was right . . . I'd let my jealousy get the better of me and behaved like an overbearing arsehole, all but knocking her over the head with my club and dragging her back to my cave. On top of that, I'd disrespected him as my brother. Aye, I didn't believe he got a say in my relationship with Juniper, but he'd deserved a conversation – an explanation – at the very least. No wonder he'd punched me.

That didn't mean he had the right to take out his frustration on the kind doctor. "Planning to stitch a wound with a broken hand?" I nodded to the swollen digits of his left hand, the skin already beginning to bruise. He'd fared far worse than I had. I'd have to teach him how to throw a decent punch once this was over.

Alistair scowled, tucking his hand into his jacket pocket as the doctor glanced between us like she expected a brawl.

The tension was starting to get to everyone. Mal couldn't sit for more than a few minutes at a time and had taken to reorganising a jar of wrapped boiled sweets on the desk. April stood at his side, offering whispered suggestions on colour preference. The jar now ranked from purple through to red through to green. Even Mum – distracted as she was – had thrown worried glances between Alistair and me.

Dr Redford turned a saccharine sweet smile up at Alistair. "I don't think we've been introduced."

"I'm *Dr* Alistair Macabe."

"It's a pleasure to meet you, Dr Macabe. I'm Amy Redford and I'm in charge of this unit. You are very welcome to come through and watch me work. I could take a look at that hand too."

Alistair frowned, then seemed to get the message that he was acting like a high-handed prick to this woman for no reason. Flushing, he cleared his throat and stepped back. "That won't be necessary."

Moving over to my parents, I dropped a kiss to the top of Mum's head and brushed a hand over Dad's shoulder, giving a light squeeze.

"We'll wait here," I promised them. Mum nodded mutely, her eyes locked on Dad as she followed him and Dr Redford from the room, like she could tether him to this lucid moment by sheer force of will. I couldn't look away, but instead of Dad, I saw Juniper in that bed, forty-odd years from now. Would I make different decisions than my mum had? Or would I be clinging on just as tightly? The truth had me rubbing the headache building in my temples. "*Fuck*."

"Language." Heather's hiss reached us before she even rounded the corner. Emily tucked on one hip, Ava barely awake, holding her mum's hand. "There are children present."

"Hey, peanut," Mal said, obviously glad for something to do, scooping Ava into his arms, immediately settling her against his broad chest.

I used the moment of hugs and explanations to pull out my phone and check over my thread of messages to Juniper.

Have you found her?

Let me know you're all right, at least.

Please, sweetheart.

I typed out a new text right below the others, watching as two ticks appeared. Then, I waited for those ticks to turn blue to let me know she'd read it.

I was still staring at the screen when Heather, shucking out of her thick coat and scarf, voiced, "Someone better tell me what the hell is going on, the tension in this room is making me antsy."

It was almost five in the morning. Hopefully she'd stopped searching and gone to bed. I doubted it. The thick, slimy feeling spreading through my gut doubted it too.

So distracted by thoughts of Juniper, I didn't even hear the conversation taking place around me until Alistair clipped, "Callum's fucking Juniper."

Mal wheezed, looking unprepared to dive between the two of us again.

April gasped in a god-awful display of shock, given her occupation.

And Heather said nothing at all.

I stared at my brother, resisting the impulse shake him. "I get that you're pissed, but I'll only say it one more time, keep her name out of your mouth. *Fucking* isn't half of what's between us."

"Oh, so you have feelings for her now?" he hit back with a sneer.

"Yes." My voice whipped dangerously. If he'd been anyone but my brother, I wouldn't even have dignified him with a response.

"Don't make me laugh, Callum, you don't take anything seriously."

It wasn't at all what I'd expected him to say, and it hurt more than I'd ever admit out loud. Absorbing the stinging blow, I volleyed my own. Words I'd regret later. "And how the fuck would you know, huh? Knowing would mean actually visiting your family once in a while, or a phone call where you aren't distracted half the time. Ava and Emily barely even know who you are—"

At Alistair's flinch, Heather jumped between us. "Woah, all right, I think maybe we should take it down a notch."

"As if you're all right with this." Alistair flung a hand at her. His good hand, I noted, the other he kept tucked inside his jacket.

"I wasn't at first but—"

"Wait, wait, wait . . ." Like a switch had been flipped, all fight drained from him as his gaze flicked between us. "You already knew about this? Since when?"

Heather's lips rolled together. I could see the gears turning in her mind, deciding whether to lie or tell the truth. She settled on honesty. "I found out a few weeks ago," she said simply. "And quickly realised it isn't my place to be pissed off."

I opened my mouth to intervene on Heather's behalf, when Mal cleared his throat. "This is probably a good time to mention that I also knew."

Fucking hell, probably could have kept that to yourself, Mal.

Alistair's expression shifted from stunned to betrayed in a nanosecond. He was a man who prided himself on always having the right answer, being last to know something so huge would hurt him deeply.

I couldn't stand that *I* was the one causing that hurt.

Sighing, I scrubbed a hand over my face. "Alistair, I'm sorry—"

"You all knew?" Alistair's chest heaved, like he was absorbing a great weight. The result trickled around the room until the air felt thick.

"It wasn't intentional."

He nodded shakily, a raw laugh slipping free. "Right."

"It wasn't," I implored, stalking closer.

His eyes were glassy when they settled on me, wounded and furious, ready to land another blow. "As you've finally decided to be so honest, this is the perfect time to come clean about Dad's diagnosis."

My stomach sank. Mouth snapping open, then closed, as my retort died on my tongue.

"What's he talking about?" Heather's voice sounded suddenly small, the way she'd sounded when she was seven years old.

"Don't." I pointed a finger at Alistair, unable to look at my baby sister. "Don't you dare use Dad as a way of getting back at me."

His jaw ticked. "They were going to find out eventually."

"Find out what?" Mal asked, his face smooth as marble, perfectly blank even as he held a sleeping Ava so carefully. Heather's arms wrapped around her middle, paler than I'd ever seen her. For the first time in so long, I floundered, without a clue what to say to my siblings.

Juniper's words came back to me from the day she'd encountered Dad in the village, *Who's taking care of you?*

Perching on my coffee table, glass of whisky in hand, she'd known the answer without me having to say it. *No one. No one takes care of me.* And I'd been okay with that. What I couldn't accept was the knowledge that tonight likely wouldn't have happened if I'd been more open with my siblings.

Heather whispered my name again and I finally faced them. "Dad—" I took a ragged breath. "*The disease* has worsened a lot quicker than doctors first predicted. His memory loss is significant and he's becoming agitated, because of that he's started wandering out of the house. That's what happened tonight."

"No." Heather shook her head. Chin raised defiantly. "I would have known, we have lunch every weekend, I would have noticed."

"Mum and I have gotten good at covering it up." Not to mention big groups overwhelmed Dad these days. He'd lost all ability to follow a conversation, he pretty much sat in silence any time we were all together.

"Why cover it up at all? You had no right to keep that from us." There was an edge to Mal's tone. Guilt perhaps, the last thing I ever wanted from him. April's arm curled around his waist, silently soothing.

Pacing to the window, I shoved a hand through my hair. "Because I didn't want to burden you."

"Bullshit," Mal shot back, the steel in his voice taking me aback. "This is classic you. You have a hero complex a mile wide, always looking for something to fix, a new problem to take on so you can avoid what's missing in your own life."

It didn't take a genius to figure out what – rather *who* – he referred to. People always said introverts were the most observant, but I hadn't realised my wee brother saw me quite so clearly.

"No more," he finally said. "We make these decisions together. As a family."

I nodded, shoulders slumping with relief. It was an easy agreement to make. I didn't want to do this alone, not anymore.

"As a family," Heather agreed, coming to my side to hug me.

Alistair's agreement came last. He stood away from the rest of us, his tone cool, posture aloof. But he spoke the words all the same – as a family – and I knew we'd be okay eventually.

36

Juniper

Digital receipt:
   Time: 02.13 a.m.
   Order Number: 27310
   Item: 1000 x missing cat posters

Something poked me in the ribs. A finger. Or the sharp end of Shakespeare's paw, perhaps. Enjoying my dream too much, I rolled over, burrowing deeper into my pillow.

"Time to wake up." A familiar voice I recognised as irritated cut through the haze, drifting too far away for me to piece together exactly why that voice would be in my bedroom.

The finger poked me again. Hard enough to force my eyes open.

My brain ninety percent mush, it took a moment to realise it wasn't my cottage ceiling above me, but the cloud-mottled sky, somewhere between black and grey as the dreich day broke. The smell of damp air and mud irritating my nose.

I blinked.

Once.

Twice.

Rubbed my eyes and blinked again.

Hovering above me, hands on his hips, his overly bushy mutton chops looking more like devil horns from his upside down position . . . was Hank.

"Dinnae make me drag yer inside, lass, my ancient back can't hack it."

Ada stood at his elbow, hands clasped over her mouth as though she were witnessing the opening sequence of a disaster movie.

I realised a few things in quick succession:

Something had crawled into my mouth and died while I'd slept.

It wasn't a hand poking me, but the toe of Hank's boot.

The pillow I clutched to my chest like a lover was Ivy House's doormat.

And I hadn't found Shakespeare.

Snapping upright, I swiped a hand over my crusted cheek, trying to get my bearings. The streetlamps still faintly glowed, the car park silent. I breathed out a heavy sigh of relief.

If Hank hadn't even started work yet, that meant it was too early for any guests to have seen me passed out on the porch. *Christ, imagine if they'd had to step over me? I'd never recover from the humiliation.*

How did I even end up here?

When I'd first come to stay with Alexander and Fiona, I developed a small habit of sleepwalking but that hadn't affected me since my teen years.

"Are you all right, love?" Ada asked, edging closer. "You must be freezing."

"I'm fine." I waved her away. I did feel fine, physically at least. Mentally . . . I stringed together my memories of last night. Jim Macabe had been injured. Callum had left for the surgery and, feeling helpless and guilty after I'd point blank refused to go with him, I'd retraced my steps to find Shakespeare. Starting at the cottage, I'd searched the surrounding area between my property and Callum's. From there, I'd cut across the hilly bank between Ivy House and the neighbouring croft, combing through the heather and knee-high grass for any sign of her, hating myself a little more with every step.

My hands were scraped raw from thistle needles and dry mud caked in heavy patches up to my thighs from the bog I'd fallen into.

Around three a.m., convinced I'd die in that stinking bog, I'd cried to the image of the poor hikers that would inevitably discover my remains in days, or weeks. It was kind of poetic, if you thought about it, how many times had I warned Shakespeare that she would be the death of me? And in a classic Shakespeare move, she'd proven me right in the most dramatic fashion.

It was only once I'd stopped panicking long enough to halt my sinking into mud did I realise I could use the long grass to pull myself free, beached whale style. Lethal disaster averted, I'd stumbled back to Ivy House and collapsed on the doorstep, meaning to phone Callum, but I'd turned my phone over and over in my hands, thinking about what I'd even say to him when he answered. I didn't want to disturb him while he was with his family, only to reveal my failure. I must have fallen asleep before deciding.

"Look at you, you're frozen stiff." Ada crouched in front of me, chafing her hands up and down my arms. "Work certainly isn't boring with you in charge." It didn't feel like a compliment, but I laughed anyway. "Now, get yourself inside, I'll put the kettle on." She threw a look at Hank that I couldn't decipher, before stepping around me and heading inside.

That's when I remembered Ada didn't start her shift for a few more hours. And her parking spot sat empty. "You and Ada drove in together?" I asked Hank, attempting to waggle my eyebrows, but my face was too cold.

"Aye." He observed me with a mixture of annoyance and begrudging concern. "What of it? She hasn't gotten her tyre fixed. Bloody woman, I have half a mind to do it for her."

"Oh." I deflated, utterly bored at the explanation. *Were the two of them going to dance around their feelings forever?* At my reaction, the deep grooves in Hank's forehead cut further into his weathered skin. "Oh, come on," I laughed. "Ada's been dropping hints at you to ask her out for years."

"She has?"

My laugh melted into a groan. "Are you serious? Last Thursday she asked if you liked her new haircut then said no less than three times that her book club was cancelled, and she'd gotten all dressed up for nothing."

"That . . . was a hint? To ask her out and such?"

He looked so uncertain I shook my head, dismayed. "My sweet summer child."

"I dinnae ken what that means." He stared toward the inn where Ada had disappeared, as though it might hold the answer. "I was supposed to ask her out on a date?"

"Yes. Or a drink if you want to keep it casual."

He looked appalled. "No, I couldnae do that."

"Date her?"

"*The drink*. If it's nae more than a drink she'll think I expect . . . other things." *Bloody hell*. Hank was actually blushing.

"That's okay too, if you both want that."

"*No.* I may not always look it but I'm a gentleman."

And they said romance was dead. "You still have time to ask her," I pointed out, doing my best not to smile as he checked his reflection in the door's glass, smoothing his unruly hair.

"Yer trying to distract me." He turned back to me. "What's really going on? Did that Macabe lad hurt yer?"

"Callum? Of course not." The opposite was true, in fact. When I was with Callum, I felt strong enough to do anything. Only when he was gone did the problems occur. If he hadn't been called away last night, I definitely wouldn't have run headlong into a bog. He'd have collected the humane trap from the practice and, like the problem fixer he was, Shakespeare would be safely at home, ruling over her domain.

He would have fixed it all . . . like he fixed everything. Did I want him to fix everything? Did I want to rely upon another man so much that I'd be left broken without him?

Callum said he loved me, and I trusted he meant it. One of my first observations of him had been his staunch honesty. It had made me uncomfortable back then, but now . . . I knew there was little life in a relationship that didn't value honesty.

Callum loved me. But could I trust that he loved me enough to stay forever? To hold my hand through this messy life – the good, the bad and everything in between? Because life hurt.

It's all pain in the end, wee one, might as well make the journey worth it. Is that what Alexander had meant? That love was supposed to devastate?

Look at April and Mal, content to enjoy every moment together, knowing April's job would always pull them apart

343

for months at a time. Love played only a small part when a relationship was built on such unstable ground. It would take *everything*.

"If he dinnae upset yer, why are yer crying?" Hank asked.

Because I love him so much it scares me.

Maybe it was the cold or the lack of sleep, but my emotions felt like the inside of a sewing box, a snarl of needles and threads of every colour. If you pulled on one, they would all tangle into a single jumbled knot.

All I could offer was a very wet, "I lost my cat."

"You mean *that* cat?"

My head snapped up, precisely as a pitiful yowl tore through the air. "Shakespeare?" Whipping around just in time to see her bounding from a hedge as though her tail were on fire, I crouched and opened my arms. No time to worry over her possible rejection. She was already in them, dry leaves and moss falling from her fur.

Her yowl became accusing, head butting my chin. *This was all your fault*, her yellow eyes seemed to say.

I held her tighter. "Don't do that again."

She purred and it felt like a suitable agreement.

Watching us, Hank wrinkled his nose. "I'll leave yer to it."

"Remember my advice," I called over Shakespeare's head.

"There was some advice between all that weeping?" But he smiled and I knew I'd won him around.

Phone in one hand, I slipped my keys into my back pocket and checked the lock on the cottage door. Giving it an extra rattle just to be safe.

After I'd settled Shakespeare safely inside, she'd demanded two full bowls of food, swallowed them down like she hadn't eaten for a year, squished her body into the mound of sofa cushions and promptly fallen asleep, where she was sure to remain for the rest of the day.

Hurriedly flicking through Callum's essay of texts, I rushed around the side of the inn to my car.

Remember to call if you need me.

Any sign of her?

I'm starting to feel like a stalker, sweetheart.

Apparently I can't take a hint, let me know if you're all right. Please.

And there, sent at six a.m. You're living up to your nickname again, harpy. I hope for your sake you've been tucked up, sound asleep in bed all night, because you won't be getting any later. I think it's about time I tied you up. Fair's fair.

Heat curled in my lower belly and I picked up my pace. It was almost seven and I was eager to get to the Minor Injuries unit in Portree. Get to *him*. I didn't want to make things worse between him and Alistair, so I'd wait outside and then, once his dad was on the mend, we could talk to Alistair together and find the path of least awkwardness.

Unlocking my car with the fob, I reached for the handle when tyres crunched over gravel.

Callum.

A taxi swung around in a small arc, and hope quickly gave way to disappointment when a small woman in big sunglasses stepped out, her hair a little more sun-streaked than its usual dark brown. Wait—

"*Fiona?*" She straightened. "I thought you weren't coming home until Tuesday?"

Beaming, she pushed her sunglasses onto her head. "I caught an early flight."

Three strides and I had her in my arms, squeezing her tighter than ever before. "I missed you."

Shock stiffened her limbs for a single heartbeat, and then her arms swept around me too, clutching just as tightly. "I missed you too, love." She pulled back, running that assessing gaze over me. "What on earth, Juniper? You're all covered in mud."

Yeah. Too eager to get to Callum, I hadn't exactly hung around to change. "That doesn't matter." Picking up her case, I all but dragged her to the door, ready to get this over with. "I need to tell you something – well, show you, really."

The flight must have really worn her out, because she was very un-Fiona-like, barely uttering a word of protest when I abandoned her luggage in reception, or when I flaked dry mud on the staircase. At the threshold to room five, I didn't hesitate, flipping the lock and pushing open the door wide with sweaty palms.

She'd either like it or she wouldn't.

Entering first, I held my breath as she turned in one slow circle, eyes skimming over the new soft furnishings and freshly painted panelling – the soft sage that made the space feel bright and airy – then pausing to dance a finger over the antique dresser. Callum had helped me hang photographs of Skye on the largest wall a few days ago, the frames all various colours, shapes and sizes. *Disordered tranquillity*, he'd said, when we stepped back to admire our handiwork.

I'd liked the phrasing then, now I worried if perhaps it were too much.

As a child, I'd always admired the way Fiona never let her emotions show on her face. On the days she'd frustrated him, Alexander . . . *my dad*, would say it was like arguing with a brick wall, you got nothing but silence and a sore head. On the good ones he loved the fact he was the only person alive who could accurately read that twinkle in her eye. I wished he was here now to read her for me, because when she smoothed a hand over the new linen bedding, easing the corner into a perfect square I could never quite replicate, I'd have given anything to know what she was thinking.

Then she noticed the pictures – the largest frame right in the very centre displaying a large swathe of Dad's tartan wallpaper. She sat down with a thump, the air punching from her lungs just as soundly.

"Mum—" The title came instinctually, if a little awkwardly. "I'm so sorry if you hate it, I . . . I should have asked you first."

Her lips wobbled into a watery smile. "Aye, probably." And then she rolled her eyes, just like I would have done. "But Hank – busybody that he is – might have pointed out that it was time I loosened the reins around here."

"You spoke to Hank?"

"Aye, a few times. He told me you had it all in hand and I should leave you to it."

Hank had actually covered for me? "So you knew what was going on?"

She laughed, tossing her thick brown hair. "Of course I did, I'm your mother. You were creeping around, taking secret phone calls, looking guilty as sin for weeks. I knew you had something planned, though I didn't know it was all this."

"If you hate it—"

"It's beautiful." Gnawing her bottom lip, she folded her hands in her lap. "I should have let you play a bigger role at Ivy House a long time ago, after your father . . . I needed something to hold onto and I thought it must be this place, but it wasn't. I . . . I needed you, baby girl, and I didn't know how to tell you." She held out her arms, her face so hopeful it tore my heart from my chest.

Crossing the room, I sank to my knees, dropping my head into her lap. "I'm sorry I've been such an awful daughter." She stroked my hair with tentative movements and I squeezed my eyes shut. "I think . . . ever since you adopted me I've been waiting for the other shoe to drop. That you and Dad would see I was nothing like the perfect child you dreamed of and then I'd be alone all over again."

"*Never* . . . you were our baby, born from me or not. You have nothing to be sorry for, love. We should have tried harder to be a part of your life. You were such an independent wee girl, forced to grow up too soon. You didn't need me to brush your hair or tuck you in at night." Her hand didn't slow. "Your dad wanted to push but I . . . I feared pushing too hard would only drive you further away from us."

Throwing my arms around her waist, I held her like I was seven years old with a cut knee. "I love you, Mum."

She whimpered, kissing the top of my head. "I love you too, baby. Always have. Your dad would be so proud of you."

The words were like a warm blanket thrown over every miserable moment in my life. Still being me, when tears rolled down my cheeks again, I wanted to stuff them back inside my eye sockets. Three people had seen me cry this morning, if you counted that sheep judging my knee-deep breakdown in the bog, and I most certainly fucking did.

I pulled back, swiping at my cheeks. "I didn't even ask about your trip, did you have a good time?"

"The best." She smiled, looking lighter. Like years of grief – hadn't disappeared exactly – but lifted some. "I think I'll do it again now that I'm stepping back as manager."

"You're what?"

"It's time. This place was mine and your father's. Now it's yours. If you want it."

Mine.

Happiness sprang like wildflowers. I didn't have to think about it. "*Yes.*" My voice wobbled. "Of course. *Yes.*"

"Good." Standing, she smoothed her skirt in that no-nonsense way of hers. "I need to wash the plane off me . . . you should shower too before you see that new boyfriend of yours."

She turned for the door and my mouth gaped. "Boyfriend? How could you know of any boyfriend?"

"I told you, Hank is a busybody." Her eyes danced. "He's a good boy, June bug. Hold onto him."

"*What?*" I said again, but she disappeared down the hallway.

The second the door closed, I slapped my hands to my face and sank to the mattress. "Feeling fucking sucks," I whimpered right before another sob wracked my body, tears free falling in an undignified mess of salt and snot.

This was all Callum's fault. He was the reason I felt so wonderfully overwhelmed. Like I'd been hit by a double-decker bus and couldn't wait for the next collision. It was exhausting.

Did people feel like this all the time?

Footsteps sounded in the hallway, a heartbeat before the door creaked.

"Sweetheart?" His voice reached me first. Then gentle hands tugged me into arms that felt like they were built for the sole purpose of holding me. Callum tucked me tightly to his chest, like he predicted I was about to break and only he could hold all my pieces together.

37

Callum

Callum: Mum, I'm sorry if I've been pushing you these past few months to make decisions you weren't ready for.
Callum: I just wanted to keep you safe. Both of you.
Mum: You have nothing to be sorry for, sweetheart. You've held us together. Been burdened with a weight no parent wishes their child to carry.
Callum: I never saw it as a burden.
Mum: I know. I've always been so proud of your big heart. So was your father.
Callum: I'm not sure I ever made him proud.
Mum: You did. All of you, even if he could never show it.
Callum: I love you, Mum, it's all going to be okay.

Juniper cried so long, I might have worried she'd drown in her tears, if my shirt weren't soaking all the moisture up.

After a minute of holding her, I lifted her into my arms, planning to set her on the impeccably made bed, then hesitated. I still wore last night's shirt and kilt and Juniper looked almost as filthy as that day with the cow. I'd get that story later, because when she sniffled against my throat, the decision was made.

In the middle of the bed, I curled her into my good side, peppering kisses into her tangled hair. "Why are you crying?"

"*Ugh*—" She started to answer, only to cut off with another round of wracking sobs.

"Take your time. I'll be here when you're done."

"Stop being sweet, you're making it worse."

I was . . . confused. The love of my life lay weeping in my arms and she didn't want me to be sweet to her? "You'll have to catch me up, sweetheart."

Her sobs kept coming in a steady stream, so I decided easy questions were the best way to handle this. I smoothed my hand down her spine to her hip, holding her body tight to mine, recalling the thousand times I'd imagined a moment just like this one. Not the crying part, obviously – but offering comfort. I couldn't bungle it now.

"You're upset about something?" *No shit, Sherlock.* She started to nod, then shook her head, strands of hair catching on my shirt buttons. "You're not upset?"

"No."

"Let me make sure I'm following . . . you're crying but aren't upset and I can't be sweet to you?"

"Exactly." She sniffled, using my shirt as a tissue.

Cupping her damp cheek, I tipped her head back, taking in the streaks of dirt and tracks of tears, waiting until her puffy eyes cracked open before I said, "There's one problem with that, Juniper. I plan on being fucking sweet to you for the rest of my life."

Her entire body melted, head tipping to my shoulder where she made this little choking sound. I caught the fresh tear with my thumb before it could fall. "This fucking sucks."

I chuckled. "A relationship?"

"All the crying that comes with it." Pushing up slightly, she swiped her hands over her cheeks. "Being emotionally stunted was so much easier."

"You weren't emotionally stunted." She shrugged like she disagreed, but I'd always seen what lay beneath the surface. It's why there'd never been a choice in loving her. "You found Shakespeare?"

She nodded. "First thing this morning. I think I was more distressed than she was."

I sighed with relief. "Good . . . that's good. I knew you would. I'll check her over later." She nodded, still lost in whatever thoughts were dragging her under. "And then your mum came home – I ran into her in the hallway," I explained at her quizzical look. "Was she angry?"

"No." She shook her head. "She loved it, that's the problem. I think I might be . . . *happy*."

She said the words like a person might say fungal infection. "Do you think it's contagious?"

"*Shut up*." She slapped my chest, and I caught her hand there. "For weeks you've been killing yourself to help me and – your dad! Shit." She suddenly gasped, throwing a hand over her eyes. "*See* . . . I've been lying here letting you comfort me and I didn't even ask about your dad. Is he all right?"

"Yes, you did. That was literally the first thing you asked me." At least I thought it was. Her speech had been too muffled to fully make out, but I'd gotten the gist around the third repetition. "He's fine. Safely back at home with only a few butterfly stitches and an order to rest."

"Your mum?"

"Shaken. I think I'm finally understanding how hard this has been on her."

"What do you mean?"

"There's always been this little resentful part of me that wondered why she stayed with him. Why she never stood up to him." I fiddled with her hair.

"She was scared of him?"

"Not in any physical way. But I think he smothered her. His personality was so big it often left little room for anything else."

Her hand met my chest, rubbing in a soothing circle. "It can be hard to walk away from a relationship like that, when you don't know how to be without them."

"Aye," I agreed sadly. And even harder to watch that person slowly slip away from you, day by day. "But she'd always find ways to make it easier on us. He used to have this stupid rule about no sugary food in the house, so every day after school she'd take us to Brown's and let us pick out whatever treat we wanted. When he eventually found out, he didn't even try to fight her on it."

"The neck that turns the head," she hummed. "What did you pick out?"

"An oat and raisin cookie. Obviously."

Her laugh brushed over my lips. "I'm impressed with the level of commitment it takes for a seven-year-old to be that boring."

I was on her in a flash, tickling her side until she squealed, but her eyes were still a little sad. "I should have come with you to Portree, you've done so much for me—"

"Nope." I could already see where her mind was taking her. Scooping her around the waist, I lay back, planting her in my favourite spot with those long legs either side of my chest. I suspected that she loved it too because her cheek immediately lowered to my heart. "None of that. You're allowed to have a crappy few weeks and ask for help."

"I didn't exactly *ask*."

"Precisely. I wanted to help you." Lifting my legs, I settled her firmly into the V. "Just like you did that day in the village with my dad, when you helped get him to the car, even after all that shit he said to you. I swear I was so close to losing it; I had no idea what to do. Then you handled him so easily I think I fell in love with you all over again." She still looked unconvinced, and I realised she truly didn't get it. "For the better part of a year I've been going through the motions, rushing between work and my family, sleeping on my parents' pull-out on the nights Mum couldn't cope alone. You were right when you said I didn't have time for all of this," I waved a hand around the room. "But I *wanted* to have the time. You woke me the fuck up, sweetheart, not a single second I've spent with you has been a chore." There was no way this woman couldn't understand her value. I wouldn't allow it. "No more waiting for the other shoe to drop. Ever."

She drew back. "You heard what I said to Fiona?"

"Aye." I pressed my forehead to hers. "There is no other shoe, Juniper. This is it. Through every awful moment I've been waiting for you, I've loved you, and I'll continue to love you through whatever comes next."

She crawled up my chest, her hair tickling my cheeks as she kissed me. The touch was achingly tender, still I felt it like a caress between my legs. "I love you too."

I didn't expect the words to feel like such a blow. Could a moment be so exquisite it almost felt horrific in its magnitude? My eyes screwed shut, tears needling the backs of my eyelids.

That was her lips' next destination, kissing beneath each eye, then tracing the line of my beard from nose to cheek.

"I love you."

That time I moaned. And when her teeth bit my earlobe, I jerked. "Sweetheart . . ." My eyes flew open, seeing only the top of my head as her mouth blazed a line from my jaw to my throat. "*Juniper*, it feels wrong to have a hard-on right now."

Her eyes flicked up, full of amusement. "Oh?" She opened the top button of my shirt. I didn't even try to stop her as my head fell back.

"I always pictured . . . *ah*." Her mouth closed around my nipple. "I pictured the moment you said you loved me to be a little more romantic." I should have taken her out to a fancy restaurant. Bought her flowers. The whole big thing.

She paused, her lips a hair's breadth from my quivering stomach. "What's unromantic about your cock in my mouth?"

"*Christ.*" Now that she mentioned it, I couldn't think of anything more romantic than coming apart under her then holding her down while she did the same.

With a wicked grin, her lips continued their torture all the way to my waistband where she paused, grabbed my hand and pressed a sweet kiss to it.

"I'm sorry about that night in Glasgow." I blew out a breath, taken aback by the sudden turn in conversation. "I think that was the night I finally started to move on . . . I was scared as hell. I'm still sorry I used you in that way."

"*Fuck.* I would have let you use me, Juniper. I kicked myself for years after, but I wanted a real shot with you, and that wasn't the way."

"That was then," she said after a heartbeat.

"And now?"

"Now . . . I want to treat you how you deserve to be treated."

"And how's that?"

"Like mine." Her hand moved up, pressing over my heart as it raced for her. "Deep down, I think you've always felt like mine."

"Always," I agreed.

Hers.

I laced our fingers together, taking a heartbeat to acknowledge the perfection of the moment before I tumbled into the next one. "Harpy, I've changed my mind about the bed." Before she could blink, I swooped up from the sheets, tossing her giggling body over my shoulder and slapping that gorgeous arse. "We should christen the new shower first."

It wasn't until we were beneath the spray, both of our hands pressing the tile while I thrust inside her that she spoke again. "Something doesn't feel right."

I immediately stilled. "The position? This might be the best thing that's ever happened to me."

"Not the position . . ." She wiggled her hips, urging me to keep moving. My hand sank between her legs, finding the tattoo from memory alone. *Lucky.* "This. Us," she continued and my hips snapped to a stop. "Don't stop!"

"*Fuck*, you just told me to."

She moaned, taking matters into her own hands and swivelling her hips in little thrusts I couldn't help but fucking stare at. "All I'm saying is perhaps we should set some ground rules."

Should I have expected anything else? "Such as?"

"We don't start being nice to each other."

I barked a laugh that had her back arching. "It would break my heart if you started being nice to me, harpy." I rolled her pert little nipple. "What else?"

"We don't move in together for at least a year." Damn. I'd actually expected her to want longer. But even with her only a hundred yards away . . . it felt too much.

"No." Pressing a hand between her shoulder blades, I urged her forward, watching as the spray hit her back and rolled down her spine, pulling back so I fucked her with shallow strokes that tortured us both. "No time stamps. We take that step when it feels right, before or after a year."

"*Shit . . .*" Her whole body quivered. "Fine. Now fuck me hard, Macabe."

I kissed the base of her neck. "You gonna say my name?"

She shook her head.

"Slow it is."

* * *

I scooped the wriggling cat back into its carrier, its black fur so like Shakespeare's I couldn't help but wonder what the little demon was getting up to. Her owner too, she'd been half asleep when I'd slipped out of bed this morning to make an emergency house call.

"That should be you until next year." I handed the carrier to the smiling owner. "Keep her out of trouble."

He laughed good-naturedly, petting the cat through the wire door. "I'll do my best, this one has more energy than me and my husband put together."

Just like another cat I knew.

Fuck. I needed to get a hold of my obsession at work, but I couldn't stop smiling.

I didn't even wait for him to exit the reception before I called out to Kelly, "Who's up next?"

She shot me a wide look. She'd been doing that a lot lately. I think the constant smiling was weirding her out. "It's your lunch hour."

"Right." I pulled my phone from my scrubs pocket, wondering if I had time to pick up lunch and make it to Ivy

357

House and back before my next appointment. No doubt Juniper would have nothing more than cereal if I didn't intervene. Then the bell sounded and . . . Alistair ducked beneath the door, head swivelling as he sought me out.

I still couldn't get used to this new look on him. Hair shaved only millimetres long, it made his sleek profile appear roughened, like he didn't spend his days in scrubs and Crocs, but doing something more outdoorsy. As did the splits across the knuckles of his still healing hand.

Meeting my eye, he stared me down, the frown on his face almost dangerous.

When did he grow as wide as me?

A loud crunch cut through the tension.

Behind her desk, Kelly ate from the bag of crisps in her hand, wide eyes pinging between the two of us, clearly ready for a show.

I cleared my throat, and her cheeks turned pink. "Let's do this out the back, shall we?"

"If you prefer." Alistair strode ahead, the portrait of casual as he disappeared into the surgery room.

"If you need me, boss, I totally have your back," Kelly whispered.

"I'll buzz twice," I joked, then laughed at her very serious salute.

I knew I should have felt nervous. But if Alistair had come to have it out again, I welcomed it. Maybe then we could move on with our lives.

Pausing to close the door, I pointed out the still healing split and yellowing bruise on my lower lip. "Come to hit me again? My face could use the evening out."

He didn't move from his reclined position against the table but his jaw tightened. "Of course not. It shouldn't have happened at all."

I shrugged. "I deserved it."

He tilted his head but didn't disagree. "Was Juniper upset that I ruined your good looks?"

Here we go. "I think she prefers it actually." My woman had claws.

"Did you ever try anything when we were together?"

"No." I winced. "Well . . . not exactly."

He huffed a laugh and folded his arms. "Yeah . . . going to need you to explain that one."

"The day I first met her at your apartment . . . I might have asked for her number on the train. I didn't know who she was." I held up my hand though he didn't try to interrupt. "She turned me down. Hard. I couldn't believe it when she showed up at your place not even an hour later. I swore to forget all about her, but I couldn't." I shrugged sadly. "I think I fell in love with her on the spot."

Jaw ticking, he mulled over my explanation. "You should have told me."

"And ruin what you two had? I'm not that bloody selfish. Juniper didn't want me, she loved you." That particular truth would always make my chest ache. But it was no longer the gaping wound it had been back then. "Nothing happened until a year after you broke up, and then again the past few weeks."

"What happened exactly?"

"Fuck off. I'm not giving you the gory details." I crossed my arms. "I'm sorry if that pisses you off, but it's not happening."

He rolled his shoulders. "You shouldn't have kept it from me."

"It wasn't my call. I should probably apologise again, but if I'm being honest . . . I'm not sorry. I'd do it all over again if she asked."

His eyes widened in surprise, like he was seeing me for the first time. "You're in love with her," he said.

"Yes." I answered simply.

He scrubbed a hand over his slightly scraggly beard. "Looking back, I should have guessed. There was always something more in the way you interacted with her, and the way she looked at you outside Brown's . . . she used to look at me like that once. I think I deluded myself enough I didn't see the signs."

She used to look at me like that once. The way he said it niggled at me, he almost sounded wistful. "Are you still in love with her?"

He was silent for long enough for that niggle to grow wings that lurched around stomach. "No. At least not in the way you think. Obviously, you know how impossible she makes it not to care about her, even when she's infuriating." We shared a small grin at that. "She's actually the reason I'm here." My surprise must have shown on my face because he drew a velvet box from his pocket that I knew extremely well. "She asked me to meet her at Brown's so she could give the ring back." He seemed unaware when his fist squeezed around it. "Then she told me to get over my shit and come and talk to you and . . . here we are, getting over our shit."

"Very mature of us."

"Wonderful. This might have been the weirdest conversation I've ever had." Heading for the door, he slapped me on the shoulder. "Don't make the same mistakes I did. Keep showing up, even when she doesn't want you to. Yes?"

"Yes." I didn't even have to think about it.

"Great." He clapped me a second time. "Let's never talk about this again."

"Agreed."

"*Oh.*" He paused with the door cracked. "I figured you'd want to know. Mum agreed to hire a night nurse three days a week. She rang and made the appointment herself; he starts next month."

It's what I'd hoped for months now, and yet . . . I didn't feel relieved. Our family would never be the same again. "I knew you'd convince her."

"It wasn't me, it's just . . ."

"Time," I finished for him.

"Aye. It's time." He nodded sadly, the world seeming to weigh on him when he turned again, as if he'd accomplished his task and couldn't wait to get out of here.

"I'm about to grab lunch if you want to join me?" I rushed to say. He paused with his back to me and I hated the distance still lingering between us. He was my little brother, the feeling to protect would never disappear.

"I can't, I'm helping Mal at the distillery this afternoon."

Instinct made me push. "That's great. If you ever want to talk – about anything at all – I'm always here. You know that?"

For a moment, I thought he wouldn't reply, but then he said over his shoulder, "I know." The door didn't shut fully behind him, I heard his murmured goodbye to Kelly and the bell ringing on the door as he left.

Sighing heavily, I pulled out my phone, already craving Juniper's voice. She'd ease all my worries with a single sarcastic comment.

It buzzed in my hand, "voice note from Juniper" flashing across the screen. Pressing play, I put it to my ear, already grinning with anticipation.

"You left early this morning." Her sultry voice made me shiver.

I hit her number.

It didn't even take two rings for the line to connect. "Macabe." She spoke my name breathily and *fuck* . . . I was instantly hard.

"Some of us can't laze around all morning," I said without preamble. "Besides, you and Shakespeare looked so cute snuggled up, I didn't want to disturb you."

"The little arsehole is actually starting to grow on me."

I laughed, imagining the adorable as fuck frown she wore whenever Shakespeare offered affection. "I think she wants the full Juniper Ross experience."

She laughed too and it lit up my insides. "Callum?"

"Aye, sweetheart?"

"You forgot to ask which colour today."

My hand curled around the phone, barely stifling my groan. I swear this woman would be the death of me. "What colour?"

"None."

I was already reaching for my keys, swinging the surgery door open with a crash that made Kelly jump. "I'm taking a long lunch." I didn't pause for her acknowledgement, ducking out onto the high street and turning my attention back to Juniper. "Don't hang up the phone and get back into bed."

"Already there," she hummed and I picked up my pace. "I've just been waiting for you."

Epilogue

Five Months Later

Juniper

"I think they kind of hate each other." Legs crossed at the ankle, I watched Shakespeare stalk the perimeter of Simon's enclosure like a panther. Wrapped in only a towel and still slick from the shower, Callum crouched beside me, flashing an exquisitely muscled thigh through the slit.

Ah, thank the mother for shinty season.

"Tease," I muttered, fully ogling him.

He winked, dragging me into his lap. And like an absolute love-sick arsehole, I went willingly, releasing something that sounded suspiciously like a sigh.

His arms tucked around my middle, holding me to his damp chest. "Everyone's still alive, aren't they? The transition is following the plan perfectly." *The plan.* How could I forget?

Callum had spent weeks researching and then forming the perfect twelve steps to introduce the two animals, including a daily behaviour chart he'd taped to the fridge. These two needed to get along if I was to move into Callum's place permanently – which he wanted sooner rather than later. He was slowly relocating all my skull-shaped mugs. They sat like little hostages in his kitchen cupboards.

What's yours is mine, harpy, we are married after all, he just loved to remind me whenever I tried to steal them back. Not that we'd shared that information with anyone outside this room.

It had been a whim on a random Tuesday last month when we'd taken an overnight trip to Inverness, like all island folk did every now and again to pick up supplies not readily available in our wee stores. As our first technical "couple trip" – even if it was only Inverness – Callum had gone all out. A romantic dinner followed by an outrageous hotel room overlooking the river. I'd taken one look at the claw-foot tub and rose-petal-scattered bed and said, "We should get married today."

Callum had brought me swiftly back down to earth. Lounging across the bed like a king, he'd reminded me that no council would offer a same day or even next day wedding licence. Yet, he hadn't attempted to disguise the hope in his eyes, or the quiver to his lower lip, when he'd asked in his next breath if I'd consider handfasting with him.

". . . it's an archaic practice and in no way legally binding . . . but I won't lie, I love the idea of tying myself to you in every possible sense."

Who the hell could say no to that?

He'd practically leapt from the bed, dragging us both to our knees on the soft rug before the fireplace. Extracting the long tie from the fluffy hotel robe, Callum had looped our crossed hands together with the infinity knot.

Those perfect minutes were a blur and yet I knew I'd never forget the way Callum looked. Eyes shining with so much love I thought my heart might combust beneath the weight of it. His voice shook around his declaration, nervously confessing he had no clue how a traditional handfasting ceremony was supposed to happen. That this was a moment so perfect, so impossible, he'd never allowed himself to dream of it.

I couldn't recall the words I'd spoken in return. I knew Callum did. That his brilliant brain had locked away every moment of it. Every breath. Every touch.

It was beautiful and messy and unconventional and so perfectly *us*.

We planned to make it legal . . . eventually. But for now, I adored our little secret. Just as I knew Callum got off on whispering, *wife*, in public, on the chance someone might overhear.

The following morning I had a little heart tattooed on my ring finger to commemorate the occasion. Callum had gotten his first ever tattoo. *Fortanach*. Lucky in Gaelic. Right above his heart.

Locked in the memory, we watched Shakespeare and Simon in silence. I didn't hold out much hope for a friendship. Callum, ever the optimist, insisted it would take a little time. *Like it took you to warm up to me, wife*, he'd say. Usually while kissing my neck.

I'd always reply, *We don't have a decade, husband*.

To be fair to Shakespeare, Simon was kind of an arsehole. Last week he'd nibbled through the toe of my favourite shoe. Callum claimed he was "temporarily acting out" because of the big changes in his life.

I still thought he was an arsehole.

"All ready for today?" Callum's fingers tracing up and down my arm brought me back to the present.

I exhaled a nervous puff, the meagre breakfast I'd choked down sitting like a stone in my stomach. "I'd rather go back to bed. Let's say we both came down with a stomach bug."

"And miss the grand reopening of Ivy House? Absolutely not." He squeezed my waist then bent, breath hot on my ear as he whispered, "I'll make you a bargain. Today I get to act like a proud, overemotional husband, watching you soak up every moment of praise you so thoroughly deserve. And in return . . . I'll let you tie me to the bedframe." He licked my pulse and I couldn't contain my tremble. "Do we have a deal?"

My eyes fell shut, back arching, breasts aching for his hands that remained resolutely at his sides. "Deal."

Tonight couldn't come quickly enough.

Callum

I made it three hours.

Three hours of watching my wife – heels in place, black wide-leg trousers that covered her arse like a second skin, my tattoo on her ring finger – from the other side of the room while she blushed and laughed. Flashing that obscene smile as she thanked the villagers who'd come out in droves to support the reopening of Ivy House.

Gossip had spread like wildfire the first few weeks of our relationship, locals staring and whispering behind their coffee cups every time we stopped by Brown's for breakfast. But even in a wee village, gossip grew boring really quick when the people involved made it clear they didn't give a fuck. As I'd predicted, Jessica Brown had been thrilled, insisting she'd always known there was something between us. She must have been clairvoyant, because she claimed to know just about everything that happened around here.

Sipping my slightly warm white wine and fighting the

urge to drag Juniper upstairs, I decided it should be illegal for anyone to look that good in business attire.

She'd worked so bloody hard for this moment. She deserved for it to be all about her.

Ivy House had shut its doors the first week of January, once the Christmas and Hogmanay rush was over, and undergone a complete renovation thanks to Juniper's freshly acquired business loan. She'd fought to make every dream in that notebook of hers a reality. From the solar panels to the wedding gazebo in the wild garden, all ready for their first wedding this coming summer.

I was so fucking proud of her.

When she'd cut through the black ribbon that I'd snuck over and tied across the front door this morning, our families had cheered and clapped while happy tears spilled down her cheeks, getting caught in her smile. I'd had to wipe at my own damp eyes.

That's my wife, I'd thought, so completely in love with her. How I'd gotten this lucky, I would never know, but I wouldn't take a single moment for granted, wouldn't waste another day of this life not telling her exactly what I was thinking.

Determined to do just that, I placed my half-drunk wine on the table. "Be right back," I said to Heather, feeling only mildly guilty that I'd barely heard a word she'd spoken for the past ten minutes, and cut across the room.

Nodding politely to those I passed, I hooked an arm around Juniper's waist just as Duncan from the hardware store left her to peruse the food table. "Fucking proud of you, superstar."

"Superstar?" Her head tipped against my shoulder, body turning pliant under my touch. "I think I prefer that to harpy."

I smiled into her temple. "What about sweetheart?"

"Definitely not. You only call me sweetheart when you're feeling all soft."

"I'm always soft for you."

"Is that so? Then what's that poking me in the arse?" She nudged her hips back, emphasising her point.

I grunted, angling my body to disguise it against her hip. "That is an unfortunate side effect of watching you thrive. I might have a praise kink, I'm so damn proud it's turning me on."

She laughed, hands covering her eyes. "That's not what a praise kink is."

I couldn't care less. This was my version of a praise kink. "You can show me later," I said, ready to move us on to safer subjects, like Hank's spread of vol-au-vents or Fiona's tentative new relationship with a tourist she'd met over Christmas, when Juniper pushed onto her tiptoes and whispered in my ear, "Meet me in room five in ten minutes."

My mouth was still gaping as I watched her climb the stairs, a seductive sway to her hips. God, she fucking excited me.

Eyes on the clock, I made it to seven minutes. Heart and cock threatening to tear through my damn clothes to get to her as I took the stairs two at a time. The thrill of fucking her only a floor above the entire party urging me down the corridor.

Slipping through the door, I found the room quiet and dim, despite the early spring afternoon. Juniper had closed the curtains and spread out across the bed, head resting on her hand as she drew shapes across the coverlet. Absolute perfection.

"Alistair didn't come today," she said, eyes finding mine.

I stopped short, trying to place her tone. Talk about boner killer. "And you're upset about that?"

"Not upset." She shrugged. "Just a little concerned. He's missed a lot of family events recently. Even your mum dropped by for an hour."

I was worried about him too, he felt like a different person most days. There was something . . . sad about him now. Guarded.

He hadn't returned to Glasgow. Other than to pack up half of his belongings and come straight back. I'd expected him to leave when things with Dad settled but he remained. Even going so far as to start working with Mal at the distillery and move into a small cottage on the outskirts of Kinleith. Anything that wasn't strictly related to Dad, he found a last-minute excuse to bail.

None of us believed him, but we enjoying having him home too much to push him on the matter. And frankly, I felt like I had no room to pry into his business, so I let it go. Perhaps the time had come for me to push.

Loosening my tie, I stalked toward the bed. "I'll talk to him tomorrow. Happy?" I balled the tie, dropping it beside her hip.

"Yes." Juniper picked it up, running the dark green silk between her fingers. "Do I get to tie you to the bedpost now?"

I grinned and it felt exactly like us. A little vicious. A little out of control. "Later. First, I want your back against the door so everyone downstairs can hear it rattle."

"Romantic." She hopped to her feet, every line of her sleek and perfect.

"Romance is my middle name."

"I thought it was Clive?"

"I regret telling you that," I said, guiding her into position and flicking open the buttons of her shirt.

"You don't mind when I shout it in bed."

Pausing just as my favourite lacy blue bra came into view, I pinched her chin between my thumb and forefinger. "I mean this in the most loving way possible, but, sweetheart, when I'm between your legs my dead grandmother could start tap dancing on the side table and I wouldn't notice."

"That is . . ." She squinted.

"Fucked up?"

"Weirdly hot, actually. You're right, we should probably fuck against the door." She curled her arms around my neck, readying to jump into my arms.

But I held her steady and dropped to my knees, tugging her trousers and underwear as I went, so she was gloriously bare to me. "Not so fast, I want to live up to my favourite alter ego first."

She grinned, eyes dancing with that mischief that had drawn me in from the very beginning. Even when it shouldn't. "Whatever you say, Ken."

My eyes found hers, right before I licked her tattoo. "Dig those nails in my back and scream for me, harpy, I'm feeling lucky."

Acknowledgements

We did it! I can't believe I'm writing the acknowledgements for my first fully traditionally published novel, and I have so many amazing people to thank for helping to put this into the world.

First, as always, my husband, Freddie. This was a dream I never truly allowed myself to dream. Thank you for believing in this when I couldn't, for being the ultimate hype man, for always letting me be the passenger princess and for showing me what unconditional love is, without you, I wouldn't have been able to write it.

SCOTLAND! For the wildness of your heart and the warmth of your people. You might not be the home of my birth, but you are the home of my soul.

To every person who has supported me this far, whether by purchasing a book or simply liking a post. All the Bookstagrammers, BookTokers and content creators for your support and beautiful posts, without your joy, creativity and generosity, no one would have ever heard of the Macabe Brothers. I'm more grateful than you'll ever know.

To the gorgeous, endlessly kind women I've met in this community, both readers and authors: Erin, Courtney, Dilan, Caden, Olivia, Zarin, Meg, Natalie, Soraya, Sam, Annabel, Mahbuba, Ronnie, Jesse, Valentina, Kate, Leti,

Georgia, Emma, Rach, Hannah (and so many more). You inspire me every day, I'm so thankful to call you my friends.

To my family for your endless support and joy in this strange career I've created for myself. My niece, Grace, who loves romance books just as much as I do, now I have someone to send recommendations to. My mum, for telling every person you meet about my books, you've probably sold more books than I have. My dad, for not reading this. My husband's family, if you read this, let's not talk about it.

Katie Fulford, for being just as passionate about Scotland, seeing the possibilities of these characters and for taking a chance on a small indie author, for working so hard to find the right home for the Macabe Brothers. I can't wait to create more amazing things with you.

My editors Olivia and Tessa, you understood exactly who these characters needed to be and worked so hard to help me get them there. The entire team at HarperFiction and Avon US, especially Lynne, Libby, Emily and DJ, for all your support and the work you do behind the scenes – it truly takes a village. To all the copyeditors, designers, formatters and audio team.

To Sam (@inkandlaurel) for the Callum and Juniper of my dreams, just when I thought nothing could get better than *Whisky Business*, you served up the sexiest cover I've ever seen in my life.

Last, but not least, thank you to Zeus. My dog, my best friend, the hardest-working office buddy a girl could ever ask for.